RANDOM HOUSE
LARGE PRINT

TOM CLANCY
ENEMY CONTACT

Also Available from Random House Large Print

Tom Clancy Oath of Office
(by Marc Cameron)
Tom Clancy Line of Sight
(by Mike Maden)
Tom Clancy Power and Empire
(by Marc Cameron)
Tom Clancy Point of Contact
(by Mike Maden)
Tom Clancy Duty and Honor
(by Grant Blackwood)

TOM CLANCY

ENEMY CONTACT

MIKE MADEN

RANDOM HOUSE
LARGE PRINT

Copyright © 2019 by The Estate of Thomas L. Clancy, Jr.; Rubicon, Inc.; Jack Ryan Enterprises, Ltd.; and Jack Ryan Limited Partnership

Published in the United States of America by Random House Large Print in association with G. P. Putnam's Sons, an imprint of Penguin Random House LLC, New York.

Cover design by Eric Fuentecilla
Cover art: Bose Collins

The Library of Congress has established a Cataloging-in-Publication record for this title.

ISBN: 978-0-593-10426-2

www.penguinrandomhouse.com/large-print-format-books

FIRST LARGE PRINT EDITION

Printed in the United States of America

10 9 8 7 6 5 4 3 2 1

This Large Print edition published in accord with the standards of the N.A.V.H.

Aut inveniam viam aut faciam.
I shall find a way or make one.

PRINCIPAL CHARACTERS

THE WHITE HOUSE

Jack Ryan: President of the United States
Scott Adler: Secretary of state
Mary Pat Foley: Director of national intelligence
Robert Burgess: Secretary of defense
Arnold "Arnie" van Damm: President Ryan's
chief of staff

THE CAMPUS

Gerry Hendley: Director of The Campus and
Hendley Associates
John Clark: Director of operations
Domingo "Ding" Chavez: Senior operations
officer
Jack Ryan, Jr.: Operations officer and senior
analyst for Hendley Associates
Gavin Biery: Director of information technology
Lisanne Robertson: Director of transportation

CLOUDSERVE, INC.

Elias Dahm: CEO
Amanda Watson: Senior design engineer

and head of security for the Intelligence
Community Cloud

Lawrence Fung: Watson's number two and
supervisor of the Red Team IC Cloud
hacking group

OTHER CHARACTERS

Liliana Pilecki: Agent with Poland's Agencja
Bezpieczeństwa Wewnętrznego (ABW)

Senator Deborah Dixon (R): Chair, Senate
Foreign Relations Committee

Aaron Gage: Husband of Deborah Dixon and
CEO and founder of Gage Capital Partners

Christopher Gage: Stepson of Deborah Dixon
and CEO of Gage Group International

Rick Sands: Former member 75th Ranger
Regiment

1

PARTIDO DE BAHÍA BLANCA, ARGENTINA

He was a Scorpion.

First Ensign Salvio was never more proud of that fact than now. He checked his watch.

Three minutes to target.

Like his men, he was kitted out in body armor, a leg-holstered Glock 17 pistol, an M4A1 carbine, and a ballistic ATE Kevlar helmet with night-vision goggles.

The noise of the whining twin turboshafts of the EC145 Eurocopter filled the dimly lit cabin. His platoon of special operators of Grupo Alacrán—Scorpion Group—was the best unit in the Gendarmería Nacional Argentina. Maybe the whole country.

Grupo Alacrán was Argentina's primary anti-terror weapon. Like Israel's Yamam—the elite police unit with whom Salvio's team had trained in the Ayalon Valley—his men were the bleeding tip of the spear.

Salvio flashed three fingers to his trusted number

two, Sergeant-Adjutant Acuña, who acknowledged with a nod and a feral grin. The two of them cut their teeth fighting armed Mafia gangs and Islamic radicals in La Triple Frontera, the border region where Brazil, Paraguay, and Argentina collided. Long a bastion of drugs, guns, and human trafficking by international and indigenous gangs, the region's violence and crime grew worse each year. The Lebanon civil war drove tens of thousands of Lebanese to the region, and with them, Hezbollah.

And with Hezbollah came Iran.

Hell, even Osama bin Laden and Khalid Sheik Mohammed had visited La Triple Frontera years ago.

His government couldn't root them out. Couldn't even stem the tide. But after OBL appeared on scene, American money and technology flooded in and brought the war on terror to La Triple Frontera. Kept the cancer contained for a few years. But then the Americans turned their attention elsewhere and now Hezbollah was on the move again. South.

Tonight's mission was proof of that.

GNA intelligence had spotted a Lebanese Hezbollah commander two days ago, and CIA confirmed. But the CIA confirmation yesterday of an actual Iranian Quds Force commander on the ground near the coastal city of Bahía Blanca put blood in their mouths.

Against his government's protests, a gathering of Hasidic youth in Bahía Blanca was scheduled for next week. Hundreds of young Jewish people from all over the country would attend. A perfect target.

And an Iranian Quds Force commander to lead the attack.

Hezbollah had killed in his country before. More than a hundred Jews in two separate bombing attacks in the nineties.

And they'd promised to do it again.

The two terrorists were holed up at a small abandoned horse ranch just twenty-six kilometers north of the city. "Capture them—alive" was his only order, straight from the mouth of the **comandante mayor**. A chance to finally break the Hezbollah network, he said. And to knock the bastard Iranians back on their heels.

So they saddled up at their base in Ciudad Evita, loading out three helicopters with twenty-three of his best troopers. The three Eurocopters took three different flight vectors, avoiding direct routes from the base to the target. He was pushing the EC145 range limit to the maximum but there was no point in making it easy for any shoulder-fired MANPADS the tangos might have with them. His aircraft would need a refuel for the flight back for sure.

"Two minutes out," the pilot said in Salvio's headset. He glanced around the cabin. Tarabini,

Gallardo, Zanetti, Crispo, Birkner, Hermann. His boys were young but well trained, good shooters and **duros**. They met his eyes with confident smiles. They were like hungry wolves in a pack.

His pack.

"Kill the lights," he told the pilot. The dim red bulbs extinguished.

Salvio switched his comms channel. "Bravo One, this is Alpha One. Sitrep."

His sniper team—a shooter and spotter posted a kilometer away in the flat, open field surrounding the ranch—replied. "Eyes on. No movement. Lights out. Good to go, sir."

"ETA ninety seconds," Salvio said, adding in English, "Stay frosty!" He logged off. Like every other Argentinian man his age, he grew up on American movies, but it was his Black Hat jump instructor at Fort Benning who'd first barked that order at him.

Time to rock 'n' roll.

Based on drone surveillance photos shot the day before, Salvio ordered the pilots to put down in a NATO "Y" formation at twelve, four, and eight o'clock relative to the broken-down main house. The only trees in the area were a few dense mesquites surrounding the house, partially blocking the view of the windows. Fence rails were down in several places, and a few ramshackle outbuildings were scattered around the now horse-less ranch that had seen better days.

Each Eurocopter flared in near perfect sync to just a meter above the hard-packed dirt one hundred meters from the house. Salvio jumped first. His men followed, boots hitting the ground on a dead run. The choppers roared away and took up overwatch, circling high and wide as the Scorpion operators raced toward the main house. Beneath the moonless blue-black sky, the ancient farmhouse was a gray shadow.

Salvio landed at the four o'clock. He whispered orders into his comms for the advance of the rest of his team, knowing full well his men could do it without him.

"Bravo One, we're on the ground," Salvio said. "Watch your fire."

"We have your back, sir." The sniper team was positioned at six o'clock, the big Barrett M95 directly opposite the front door, ready to put a .50 BMG slug through any **cabrón** that stepped into its night-vision glass.

Salvio's squad advanced at a slow, crouching trot, as did the others. Out in the open on the flat, grassy plains there was little chance of finding cover, so dropping in close was the only choice. He'd chosen the night, hoping the fighters inside didn't have night-vision capabilities.

The twenty-four troopers closed in rapidly from three directions, weapons high, rounds chambered, safeties off. Heavy boots thudded onto the rickety wraparound porch, where the squads split up, stacking on either side of windows and both doors, front and back. Flash-bangs were pulled.

Salvio took the front door. Arab music blared from a tinny radio inside. He whispered another order into his comms. Flash-bangs crashed through window glass in six places simultaneously. The men closed their eyes and opened their mouths just as the grenades detonated.

Doors crashed open under their boots and Scorpions poured through into darkened rooms. The tactical light on Salvio's Glock 17 illuminated the living room, as did the swiftly panning lights on the carbines around him.

"**Clear!**" one of his **sargentos** shouted from the back of the house. Other shouts of "Clear!" soon followed. Soon, Acuña appeared, disappointment in his flash-lit eyes.

"All clear, sir. Nobody's home."

Salvio swore as he holstered his pistol. **Where the hell were these bastards?**

"**Aquí!**" a man shouted from the kitchen. Salvio and Acuña dashed in. Private Gallardo's lighted weapon pointed at the floor inside a small pantry closet. A trap door. Salvio tore it open and pulled out his pistol, activated the tac light on the barrel.

"Gallardo, Hermann, with me," Salvio ordered as he dropped into the darkened tunnel.

Salvio and the others returned to the kitchen entrance empty-handed. The tunnel ran seventy or so meters to an empty outbuilding. The terrorists must have fled from there, out of sight of his sniper team.

Salvio checked in with the chopper pilots on his comms, all deploying night vision and thermal imaging. "See anything?"

"No, sir. Not even a rabbit."

Damn it!

He was supposed to report the capture of the two terrorists to the **comandante mayor** as soon as it happened. The old man would be pissed. All he had in his hands at the moment was his own swinging dick. Not exactly what HQ was hoping for.

Salvio barked orders. He'd tear the place apart for intelligence. Maybe come away with something to show for their efforts.

They ripped through the house front to back, flipping mattresses, tossing drawers, pulling rugs, tearing up floorboards. The place looked like a debris field after a tornado.

Somebody had been here—trash and butts on the floor, a filthy, unflushed toilet.

But not one shred of intel to bring back for a trophy.

While his men stood around gulping water from their hydration packs and scarfing down protein bars, Salvio called his pilots, ordering them to land for exfil. Might as well get back to barracks at Ciudad Evita and call it a night.

Ten minutes later, his unit's three Eurocopters touched down, their turbines slowed. His men ducked low to avoid the carbon-fiber rotors raking the air just above their heads and piled into the choppers. They made room for the sniper and his spotter, who'd had to hump in six klicks by foot the day before to avoid detection. The sniper grabbed a spot on the floor at Salvio's feet.

At least the men were in good spirits, Salvio told himself. They laughed and joked among themselves as young men do for release after the adrenaline rush of a combat operation.

Even one where no shots were fired.

"Ready, Ensign?" the pilot asked.

"Let's get back to the barn," Salvio said, in English. Just like his instructor at Fort Benning used to say. **"Rápido."** Salvio's son, a striker, was finally starting on his **fútbol** team. With any luck, the refuel would go fast and he'd make it home in time to catch his game.

The turbines whined as the choppers lifted in unison, arcing into the warm, starlit sky, streaking for home in single file.

A heartbeat later, alarms screamed.

Missile lock.

Salvio grabbed a handhold as the helicopter plunged violently to escape, blowing auto-chaff in a steep banking turn. Through the gunner's door he saw a fiery streak slam into one of his choppers and erupt in a cloud of flaming metal.

The last thing Salvio heard was the roar of the exploding HE charge that tore his aircraft apart, killing most, including him. The screaming survivors perished when the burning wreck slammed into the ground five hundred meters below.

In the space of thirty seconds, the entire Scorpion platoon ceased to exist.

Proof of concept number one.

2

CRISFIELD, MARYLAND

Jack pulled up to the curbless street in front of the modest one-story white frame house and killed the engine. It brought back memories. He hadn't been here since his freshman year in college, when Cory's mom cooked the two Georgetown students a roast. "Stick-to-yer-ribs food, Jack. That's what you boys need if you're sailing today," she'd said. Taking the skiff Cory's dad built out onto Daugherty Creek was one of Jack's favorite memories.

Cory's working-class family was a lot like that little house. Solid, sturdy, dependable—and certainly nothing fancy. But Cory had been a good friend, and the memories Jack had from the summer road trip they took in their sophomore year, hiking fourteeners in Colorado, still made him laugh.

Jack approached the front door with trepidation. He hadn't seen Cory in years. Always meant to, but they both got busy. When his father died in his junior year, Cory gave up his dream of law school and dropped out of Georgetown to take over his father's hardware store, and to care for his ailing mother. Jack made it out a few times that year, but Cory was too tied up with customers and inventory to really do anything but shoot the bull over coffee at the store. Jack's academic plate was also overflowing. No hard feelings. Just a fork in the road. They went their separate ways.

Jack found his dream job with Hendley Associates and The Campus.

Cory stocked lumber and bird food.

Cory's mother died a few years back, but Jack missed that funeral—he didn't even know about it until a year after she was buried. He meant to call Cory and offer his condolences, but it just felt too damn awkward after so much time had passed.

Yeah, awkward.

Some friend, asshole.

Jack rang the doorbell. A moment later, a smartly dressed middle-aged nurse in blue scrubs opened the door. Jack noticed her lapel pins. Mary Francis was an RN and a nun. She smiled.

"You must be Jack. Cory's expecting you."

"Thank you, Sister."

Jack followed her through the neat and tidy home, the old wooden floors creaking under his two-hundred-pound muscled frame.

"How's he doing?" Jack whispered, as if in church.

"As well as can be expected," she replied at full voice. "It won't be long now."

He followed her down a narrow hallway. A dozen family photos in cheap frames hung on the walls. One of them was a picture of Jack and Cory standing next to that skiff so many years ago.

Ouch.

"This way," the nun said, pushing open a bedroom door. An invitation for him to enter alone.

Jack halted for a second. He would've felt more comfortable charging blind into a Tora Bora cave with an empty pistol than dealing with what he imagined was waiting for him inside.

"Jack, you came."

Cory smiled broadly, sitting up in his adjustable bed. He held out his hand. Despite the pallid skin and skeletal frame, he exuded warmth and grace.

Jack sighed with relief. He crossed the room and took Cory's soft hand. Jack was six-foot-one and powerfully built. More so now than when they were in school together. But back then, Cory had been six-four and two-twenty. A state champion lacrosse player. A real beast. Hard to believe the frail wraith in the adjustable bed had once carried a 175-pound Jack a mile and a half down a Colorado slope on his back after he twisted his ankle. Now Cory was half his former weight, if that, and could barely hold up his own arm.

"Good to see you, Cor."

"Sorry for the long drive out. I know you're a busy guy."

Ouch. Again.

Cory saw the flinch. "Sorry, I didn't mean it that way. I know working for a financial firm like Hendley Associates must be an eighty-hour-a-week job."

"Sometimes I bring a cot to the office. Better to sleep than commute."

"Good for you." Cory lay back on his elevated bed, obviously fatigued by his efforts.

Jack glanced around the room while Cory got comfortable, adjusting the IV needle taped to the back of his bruised and sallow hand. A large crucifix hung on the wall opposite the foot of his bed. Next to it was a framed wedding photo of his parents. Cory was an only child.

Standing next to the bottles of pain meds was a framed novena—"Our Lady of Good Remedy." A rolling IV stand with a bag stood on the far side of the bed.

"So, I like what you've done with the place," Jack said.

"My designer calls it Medical Modern. Sort of like **Mad Men,** but with drugs instead of booze."

"I need to call her."

"Just wait a few more weeks. I know a place where you will be able to get all of this stuff dirt cheap." Cory winked.

Jack chuckled. He never knew anybody funnier than Cory. Or scarier, when he threw a punch. Fists like cinder blocks tied to tree trunks. Two bikers in a Jackson Hole bar discovered that side of Cory the hard way.

Jack suddenly felt very self-conscious, his full beard and head of hair in stark contrast to Cory's naked scalp. Chemo took that thick mane of curly blond hair, no doubt, but not the fire in those dark brown eyes.

Cory reached for a plastic cup full of ice water, but it was too far away. Jack snatched it up and brought it close.

"Thanks." Cory sipped cool water through the straw.

Jack's eyes drifted back to the prayer card. **"Dear Lady of Good Remedy, source of unfailing help, thy compassionate heart knows a remedy for every affliction . . ."**

"You go to church much, Jack?"

"Me? Not enough. You?"

"Kinda hard to wheel this bed down the aisle these days. But I do have my own nun, don't I?"

Jack glanced back at the large crucifix. He thought about the coeds that used to draw to Cory like flies to honey, and the beer kegs he'd polished off, almost single-handedly. "I guess you got some religion lately."

"No, I got some cancer lately. My faith renewed is the payoff."

"That's great," Jack said.

Cory heard the cynicism in Jack's voice. "Yeah, I know. Foxhole prayers and all of that. But I'm serious. There's something about facing your mortality that brings eternal things into focus."

"Sure, I suppose it would." Jack didn't mention he'd stared death in the face a few times lately. Quite a few times. He had a hard time finding faith in the dark abyss of a pistol barrel shoved in his face.

"Don't be like me and wait until something like this wakes you up."

"Now you sound like my sister."

"I liked your sister. She doing okay?"

"A doctor now, just like Mom. Same hospital, even. Married a great guy."

"Good for her. Your folks okay? I don't watch the news much these days."

"They're doing well. Thanks for asking."

Cory coughed violently. Thick gobs of phlegm rattled in his throat. He lurched forward, gasping for breath, his pale face reddening with the effort.

Jack reached for a clean spit tray on the table and held it up to Cory's lips with one hand while supporting his bony back with the other. Cory coughed and spat until a spoonful of yellow gel finally dropped into the pink plastic tray.

The nurse burst into the room.

"Cory?" She rushed over to the bed as Jack

gently lowered him. She took the spit tray from Jack's hand and set it down.

"Thank you, Jack. Perhaps you can wait outside for a minute," she said as she wiped Cory's mouth with a tissue.

"Sure, no problem."

Cory shook his head and waved a frail hand. "No, wait, Jack, I'm fine."

"You sure? I've got plenty of time."

Cory took another sip of water with the nun's help. It surprised Jack how much effort it took him. He finished and sighed with exhaustion.

"I'll be right outside," the nun said. "But call me before you need me, okay?"

Cory smiled. "Okay."

She left, closing the door gently behind her.

"So, Jack. Remember those fourteeners we climbed in Colorado?"

"Sure do. I was thinking about that when I pulled up."

"Good times, man. Can't tell you how often I thought about those days when I was counting pallets of drywall and roofing nails. Got me through some dark patches."

Guilt fell all over Jack like a bucket of warm motor oil.

"I'm sorry about that, Cory. I should've—"

"Oh, man. No. I wasn't saying anything. I just mean climbing those mountains meant a lot to me. That high up. Clean air. And the quiet!"

"Yeah, good times for sure."

"I've had a lot of time to think about my life lying here, ya know? Things done, and things undone. And to be honest with you, I wouldn't change a lot. Don't get me wrong. Arguing a landmark case in front of the Supreme Court would've been awesome, but it wasn't meant to be."

"It must have been hard on you."

"It was, and it wasn't. I just did what I had to do to take care of my family. You would've done the same thing for yours. I know you would have."

Jack nodded. He sure as hell would have. There wasn't anything he wouldn't do for his family, especially his mom and dad.

"So really, no regrets. Well, except one. I never told you this, but I made two promises to my dad when he was on his deathbed. I'm proud to say I kept one of them—finishing my pre-law degree at Georgetown last year."

"That's freaking awesome. Congratulations."

Jack stuck out his hand. Cory took it as best as he could.

"Thanks, man. Summa cum laude, too, by the way."

"Not surprised." Truth was, Cory was the sharpest knife in the drawer.

"But I didn't keep the other promise. And it's killing me."

"You do look like shit. But I thought that was the cancer," Jack said, hoping for a laugh.

He got one.

"Ouch, man," Cory said, touching his stomach. "Don't do that. It makes me hurt."

"Sorry."

"No, you're not."

"No, not really."

They bumped fists. Friends again. For life.

However long that was.

"So, what's the promise you didn't keep?"

Cory told him.

Jack didn't bat an eye.

"It's a lot to ask, I know," Cory said. "But I couldn't think of anyone else I could ask, let alone pull it off. But I hate to disappoint my dad, you know?"

"Yeah, I know. But I think he'd understand."

"He probably would. But this is about me. I want to keep my word. And you're my only shot."

Jack fought back the tears welling up in his eyes.

"It would be an honor."

Sister Mary Francis brought in a bottle of twelve-year-old Macallan single-malt whiskey and two glasses Cory had purchased for the occasion. The bedridden man sipped water out of his glass while Jack worked his way through a couple fingers. They laughed and told stories like old college buddies do, but the light began to dim outside and Cory's eyes began fluttering with fatigue.

Jack left the room with Cory gently snoring and Sister Mary Francis's heartfelt thanks.

"If he needs anything at all, please call me," Jack said, slipping her a business card. She handed him one of hers as well.

"I will. Safe travels, Jack. And God bless you for coming."

Jack was surprised when his phone rang with her number just three and a half hours later as he sat at his desk, poring over a spreadsheet.

Cory Chase was gone.

3

Arnie van Damm, President Ryan's chief of staff, sat in the office of Senator Deborah Dixon. There was something bigger than the massive, hand-carved antique desk separating them at the moment.

As the chair of the Senate Foreign Relations Committee and a former chair of the Senate Foreign Relations Subcommittee on Europe and Regional Security Cooperation, Dixon was one of the most powerful people in the Senate and arguably the most important foreign policy legislator. Treaties lived and died on her watch.

Except this time, a bill didn't "die," it was killed—shot in the head and bled out by Dixon herself, a fellow Republican. It had been a straight party-line vote—except for Dixon, who crossed the aisle and voted with the Democrats.

Arnie was furious. More important, so was President Ryan, along with Secretary of State

Scott Adler, Secretary of Defense Robert Burgess, and the Army chief of staff. President Ryan himself had spent months carefully planning and negotiating a bilateral treaty with Poland to build and maintain a permanent army base on Polish soil. That base would serve as a forward defense against encroaching Russian expansion in the region in the face of a weakening Western European commitment to NATO's defense.

As chief of staff, Arnie had the task of greasing the wheels on Capitol Hill for any piece of legislation, including the one Dixon murdered. The senator was an old friend and a reliable colleague. Or so he thought until this morning. He polished his steel-rimmed glasses, trying to calm himself.

"You're kind of cute when you're angry, Arnie. Anyone ever tell you that?" Dixon said. She was fifty-six trying to look thirty-six and nearly pulling it off. Pilates five times a week, Botox three times a year, a strict Paleo diet, and the best hair colorist in the District went a long way, but good genetics didn't hurt. She was a striking woman, but it was her razor-sharp mind and not her head-turning figure that got her where she was today.

Well, mostly.

"If you think I'm cute when I'm angry, then I must be damned beautiful right now, Deborah. A fucking Adonis. I thought we had a deal." Arnie's bald scalp pinked with anger.

"Well, you thought wrong. We had a lengthy

discussion and I considered your words carefully. The subcommittee examined the matter from all points, including expert testimony both for and against. You know, Arnie, I do have a job to do. I'm a sitting U.S. senator, not a GOP apparatchik. I'm supposed to 'advise and consent,' not just roll over and wag my tail whenever the Ryan administration whistles."

"Cute speech, Deborah. You write it yourself?"

"Let's cut the shit, Arnie. What do you want?"

"To begin with, I want a public apology. You embarrassed the hell out of the President—he's already scheduled for a meeting with the Polish president in Warsaw next month to break ground on the base."

"First of all, I'm not apologizing for living up to my sworn constitutional responsibilities, and second, don't blame me because you already ordered your golden shovels for Fort Ryan."

"Damn it, Deborah, that's not fair and you know it. No one's asking you to shirk your duties. But if you had concerns, you should have brought them to us, privately, and we could have worked something out. But you know that and you didn't say a thing. What the hell happened?"

"Nothing 'happened,' Arnie, other than I performed due diligence."

"And what did your 'due diligence' uncover that we hadn't already discussed ad nauseam?"

"C'mon, Arnie. We're adults here. Let's get real.

This is rah-rah bullshit. A giant photo op. This treaty sends exactly the wrong message at the wrong time to the Russians. It's time to deescalate, especially with a new Russian president. Give him a chance to settle in. Putting a forward base on his perimeter forces him to respond. Otherwise, the Kremlin hardliners will have his head, literally if not figuratively."

"Si vis pacem, para bellum," Arnie said, leaning in. "If you want peace, prepare for war."

"Si vis pacem, para pacem," she countered. "We should try diplomacy for a change, instead of provocation."

"We're not the aggressors here. We aren't the ones who put troops over the borders in Ukraine and Lithuania." Arnie was referring to the recent Russian incursions, pushed back or at least halted by a force of mostly American arms. "But you know that. What's this really all about?"

"I think I've made myself perfectly clear. This bilateral treaty—which is already pissing off our most important NATO allies, Germany and France—isn't going to do anything but provoke another war with the Russians. We keep encroaching on their periphery, despite our promises to the contrary."

"The Russians are just making excuses—"

"No, Arnie. Think about it from their perspective. The Russians agreed to allow Germany to reunify, but only after a NATO promise not to expand eastward. What happened? Germany unified—Russia's worst strategic fear, at least on the Continent—and NATO expanded eastward anyway."

"That was before President Ryan's time."

"But he still stands by it. It's not like he's pulling back our NATO commitments in the East. Croatia? Albania? For chrissakes, Arnie, Montenegro? You think we need Montenegro for strategic defense in depth? Don't bother to answer that. We both know the answer. So do the Russians. You're one of the President's whiz kids. Tell me, what would you do if you were the Russians and the shoe were on the other foot?"

"I sure as hell wouldn't be invading my neighbors."

"Really? If Cuba suddenly got nuclear weapons? Or the Russians staged Bear bombers on bases in Canada? You'd advise the President to be patient? To not see any of that as a threat?"

"But we're not the Russians!"

"Russians." Dixon shook her head in a pitying gesture. "What is it with you neocons and Russia? It's a glorified gas station with nukes that they'll never use. A third-rate power, at best."

"Tell me, Deborah. What's the color of the sky in your world? Because in mine, it's blue, and in my world, the Russians are an aggressive and dangerous nuclear power that won't stop expanding unless someone stops them. The Germans sure as hell aren't going to do it. The Poles will—or at least help us stop them."

"Our current defense budget is ten times larger than Russia's, and larger than the combined defense spending of the next eight countries, including Russia and China. Hell, our defense budget is three times larger than the rest of NATO combined. You think one more American base in Poland will finally do the trick?"

Arnie sighed. "We used to be on the same page. I don't quite get you. So tell me, straight up, what do you want?"

"What do I want?" Dixon stood. "I'll tell you what I want. A bourbon and rocks. You want one, too?" She crossed over to her office minibar.

As Dixon dropped ice in her glass, Arnie rubbed his head, thinking, **What's her game?**

He scanned the walls absentmindedly. He'd seen the photos before. Dixon with kings and presidents, popes and CEOs. In one, she knelt by the bedside of a double amputee at Walter Reed. In another, she sat in the cockpit of an F-35, and in a third, her eyes were glued to the periscope of a **Los Angeles**–class attack submarine.

There were also photos of projects in Africa and around the world paid for by the Dixon-Gage Charitable Trust.

The wall of photos said it all. She was an effective legislator, a compassionate leader, a foreign policy expert and, to judge from her tailored Fendi suit and Manolo Blahnik Estipulas, a woman of expensive tastes married to big money.

She was, in a word, ambitious.

Dixon took her seat behind her desk and sipped her bourbon. "Where were we?"

"I need you to know that this will not stand. President Ryan is determined to get this treaty passed. He reached out to you before and now you've bitten his hand. That's a stupid mistake, especially for someone who has her eyes on the prize."

Dixon snorted. "Hell, Arnie. I once caught a White House janitor sitting in the President's chair. Everybody in this town has their 'eyes on the prize.' The question is, what would any of them do with it if they actually got ahold of it?"

"Defend the nation from all enemies, foreign and domestic. Or so I hope."

"At least we agree on something. The devil is in the details."

"Look, Deborah. You want to run for President? Fine. But you're better off with a Ryan endorsement than without one."

"Is that something you're guaranteeing today?"

Arnie shook his head. "You know I can't do that. The President will endorse whom he thinks is the best man or woman for the job."

"Then the choice is clear, don't you think?"

"Running for the presidency against this

President's agenda is a mistake, especially the President of your own party."

"You know I've never been a party hack. I'm an independent thinker."

"Then you can run as an independent."

"And lose? No, thank you. I need the GOP nomination if I want to win."

"Then mind your manners, wait your turn, and get in line with the President's agenda."

Dixon's face visibly reddened behind the bleached white smile.

"I'll take that under advisement."

"Good. And consider the consequences if you don't." Arnie stood. "I've got another meeting, Senator. Thank you for your time." He turned on his heel and left, not waiting for her response.

Dixon sat back in her chair, rolling the bourbon glass in her fingers, fuming. President Ryan was pissed off. She knew he would be. But that was part of the price she was willing to pay. Besides, she had no choice. On the Polish treaty, her instructions were made crystal clear.

And she had no intentions of waiting her turn.

She sipped her bourbon thoughtfully. The idea of Ryan coming after her sent shivers down her spine.

But the alternative was far worse.

4

TEHRAN, IRAN
MINISTRY OF INTELLIGENCE
AND SECURITY (VEVAK)

SATISFIED?

Dr. Mehdi Mohammadi, head of VEVAK, Iran's intelligence ministry, had been staring at that single-word query on the computer screen for more than a minute. It was an interesting question, full of possibilities.

And dangers.

The countdown clock didn't help clarify matters. Forty-two seconds to go.

"Sir?" The bearded young technician smiled hopefully. He liked his job. He liked breathing even better. Crossing Dr. Mohammadi threatened both.

"I'm still thinking." Mohammadi stroked his gray beard with his one good hand.

In truth, he was satisfied. The intel provided by CHIBI was as good as promised. Perhaps too good.

On the one hand, it had allowed the Quds Force to set a trap and wipe out the Argentine crusaders, opening the door for further Hezbollah actions in that country and, perhaps, the entire subcontinent, providing yet another distraction for the Americans and Israelis in the war they could never win against the Most High.

"Thirty seconds, sir."

"Even with one blinded eye, I can still read a clock."

VEVAK—Vezarat-e Ettela'at va Amniat-e Keshvar—was the largest, most powerful, and best-funded agency in Iran, and Dr. Mohammadi reported only to the Supreme Leader, Ayatollah Yasseri—even the Assembly of Experts had no say in his affairs. His agency was second only to Mossad in the region, and nearly equal to the other great power services. Intelligence was key to everything. His Unknown Soldiers of Imam Zaman carried out clandestine intelligence-gathering operations all over the globe. But never had they gathered this kind of intelligence.

The kind of intelligence that would change everything.

Intelligence of inestimable value.

And how did CHIBI come by it? A single, anonymous e-mail—his best technicians still couldn't trace the source—with a simple offer. "A free sample," it promised.

Mohammadi's first thought was that it was

a trap, some kind of elaborate ruse by the Americans or Israelis to expose Quds Force and Hezbollah operations in Latin America.

But even the Americans wouldn't sacrifice more than two dozen Argentine special operators for an act of deception.

This all seemed too good to be true. But Allah was known to confound the minds of the infidels. And every intelligence professional knew that the greatest intelligence coups of the Cold War didn't come from traditional methods but rather through persons choosing to walk in the door and deliver the goods of their own volition, motivated by their own sense of ideology, ego, or greed.

Was this the case now? Or was this, indeed, an elaborate and bloody trap designed to finally destroy the Revolution? And if so, by whom?

The Persian Spring operation had been an utter fiasco. Thanks be to Allah that he had opposed it from the start, Mohammadi thought. But that fool Ghorbani had won the argument. His death was Allah's judgment, surely, but the Russians were badly burned by the failed operation. Perhaps they were seeking some sort of revenge for Reza Kazem's failure?

If Mohammadi passed on this opportunity, he risked losing the greatest sword Allah could ever have put in his hands to defeat his crusader enemies. Perhaps Allah would not forgive him if he foolishly refused the generous offer.

The Ayatollah surely would not forgive him if he refused it. Mohammadi cast his one eye not blinded by the Shah's SAVAK torturers at the technician seated next to him. Did the young man realize his life hung in the balance of the next few seconds?

There was another possibility. Could this be the devil's sword, aimed at the heart of the Republic? A sword plucked out from the fires of hell by his own hand because he had allowed himself to be deceived by the infidel on the other end of this computer connection?

Risk versus reward. Isn't that how the Americans would view this?

Dr. Mohammadi touched the knot of fused bone and melted flesh that used to be his left hand. Another gift of the CIA and Mossad-trained SAVAK scum that tried to strangle the Revolution in its mother's womb. His hatred for the Americans and Jews knew no bounds. Allah had used his suffering to make him as hard as the stump at the end of his arm. His study of the holy texts taught him many things, but none so important as the truth that **there are no cowards in Paradise**.

Just four seconds left on the clock.

"Type, 'Yes, quite satisfied,'" Mohammadi finally said.

The tech sighed silently and typed quickly.

They worked in English, the language chosen by CHIBI. When he was still a young Islamic scholar, Mohammadi fled to Canada to escape the Shah's murderous reach. He became fluent in both French and English in his years there before SAVAK found him and brought him back to Tehran for extensive interrogation.

Another proof of Allah's omniscient guidance in his life.

"Now ask, 'How much?'"

The tech typed again.

A response appeared instantly.

YOU KNOW THE TERMS.

"Name your price," Mohammadi replied.

YOU KNOW THE TERMS.

"At least tell me whom I'm bidding against." Mohammadi feared that someone else would win the auction and wield this weapon against the Republic. But he also feared paying too much. Iran's economy was in shambles now. He would have to ask the Ayatollah for ungodly sums of money if he wanted to guarantee a win. But what if the other bidders were lesser agencies?

YOU KNOW THE TERMS.

Clearly, CHIBI was being careful. Syntax, vocabulary, and logical arguments could give away his identity.

"Enemies of the Revolution?"

YOU KNOW THE TERMS.

He did. Anonymity of the bidders had been guaranteed. But the other bidders must be the other major intelligence agencies locked in battle with the Americans. Who else would want what CHIBI was selling?

YES OR NO?

"Yes. I will send a representative to London on the date specified."

INSTRUCTIONS TO FOLLOW.

CHIBI disappeared from the screen. Another digital jinn in the wilderness of the Dark Web.

A quick, cold look from Mohammadi's blinded eye sent the tech scurrying out of the air-conditioned room. The intelligence chief sat alone in the underground bunker, surrounded by the hum of a dozen large-screen monitors, rubbing his stump and thinking.

CHIBI was a genius. A single, silent bid in an anonymous auction would guarantee maximum profit. If CHIBI offered the same quality "free sample" to the others as had been offered to him, they would all be champing at the bit—and bidding high.

Time to meet with the Supreme Leader. He stood, brushing away the wrinkles in his clerical robe.

With the economy in shambles, it would take some effort to gather the vast sum he had in mind.

Priceless didn't come cheap.

Inshallah.

5

FORT MEADE, MARYLAND
NSA HEADQUARTERS

Dead rats. Sometimes pigeons. But dead, desiccated rats were better. We slathered them with hot sauce to keep the feral cats away and stuffed film rolls or transposition ciphers in them for dead drops. That was how we did it in Moscow back in the day."

So said Director of National Intelligence Mary Pat Foley, sitting at the head of a large mahogany table in the fourth-floor conference room. Her husband, Ed Foley, had been the youngest CIA Moscow chief of station ever. They served together. Brought and raised their kids over there. It was the late eighties. It was the Cold War.

It was a long time ago.

Mary Pat glanced around the room. Polite smiles, mostly. Indulging the boss, no doubt.

The faces were all so young. Forties, mostly, a few even younger. On either side of her sat the security department head or their representative from each of the sixteen agencies that comprised the Intelligence Community (IC) Cloud, as well as the rep from her own office, the ODNI. The room's glass walls were electronically shaded from the dozens of NSA analysts at their workstations on the floor beyond. Total security all around.

She used to be the youngest person in every room. More often these days, she was the oldest.

When did that happen? she thought.

One fleeting day at a time.

The youngest face in the room sat directly opposite her on the far end of the table. Amanda Watson was also the most attractive. Blond and athletically built, the thirty-three-year-old computer savant looked more like a Fox News anchor than CloudServe's senior design engineer and principal architect of the IC Cloud. Watson was also in charge of IC Cloud security and personally ran the Red Team hacking group that routinely assaulted the IC Cloud, searching for any hardware or software weak spots to exploit. Who better to do this than the woman who had designed the world's first "unhackable" cloud network?

"Rats? Sounds kinda gross," Watson said, flashing a perfectly engineered smile. "But I'm guessing it worked."

"Like a charm."

Foley scanned the room again. She was trying to find a way to make her point. The average technical IQ around the table was several orders of magnitude beyond hers, especially Watson's. Who was she to challenge these brainiacs?

The decision to put all IC intelligence onto a single "cloud"—really, just racks and racks of servers in a secured data-storage facility—was made by people smarter than she was and who assured both her and President Ryan that this was the future of intelligence processing, sharing, and security. No more firewalls or turf wars that prevented one federal agency from knowing vital information that another agency had. No more missed opportunities. No more FUBARs. Everything the IC departments did—ELINT, HUMINT, and SIGINT—was uploaded to the cloud. Everyone had access. Everyone would be on the same page. It was exponentially more efficient for information sharing among all IC agencies and organizations, rendered enormous cost savings, and increased computer security by reducing the number and complexity of machines and access nodes.

On paper, it was a brilliant idea.

And all of it more secure than ever before. Or so they said. As one of her aides explained to her, instead of having a bunch of little banks scattered all over the country, where every local bank robber had a chance to break into any one of them, now you had a giant Fort Knox where all the money was kept.

And nobody could break into Fort Knox.

Right?

"Rats were great because nobody likes rats, not even Communists, especially dead rats dropped around garbage cans."

Watson's flawless brow furrowed with an unspoken question. **And your point is?**

"You all are digital natives," Foley said. "You grew up with this stuff like a second language. You're fluent in 'Hadoop nodes' and 'bit lockers' and 'SaaS.' My generation are digital poms."

"Poms, ma'am?" the young analyst from the FBI Intelligence Branch asked.

"Poms. Pomegranates. Rhymes with 'immigrants.' It's an Aussie word I picked up recently. It's a tiresome way for me to say I'm a digital immigrant. I came to all of this late. I know it's the future—heck, it's the **now**—but I'm analog. I know what works for me."

"I assure you, Madame Director, the IC Cloud works, too." Watson didn't pile on. They'd just spent the last two hours reviewing the stunning successes of the system in today's quarterly meeting. Perfect operability, zero breaches.

Foley touched her tablet. "I know it does. Your data prove it."

"But you're still concerned," Watson said. She was the only private-sector person in the room, and her company's future depended on making and keeping her federal government clients happy.

"A professional habit," Foley offered with a weary smile. She hadn't been sleeping well lately, another hazard in her line of work. What was really bothering her? Was it her own insecurity she was worried about? Unable to keep up completely with all of the technobabble? Just feeling her age?

It was easy to dismiss someone as young and pretty as Watson. Women Foley's age often did, for all of the wrong reasons. Youth and beauty were still the coin of the realm. But that would be a mistake. Foley had studied Watson's file.

She was, without question, brilliant.

What had made Watson particularly interesting to the Ryan administration was her unreserved patriotism, a lamentably rare thing in the privileged corporate boardrooms of the San Francisco Bay Area. Amanda's brother, Kyle "Rex" Watson, was a Delta sniper, killed by an eighty-two-millimeter mortar strike along with his spotter "Mutt" in Sevastopol just a few years ago during the Russian invasion of Ukraine. Since his death, Watson had worked tirelessly on behalf of wounded veterans and their families, winning numerous awards for her charitable work. Mary Pat's sources told her that Watson even visited his grave at Arlington National Cemetery before today's meeting.

No one in the room doubted Watson's skill sets, intelligence, or patriotism, least of all Foley. But it wasn't Watson that Foley was worried about.

A few years ago, China's premier cyberwarfare unit, Ghost Ship, had been destroyed in a heroic bombing run by Marine Corps fighter pilots on the Chinese mainland. But China's electronic warfare and cyberespionage cadres, including the infamous People's Liberation Army Unit 61398, had only expanded in numbers and capabilities in recent years. It wasn't a surprise. China produced more than four million STEM graduates every year on the mainland, and many thousands of STEM students in the United States were actually Chinese nationals, some of whom were guilty of spying on the U.S. corporations and research institutions that hired them.

American corporations lost an estimated $300 billion of intellectual property to China's cyberespionage programs, which had also successfully stolen plans related to advanced American weapons systems, including the F-35 Lightning II.

"Chinese army's APT"—advanced persistent threat—"units have upped their game recently, investing heavily in AI-assisted hacking attacks that are escalating exponentially in frequency and scope. Tell me, Ms. Watson, doesn't that concern you?"

"Yes, of course it does. China is, without a doubt, the single greatest cybersecurity threat we face. But right behind them are the Russians, the North Koreans, the Iranians—the list is endless. The IC Cloud's standardized, automated, and air-gapped cloud computing system has proven to be impervious to their attacks, as I know you're well aware, Madame Director."

"But here's what's keeping me up at night, Amanda," Foley began. "All U.S. intelligence is stored and analyzed on the IC Cloud. But the U.S. IC is intimately connected to the Five Eyes program, the Club de Berne, and EU INTCEN, among others. In short, the entire Western intelligence apparatus would be exposed if the IC Cloud was ever compromised. I can't shake the feeling that having put all of our eggs in this one basket has created an awfully tempting target. The math isn't on our side. The IC is currently defeating tens of millions of attacks every year—and I congratulate all of you around this table for that—but if just one of them succeeds, just one, we could suffer the most catastrophic intelligence failure in the history of the world."

Watson nodded patiently. "Forgive me, but I think the math actually is on our side. I would suggest that the **failure** of tens of millions of these attacks so far this year is evidence that the IC Cloud is doing its job perfectly, and there is every reason to believe it will continue to do so."

Watson leaned back in her chair, tenting her fingers. "Believe me, Madame Director, you're not the only one who wakes up with panic attacks in the middle of the night. That's why my Red Team hackers work so hard to find any potential vulnerabilities. My department is constantly up-dating your hardware and software, and there isn't a line of code or a single circuit diagram upgrade that doesn't land on my desk. I check and double-check everything after it's all been thoroughly tested by my team—the best in the world, I might add. To borrow a quote, you have nothing to fear but fear itself."

"You sound pretty confident."

"I can't guarantee the sun will rise tomorrow morning, either, but I believe the IC Cloud is just as reliable." Watson leaned forward on the table. "I love this country too much to put it at risk. If there is ever a whiff of a potential problem, you will be the first to know, Madame Director. You have my word on that." Watson smiled warmly. "Until then, leave the worrying to me."

Foley offered a tired nod. She came in wanting assurances. Watson gave her at least a few.

"I'll do my best. I suppose I have enough on my plate as it is." Foley addressed the room. "Again, thank you all for your time and attention." She stood. "Especially to you, Ms. Watson. And please give my regards to Elias. Meeting adjourned."

As the others began filing out, Watson asked, "A private word, if I may?"

Foley smiled. "Of course."

———

The room emptied. Amanda Watson approached Foley. Both remained standing after hours of sitting through the long session.

Foley admired the younger woman. She'd studied her security audit files closely.

Watson was recruited heavily by Silicon Valley firms out of grad school at UC Berkeley, where she earned her master's degree in computer engineering, graduating at the top of her class at the tender age of eighteen. The head of the NSA had personally flown out to the West Coast to invite her into the fold after Watson passed a secret FBI vetting with flying colors. But she turned him down cold for the far more lucrative offer made by Elias Dahm, seduced by both the cash and the playboy's well-known sexual charisma.

The two lovers went on to build the world's largest and most trusted cloud computing company over the course of the next decade. A brilliant engineer in his own right, Dahm was the headline-grabbing salesman and Watson the quiet technical genius, an updated version of Apple's Jobs–Wozniak dynamic.

After Elias Dahm had moved on to other romantic and business interests—particularly SpaceServe, his rocket subsidiary—Watson kept a steady hand on the tiller at CloudServe's engineering department. Watson wasn't on the CloudServe board, but she was number four in the company's organizational chart after Dahm, the COO, and CFO, respectively, and she owned approximately $240 million worth of CloudServe stock. It was as much her company as his, at least in intellectual pedigree, though not in legal reality.

"How may I help you, Amanda?"

"Just a quick word. Elias asked me to inquire about where we stood on the JEDI War Cloud project?"

Watson was referring to the Joint Enterprise Defense Infrastructure program the DoD was seeking to implement. The JEDI War Cloud would consolidate the DoD's four hundred data centers to just one integrated cloud-based system with real-time monitoring of all activities. The biggest tech names—Google, Amazon, Microsoft—were also bidding for the contract, but CloudServe had the inside track, thanks to its successful implementation of the IC Cloud. Watson wasn't a saleswoman, but she knew that part of her job today was to wax the skis for CloudServe's JEDI bid.

"I'm sorry Elias couldn't be with us today," Foley said, hiding her annoyance. The federal government was CloudServe's biggest client and they stood to gain even more business if the War Cloud project moved forward.

"I apologize, Madame Director. The next Space-Serve launch is less than two weeks away and it has his full attention. Besides"—she grinned—"I'm a much better engineer than he is, anyway. It made more sense for me to be at this meeting today."

"You and your team are doing a fantastic job, and I really do want you to know how much I appreciate all that you've accomplished despite the hand-wringing you witnessed today."

"The entire IC is to be commended. You have some really top-drawer people running the show. But I promise you, we won't relax. You're absolutely right to worry about the Chinese and the rest of the bad guys out there. They're relentless, but so are we."

"Please convey my best wishes to Elias. I hope the launch goes well."

"And what may I tell him regarding our War Cloud bid?"

"Tell him that all bids have been submitted and are being reviewed, just as the law requires."

"Yes, of course. I'll do that."

They shook hands. "Have a safe trip home, Amanda."

Foley resisted the temptation to play mother and advise her that a schoolgirl crush on the high school quarterback was no way to organize one's life.

6

BERLIN, GERMANY

Dieter Hansemann exited the Blissestrasse U-Bahn station, the last train of the night. He jammed his hands into his coat pockets against the slight chill breeze and headed south until he reached the Mexican restaurant on the corner and turned left onto his street.

The late-night auditing marathons over the last month had become a predictable thing, and had taken their toll on the thirty-five-year-old banker. But it was worth it. He was close to finally nailing down the project he'd been assigned.

Very close.

Mature elm trees lined both sides of the narrow street, spreading their branches high over the asphalt, bent over and nearly touching like the angels' wings on the Ark of the Covenant.

A small fenced park stood on his side of the street, a pleasant place to jog when he actually had the time to do it. He looked forward to the day he'd be there again. He hoped before it began snowing in the next month or two.

Passing by a park entrance gate, he heard a commotion. A woman's plaintive cry against a man's harsh, accented voice. Dieter stopped in his tracks and squinted through the gloom. The couple were little more than shadows in the distance, partially hidden from the street. The tall man raised an arm high before swinging it down with a curse in Arabic.

Dieter hesitated. Nothing could put his work at risk. But honor won out in the space of a single breath, and the athletic German dashed toward the fighting couple.

When he got close he shouted **"Halt!"** but kept at a dead run straight for the bigger man's broad torso. The woman, a redhead, cried out, **"Hilf mir!"** just as the bearded **Araber** backhanded her across the jaw. She tumbled to the ground in a whimper as the man whipped around, facing Dieter down with a crooked smile and a sharp blade.

The banker didn't slow. He juked left, then right, forcing the other man—an Egyptian—to shift his weight. Dieter juked left again, and just at the moment when the bearded man transferred his weight between his feet, Dieter lunged forward with speed, blocking a weak strike by the other man with his left forearm and smashing his right elbow into the side of his skull.

Dieter's strength and momentum put the man on his back, scattering the blade. The German's

CQB training took over. Straddling the Egyptian between his thighs, Dieter pinned his neck to the ground with his left forearm as he launched right-elbow strikes at his face, partially blocked by the bigger man's counterpunches.

The German's furious attack ended with the explosion of white-hot pain in his back. Instinctively, he rose up and reached for the wound, only to feel the heavy knife blade plunge again between his shoulders, this time severing his spinal cord. He was dead before his face smashed into the pavement.

"About fucking time," the Egyptian said. He rubbed his swelling face.

The redhead reached a hand down and helped him to his feet.

"I'll grab his shit," she said, wiping the bloody blade on the back of Dieter's tweed coat.

She robbed him of his wallet, iWatch, iPhone, and a gold crucifix hanging around his neck.

"Too bad," the woman said. "He is a beautiful man. **Sehr schön**."

"Let's get out of here." The man held one hand to his aching face.

"Wait." She rolled Dieter onto his back with her booted foot and snapped photos of his lifeless face with her Galaxy phone.

"Now we leave."

The two of them sped quickly across the park, but not at a run, lest they draw attention to themselves. They climbed into a 2018 silver BMW 5 series sedan and drove away, careful to obey the laws.

The couple knew the Berlin **Polizei** would no doubt conclude that banker Dieter Hansemann had been killed during a robbery, far from any surveillance cameras and witnesses. When the police detectives learned he was actually a deep-cover agent for the BKA, or Bundeskriminalamt—the German version of the FBI—they would know he was murdered, but not the reason why.

Dieter Hansemann's corpse was proof of concept number two.

7

WASHINGTON, D.C.
THE OVAL OFFICE

President Ryan sat in one of the new tufted leather chairs, his back to the Resolute desk, his suit coat on the rack, tie loosened, and an iced coffee in hand. It had been a helluva long day, and the news Arnie van Damm was bringing was making it even longer.

SecDef Burgess and SecState Adler sat on opposite Chesterfield couches while Arnie took the other chair across from the President. The rich, caramel leather didn't swallow them up like the old sofas had. The round silver carpet with the bold presidential seal lay between them.

"You can't blame her. The Senate is just a hundred little Presidents waiting to run," Adler said.

"I don't fault her for her ambition, per se," Ryan said. He was still smarting from Senator Chadwick's unwarranted and vicious partisan attacks in the past few months. Vain and unscrupulous, Chadwick at least was a member of the opposing party. "But ambition needs to have its limits."

Everybody in the room knew that Ryan never asked for the presidency. A suicidal Japanese airline pilot was the reason he was first thrust into the Oval Office. "But she isn't President yet," Ryan said, "and I don't like the way she's trying to hijack my foreign policy agenda."

"I just don't get why she did it," Burgess said. "We kept her in the loop the whole time."

"Maybe we should've put her out front and center. She likes her picture in the papers," Adler said. "And Instagram Live."

"We offered her the opportunity to run point on this. She said she had other legislative priorities," Ryan said. "I took that to mean she wasn't interested—not hostile. Maybe she was telegraphing and we missed it."

"No way. I kept in touch with her office all the way through. Never a peep of concern," Arnie said. "And frankly, it's damn disloyal."

Ryan couldn't help but smile. His chief of staff was as loyal as they came, a virtue he greatly appreciated, along with the fierce intelligence lingering behind his pale blue eyes.

"Loyalty? That's becoming as rare as honor in this town—and shame took the five-thirty Greyhound out of here a long time ago," Adler said.

"Something happened," Arnie said.

"Like what?" Burgess asked.

"Somebody yanked Dixon's leash." Arnie pulled a handkerchief from his pocket to wipe his wire-framed glasses.

"Meaning?"

Arnie fogged one of his lenses with his breath. "I think she's dirty."

"Whoa, hold on there. That's quite a charge," Ryan said.

Arnie tapped the side of his nose. "I'm telling you, I can smell it."

"As beautiful as it is, I don't think we can call on your honker to testify in open court," Ryan said. "You have any proof?"

"None. But common sense and thirty years up to my neck in this filthy swamp of a town has taught me a few things. She T-boned the shit out of us— the political equivalent of a hit-and-run. Why? What does she get out of it? Especially knowing what she's risking by crossing you."

Ryan shook his head. "I'm not a Mafia boss, Arnie. I'm the chief executive and I'm just trying to do what's right for this country and our national security. It's not like I'm going to put a hit out on her." He took a sip of his iced coffee. "But I will promise you this: If she's committed any kind of crime or done anything to harm this nation, she'll answer for it."

Arnie fought back a smile. He knew his boss and his friend as well as any man in Washington.

There wasn't a vengeful bone in his body—for him, politics wasn't personal. But he had a profound sense of justice, and when anything threatened the things he loved most, he was ready to fight. President Ryan wouldn't sucker-punch anyone, but he was one hell of a counterstriker.

The SecDef shifted his weight on the leather sofa. "I'm with Arnie. I can't for the life of me figure out what she gets out of killing this bill. The Poles are paying for the base and its maintenance, NATO gets a forward defense, and the Russians are kept back on their heels—a tangible, kinetic deterrent to further aggression."

"**Cui bono**, gentlemen," Ryan offered. The Georgetown Jesuit profs had drilled that into his skull early on. "It always comes back to that. If we can't figure out what she gets out of it, let's figure out who else might benefit from her decision."

"Well, the Russians, certainly," Burgess said. "They sure as hell don't want a U.S. armored division on their doorstep."

"I don't think the Russians are behind this play," Ryan said. "No one has been more vocal in the Senate calling for stiffer Russian sanctions than Dixon. Who else?"

"Come to think of it, the Germans didn't exactly come running to the table on this—we had to drag them by the elbows to get them to sign off," Burgess said.

"Nor the French," Adler added.

"If this makes NATO stronger, why would the French and Germans **not** want this?" Arnie asked. He was focused on domestic issues and legislative affairs. He left the foreign policy heavy lifting to Ryan's cabinet.

"Because they don't want to piss Moscow off—the Germans especially are dependent on Russian natural gas," Adler said. "But in truth, the total volume of trade between Russia, Germany, and France isn't significant."

"But it is there," Burgess said. "Despite all of the recent troubles with Russia."

"Nothing new on that account," Adler said. "All through the Cold War, the Europeans were more than happy to have us spend billions running NATO while they traded heavily with the Soviets. I don't know if that made them hypocrites or us just plain fools."

"Why not both?" Ryan offered with a mocking smile.

"And if, in the spirit of full disclosure, we use Russian RD-180 engines on our Atlas V heavy rocket," the SecDef said. One of the many infuriating, ironic compromises of the modern world.

Ryan scowled. Signing the bill that exempted Russian rocket motors from the sanctions list had left a bad taste in his mouth, even though it was necessary at the time. "We need to fix that, Arnie. Let's put that at the top of the Security Council agenda tomorrow."

"Done."

Burgess asked, "So, if this isn't about European trade with Russia, why did the French and Germans resist this base treaty?"

"To be fair, they resisted, but they eventually signed on," Adler said.

"But why the reluctance?"

"My sense is that it wasn't about the base, it was about Poland. The bureaucrats in Brussels are far more worried about European nationalism than Russian expansion, and Poland is one of the most self-consciously nationalist countries in Europe."

"And the EU views nationalist movements as a threat to deepening European integration," Ryan said.

"Not just slowing integration down but actually unraveling it. Brexit, the Italians, the Hungarians—the peasants are sharpening their pitchforks."

"And they saw a bilateral treaty between two NATO member nations as a threat to the borderless European Union?"

"It was never expressed that way officially, but it was loud and clear in the European media," Adler said. "There's always been a radical element that saw NATO as a barrier to European integration, especially since it so heavily relies on our participation—and funding."

SecDef Burgess chuckled. "Last year, six out of six German diesel submarines were in dry

dock—and they could only field ninety-five Leopard 2 tanks. The Russians have twenty thousand
tanks and IFVs active or in reserve. Bundeswehr
helicopter pilots are borrowing civilian choppers
to practice because the military ones aren't available, and only half of all French aircraft and a
quarter of their helicopters are flying at any given
time. And don't forget that incident a few years
ago when the Germans used broomsticks for rifles
on a training exercise because they had a shortage
of the real ones."

Adler shook his head. "Neither Germany nor
France nor half a dozen other NATO partners
have lived up to their NATO spending obligations. We've been footing the bill since the beginning even though the EU is our biggest trading
competitor next to China."

"If you go to a party and people keep kicking
you in the ass, you're probably the guy with the
KICK ME sign pinned to his back," Adler said.

"So how do they expect to defend themselves
against Russian aggression if NATO isn't ready?"
Arnie asked.

"You'd be surprised how many Europeans
think it's American and NATO aggression that
provokes Russian hostility. Get rid of NATO and
your Russian problem is solved, or so they think,"
Ryan said.

"A few Americans think that, too," Arnie added.

"So, to bottom-line this, you think Dixon is dancing to the tune set by Berlin and Paris?" Burgess asked.

"I think it's worse than that," Ryan said. "Let's finish the exercise: Who else benefits from a canceled Polish army base?"

"Maybe it's not about the Polish army base. Maybe it's really about us," Adler said.

Ryan nodded, always the college professor. "Agreed. Go on."

"And the list of people who stand to benefit at our expense is a mile long."

"And who would you say would be at the top of that list—besides the Russians?"

"The Chinese, no question," Burgess said.

"Exactly."

"I'm sorry, Mr. President. I'm not following. How would China benefit from killing this deal?"

"You want the short answer or the long one?" Ryan grinned.

"I think you'd be disappointed if I didn't say 'both.'"

"The short answer is the BRI."

"And the BRI is . . . ?" Arnie asked.

Adler jumped in. "The Belt and Road Initiative. It's China's comprehensive infrastructure plan to link two-thirds of the world's population and half of global GDP with new roads, rail, and shipping arteries stretching north–south from New

Delhi to Murmansk and east–west from Shanghai to Lisbon. Think of it as a modernized version of the ancient Chinese Silk Road.

"Of course, the Chinese will kindly loan participating countries the billions of dollars those countries will need for mostly Chinese firms to come and build that infrastructure at usurious rates."

"Unlike us, who spend ourselves into oblivion giving stuff away," Arnie said.

The President nodded grimly. "It's the China Dream—the means by which the Chinese Communists plan on achieving global hegemony."

"How will cheap diapers and alarm clocks do that?" Arnie asked.

"How much of your European history do you remember from college?" Ryan asked.

"Not as much as the guy with the Ph.D. in history who taught the subject at the Naval Academy, I suspect."

"The ancient Persians dreamed of an empire stretching from Asia to Europe, and they would have pulled it off, were it not for a few stubborn Greeks. Fast-forward as far as you want to— Napoleon, Kaiser Wilhelm, Hitler, Stalin. They all tried it as well. Nothing would be more powerful or destabilizing than a united Eurasian landmass. It's Mackinder's Heartland Theory: Whoever rules Eurasia rules the world. American security policy for the last hundred years has been designed to keep that from happening."

"The Chinese certainly don't have the military means to do so, at least not yet," Burgess said.

"But they do have the economic means," Ryan said. "And the will. What did Lenin say? 'A capitalist will sell you the rope to hang him with'? BRI is a very clever and profitable way for China and Russia to unite against us, right under our noses, with most of the West European globalists cheering them on."

Ryan leaned forward. "And just maybe at least one U.S. senator."

"And so we're back to Dixon," Arnie said. "Right where you wanted us to be."

"Yes, I see it now," Adler said. "Maybe not her, directly, but her husband—what's his name?"

"Aaron Gage," Ryan said. "Founder and CEO of Gage Capital Partners. His firm has made a lot of money doing business with the Chinese."

"He's made a lot of money doing business with everybody," Arnie said. "He and Dixon are multi-millionaires, thanks to him."

"You have a problem with millionaires, Arnie?" Ryan asked with a smirk. He was a one-percenter himself.

"Not with millionaires who earned it the old-fashioned way in the private sector **before** they got into politics," Arnie said.

"So we think she's fronting Chinese legislation to benefit her husband's firm?" Burgess asked.

"She wouldn't be the first. This whole town stinks of legal nepotism," Ryan said. He was referring to the dozens of siblings, children, spouses, and other relatives who actively lobbied the Hill—though never their family members directly, in order to avoid the strict letter, if not the spirit, of the law.

"Money rules this town," Arnie said. "The average senator needs to raise fourteen, fifteen thousand dollars a day, every day they're in office, just to pay for their reelections."

"This isn't just about campaign finance," Ryan said. "It's about the whole damn system. The sweetheart contracts to family members, the revolving doors between elected offices and corporate boardrooms, the donations to family charitable trusts. Lobbyists who become staffers, staffers who become lobbyists. I read the other day that nearly half of all ex-senators and nearly a third of ex–House members become registered lobbyists—and a whole bunch more of them aren't registered as such but still work the cocktail circuit. It's all perfectly legal, but legal corruption is still corruption, especially when it's the lawmakers themselves who make this stuff legal. I hate it, and it's why Congress is becoming less functional every day."

"You can't expect the foxes who run the hen-house to rewrite the rules to protect the hens, boss," Adler said.

Ryan dragged a hand through his hair, obviously frustrated. "Another battle for another day, I suppose." He took his last sip of cold coffee, the ice tinkling in the bottom of the glass.

"I know you don't think much of my proboscis, but I still think we should look more closely at Dixon's family finances."

"Do you honestly believe a sitting U.S. senator is on the Chinese payroll?" the SecDef asked.

"I won't use federal resources against an elected official without probable cause," Ryan said. "Besides the fact it's not ethical, it's bad optics. How would it look to the country if I put FBI investigators on the trail of a a likely presidential candidate I'm at odds with politically? Am I clear on this?"

"Clear as rain, boss," Arnie said. His blue eyes smiled behind his glasses. "But you don't mind if I ask around a little, do you?"

8

BEIJING, CHINA

Chen Xing hung up his phone.

The traitor was dead.

Such unfortunate news.

As the head of the ultrasecretive International Counterterrorism Division of the Ministry of State Security, Chen was a man to be feared. But he was no fool. Facts were the best weapons in his line of work. The only thing his subordinates need fear was failure. Reporting bad news carried no penalties for the message bearer.

From an intelligence perspective, the death of the treasonous physicist mattered little. Electric batons and ultraviolet-ray shocks had already squeezed everything out of him they could. They had also overwhelmed an undetected heart condition.

The scientist had no network to roll up, no family to exploit. Chen only wanted the scum to live longer so he could suffer more. Nothing was more delightful than to watch a sobbing prisoner concoct fantastical confessions in hopes of stopping

torture that had no purpose other than the inflic-
tion of pain.

What Chen had discovered was that the snivel-
ing bastard had sold out his country in exchange
for the promise of Canadian citizenship and a
modest two-story home in a Vancouver suburb.

The physicist's only mandate was to collect data
as opportunity arose, paying the utmost attention
to his personal safety. He worked in the Quantum Science Satellite program at the University of
Science and Technology in Hefei, passing along
invaluable state secrets to the Canadian assistant
trade representative, a Canadian Security Intelligence Service (CSIS) operative.

His Canadian handler made the mistake of
agreeing to a CIA request for specific information regarding a recent test. To Chen's surprise,
an unsolicited text from CHIBI arrived on his
encrypted phone, providing the CIA data request
along with the physicist's name, address, and drop-
off location—and a proposition.

It was exceedingly rare for a foreign asset to walk
in the front door with actionable intelligence. On
the other hand, some of the greatest intelligence
coups in history happened precisely this way—
John Walker, the U.S. Navy chief warrant officer
sailor; Aldrich Ames, the CIA operative; Jonathan
Pollard, a civilian Navy intelligence analyst; and
FBI agent Robert Hanssen all came to mind.

Of course, CHIBI didn't walk into his office

literally; rather, it was a brief, digital introduction and actionable intelligence that proved highly valuable. But Chen found CHIBI's proposition unpalatable.

Under any other circumstance, Chen would have leaped at the opportunity to continue working with an intelligence gold mine like CHIBI. But CHIBI didn't want cash—at least, not immediately—or honorifics. Not even an exchange of intel. Chen detected no bitterness in this mysterious person, no ideological motivations for his actions. Ego? No question. Who would have the balls to reach out to the MSS and play such a dangerous game unless they had an inflated ego?

Except, CHIBI's ego wasn't inflated. He was as good as he thought he was. Chen's comrades in Bureau 7 were unable to identify or locate him through digital or other means, which suggested that CHIBI had superb if not insurmountable OPSEC capabilities. Of course, this implied an equally capable offensive threat profile, his technical experts suggested. Prying into CHIBI's whereabouts further could provoke a damaging counterattack, one that at the moment the MSS would be unable to defend against.

But what to do? Accept CHIBI's invitation to the auction, or pass?

Chen didn't believe in rogue intelligence operations. The resources required were too great for an independent organization, let alone an individual, no matter how gifted.

Who would have reached out to him with such an unusual offer other than another intelligence service? He couldn't imagine it was a Canadian operation. They wouldn't allow themselves to sacrifice one of their own assets under any circumstances, let alone in a "proof of concept" demonstration. Not only would it violate their own sentimental notions of so-called individual rights, but it would also discredit them in the eyes of future potential assets. Trust was the most important currency in the spy business, especially in the field.

The Americans and other Western powers were equally unlikely candidates, for the same reason. The Russians, as good as they were, didn't have this capability. Of this he was certain. The same with the North Koreans, Iranians, and Indians.

So, if not one of the competing intelligence services, then who?

CHIBI was a dangerous enigma and a loner. A single individual with the "keys to the kingdom," as he'd put it in his proposition.

And the name. CHIBI. An obvious reference to the Battle of Chibi, aka Red Cliffs. A name as familiar to Chinese history students as Thermopylae or Agincourt was in the West. An eighteen-hundred-year-old battle personifying Sun Tzu's principle that all warfare was based on deception.

A war that saw the smaller power overthrow the greater power. Chibi was a touchstone for all Chinese strategic thinking, both military and economic.

Did that mean CHIBI was actually Chinese?

Impossible.

Or was it?

Despite the obvious draw—the offer of total access to Western intelligence sources—Chen declined the offer to attend the London auction for one simple reason.

He hated enigmas . . . especially ones that could get him killed.

9

HIGH OVER MONONGAHELA NATIONAL FOREST, WEST VIRGINIA

The CloudServe Bombardier Global 8000 business jet streaked across the night sky with its single passenger curled up in one of the luxurious leather seats, shoes off.

Watson already had her first vodka tonic in hand as she reviewed her notes from the meeting with Foley.

Her phone rang. A familiar ringtone.

"How'd it go?" Elias Dahm asked. He breathed heavily on the other end.

"They hate the cloud, they've fired us, and they're sending you to jail."

"Ha, ha. Funny. Seriously?"

"It would've gone a whole lot better if you had been there."

"I doubt it. You're the brains in this outfit. I'm just the pretty face."

"Yeah. That's why they kept asking, 'Where's Elias? Did he go to Burning Man this year? When's the next rocket launch?' I swear, sometimes I feel like I'm working for Mick Jagger."

"You know how it is. It's all about marketing." Wind buffeted Elias's phone.

Yeah, but you actually have to have something to market, she wanted to say. "Foley really wanted you there. I think she's pissed."

"Yeah, well, screw her. I've got a lot going on and no time to waste on circle-jerk meetings like that."

Oh, but I do? Watson said to herself.

"What did she say about our War Cloud bid?"

"That our bid is being considered just like all the others."

"Goddamn it. We need that contract."

Watson understood his frustration. The name of the game in tech was cash flow, and CloudServe needed some badly. "She doesn't run the DoD. It isn't up to her."

"But she has her ear to the ground and she sure as hell could pull a few strings on our behalf if she wanted to."

"She strikes me as a straight shooter."

"Then why in the hell am I paying an army of lobbyists to make this happen?"

"That's your end of the business, not mine. But you might want to give her a call and reassure her a little."

"About what?"

"She's nervous about her cloud security."

"She has every reason to be, if things go wrong."

Watson's temper flared, but she bit her tongue. "I won't let that happen."

"I know that. Believe me. I'm your biggest fan."

Watson let that one go, too. She waved her empty glass at the flight attendant, signaling for a refill.

Watson frowned, more annoyed than concerned. "You okay? You sound like you're having a hard time breathing."

"Yeah, sure. I'm fine."

MARIN COUNTY, CALIFORNIA

Elias stood on the manicured lawn of his seaside hilltop estate while he was speaking on his earbuds with Watson, three thousand miles away.

Broad-shouldered and movie-star handsome, Elias was dressed in full kendo gear—black **gi** jacket, **hakama** trousers, body armor. He was still holding the bamboo-stave **shinai** practice sword in one hand while his sensei, an all-Japan kendo champion, smoked a Marlboro, waiting for the call to end so they could resume their practice.

Elias absentmindedly waved the sword in the air as he spoke. Two dozen tiki torches flickered in a gusting ocean breeze rattling the ancient cypress trees. His bright, piercing eyes were nearly the same gray-green as the Pacific Ocean crashing on the rocks below.

"Anything else?" he asked.

"Less than three weeks until the TechWorld conference. You ready?"

"I was born ready."

"You can't just wing it, you know. You're giving the keynote speech."

"I'm working on it," Elias said, pointing his sword at his sensei. The Japanese swordsman nodded curtly and flicked his cigarette butt away before reaching for his sword and mask.

"Look, I gotta run, Amanda. Hey, take tomorrow off. You deserve it."

"I wish I could."

"Call me when you land so I know you're okay."

"I will. Thanks."

She rang off, a tinge of sadness and longing in her voice. Exactly as Elias desired. He forgot about her as soon as the call ended.

Elias grabbed his padded fighting gloves, peppering his sensei with a dozen technical questions about **suburi** in faultless Japanese as they both geared up. He couldn't wait for their next round to begin, each strike of his bamboo sword a blow against the mountain of worries looming over him.

10

ALEXANDRIA, VIRGINIA
HENDLEY ASSOCIATES

Jack Ryan, Jr., sat in his cubicle, staring at the Excel spreadsheet and scratching behind his ear, a nervous habit. It wasn't really itchy. But ever since it had been nearly torn off that night in Afghanistan by the sticky-bomb explosion and sewn back on with nine stitches of catgut by an ISIS drug smuggler, Jack couldn't shake the feeling it was going to fall off. His finger kept gravitating to the stitch line the same way his tongue would automatically float to the empty space where a tooth fell out when he was a kid. Or the way it did now, touching the capped tooth that had been chipped in the same explosion.

He'd fully recovered from the aches, pains, and sprains of one of the hairiest ops he'd ever been on, grateful to be alive. He was even more grateful that Ysabel Kashani was in his life again.

Sort of.

She was back in London with her family, partly recovering from their operation together in Afghanistan and Iran, and partly to figure out where she was with everything, including Jack. She had been working with the United Nations Office on Drug and Crime when he found her again in Afghanistan, but after everything that happened over there, she couldn't possibly return to either the land of her birth, Iran, or Afghanistan.

"I just need some time, Jack," she'd said, and in truth, so did Jack. He thought she'd been married and had a kid—a clever cover he'd stumbled across on social media, and, like an idiot, he'd swallowed it hook, line, and sinker. He figured he'd lost her forever, and now she was back. But neither of them was exactly sure what that meant or what the future held.

Just one of the many reasons he was glad for the current assignment.

Jack rubbed his tired face. It was getting late. The numbers swarmed on the screen like ants on a candy bar. He'd been staring at the electronic spreadsheet for hours, trying to puzzle out this company's Rubik's Cube of international bank accounts, wire transfers, and conflicting calendar dates against the data presented in the 10-K annual filing. Something just wasn't adding up.

Jack was a financial analyst with the "white side" Hendley Associates but also a field operative with the "black side" Campus. The Campus was an off-the-books intelligence agency designed to carry out missions on behalf of the United States when traditional security agencies couldn't be called upon.

But when Jack was back home, he was still responsible for helping Hendley Associates accomplish its mission as one of the world's premier private equity management firms. After all, it was the money Hendley Associates earned that paid the bills for all Campus operations.

Jack had started out as a financial analyst and he loved the work, though if he had to choose between the two jobs, he would prefer being an operator for The Campus. But in truth, he enjoyed the downtime as a financial analyst, using that part of his brain to decompress from the high-adrenaline stress of close-quarters combat and large-caliber gunfights.

In fact, he needed it. Jack had no problem carrying his share of the load on a mission. Thanks to John Clark's training, Jack liked to think he handled himself well in tactical situations—though there was still much more for him to learn—and he was proficient with small arms, CQB, and even knife fighting.

But like his dad, Jack's mind was his best weapon.

Jack ran a hand over his neatly trimmed beard absentmindedly as his eyes scanned the screen, searching for clues. He needed to crack this nut before he could move on with the project, an investment opportunity in Dubai that as of now was looking more and more like a shady deal.

He and his dad shared a lot of qualities, but lately Jack had been taking stock. At just about his age, his father had already been medically discharged as a lieutenant from the Marines, married his mom, had two kids, earned a fortune as a trader at Merrill Lynch, completed a Ph.D. in history, taught at the Naval Academy, and joined the CIA.

If life was a race between him and his dad, his dad was lapping him badly. Heck, Jack felt like he was still stuck in the starting blocks. He pulled off his reading glasses and pinched the bridge of his nose, willing away the headache boiling up behind his blue eyes. His desk phone rang. Surprising, given the hour. It was Gerry Hendley, his boss. His dad had persuaded Gerry to found Hendley Associates and The Campus years ago.

"Hello, Gerry."

"Jack, I was wondering if you could spare a few moments."

"I'll be right up."

Gerry Hendley, the former senator from South Carolina, clapped Jack on his broad back as he stepped into the fourth-floor office. He pointed him to one of the two chairs in front of his spotless desk and took the other one himself.

"Thanks for coming up, son," Hendley said, in his honey-baked southern drawl. "I know you're on a deadline on that Dubai deal. How's that squaring up?"

"Dad always said when something looks too good to be true, it probably is. I just can't quite put my finger on it yet."

"I know you're as stubborn as your father, which is a virtue in this line of work. Coffee?"

"I'm fine, thanks. What can I do for you?"

Hendley's tailored shirt with French cuffs and diamond links was as immaculate as his mane of silver hair. The former senator was a shrewd financial expert in his own right, and Hendley Associates was one of the most profitable firms in its industry. But the ex-senator's passion was still national security. Like Jack's father, Hendley was an old-fashioned patriot, and unashamed to say so. More important, he was willing to back up his sentiment with something more than words. The one hundred presigned presidential pardons sitting in his office safe were for the protection of his employees, not himself.

"I just had a long and interesting conversation with Arnie van Damm. Did you hear about what happened on Dixon's committee today?"

"No, sorry. I've been buried in reports."

"I won't bore you with the details, but the long

and the short of it is our shared concern that
Senator Dixon might be playing ball for the Red
Chinese."

Jack frowned. "That's quite an accusation."

"More of a hunch, actually."

Jack nodded. If his father had actual proof, the
woman would already be in jail awaiting trial, senator or not.

"She's probably not the only one. There's a lot of
Chinese money floating around D.C. these days."

"But few are as powerful as Senator Deborah
Dixon. If it's true, it's a real problem."

"How do I fit in?"

"I know your plate is full right now, and you've
got a leave of absence coming up in a few days, but
I'm asking you to put everything aside and take a
look at Senator Dixon's financial situation."

Jack shifted in his chair. Finishing the Dubai
project was a high priority for him, but his leave
of absence was essential. He'd made a promise to
Cory and he was determined to keep it.

"We have a deep bench of financial analysts who
are every bit as good or better than I am. Can't
one of them take this on?"

Hendley flashed a wide smile. His perfectly
aligned teeth sparkled with porcelain veneers. The
effect was a cross between a kindly grandfather
and a great white shark. "You have a unique skill
set in this regard, my boy. You have a doggedness
to you that can't be taught, and, more important,

the political savvy to know when to tread lightly, if you catch my drift."

"In other words, snoop inside her sock drawers, but don't get caught doing it."

"Not even a whiff of suspicion. Especially after the Chadwick fiasco. We need to keep as low a profile as possible."

Nobody in the Ryan family was particularly fond of Chadwick. Her irrationally unjustified personal animus toward the President had been expressed frequently in private and public venues until just recently. Her accusation that the President maintained a "personal assassination squad" was almost comically stupid and unbelievable to all but the most intractable Ryan haters, but it had struck perilously close to the truth. The Campus was, indeed, a secret weapon available for rapid deployment by his father to defend the national interest when normal security resources couldn't be used. The Campus was only as effective as it was unknown. They needed to keep it that way.

Jack sighed, frustrated. "Understood."

"I wouldn't ask you if it wasn't of the utmost importance, or if there was someone else I could trust with the assignment. And you know your father. He won't countenance the thought of deploying the FBI against an elected official without probable cause."

"And it's up to me to find it."

"That about sums it up."

"It just comes at a really bad time."

"So do most things that matter."

Jack nodded. "Then I'd better get after it. Any ideas about where to start?"

"Senator Dixon won't leave any low-hanging fruit and sure as hell won't even come close to breaking any laws. If anything, I'd take a look at her husband, Aaron Gage. He's done a lot of business with the Chi-Coms over the years, and he's tied in with the Belt and Road Initiative."

"Chinese trade pushed through global infrastructure projects financed with Chinese money."

"Exactly. The senator's husband owns a private equity firm that invests heavily in infrastructure. I'd say that would be a good place to start."

Jack stood. "I'll get right on it."

11

WASHINGTON, D.C.

The elegant two-story Tudor-style home stood on a hill in leafy Kalorama Heights, bordering the park below. The sturdy, hand-cut stone walls and antique wrought-iron gate were more decorative than functional but perfectly complemented the $5 million residence. Senator Dixon and her husband, Aaron Gage, relied instead upon the discreet services of a private contractor employing former spec ops personnel for 24/7 security.

After their Guatemalan housekeeper cleared away the plates from a late dinner of Chilean sea bass and mint-pea puree, Dixon poured fingers of scotch rocks for both of them in the privacy of her husband's library.

"Long day." Dixon sighed as she fell back into the sofa. She plopped her bare feet on his legs and took a sip of her drink.

"Must have gotten a little longer after van Damm showed up," Gage said, chuckling, rubbing her feet with his powerful hands.

He was sixteen years her senior, but the

seventy-two-year-old financial guru kept fit by submitting himself to a daily torture routine on his fifteen-thousand-dollar ROM total body work-out machine. He kept one in each of their several homes around the country.

They first met when she was a freshly minted Wharton MBA and the vice president of marketing in a small firm his company had just acquired. Still smarting from a nasty divorce, Gage wasn't looking for a new relationship at the time, but Dixon was single, attractive, and whip-smart, and the chemistry between them was obvious from the start. They found they enjoyed each other as much in the boardroom as the bedroom, and from day one had formed an incredibly strong partnership that proved mutually beneficial.

"You were smart not to get into politics," Dixon said over the top of her glass.

"Everything is politics," Gage said, driving his thumbs into her arches. "Especially finance. I just get paid better. Anything you want to talk about?" He reached for his glass.

"Arnie was pissed—I mean, really fired up. Which means Ryan is fired up, and that scares the hell out of me."

"You? Scared? Since when?"

"Since I decided I wanted to be the next POTUS."

"Ryan is a lame duck and he has his share of enemies. We've talked about this."

"But Ryan isn't distracted by retirement plans. He's laser-focused on his job and I don't want to be his next target."

"Why would you be? You've dotted your **i**'s and crossed your **t**'s. A dozen lawyers from the best firms here and overseas have signed off on everything. We're watertight and ironclad. Let Ryan rage against the night. What the fuck do we care?"

Dixon took another sip. "It's not me I'm worried about."

The silence hung in the air like a fog.

Gage darkened. An old wound. "I wouldn't worry about Christopher."

"I didn't say anything about him."

"You didn't have to." Gage gulped the rest of his scotch.

After his divorce from his alcoholic ex-wife, Gage retained custody of his only son. Dixon understood that marrying Gage was a package deal, but being a stepmom taxed her nominal maternal instinct. The chore eased considerably after Christopher Gage was carted off to boarding school.

Despite his high IQ and athletic promise, the young man had a penchant for bad decisions and worse friends, both of which got him expelled from several elite prep schools. Thanks to pricey attorneys and thick wads of cash, the troubled boy avoided well-deserved jail time.

Seemingly "scared straight" after a near-death DUI incident in his freshman year in college,

Christopher eventually graduated from Stanford Graduate School of Business with high honors. Within a decade he had joined his father's firm, Gage Capital Partners, and become the CEO of its public infrastructure and transportation subsidiary, Gage Group International. Currently, Christopher was operating in Poland with his own venture, Baltic General Services.

But Dixon remained suspicious. The boy—a thirty-eight-year-old man, she had to remind herself—had too many close calls, and she had a long memory.

But her husband, Aaron, had a short fuse. He was not a man to be crossed, not even by her.

Dixon pulled her feet off her husband's lap, stood up, grabbed his glass, and headed for the bar. "How's Poland shaping up?"

"Christopher is doing a good job. Still scouting things out, making connections."

Dixon poured another drink for them both. "He's a smart boy. I don't doubt he'll make you proud." She crossed back to the couch and handed him his glass.

"I just wish he'd settle down and get married. I'd like a grandson to play ball with while I still have my marbles."

"Maybe he'll find one of those beautiful, long-legged Polish girls."

"I'm sure he's looking as hard as he can." Gage chuckled, taking another sip.

Like father, like son.

"I'm just asking him to be careful over there. I'm sure you understand my position." She smiled. "Our position."

Gage took another sip. "He knows the lines he can't cross."

Dixon remained standing over him. "Even when the lines keep moving?" she said over her glass.

"So long as we're the ones moving the lines, it shouldn't be a problem."

"Does he understand what's at stake?"

"He's my son, isn't he?"

"Thank God for that." Dixon smiled. "Thanks for letting me vent. It's been a long day." She finished her drink.

"Trust me," Gage said, finishing his scotch. "He's fine." He stood, yawning. "I'm off to bed. You?"

"I have some committee work to read, but I'll be up soon."

Gage leaned over and kissed his wife on the cheek. "Good night."

He headed for the stairs leading toward their bedroom, making a mental note to call his son first thing in the morning.

Before it was too late.

12

SAN FRANCISCO, CALIFORNIA

The carmine red Porsche 911 Targa 4S slid into its designated five-hundred-dollar-a-month parking space in the basement of the glass-and-steel building near the Embarcadero.

Lawrence Fung, a lean, handsome thirty-year-old, dashed from his vehicle to the elevator, clutching his laptop case. He stabbed the up button furiously, willing the doors to open. He checked the time on the oversized TAG Heuer watch strapped to his narrow wrist.

Shit!

The doors finally opened, and the fast elevator whisked him to his expansive Bay-view condo on the thirteenth floor. Fung punched the keypad on his keyless door, but the lock beeped. He cursed his clumsiness and punched the code again. The door clicked open and he pushed his way through, kicking off his calf-leather loafers and dropping the Porsche key fob into a sterling-silver bowl on the hand-carved entryway desk, along with his polycarbonate slim wallet.

Fung sped barefoot across the bamboo floor toward the kitchen, conscious of the precious few minutes remaining. He was starving, but there wasn't time to make anything, not even a cup of tea. He yanked open the Viking refrigerator and pulled out a bottled organic protein shake, cracked it open, and guzzled it before heading for his bedroom.

He fell down into his chair just as his timer beeped, and powered up his desktop, ignoring the stunning view of the Bay Bridge lit in the low fog on the dark water below. He opened up Skype, scrolled down to his contacts list, and selected the video button. His face popped up in a small window on the screen. Not liking what he saw, he brushed his hair with his fingers and wiped his lips to make himself more presentable as the international phone line chirped and buzzed. An image popped up.

"Sweetheart," Fung said. "It's wonderful to see you."

A brooding, handsome face loomed on the wide monitor. Torré was mixed Korean, Haitian, and Irish. He broke into modeling on his exotic looks years ago as a teenager, but a vicious drug habit ruined his career. He was now in recovery, his ambitions turned elsewhere, convinced that modeling was a one-way ticket back into addiction hell.

"Hello, Larry. How are you? You look exhausted."

Fung hid his frustration with the failing VoIP tech. Torré's lips weren't synched with his voice, like a bad kung fu movie, and his voice crackled and reverberated on the speakers. Bad connection.

"Miss you."

Torré's brooding face softened. "Miss you, too."

Fung's heart leaped in his chest. The face in the monitor was beyond handsome—beautiful, really. He'd forgotten how much he missed Torré. Sunlight dappled the palm trees in the open sliding glass door behind his lover as the crashing ocean waves washed through the scratchy speakers.

"Thailand looks gorgeous."

Torré sighed. "Yes, I suppose it does."

"That terrible, eh?" Fung chuckled, trying to lighten the mood.

"How's the city?"

"Same. Busy, crowded, cold. More shit and needles on the streets than ever." Fung quickly added, "Can't wait to come visit you."

"Yeah, that would be great." Torré shifted in his chair, adjusting his sheer linen robe.

Clearly, it wasn't.

"Something wrong?"

"Some friends are leaving for a week's vacation to Tokyo tomorrow."

Fung frowned with concern. "They'll be back before you know it."

"I know. It just gets so boring around here sometimes. I hate to miss out on the fun."

"It can't be that expensive to go."

"I've already spent this month's allowance."

"Oh, wow."

"But no worries. I know how it is. You've already done so much."

That's putting it mildly, Fung thought.

The cost of Torré's gender transition kept escalating. The hormone therapy was expensive, and the anticipated surgery even more so. Thailand performed more gender reassignment surgeries than any other country in the world, followed by, of all places, Iran, which viewed homosexuality as a Quranic evil. But rather than punish gay people, the Revolution gave them the "opportunity" to change genders rather than suffer prison sentences.

Given the choice between Thailand and Iran, Torré chose the Southeast Asian paradise. Both countries were cheaper alternatives to anything offered in the United States, where medical procedures alone added up to six figures. Unfortunately, Fung wasn't saving any money, because the lifestyle Torré insisted on maintaining in Thailand was more expensive than the medical bills themselves.

"You still have the credit card, right? Just use that."

"Are you sure?"

"Absolutely. What's the point of denying your-self a little fun?"

"I hated to ask, but thank you. You're just the best." Torré smiled shyly. It was quite charming. The hormone therapy was really taking effect now. He was completely androgynous at this point. Fung could only imagine the beautiful butterfly that would emerge from that delicious caramel cocoon over the next several months.

With the ice between them finally thawed, Fung hoped the conversation might turn more **interesting**—even if only virtually. Fung's heart raced with anticipation. But before he could open his mouth, an encrypted text notice slid onto his monitor.

Now what?

"Hey, babe," Fung said, staring at his phone screen. "I gotta run. Something's come up. Maybe we can talk again tomorrow."

"I'll call you from Tokyo—"

But Fung had already hung up and was pulling up the text.

13

WHY NOT? CHIBI asked in the dialogue box. Fung's cursor flashed on his screen. What could he say? The truth, he supposed. "I'm afraid."

OF WHAT?

"I know I'm being watched."

SHE WATCHES EVERYBODY.

"You know what I mean. She's been acting very suspicious. Double-checking my logs."

I UNDERSTAND. I WOULD NEVER WANT YOU TO DO ANYTHING THAT PUTS YOU AT UNNECESSARY RISK.

Fung sighed, relieved. He'd hoped the nature of this relationship would have changed over time. He didn't want it to end, though. It was too wrong not to be enjoyed.

"Thank you for understanding. Maybe next time," he typed.

SADLY THERE WILL NOT BE A NEXT TIME. I NEED SOMEONE I CAN COUNT ON WHEN IT MATTERS MOST TO ME.

Fung's stomach roiled with anxiety. He was losing CHIBI. His thumb tore across the virtual keyboard on his phone.

"NOBODY can give you what I have."

BUT YOU WON'T GIVE IT TO ME ANYWAY. SO WHAT DOES IT MATTER?

"I didn't say I wouldn't. I just said I couldn't. Not now."

WHY? BECAUSE SHE IS WATCHING YOU? YOU DO NOT EVEN KNOW IF SHE IS. YOU MAY NEVER FEEL SAFE. YOU MAY NEVER BE ABLE TO HELP ME AGAIN. I UNDERSTAND YOUR CONCERN. BUT I CANNOT WAIT AROUND.

"Please don't play games with me. I hate that shit."

I AM NOT PLAYING GAMES WITH YOU. I AM YOUR FRIEND. BUT I HAVE OBLIGATIONS TO MEET. IF YOU DO NOT WANT TO HELP ME THAT

IS FINE. WE CAN STILL BE FRIENDS. BUT YOU
DO NOT WANT ME TO GET IN TROUBLE DO
YOU?

"What kind of trouble?"

NOW WHO IS THE ONE PLAYING GAMES?

Fung cursed himself. He really was playing
games. He knew there was a lot at stake. Had to
be, with all of the money that had been tossed
around. But he was genuinely afraid, too.
But the money. The damn money.
"I'm sorry. You're right. I don't want to put you
in a bad place."

DO NOT WORRY ABOUT ME. YOU ALREADY DO
SO MUCH FOR SO MANY PEOPLE. I DO NOT
WANT YOU TO RISK ALL OF THAT. I WILL BE
FINE. THERE ARE ALWAYS OTHER OPTIONS.

"But no option as good as me. Let me do this
one last time. I don't want to leave you hanging."

NO. I DO NOT THINK IT IS A GOOD IDEA. TRUST
YOUR INSTINCTS.

"Please? I'm just having a bad day, that's all.
Really, I want to do it."

BUT YOU SAID THERE IS EXTRA RISK INVOLVED,
RIGHT?

"No more than usual."

I DO NOT BELIEVE YOU. HOW ABOUT THIS: I
CAN PAY AN EXTRA 25K FOR THIS JOB. WOULD
THAT HELP ALLEVIATE THE RISK?

Hell, yeah. Fung couldn't believe it. "I wouldn't
say no.😊 That's very generous of you."

BUT ONLY IF YOU ARE SURE. DO NOT LET THE
MONEY PERSUADE YOU.

"I'm not. I'm sure it won't be a problem."

THANK YOU. YOU ARE LITERALLY SAVING MY
LIFE.

"Glad to do it. Give me the details."

CHIBI sent Fung the particulars.

Very doable, Fung decided. But precautions
were in order. He was being watched. He could
feel it. But he needed the money, and he needed
this. Something secret, something important. The
big "fuck you" to everyone around him. To everyone who doubted him.

And he'd do anything to keep it.

Fung licked his lips. Twenty-five thousand extra

would come in handy. He had a head for numbers, sure, but not money—or, at least, spending it. He was out of control and he knew it. The more he made, the more he spent. All the bills got paid, but only at the last minute.

CHIBI knew this. It was why he had reached out to Fung. Fung was frightened at first. To have been watched, studied, probed. Kind of embarrassing, actually. He was a cybersecurity expert—a professional hacker!—and he'd been hacked. That was a neat trick. Fung had been certain his personal financial information was secure, at least on his end. But CHIBI must have hacked the losers at his bank and mortgage company and who knows who else.

His first instinct was to shut everything down. Go dark. Contact his boss, tell her what happened, humiliating as that would be. Or maybe even call his friend at the FBI's Cyber Division. Another humiliation, for sure, but maybe he would know a way to get out from under this asshole without losing his job. Either of those would have been the smart play.

But something clicked inside him. CHIBI could have robbed him blind or blackmailed him into service. But he did neither. He just wanted to talk.

And they did.

After the initial shock and embarrassment, Fung warmed to the idea of being known by this mysterious stranger. A stranger with a serious skill set.

A master hacker who had reached out to him for help. No threats. Just cash.

And the thrill.

Thrilling, because CHIBI was most likely a Chinese agent. Possibly even with Unit 61398. Had to be. Those guys were the best.

Fung was born in Alameda, California—an anchor baby, by design. His mother had flown over from Guangzhou when she was seven months pregnant. She took up residence with four other pregnant Chinese nationals at an illegal "maternity hotel" in a suburban residence owned by a Chinese expat maternity nurse charging exorbitant fees to her desperate countrymen and not reporting that income to federal authorities. The fourteenth amendment to the American Constitution, not anticipating global jet travel, apparently determined that anyone physically born in the United States was automatically an American citizen, and tens of thousands of Chinese mothers had taken advantage of this quirky law over the last twenty years, including Fung's, who lied about her pregnancy status and the duration of her visit. Both lies rendered her entry status illegal. Two months after he was born, she returned to the mainland. Within two years, she and her husband were allowed to immigrate to the United States with visas in hand, owing in part to Lawrence Fung's illegally contrived citizenship and sponsored by distant family members already living in California.

The Fungs did well for themselves in their new country, at least initially. His mother was a civil engineer and his father an economist, and within a decade they had managed to climb the first few rungs of the American dream ladder. Lawrence was raised in a Mandarin-speaking home, and he quickly picked up Cantonese from his expat Hong Kong friends. His parents' social circles were limited to other Bay Area Chinese families, of which there were many.

His parents taught him all of the myths and stories they had grown up on, including the ones that portrayed the Chinese Communist Party heroically, the vanguard of the Revolution against Western imperialism.

His mother and father didn't leave the Red mainland for ideological reasons but green ones—dollar bills, to be exact.

Outwardly and legally, Lawrence Fung was as American as apple pie, secretly listening to Alanis Morissette, Jay-Z, and Limp Bizkit and smoking dope along with the rest of his non-Asian skater friends after school. But inwardly, he was Chinese to the core. Part of the great Han diaspora. Every year it became more and more obvious to him that the twenty-first century belonged to China, and, no doubt, the centuries after that. In his heart, he'd always hoped his motherland would reach out to him.

When Lawrence turned sixteen, he told his

ultra-traditionalist parents he was gay. They disowned him. At seventeen, he left home—technically, he was thrown out—and entered the UC Berkeley mathematics program. Not easy for an Asian kid to do back then, with all of the admissions biases against Asians, who dominated GPAs, test scores, and extracurriculars relative to other ethnic groups. Cut off from his parents, he paid for everything along the way with student loans, including extensive international travel, a lavish lifestyle for him and his friends and paramours, top-of-the-line computer and audio equipment, and, best of all, cars.

By the time Fung had finished graduate school, he was almost three hundred thousand dollars in debt, and according to the law, none of those educational loans could be discharged through bankruptcy. One more reason to hate the U.S. government, as far as Fung was concerned.

His penchant for getting hired on at Silicon Valley "unicorns" that failed was a running joke among his so-called peers who couldn't code their way out of a bento box. But he made enough quick cash to pay off all his debts and accelerate his already lavish lifestyle. Giving up his dream for a fast score with another startup, he finally relented and joined a boring but reputable firm two years ago and began making seriously good and **stable** money for the first time in his life.

Money he couldn't help but spend.

CHIBI knew all of this. And more. Fung didn't care. In fact, it was a relief. And deeply satisfying. An intimacy he shared with no one else in the world but this mysterious brother on the other side of the planet. Another dark and dangerous secret he kept from the people around him who thought they knew him. Only this time, he would never out himself. And neither would CHIBI. What would be the advantage of doing so?

Fung feared being discovered. The idea of going to jail terrified him. The idea of getting caught by his inferiors humiliated him. He knew the shame that would fall upon his parents would be unbearable for them—and for him.

"I'll make it happen," Fung typed.

THANK YOU. AGAIN.

CHIBI logged off.

So did Fung. He'd saved his connection to his mysterious friend. But now he was in deep shit.

Drowning in it.

And for all of his bravado, he'd probably get caught.

How in the hell would he pull this off?

He wanted to call Torré and bare his soul. But his lover was so damned moody these days, and a bad Internet connection only made things more frustratingly awkward. Even if he did pick up, what would he say to him? He had to keep Torré in the dark to protect him, just in case.

Fung sighed. It didn't matter. His lot in life was to bear everyone else's burdens all by himself. He just had to accept it.

Fung stood and shuffled toward his shower. The thought of pleasuring himself beneath the steaming twin rain heads crossed his mind, but he was too damned tired. Instead, he poured himself a glass of Beringer Private Reserve Cabernet Sauvignon and popped a couple Ambien before falling into bed, exhausted and depressed.

14

WASHINGTON, D.C.

After Senator Dixon had left for her office the next morning, Aaron Gage entered his library, closing the door behind him. The housekeeper wouldn't arrive for another hour and he had the place to himself. Plenty of time before his driver would take him to his private jet for a flight to corporate headquarters.

Five years ago, Gage Capital Partners had relocated to Dallas. He didn't particularly care for the city, its weather, or its inhabitants, but it was a great place to do business. Texas had extremely low corporate franchise taxes and zero personal income taxes, and that counted for a great deal in Gage's book. Taxes were for little people, and the morons too stupid to know how to avoid them.

These days, he seldom traveled to the firm's twenty-second-story downtown office because the day-to-day operations were handled by a cadre of vice presidents and the people under them. GCP employed a small army of talented quant heads, contract lawyers, and technical analysts recruited from all of the best grad schools. They did all of the number crunching and contract writing, conducted the 24/7 searches for promising new market opportunities, and sniffed out tax loopholes, or created them, thanks to their lobbying efforts.

In his youth, Gage had excelled at most of those activities, but now he was bored by them. He made his first $10 million pitching his investing services to big family trusts, pension funds, and high-networth individuals. But he soon figured out that the real money lay elsewhere.

Real being loosely defined.

He negotiated big contract purchases of muni bonds, commodities futures, and stock options, ferreting out the last quarter-point of interest rate return, fee reduction, or tax deduction he could find. All of that work added up to millions of dollars for his largest clients and, ultimately, for himself.

But the really big money was in government. Socialism was dead, but so was capitalism. Western liberal governments borrowed trillions of dollars of fake money—ones and zeroes created out of thin air in computers run by central banks—to buy votes rather than balance budgets, enslaving future generations with debt they could never repay.

Gage concluded it was better to do business with the people who created money than with the peasants who merely scrapped over bits of it.

Central banks and governments weren't the only wealth creators. Trillions of dollars were siphoned away from public and private coffers by criminal syndicates, and many billions more made in illicit trade.

Aaron Gage wanted as much of that free and dirty cash as he could lay his hands on. Millionaires were a dime a dozen these days. He wanted billions.

Gage Capital Partners played a key role in his plan. It continued to provide the legitimate cover of conventional business. It was also the platform that allowed Gage to do the really important work of cultivating strategic relationships with business and political elites around the world. These relationships allowed his business to grow in power and influence, which led, ultimately, to everincreasing wealth, which, in turn, was its own source of power and influence.

It was the greatest game of all, and his wife had proven to be an important cog in his machine. She knew her part and played it well, even if she didn't fully grasp the scope of his vision.

Christopher, however, did see the big picture, Gage reminded himself, as he stepped into a large walk-in closet, modified to protect against electronic eavesdropping.

The boy had made some serious missteps in his youth, to be sure, but Gage knew it was far easier to put a saddle on a stallion than it was to turn a mule into a racehorse. Christopher was headstrong but smart—damn smart. And when Gage finally broke through his son's hormonally challenged adolescent fog, the tumblers all fell into place behind the dark, impenetrable eyes.

His wife was right to be worried. Even when he finally came around, Christopher always played right up to the edge.

Gage's phone finally engaged Christopher's encrypted cell, to judge from the long, tonal pulse common to European phones.

"Hello, Father."

"Can you speak privately?"

"Yes. I'm at home."

"You know that 'vacation' we had coming up? The one you've been planning lately?"

"Yes, of course."

"Well, I need you to postpone it."

"Why?"

"It's a bad time. Your mother—"

"The senator isn't my mother."

"Your stepmother is preoccupied at the moment."

"She's always preoccupied. She's a senator."

"She's particularly preoccupied at the moment. The vacation won't work right now."

"I thought she didn't want to go on vacation with us."

"She doesn't. But that means it's not a good time for me, either."

Christopher was silent on his end for a moment, processing.

Aaron added, "We can do it later. Just not now."

"But you don't understand my situation. I've already purchased the tickets. The reservations are set. And there aren't any refunds."

"That can't be helped."

"The people I've made arrangements with will be extremely disappointed."

"I guess you're not hearing me. Cancel the damn vacation. Today. **Capisce?**"

"Yeah, sure. Understood."

"Good. We'll talk again soon. Stay safe."

"You, too."

Gage ended the call. He smiled.

A fucking stallion.

He just needed to keep the reins tight.

15

SAN FRANCISCO, CALIFORNIA

Fung stood at his workstation in his private glass-walled fourth-floor office, a perk of the job and a nod to his exalted status in the organization. His oversized monitor faced away from the door.

The rest of the team had gone to lunch at a new Asian fusion pho joint a few blocks away. Fung passed, citing work deadlines and a weak stomach, both of which were true. More than three hundred e-mails sat unopened in his inbox, and his irritable bowel syndrome was boiling his guts. Why in the hell did he agree to do this? An extra twenty-five thousand wouldn't mean jack shit if he was rotting away in a federal supermax somewhere.

His eyes scanned the open work floor again. Most of the desks were empty. The programmers that remained were midwits scrambling to finish a project for a northeastern grocery chain.

Losers.

Fung's fingers hovered over the keys to his

computer. A few keystrokes and he could once again invisibly slip into the National Reconnaissance Office desktop that linked to a CIA comms satellite. Fung was able to mirror one particular NRO machine without the operator knowing it or alerting the security algorithms monitoring workstation activity. It was a clandestine version of Apple tech support screen-sharing with a customer and manipulating the computer during a service call.

In fact, any action Fung took was automatically hidden from the NRO station logs as well, so that any digital footprints he theoretically might have left were never recorded.

But even knowing he couldn't be caught and with six figures riding on the transaction, Fung still hesitated. His boss wasn't stupid. She was a worthy opponent. What if she had uploaded some new security package overnight and he was walking into a trap?

"Larry? I thought you'd be at lunch."

Fung nearly jumped out of his skin. Amanda Watson, his immediate supervisor at CloudServe, stood in his doorway.

"Oh! Amanda. Hi." He tapped a function key that pulled up a fake desktop image.

Watson frowned with concern. "You okay? You look like you've seen a ghost."

"Sorry. Not feeling one hundred percent." Fung felt beads of sweat forming on his forehead.

"You look sick. Maybe you better get home and take care of yourself. I can't afford to lose my number two."

"I'm fine, really. I just need to grab some aspirin."

"I've got some in my desk. You want me to get it?"

"Uh, yeah. Sure. If you don't mind. That would be great."

Watson smiled. "Glad to. Be right back with that aspirin and a Fiji."

"Thank you."

Fung watched her march toward the break room to fetch a bottled water.

Damn, that was close.

But Fung suddenly had to fight the urge to laugh.

The stupid bitch didn't realize how close she was to the man who had hacked her "unhackable" cloud. She knew the system's vulnerabilities and had given those to her Red Team, which included Fung. She had suggested multiple lines of attack, and the strategies to exploit them, over the last year. What she didn't realize was that Fung had managed to find the single crack in the system, and to break through it just over a month ago. The resulting dopamine rush was pure ecstasy. He had beaten the system, which meant he had beaten her. His first urge that day was to rush into her office and rub her face in it and show her who really was the smartest person in the building.

But he didn't.

Why tell her? It was his perfect, delicious secret. Gloating over her would have given him temporary satisfaction. But hiding the golden key from her and everyone else? That was more than satisfying. It made him feel absolutely dominant.

And when CHIBI came calling again and again, asking if he could find something for him for big bucks? And never getting caught?

Better than sex.

But Watson had been acting suspiciously lately. Hovering over him, always seeming to keep her eyes glued to him. Did she know? No, it wasn't possible. He'd already be in jail. But did she suspect something? Maybe.

Fung checked the original Seth Thomas mid-century sunburst clock on his wall. Time was running out. His assignment was time-specific. But he also knew that Watson would be leaving for the gym shortly. She was as regular as a metronome when it came to her Pilates class. He could afford to wait a few more minutes and enjoy a few sips of cool Fiji water in the meantime.

Watson returned, handing Fung a bottle of water and a packet of aspirin.

"Thanks."

"My pleasure." Watson leaned on the doorjamb.

"You do so much for so many people. Are you sure you're taking care of yourself?"

"Just a little behind on my sleep is all."

"Anything I can do to help?" She nodded toward his workstation.

"If anybody has too much on her plate around here, it's you. But I really appreciate the offer."

"I can pull somebody else in to assist."

"Everybody around here is slammed. I'll turn the corner here in a few hours. Maybe I'll head home after that."

Watson shrugged. "Well, don't hesitate to ask. We're all on the same team, aren't we?"

"Absolutely."

Watson's iWatch alarmed. "Time for Pilates."

"Have a great workout." Fung winked. "You know where to find me."

Watson winked back and sped away toward her desk to grab her car keys. When the elevator doors finally shut, Fung was already back on his screen.

Time to get to work.

16

GDAŃSK, POLAND

They were princelings.

Christopher Gage, the stepson of one of the most powerful women in the world, Senator Deborah Dixon, and Hu Peng, the son of a high Party official and a director of China's largest state-owned bank.

The two men, both in their late thirties, shared many of the qualities common to princelings everywhere, not the least of which was the compulsion to prove themselves worthy of inheriting their respective kingdoms.

Gage's father had proven easy to please, particularly after Christopher's graduation from the Gage alma mater, but nearly impossible to satisfy. Hu Peng was in no better a position, and, arguably, a worse one. It was Peng who insisted they meet inside the angular composite steel walls of the European Solidarity Centre near the port and leave their phones in their offices on the tenth floor of the Citi Handlowy building in Gdynia some twenty kilometers away. Gage was wary of all electronic communications but took precautions. Peng, however, was paranoid about it. Especially when discussing matters that might displease his superiors or, worse, reach his father's ears.

It was also Peng who taught Gage the useful but awkward practice of surveillance-detection routes, and using his peripheral vision to check for tails in the reflections of door mirrors and office windows.

They stood in front of the hanging display of two large plywood sheets listing the twenty-one demands of striking Polish workers against the Communist government in 1980—the Polish equivalent of the American Declaration of Independence and Bill of Rights combined. These demands, and the workers' refusal to back down from them, led to the formation of the independent Solidarity labor union and marked the beginning of the end of Communism first in Poland and, soon after, in all of Europe, including the Soviet Union.

Both Gage and Peng wore English language headsets but with the volume turned off. They stayed close to a group of bored but chattering middle-school kids for audio cover.

"I'm sorry," Gage said in English. "It can't be helped."

"The wheels are already in motion—"

"I explained that to him." Off of Peng's concerned reaction, he added, "Not in any detail, of course."

Peng's eyes constantly scanned the room. It wasn't hard to pick out any Chinese who might be trailing them in a place like Poland. He knew each of the Chinese consular officials in Gdańsk on sight, including the MSS officers stationed there, but none were present here today. His superiors would never use Chinese operatives in a Caucasian nation for undercover work to spy on him.

"Did you explain to him the consequences we'll face if we stop this?"

"Not in so many words."

"Then perhaps you should," Peng said, drifting behind the jabbering students and toward the next exhibit. His English accent betrayed the fact that he'd learned the language from Oxford-educated tutors in China, and reflected the two years he spent drinking in pubs and sleeping with English girls while earning his master's at the London School of Economics.

"There must be alternative routes."

"We're not talking about changing a bus schedule."

"Well, it's a no-go. Call it off."

"Because your father told you to? Or your mother?"

"**Step**mother. And don't blame her. It's Ryan that's yanking her chain."

"Then let her worry about him. You have bigger worries at the moment. So do I."

"You don't know my father."

Peng darkened. "You don't know mine."

They moved toward a corner, away from the group. The room was still filled with their incessant noise.

Peng lowered his voice. "You are five thousand miles away from the two of them. They don't have a knife to their throats like we do. Besides, there's no way this shipment will be a problem. Everything is arranged, everything is accounted for. We just need to be patient for a few days more. Nobody will know a thing."

Now it was Gage's eyes that scanned the room, half expecting his father to march into the gallery. In truth, his father didn't fully understand what was going on, or what was at stake—including his life. But the payoff would be huge, and a chance to step out of his father's long shadow. Maybe even to earn his respect.

Failure was not an option.

A careful planner, Christopher had other safeguards in place, the biggest one being his dearly beloved stepmother, whether she liked it or not.

Only she didn't know it.

"Fine. But so help me God, this better not blow up in our faces."

"How could it? You and I are the only people in Poland who know about this. Grow a pair and relax." Peng smiled. "Let's get out of here. I'm starving."

"To hell with food. I need a drink."

"There's a new place not far from here, and the Ukrainian girls there are super hot."

The princelings stripped the audio guides off their heads and sped for the exit.

17

ALEXANDRIA, VIRGINIA

Jack's brain was busted.

After ten uninterrupted hours poring over an extensive LexisNexis search, including records of incorporation, liens, business licenses, and even boat and aircraft registrations, Jack was both bleary-eyed and frustrated. Aaron Gage's record was squeaky clean.

He suspected as much going in, but he had to do his due diligence. Besides the fact that Aaron Gage was both smart and cautious, Jack also knew that most of Gage's business dealings were conducted within the framework of his private equity firm, Gage Capital Partners. The details of those transactions were not required to be disclosed under the rules governing private equity firms either here or abroad. Private equity firms like GCP were the perfect place for shady dealers to hide in plain sight, if they so desired.

Jack's only recourse was to turn to OSINT—open-source intelligence, otherwise known as the Internet. Also a mind-numbing exercise, as it turned out. Aaron Gage and GCP had been in the news for decades, the beneficiaries of a carefully orchestrated PR campaign dating back as far as the Reagan administration.

In the last ten years, PR turned to the socially conscious efforts of the Dixon-Gage Charitable Trust, featuring frequent donations to women's shelters, symphony orchestras, inner-city schools, breast and ovarian cancer research initiatives, and a host of other programs supporting Senator Dixon's political platform. The trust had also served to bolster the image of GCP as a socially conscious civic entity. In the last five years, the Dixon-Gage charity expanded to Africa, building schools, digging wells, and microbanking.

But Gerry had pointed Jack toward the China connection, and that was where he focused his latest efforts. He started by refreshing his memory of U.S.–China trade relations for context, especially after 2001, when China was admitted to the World Trade Organization, owing, in part, to then-Congresswoman Dixon's strong advocacy for it and her promise that capitalism would democratize China. Just the opposite occurred. "Red capitalism" actually strengthened the power of the Chinese Communist Party at home and abroad. It leveraged WTO membership to acquire extensive foreign investment and technology to launch the greatest manufacturing and export boom in the history of the world at the cost of more than three million American manufacturing jobs. China also used its enormous trade surpluses with the United States—currently in excess of $300 billion per year—to fund a massive military buildup. In less than a decade China had become number two in the world, both economically and militarily.

The Chinese Communists clearly used trade policies such as WTO membership and the BRI as tools to further their national interests, and many of China's largest global corporations were SOEs—state-owned enterprises—under the control of the Party. American corporations, on the other hand, appeared to influence U.S. foreign policy mainly as a means to enrich themselves.

But all of that was above Jack's pay grade. Right now, he had smaller fish to fry.

Like many other American and European companies, Gage Capital Partners had rushed into Beijing to start doing deals.

After all, the business of America was business, wasn't it? Still, it bothered Jack that so many corporations put their profits before their patriotism. Offshoring manufacturing, importing subsidized commodities, utilizing corporate inversions—moving overseas to avoid paying American taxes—and demanding cheap labor on American soil all added to the corporate bottom line. All perfectly legal, because senators like Dixon wrote the laws that made them legal.

What angered Jack was the hypocrisy. Those same corporations that dodged American taxes legally and offshored American jobs legally would appeal to the aid of the U.S. government—paid for by federal taxes on American workers—for protection against hostile governments and terrorist groups.

Didn't that require some measure of loyalty to the American worker? To American jobs? The American taxpayer?

Apparently not.

Jack rubbed his tired face. He knew his brain began wandering down these long, speculative corridors when he got tired. He needed to stay focused.

One particular item in his OSINT research grabbed his attention. The Stanford Graduate School of Business alumni newsletter announced Christopher's promotion to CEO of Gage Group International—a transportation and infrastructure company.

Interesting.

Following that announcement, Jack discovered that in the last three years, it was exclusively Christopher Gage who traveled to Beijing.

Whatever the Gages were now up to in China, Christopher was the point man.

Gerry steered Jack in the direction of China's

Belt and Road Initiative. But he had also mentioned that Senator Dixon killed the Poland
deal—and that was the whole reason for Jack's
investigation.

Was there a connection between BRI and
Poland?

Jack kept digging.

He discovered that the BRI was firmly estab-
lishing itself in Gdańsk, Poland, one of the most
significant ports on the Baltic Sea.

Interesting.

Millions of dollars of Chinese loans were being
arranged for upgrades to port, rail, and road facilities in the ancient seaport. For centuries, the
city—formerly known as Danzig, especially when
under German occupation—was one of the largest and wealthiest trade centers in all of Europe.
For many centuries it was long coveted by major
powers in the area, including the Teutonic
Knights, who captured it in 1308. Now the
Chinese had their eye on the Baltic jewel. Perhaps
it was destined for greatness again.

And then Jack found it.

An announcement that Christopher Gage's new
company, Baltic General Services, was searching
for property in Gdańsk.

But did it mean anything? Or just a coincidence?

Jack put it on a sticky note and posted it on his
monitor, one of several staring him in the face now.

He hoped one of them would pay off soon.

18

She put two .380 rounds right between the man's eyes.

"God, I love this laser," Dixon said.

The paper target hung limply in the air some thirty feet away on the indoor range. The beam from the red targeting laser attached beneath the short barrel of her SIG Sauer P238 pistol still danced on the silhouetted head.

"Good shooting, Senator."

"Well, you trained me, didn't you?" Dixon smiled.

Dixon and Sandra Kyle were the only two shooters in the subterranean range at the moment. Dixon preferred both highly personalized and private instruction from Kyle, who was happy to oblige. Kyle was a former undercover officer in the U.S. Capitol Police who had been detailed to Dixon's office when she was in town. Now retired, the attractive African American woman had purchased the gun range and specialized

in self-defense and concealed-carry courses for
women. She also ran a private detective agency.

Dixon dumped her empty mag and double-
racked the slide to ensure the weapon was
completely empty before setting it down on
the shooting table, barrel pointed downrange.
She pulled off her headphones.

Kyle removed her ear protection as well. The
empty, soundproofed room was the perfect place
to hold a private conversation.

"I have a little problem I need you to look into,"
Dixon began. She rather liked the smell of burnt
gunpowder hanging in the air.

"Happy to oblige."

"You haven't asked me what the problem is yet."

Kyle shrugged. "I owe you, whatever it is."

Dixon shook her head. "You don't owe me a
thing. If anyone's in debt, it's me to you for all the
years you've kept me safe."

Dixon had received numerous death threats
while in office, most of them nothing but noise.
But on the few occasions when the threat profile
escalated, Kyle was always there, rain or shine, no
matter the time of day or night.

But that was Kyle's job. Her sworn duty as a
U.S. Capitol Police officer. In truth, she never had
to face actual combat on Dixon's behalf or anyone
else's, not even as an active-duty Air Police officer on her single tour in Kabul. But she was well
trained and very loyal, eager to carry out the side

jobs Dixon occasionally assigned to her, mostly involving gathering embarrassing intelligence data on political opponents as the need arose.

More to the point, when Kyle was arrested on a DUI in Virginia, it was Dixon who intervened, saving both her career and her generous public pension. Aaron had also provided the interest-free capital Kyle had needed to purchase the Alexandria gun range. So, in fact, Kyle did owe Dixon in perpetuity, and both women knew it.

Dixon hit the retrieval switch. The punctured paper target fluttered as it sped toward the shooting bay on a whirring steel cable. It snapped to a stop just inches away from her.

"Aggressive shooting, Senator. I assume this has something to do with POTUS?"

"Indirectly, yes."

Kyle nodded at the shredded target. "Nothing quite so dramatic as that, I hope."

Dixon laughed. "Just venting some frustrations."

"So long as I don't have to break into the Oval, I'm okay with whatever you have in mind. So, what is it?"

Dixon pinched the spring-loaded clips that held the target in place. "You know Ryan's a Boy Scout. He has very specific ideas about his own versions of right and wrong."

"Sure. I've seen him in action."

"Well, I have it on good authority he's terribly

interested in me at the moment. He sees me as a political threat, and I know he's looking to find dirt on me, any way he can." Dixon laid the target on the gun table while she spoke.

"Is there any dirt for him to find?"

"No, of course not. But he will look, and as you know, anything he finds, even if it's clean, can be turned to mud if put in the proper hands in the media."

"So how can I help?"

"Put on his shoes for a minute and answer me this: If you were Ryan and your high-minded morals wouldn't let you use federal resources like the IRS or the FBI to dig for dirt on your political opponent, how else would you do it?"

"He's a pretty damn good analyst all on his own, as I recall," Kyle said.

"I doubt he has the time."

Kyle tapped her chin with a red-lacquered nail, thinking. "There's an outfit that Gerry Hendley runs, Hendley Associates. Have you heard of it?"

"Yes. It's a top drawer financial firm. Hendley was a legend on the Hill—still is, really. The senator and I conferred on a few bills together when I was still in the House before he . . . well, you know."

Kyle nodded. She was an officer on patrol duty when she first heard the news that Gerry Hendley's wife and three children had been killed in a horrible collision with a tractor-trailer on I-85.

Torn up by the tragedy, Hendley effectively threw away his Senate career in a halfhearted reelection bid he lost badly. After he recovered his bearings, he eventually founded Hendley Associates. Despite being a lifelong Democrat, Hendley worked hard on behalf of the Ryan administration while he was in the Senate, willingly crossing the aisle on matters of national security, putting petty partisanship aside for the common good.

"I'm glad he landed on his feet," Dixon said. And she meant it. She had admired Hendley back in the day and though he was no longer in office, he was still a force on the Hill. "It's a first-rate firm, according to my husband. But how does that answer my question?"

"Hendley employs a guy by the name of John Clark. Do you know anything about him?"

Dixon shook her head. "Should I?"

"He's a former Navy SEAL, ex-CIA. He's getting a little long in the tooth, but he's a guy you definitely don't want to fuck with—pardon my French—and he's a friend of Ryan's."

"Why does a financial firm employ an ex-spook? Security?"

"That would be my guess. Probably for Hendley."

"Or someone else employed there."

"Are you thinking about someone in particular?"

"Jack Ryan, Jr., is a financial analyst there." Dixon felt a tingle on the back of her neck. That would be another direct link to President Ryan.

And a retired operator like Clark had other implications. She frowned. Maybe Senator Chadwick really had been onto something.

Kyle nodded. "I'll get right on it."

Dixon folded up the decimated target and pocketed it.

"If Hendley Associates is after me, I want to know about it. But be discreet. I don't want Gerry to know you're sniffing around. There would be hell to pay if he found out."

"Understood, ma'am."

19

ALEXANDRIA, VIRGINIA

Jack carefully placed his folded clothes into the carry-on backpack. The weather in the southern hemisphere was turning warmer and he didn't want to check any bags, especially on a commercial flight with multiple transfers.

His phone rang in the other room. He checked his watch. It was Gerry. Jack popped in his AirPods as he tapped his phone.

"Hi, Gerry. What's up?"

"Just rereading the report you sent over last night. Had a few questions. Am I interrupting anything?"

"Just packing. Shoot."

"You discovered a connection between Senator Dixon's stepson and this Chinese partner in Poland."

"Yeah. Found a little smoke, but no fire." Jack dropped a couple of pairs of socks into the bag.

"But if I'm reading between the lines, you think there might be something worth digging into."

"I wouldn't be surprised. But I exhausted all of my online resources. That's why I recommended

Gavin taking over from here. If anyone can find something, it's him." Jack ran the zipper, shutting the bag.

"Unfortunately, Gavin and his team are tasked to something else at the moment. That's why I'd like you to catch a flight over there and see what you can find on the ground."

"Me? I've never been to Poland. I don't have any contacts there, and I sure don't speak the language. Why not send Midas? He's fluent in Polish."

"Midas is out of country right now. And before you ask, Dom and Adara are at Coronado, training in hand-to-hand fighting with some ex-SEAL instructors there. Ding and Clark are also indisposed at the moment."

"Which leaves just me."

"Not to worry. I've already arranged an excellent contact for you. An agent with the ABW—Poland's version of the FBI."

"Well, to be honest, you already approved my ten days of R-and-R. In fact, I'm heading out tomorrow." Jack didn't want to mention that his trip was all about the promise he made to Cory.

"Can't you postpone it a few days?"

Jack hemmed and hawed. He didn't like putting Gerry off. But keeping Cory's promise was important. Damned important. A man keeps his word.

"I mean, I've already purchased the tickets—"

"I'll pay the difference if they charge you for changing the dates."

"That's generous of you, but, well . . . it's important."

"Is your personal vacation time more important than the national interest?"

Not if you put it that way. "No, of course not. But snooping around for dirt on Dixon reads more like a Raymond Chandler novel than a national security matter."

"That's your dad's call, not ours."

Ouch.

"I guess I can put off my trip for a few more days. It's not exactly time-sensitive."

"Good. I've already contacted Lisanne to make the arrangements. You'll be leaving tomorrow. She'll be in touch."

"You know this is a long shot, right?"

"I read as much in your report. But right now it's the only one we have."

"Any ideas you can throw my way?"

"I don't have to tell you that D.C. is a political town. I need you to tread lightly over there. Don't make any waves, don't cast any aspersions. If Dixon even gets a hint that somebody is after her, or, worse, that your father is behind any of this, there'll be hell to pay."

"Understood. I'll do my best."

Gerry chuckled. "I know you will. That's why you're on the payroll, son."

"I'll find out what I can and stay in touch."

Gerry rang off and Jack unzipped his bag to unpack.

Poland was going to be colder than where he had been planning to go and a backpack wasn't going to cut it on a Hendley Associates business trip.

20

SAN FRANCISCO, CALIFORNIA

Fung was at his standup desk in his office at CloudServe. His fingers flew across the keyboard as he punched his way through a new coding algorithm. His phone rang.

Oh, shit.

"Hi, Amanda. What's up?"

"Do you mind stopping by my office for a few minutes? There's something I want to discuss with you."

"Sure. Be right over."

Fung hung up. He swallowed hard. It had been only a couple days since he pulled the most recent data for CHIBI. No word from him, but that wasn't terribly unusual. The deposited money was all the confirmation he needed that CHIBI was satisfied.

Fung glanced past his glass wall and out at the work floor. The place was packed today. They all hated him, he was sure. Even the members of the

Red Team he helped run for Watson. They were all jealous of him. He could only imagine their smirking faces as the FBI perp-walked him in handcuffs out of his office. He couldn't bear the idea of it.

To hell with them.

Fung pulled out his slim wallet. Four credit cards. One was maxed out. He had Google Pay on his phone, too, linked to a fifth. Two hundred and change in cash. He could march out of his office right now, head home, snag his passport and a few clothes, then get the hell out. But where would he go? Thailand, to be with Torré? No. Too obvious. That would be the first place they'd look.

"Just . . . breathe," he told himself. He was getting way out over his skis on this. Watson's call was probably nothing.

Probably.

Fung approached Watson's desk.

She was on the phone. He made a gesture that he could come back later. She scrunched up her face and shook her head, indicating the call wasn't sensitive and motioning for him to grab a seat.

Fung fell into one of the springy plywood laminate chairs in front of her desk. Her corner-office view was something to die for. Of course she had the corner office. She was Dahm's favorite, wasn't she?

Fuck her. She was too stupid to know she had given him the keys to the IC Cloud, or, at least, a part of it, by showing him how to access the CIA comms satellite.

His eyes drifted to the framed photos on the wall behind her. Most were of Watson and the celebrity actors, musicians, and politicians who joined her, hammers and saws in hand, framing houses for disabled and homeless veterans in the Homes for Heroes charity she founded in honor of her dead brother, killed in some stupid war.

The most prominent photo was of Watson, Senator Dixon, and Aaron Gage smiling broadly for the camera, each in hard hats and safety glasses. The Dixon-Gage Charitable Trust was the biggest donor to Homes for Heroes, and Watson never let anyone forget about it. It was priceless publicity for her and for them. Hell, he wasn't stupid. He'd even contributed to Watson's charity. Office politics, and all of that.

There was also a framed American flag on the wall, presented to her by a local chapter of the Disabled American Veterans, with a plaque indicating it had once flown over the USS **Arizona**.

The wall also featured a case of her brother's

military patches, medals, and ribbons next to another picture of her brother in an Army uniform.

Good-looking guy. **What a waste,** Fung thought.

"Sorry to keep you waiting," Watson said, hanging up the phone. "Thanks for coming."

"No problem. What's up?"

"First of all, how is your father doing on the chemo?"

A jolt of anger shot through Fung. He hoped it didn't show. His father had insisted on an experimental cancer treatment that wasn't covered by his health insurance. Naturally, he expected his dutiful son to cover it. That, and the Hawaiian cruise his parents were taking next month.

"He's good."

"If you don't mind my saying, your reaction says otherwise. Anything I can do to help?"

"Only if you can convince my father to quit smoking. He keeps bribing his home health aides to sneak in packs of Newports. I've had to fire two already."

"Parents," Watson said, shaking her head. "Hard to train them. Even harder to pick them. Sorry about that." She took a sip of herbal tea from a Homes for Heroes–branded cup she kept on her desk.

"Comes with the territory."

"And how's Torré?"

Fung brightened. "I spoke to him just last night.

Everything's going great. Three more months of HRT until he can get his surgery."

"That's wonderful. I'm very excited for both of you."

"Anything to make him happy. I just wish he wasn't so far away. But Thailand really is the best option for him."

Watson leaned forward on her desk. "You're a very generous person, aren't you?"

Fung pointed at the picture wall. "It's why we're all here, isn't it?"

Watson smiled, leaning back. "Yes, I suppose so. I could still learn a lot from you."

"Look who's talking. Someday you'll have to show me how to set up my own foundation."

"Sure, anytime." She reached over to her purse and pulled out a business card. "Scott Shelby is a JD and a CPA. He did all the paperwork for Homes for Heroes. He's the perfect guy to talk to."

Fung studied the card politely before saying "Thanks" and pocketing it.

So far, so good.

"I never did hear how your meeting in D.C. went," Fung said.

"Oh, fine. Great, really. The IC Cloud is airtight and running like a Swiss watch. Which is why I wanted to talk to you today."

Here it is.

"About what, exactly?"

"About IC security. It's too damn good."

"And that's a problem?"

"It is. For them as well as for us."

"Why for them?"

"I got the sense that some of those department heads are getting a little too complacent. They need to remember they're as responsible as we are for their own security."

"Makes sense. But how does that affect us?"

"If Foley and the department heads ever come to believe they're invulnerable, they won't see a need to keep us around anymore. At least, not for security. And I don't need to remind you that our highest profit centers are in services, not hardware and software sales."

"So basically we're cops who are going to break into the mayor's office so that he keeps putting cops on the city payroll."

"Or, ideally, hires even more. Anyway, that's why I wanted to talk to you about the next Red Team attack. Where are we on the PassPrint program?"

Watson was referring to the CloudServe research program Fung was heading up, using AI to create a master "passkey" of AI-generated fingerprints.

In theory, every human fingerprint was unique, and in theory, only the human possessing the unique fingerprint could pass through a biometric screener. The intelligence community had fully embraced biometric security, and their fingerprint scanners were top-drawer.

However, a couple flaws existed in every biometric scanner, even the high-dollar ones favored by the federal government, including the one on Watson's desk.

Just like computer virus scanners, fingerprint scanners worked by comparing data inputs—a finger placed on a screen now compared against a known database of fingerprints. If the new scan matched the prints on record, entrance was granted.

The problem was that most people didn't provide **complete** fingerprint scans for the database for all kinds of reasons, most of them human error, such as oily fingers or dirty recording glass. The same was true on the other end, too: Oily fingers and dirty scanner glass on security machines read only partial prints.

Therefore, all biometric scanners were only able to compare partial prints to partial prints.

It also turned out that while every complete human fingerprint was unique, **portions** of every fingerprint—arches, tents, whorls—were startlingly similar.

The Red Team decided to try to exploit these flaws by designing an AI-driven program that built millions of fake fingerprints into a single master passkey, not unlike the ones maids used to enter hotel rooms, even though each door lock had a unique passcode. By generating enough digital arches, tents, and whorls, the PassPrint passkey would display enough fingerprint similarities to fool any biometric system.

"I just ran the last of the simulations last night," Fung said. He smiled. "I think we have a winner on our hands."

"That's fantastic. Because I think I know the perfect way to deploy it."

21

eploy the PassPrint how?" Fung asked.

"When I was at the Fort Meade conference with Foley, there was an analyst, Steve Hilton. Very quiet, very smart. He's the IT director at the Department of the Treasury's Office of Intelligence and Analysis. We struck up a conversation over coffee and he happened to mention his department needed a new printer, but there was some snafu in the paperwork and it wouldn't arrive for another two weeks."

Fung shrugged, irritated. **Is there a point to your stupid story?** "Okay."

"I want to put a worm on his wireless printer that will jump from there to his computer."

"How? The Feds have bulletproofed their wireless devices." Fung frowned. "But you already know that."

Watson accepted the compliment with her own shy smile.

In her first meetings with Foley and the IC Cloud committee, Watson pointed out the unbelievable fact that throughout the federal government there was no comprehensive program in place to ensure that civilian or military systems didn't contain integrated circuits with malicious functionality. American combat jets could be firing missiles at Chinese fighters with microchips designed by the PLA—and designed to fail. These malicious integrated circuits, if they existed, could be installed anywhere, including combat systems, medical devices, communication networks, and, of course, the computers used throughout the intelligence community.

As seemingly insurmountable as that problem was, Watson was even more concerned about the fact that there were literally millions of devices throughout federal government offices with the potential for spying applications.

The federal government didn't manufacture the everyday devices required to run a modern office. Printers, phones, computer monitors, HVAC thermostats, and other commercial off-the-shelf (COTS) devices were manufactured and distributed by thousands of private vendors. Many, if not most, were not only manufactured overseas, but contained software or firmware created without any kind of security protocols.

Worse, most of these machines were created to function wirelessly, not only for automated "machine-to-machine" software and firmware updates, but also for energy and work efficiencies.

Globally, the so-called Internet of Things (IoT) comprised more than twenty **billion** devices, and that number increased exponentially each year. Millions were already in operation in the United States. Many of these IoT devices might already be compromised by foreign actors with bad intent.

Watson had no solution to the first problem of compromised integrated circuits; she learned later that DARPA was launching the TRUST in integrated circuits program to address it.

But Watson did have a very practical solution for the IC regarding the problem of a compromised IoT—get rid of every device and start over with certified equipment protected by IoT security protocols. It was an expensive solution, but far cheaper than the cost of a compromised intelligence community.

Foley agreed, and under her leadership, closed-door congressional budget committees were dragged across the finish line and the costly cleanup process nearly completed.

In short, it was impossible for Watson's IoT worm attack to succeed.

Or was it?

"'Bulletproofed' is exactly what I'm talking about," Watson said. "Foley and her people think that the IoT problem is solved now. That means they're not looking in that direction, so that's where I want to hit them."

"How? Every federal vendor is registered and must pass through their biometric security system. It isn't possible unless—oh, snap." Fung grinned. "Our guy will use the PassPrint device to get past security."

"Exactly. And with the compromised printer in place, we can count on Mr. Hilton to hand-deliver our worm into their system."

"After it's in his computer, the worm could go anywhere in the building, and, hell, after that, the entire IC. God, I love it."

He really did. The spy stuff gave him a real boner. It was why he loved this job. Better still, Watson clearly wasn't sniffing him out for anything suspicious. It was like she was describing the tantric sex the two of them were going to have that night without her realizing he was already sleeping with her boyfriend.

Awesome.

Watson added, "I know it's a long shot and there are a lot of moving parts, but if we can pull this off, we'll nail that new multiyear contract with the Feds we've been angling for."

"This is so very John le Carré of you. I'm impressed."

"Thank you."

Fung rose. "I'll get right on it." He turned to leave, eager to jump into a project that he could get excited about and dodging a bullet all at the same time.

"Oh, wait," Watson said. "There's just one more thing."

Fung turned around, grinning. "Yes?"

"I was lying in bed last night and it suddenly occurred to me that there's an issue we never got resolved. I came in early this morning and looked at my notes and I don't see a conclusion."

"What issue is that?"

"We talked about an exploit that we thought might have existed in the CIA comms terminal at the NRO." Watson frowned. "If someone broke into that terminal, they would have eyes on every piece of secured intel throughout the IC. It would be another disaster."

By "another disaster," Watson was referring to the breach several years prior of the CIA's Internet-based secure comms program in Iran. It had been compromised by a double agent and, of all things, a simple Google search. A similar breach occurred in the same system deployed in China. Agents, assets, and networks were rolled up in both countries before anyone knew what had happened, putting all global clandestine operations at risk. A number of invaluable in-country assets were either imprisoned or killed as a result, undoing decades of fieldcraft.

The Feds abandoned the flawed Internet-based system and instead put laser focus on securing all IC communications behind the impenetrable IC Cloud.

If that system were subsequently breached?

"Yeah, a disaster for sure," Fung echoed, his mind racing as fast as his heart.

But panic was the mind killer, and his mind was his best weapon. He took a deep breath through his nose, willing his heartbeat to slow.

Think, damn it!

Does she know? Is she just fishing? Testing my response? Trying to get me to confess?

No. If she knew anything for sure, I'd already be in handcuffs. Hanlon's razor applies here, or Occam's.

After all, she was the one who pointed out the flaw to me—it's how I found it in the first place, and exploited it. She raised it before, and now she wants to close the books on it, that's all.

"Oh, that's right. I remember now. We thought there was a problem in the code that would have allowed an external machine to read into the mirroring function. I double-checked it. There wasn't a problem. The security protocol was just in a different part of the script."

"Did you test it?"

"Yes."

"How? You can't access the NRO machine remotely. Did you go out to Virginia?"

"No. I was too under the gun around here for that. I just uploaded the code into one of our simulators here on premises and tried to break into it from my workstation. Couldn't do it."

"You think that's good enough?"

"I'd bet my life on it."

"Whew. That takes a load off. I'll make a note in my records. Thanks for taking care of that."

Fung shrugged. "It's my job."

Watson leaned back in her chair. "You really are always one step ahead, aren't you?"

Fung smiled. "I try, boss. I try."

22

SAINT PETERSBURG, RUSSIA

The port of Saint Petersburg was a twenty-four-hour-a-day operation, the busiest commercial terminal on the Gulf of Finland, feeding into the Baltic Sea.

At some sixty million tons of cargo a year, Saint Petersburg was also one of Russia's busiest ports, but with a variety of Western embargoes in place, that wasn't saying much these days. Rotterdam—Europe's busiest port—serviced nearly seven times as much. Saint Petersburg hosted all kinds of shipping traffic, including big cruise liners, tankers, and RoRo ships. But container ships and their standardized intermodal containers made up the bulk of operations.

The big steel boxes had revolutionized commercial shipping traffic, expediting loading and unloading from ships to trucks by many orders of magnitude. That was the reason more than twenty million containers were in service around the globe.

Thousands of them were neatly stacked and organized according to ship destination in the first cargo area of the Saint Petersburg harbor. But tonight there was only one intermodal container that Officer Sergei Burutin was worried about.

The one right in front of him.

Burutin was perched on top of a rolling ladder. The container in question was the second of three in a stack eight meters high in one of the four orderly rows demarcated by a numbered yellow line. The thousands of multicolored stacks of steel containers all across the first cargo area were similarly organized and all precisely arranged like a giant English garden maze. Each intermodal container bore an ISO code—the international standardized letter and numbering system identifying country of origin, container type, owner/operator, serial number, and check digit.

The still night air was chill and damp, the stars hidden behind a bank of low clouds bathed in the yellow glow of the port's blazing sodium lamps. Men shouted over the din of rumbling cranes, clanging steel containers, and revving diesel engines at the busy facility.

The anti-smuggling inspector checked his handheld RFID reader again and cast yet another glance back up at the overhead security camera—out of order for more than forty days now, according to the maintenance report he checked earlier.

Strange.

The camera covered operations for a thousand square meters of the staging area, an absolute necessity for his department, always seriously understaffed by the pencil pushers back in Moscow. He was new to this side of the port—in fact, this was his very first day of duty as a newly commissioned inspector—but he had a hard time believing they were any less concerned about the illegal transportation of chemicals, weapons, or persons in Saint Petersburg as they were back at the training academy.

"Is there a problem, **tovarich**?" a man asked from down below.

Burutin turned around. A large, bearded man in beige maritime coveralls and a light winter coat smiled broadly at him as he approached. A slightly built Asian man, ten years younger and half a head shorter, followed right behind him, similarly dressed.

Burutin climbed down the ladder and shook the older man's extended hand, lowering the pistol-gripped RFID reader by his side.

"Name's Voroshilov." The bearded Russian threw a thumb over his shoulder, pointing at a rusty blue-and-white freighter docked a hundred meters behind him. It rode high in the water, its first container not yet loaded. "I'm the captain of the **Baltic Princess**." He nodded to the Asian. "And this is my chief mate, Mr. Wu."

Wu nodded with a forced smile.

The smooth-faced young inspector's small hand was crushed in Voroshilov's iron grip. He returned the same as best he could. "Sergei Burutin, at your service."

"We haven't met before," the captain said.

"It's my first day on the job."

"In Saint Petersburg?"

Burutin squared his shoulders, trying to hide his insecurity. "Anywhere."

"Congratulations. It's an important job."

"Thank you."

"Where is Oleg? He's supposed to be on duty tonight."

"Officer Konev called in sick earlier. I'm his substitute."

"Oleg is a good man. Keeps things moving around here."

"I've never met him." Konev was out with a hangover, according to one of his comrades back at the office. Not an unusual thing.

The burly Russian captain wagged his head, thinking. Finally, he pointed up at a red steel container. "It looked as if you were having a problem with that container."

"Yes, as a matter of fact."

Burutin climbed back up the ladder. The lock-box on the double doors was padlocked, but the four vertical lock rods were not, as was customary. But one of the lock-rod handles was shut tight with an anti-terrorism supply chain device known as a CTPAT bolt. The certified bolt seal was embedded with an RFID chip and set through the catches. The RFID chip contained all of the data needed to identify the interior contents, content origin, and destination.

In most cases, the cargo shippers themselves installed and removed the CTPAT bolt seal in order to ensure accuracy and security in transit. But containers subject to legal inspection could be resealed only with new bolt seals and identified as such.

Burutin flashed the RFID gun at the bolt seal again, then came back down and showed it to the Russian and chief officer. The RFID readout flashed another error message.

"You see? The contents of this container don't match my database." The three of them were standing at the foot of the ladder.

"What do you mean?"

"This container was inspected by my department yesterday and bolt-sealed by us, but this is not the bolt seal that was attached yesterday, according to the reader. That's illegal."

The chief officer pointed at the RFID device. "Perhaps your reader is malfunctioning."

"The error message indicates a problem, not that the reader is malfunctioning."

"I'm sure there's an explanation. But I assure you, the contents are legally registered and the container was inspected by Oleg—excuse me, Officer Konev—and myself just yesterday."

"I'm sure you did. But that doesn't alter the fact that the bolt seal has been changed."

"It couldn't have been changed. I'm in charge of all cargo operations. I would know about it."

The inspector smiled thinly. It was just possible this was a test. He had heard of such things at the academy.

"Yes, you would know about it, wouldn't you? Still, I must insist we open the container and re-inspect."

"There is no time for that. We'd have to wait for a forklift—if we can even find one; they're all busy right now—take the stack apart, and pull out crates of machine parts that would each have to be inspected. It would take hours, and we're due to begin loading in thirty minutes."

"I'm sorry, but the law is quite clear. That, or you leave the container behind."

"That wouldn't be possible, either." Voroshilov chuckled. "I see you have been well trained. And I respect that. I'm a licensed professional myself, and I take my cargo security seriously. Here, let me show you my credentials."

The Russian reached into his coat and pulled out a thick leather billfold and handed it to the inspector. Burutin opened it. On one side of the billfold was Voroshilov's maritime license, with photo and rank and ratings. On the other side was a thick wad of large-denomination rubles. About a month's worth of Burutin's wages.

"Everything look in order?" Voroshilov smiled broadly.

The inspector glanced back at the wallet. He was newly married, living in a cramped one-bedroom apartment with his mother-in-law, who slept on the couch. The cash was very tempting, and no doubt more would follow if he cooperated on this occasion. Konev must have worked a sweetheart deal with this man a long time ago. Mafia, maybe? It didn't matter. It's not the way his father had raised him.

The inspector shook his head as he handed the billfold back to the barrel-chested mariner. "I'm sorry, but I'm afraid I must do my duty."

"I understand completely," Voroshilov said. "And I'm truly sorry."

Burutin's eyes flashed blinding white as the wrench slammed into the back of his skull. The white-hot agony crashed his central nervous system, dropping him to the cold, wet asphalt.

The gentle rocking woke him. His eyes fluttered open.

Burutin's throbbing brain ached unbearably, each beat of his heart another nail driven into the deepest recesses of his skull. He was just one step removed from unconsciousness. The rocking motion stirred him like his wife's gentle hand on a cold, frosty morning, easing him out of bed.

As his mind opened further, his nose filled with the stench of chemicals. The rest of his body protested, too—aches and pains everywhere. His wrists especially. Tied, perhaps? He glanced down at them, but it was too dark to see.

A slight twist of his battered head revealed a series of jagged patches of dim light. Holes. Stabbed into the wall in front of him. Another twist of his aching neck showed holes above as well.

Now he felt the contours of his body—he was twisted up and nearly fetal, his shoulder pressing hard against a smooth, curved surface. His legs? Numb and bent beneath him.

He tried to reach up with his dominant left hand, but it was weighted down, zip-tied to his other hand. He lifted his bound hands together with a groan and touched the oily, round surface with the holes in front of him. Cold, like metal.

He was inside of a steel drum.

Panic shot through him like an electrical current. His breath came in short, sharp gasps.

"Calm yourself, idiot," he whispered through clenched teeth. "Think!"

The rocking motion told him he was being transported. How? A car? No. Too small. A truck. He glanced back up. His blurred eyes couldn't make out the distant shapes passing through the holes.

Why the holes?

Air holes.

"Good," he told himself. They didn't want him to suffocate. That was something. But where were they taking him? To kill him? No, they would have already done that. "Good," he told himself again.

But he couldn't just lie there, cramped and broken in the dark. What should he do?

He reached up toward the holes above him with his bound hands. Perhaps he could push the lid off? He pressed as hard as he could, shooting pain throughout his torso. Nothing. His numbed legs and back robbed him of any leverage. He raised his hands again toward the holes—

"Damn it!" The jagged steel sliced through the tips of his fingers. His hands jerked back, the sudden movement shooting even more pain through his cramped and injured body.

"Hey! HEY! Can anybody hear me?"

The steel barrel suddenly tipped forward as it clanged to a stop, his head smashing perilously close to the jagged air holes in front of him.

Burutin pulled his face away from the steel wall. He suddenly realized the barrel had been tipped at an angle before, and now it was vertical.

And still.

What did that mean?

The sound of scraping metal screeched beneath him as the barrel jolted forward a few inches, then came to rest again.

"HEY! HELP ME! GET ME OUT OF—"

The drum pitched forward again. Burutin's entire body fell against the steel wall, as if laid down to bed. A heartbeat later a tingling sensation ran down his spine and exploded in his gut as his body floated away from the steel wall, weightless.

What the hell?

His battered brain suddenly understood. He opened his mouth to scream—

WHAM!

The curved steel wall smashed Burutin's face like a hammer blow, breaking his nose. Cold water poured through the air holes, seeping in from the sides, gushing in from the top, filling the barrel quickly.

Not air holes, he realized in his blind panic.

Burutin cried and mewled, kicking his bound feet uselessly against the drum floor, which was layered in rough concrete for added weight. He slammed his hands against the lid, shredding his fingers like a serrated knife. All wasted effort. Nothing budged.

Water poured in faster. What shadowy light remained melted away. The drum righted as the ice-cold sea flooded in, leaving an air pocket at the top, just enough for Burutin to scream his last in the dark before the barrel finally slipped beneath the waves.

Burutin's death was slow. His last cries were baffled by the frozen seawater sucking into his lungs, burning his sinuses. Trapped in the blinding dark, mindless terror crushed his chest as his spasming throat locked up, pushing iron-blue salt water deep into his belly. His eardrums burst as the barrel plunged deeper into the watery abyss.

The drum finally settled in the rocky slime some nine hundred feet below the surface of the merciless sea, his lifeless mouth opened in a perpetual, silent scream.

23

SAN FRANCISCO, CALIFORNIA

Fung was at his standing desk, coding. Or should have been. He was exhausted, mostly from worry. The conversation he'd had with Watson two days before still haunted him. When he'd left her office to chase down the IoT printer project, he was certain he'd satisfied her curiosity about the NRO workstation.

But as the days passed, he began to question his assumption. Maybe the enormous relief of just not being arrested on the spot had clouded his judgment. At the time, he thought he might have been suffering a panic attack. But her query was easily dismissed, and he thought no more about it until he woke up in a cold sweat that night.

A coincidence? The fact that the very workstation he was stealing information from was the one Watson had a question about? Sure, she had put him onto the task to fix it in the first place and it was reasonable for her to follow up with him on

it. Natural, even. At least that's what he had decided at the time.

But then it dawned on him: It was also natural
for her to suspect him of breaking into that computer, since she was the one who sent him off in
that direction.

Was she onto him after all?

No. She couldn't be.

Fung stared out his window. It was late, but
there were still office lights on in the building
across the street, though not many. Worker ants,
just like him. He wondered how many of them
were coding just like—

Fung jumped out of his skin at the sound of the
knock on his glass door.

"Larry? Still here?" Watson leaned in.

"Yeah, sort of. Starting to run out of gas."

She stepped into his office. "It's Saturday night.
You should be out enjoying yourself."

"I am enjoying myself," he said, pointing at a
duplicate printer standing next to his desk. "I love
this spy shit. Besides, look who's talking."

She snorted. "Guess we are the last two in the
office."

"Don't you have a date or something?" Fung's
eyes raked over her body. If he wasn't gay, he
would definitely be into it.

"Hiking Mount Tam tomorrow with an old college buddy."

"Is he cute?"

She almost blushed. "Very. You have any plans for tomorrow?"

"Just sleep. And a little Skype time with Torré."

"That's good to hear. Tell him I said hello."

"I will."

"Don't stay too late. The bad guys gotta get their sleep, too."

"I won't. Good night."

"Good night." Watson turned and left the office, heading for the elevators. Fung watched her enter and turn around. She shot him one last furtive glance, but he caught it. She threw an awkward wave and forced a smile. Fung smiled back as the doors slid shut.

Bitch.

Thought you would never leave.

Time to buy some insurance.

He bailed out of his programming software and pulled up the building's security cameras. There weren't any located on his floor, where most of CloudServe's security clearance work took place. CloudServe was as paranoid about camera hacking as anyone on the planet. But the cameras the building security deployed in the lobby showed that the two security guards on duty were both seated at the lobby desk, so no chance of them wandering in unexpectedly.

Fung dashed over to Watson's office, careful to leave the lights off. He powered up her machine and pulled out the PassPrint device. It recognized her fingerprint, or, at least, interpreted one of the tens of thousands of fake ones scrolling through the device as one of her prints.

Once inside her computer, he accessed the mirroring program on the NRO computer. But unlike his own setup, there was no automatic log erasure, so his time spent there right now would be recorded as her time spent there.

He glanced around the darkened office and the well-lit floor outside. No signs of life. **Good.** He turned his attention back to the screen. Maybe there was something that CHIBI could use. But the only thing on the NRO screen at the moment was a conversation about an air drop of Romanian AK-47s to a Tuareg militia unit by the Italian Air Force that was to take place tomorrow.

Interesting, Fung thought. But since he wasn't getting paid for it, he decided against recording it with the HD digital video camera hidden inside his big analog TAG Heuer watch. Even in broad daylight, it was the most natural gesture in the world for him to put his elbows on the desk and clasp his hands together as if in thought, studying a computer screen, and a simple matter of sliding a finger over and tapping the crown to begin recording, storing the files on a miniature one-terabyte drive embedded behind the face. If anyone were watching him, they would never suspect what he was up to, not that anyone ever did.

The immaculate watch was an awesome device

sent to him by CHIBI, his Chinese hacker friend. Fung agreed with the enclosed instructions that the video watch was a far safer approach to data transfer than downloading files onto a suspicious thumb drive, wireless or otherwise. Besides, the fewer actions taken on a computer, the better. The NRO might have been installing their own security systems without him knowing about it.

Fung did, however, spend the next few minutes rooting around recent communiques between the CIA and other agencies, including assets in the field. He wasn't looking for anything in particular; he just wanted to leave as many incriminating footprints as possible. If the whistle were ever blown, Watson would be the one with mud on her shoes, not him.

Ten minutes later, he shut everything down, careful to wipe his own fingerprints off of anything he might have touched. With the floor still clear, he headed back to his desktop and pulled up the building's security logs. He scrolled through the list of people leaving the building and found Watson's name registered and a departure time of 9:28 p.m. He checked his watch. It read 9:49 p.m. It would take him five minutes to shut down, and less than ten minutes to get to the lobby to check out. He added a few more minutes and changed Watson's checkout time to 10:14 p.m. His own computer automatically wiped away any digital footprints he might have left behind on the building's security computer, so no chance of that blowing back on him.

Satisfied, he shut down his computer and headed for the lobby with a spring in his step. His escort service had scheduled a date for him with his favorite, Roberto, for a weekend debauch in the bridal suite at the Fairmont in less than an hour.

Fung was on fire.

Roberto had better be ready.

24

AFRIN DISTRICT, SYRIA

Captain Akar studied his map in the lamplight inside the cab of his Kobra command vehicle, the Turkish version of the Humvee. The "Maroon Berets" Special Forces commander never could sleep before a fight, even one this lopsided.

He kept the motor running for heat against the night chill. He took another long drag of his cigarette and checked his watch. Just after three a.m. The assault on the sleeping village wouldn't begin for another two hours, covered by Italian-engineered T129A ATAK helicopter close-air support. A platoon of his best commandos was leading a group of a hundred fifty Chechen fanatics—former ISIS fighters now converted to the Turkish cause against the Syrian regime.

For the past two weeks, his combined unit had raided regime-friendly villages behind the lines, gunning down any resistance they encountered, burning down houses and farms, and leaving the women to the tender mercies of the Chechen savages. He was tasked with neutralizing armed opposition and terrorizing the countryside along the northern border to erode the morale of the obstinate Syrian Army. With any luck, this part of the border would be absorbed by his own country within the next few months.

His battle-weary troops were still bedded down in the barn and outbuildings around the small, vacated farm they would burn down later in the day. Better to let them sleep for a few more minutes, he decided. Their bellies were full after yesterday's air drop by a Lockheed C-130 Hercules cargo plane based at Incirlik. Resupplied with food, water, and ammo, they were well equipped to resume their terror campaign.

The captain yawned and stretched. Time to check with the sentries and fetch another cup of strong black coffee. He stepped out of the cab into the cool night air and crushed the last of his cigarette into the dry dust. The velvet black sky was strewn with a thick blanket of shimmering stars. It nearly took his breath away. It seemed a shame so much ugliness should thrive beneath such quiet beauty.

But such was the will of Allah, was it not?

EASTERN MEDITERRANEAN SEA

Captain (2nd rank) Nikulin studied the drone's live FLIR feed on the LCD display in the low blue light of the humming CIC. The Project 21631 missile corvette **Vyshny Volochyok** was one of the Russian Federation's latest **Buyan-M**-class vessels, specially dispatched from duties with the Black Sea fleet for this particular mission.

The high-altitude black-and-white FLIR imagery displayed the heat differentials of the ground targets below. Chimneys glowed with heat on two of the buildings. Four sentries—or at least the parts of them not covered by uniforms—stood like white ghosts against the dark, cold ground. One figure stood off in a dark patch away from the others, a widening white puddle forming at his feet. **Pissing like a cow,** Nikulin thought. **Enjoy it while it lasts.**

What caught the captain's eye was the brightest image on his screen: a vehicle with a warm motor glowing white hot.

The FLIR imagery was a clear visual confirmation of the bandit column the FSB report had promised.

Better still, the GLONASS tracking device implanted by an FSB agent into the air-dropped ammunition supply was operating perfectly, according to his electronic warfare officer.

Two confirmations were more than enough in his mind. It was time.

Nikulin gave the order to his weapons-control officer. Alarms rang.

The first of eight vertical launch tubes burst with a fiery flash of blinding light as the booster engine of the SS-N-30 Kalibr cruise missile fired in a deafening roar, leaving a trailing plume of white exhaust as it leaped into the dark morning sky thick with stars. Seven more missiles followed in rapid sequence.

Seconds later, the boosters fell away and the solid rocket motors of the turbojet engines engaged. Capable of reaching speeds in excess of half a mile per second, the supersonic cruise missiles would strike the objective in northern Syria in less than four minutes, delivering each of their 450-kilo high-explosive warheads on target by GLONASS satellite navigation.

AFRIN DISTRICT, SYRIA

Captain Akar stood at the back of the 4x4 Mercedes Axor truck, finishing off a cup of steaming black coffee as his bleary-eyed first sergeant lit a cigarette. He lifted up the pot. "More, sir?"

"No. I'll just have to piss," the captain said. He

slapped the sergeant on the shoulder with a grin. "Time to wake the men!"

The sergeant nodded eagerly, the cherry tip of his cigarette bobbing in the dark.

The two men turned to leave but froze in place. The unmistakable sound of turbojet engines roared in the distance.

"Captain—"

The first missile struck, vaporizing both men in a ground-shaking explosion that lit the sky in a fiery dawn. Seven more followed in as many seconds.

The last explosions of the burning ammo truck echoed in the low hills minutes later. Amid the flames, the screams of the few surviving wounded pierced the night.

Proof of concept number three.

25

Lost him," Tyler said.

Sandra Kyle tapped the mute button on her cell phone and swore.

Tyler was the newest man on her team. She was shorthanded at the moment, and the Ryan project was top-drawer because Senator Dixon was her top priority. Kyle assumed that basic surveillance for an ex–Pinkerton contractor like Tyler wouldn't be a problem.

Apparently, she was wrong.

The acne-scarred contractor had lost his target. She unmuted her phone. "He knew you were following him?"

"I don't think so. Just running a vehicular SDR."

"Just for the hell of it?" Kyle couldn't wrap her mind around Clark running a random surveillance detection route.

"It's normal SOP for high-value targets in high-threat environments to run them."

"I wouldn't call Clark a high-value target, and D.C. isn't exactly the Green Zone."

"Maybe Clark isn't the high-value component."

"Who's with him in the vehicle?"

"Unknown male. Late twenties, maybe early thirties. Bearded, short hair, clean cut. Blue eyes, dark hair. Six-one or so. Athletic build, maybe one-ninety or two hundred pounds. Carry-on leather satchel and a computer bag."

Kyle drummed her fingers on the desk. She ran a few dates in her head. Everything but the beard made sense.

Kyle had actually met Jack Junior—a college kid at the time—when she was still with the Capitol Police. Nice kid. Good-looking. Kind of bookish, too, as she recalled. Georgetown, wasn't it? Yeah, that was it. Just like his old man. That meant he was smart.

It wasn't completely crazy that someone like him would work for a financial outfit like Hendley Associates. Gerry Hendley and President Ryan went way back. She could see the President picking up the phone and asking Gerry to do him a favor and hire his kid. Good connections for Hendley, too.

But why was Clark playing chauffeur to a suit monkey like Junior? Clark must have been, what, seventy-plus years old by now? Too old to be a bodyguard, and besides, that's what the Secret Service was for.

So where in the hell was the Secret Service?

Something was definitely off about all of this.

"You get any pictures of the passenger?"

"Sending now."

A moment later, her phone dinged. She checked the photo.

Yeah. That was Junior for sure. Interesting.

The President's son.

"Where did Clark pick him up?"

"At an apartment in Alexandria. They left there and headed back over to Hendley Associates. Pulled into the underground parking lot. I couldn't follow. About twenty minutes later they pulled back out and headed west."

"West?"

"Yeah. Surprised me, too. I assumed they were headed for the airport. That's when they started their evasion route. After three turns, I broke off, as per **my** SOP."

Kyle sighed. There wasn't any way to run mobile surveillance with just one vehicle on a determined target. Breaking off was the right move. Maybe Tyler wasn't a complete idiot after all.

"Did you get the plate number?"

"Sending now."

Kyle's phone chirped again. "Good job. You can call it a night."

"Sorry I dropped the ball, chief."

"This one's on me. I'll take it from here."

Kyle rang off, then dialed another number. A captain in the D.C. Metro Police Department owed her a favor. Last year, his wife contacted

Kyle's agency, wanted a surveillance on her husband, whom she suspected of having an affair. She wanted evidence—or, more accurately, her divorce attorney did. Kyle agreed. Came back empty-handed.

"You sure?" the captain's wife replied, stunned and disbelieving.

"I never caught him with another woman" was Kyle's honest answer. Honest, because Kyle was the woman the captain was sleeping with, and there was no other woman besides her that she ever saw. Saved the captain half of his pension and six figures in legal fees.

"Sandra? To what do I owe the pleasure?" the captain said.

"Need a favor."

The gravelly-voiced captain chuckled. "The long favor or the short one?"

"I thought you and your wife were back together."

"We are. But you know how it is."

"Well, the favor I'm asking for is vertical, not horizontal. I need you to track a vehicle for me on the DAS—and on the down-low."

"I'm just about to leave my shift."

"It's important."

"Give me the details."

Kyle gave the captain the plate number, along with the make, model, and color of the vehicle. She also suggested its final destination.

"How long will it take?"

"Depends on where it lands. If you're right, probably no more than thirty minutes."

"Thanks. I owe you one."

"And you know how I'll want it paid back, don't you?"

"Horizontal."

"Next Tuesday. My place in Georgetown. Eight o'clock."

"Deal." She didn't mind. Captain Merriweather was a legendary lay.

Twenty-three minutes later, Merriweather called.

"I just texted you a file. Your car arrived at Dulles ten minutes ago. Headed for the charter jet FBO."

"Thanks, DeAndre."

"Next Tuesday. Don't forget."

"I'll be there with bells on."

He laughed at the imagery. "Hope we don't wake the neighbors."

He hung up just as his text message arrived. It was all pictures, each taken from the D.C. DAS—the Microsoft-branded Domain Awareness System. The technology was straight out of the television show **Person of Interest**. The DAS was a surveillance software package that linked thousands of D.C. metro area cameras, allowing law enforcement to track the movement of people and vehicles in real time. It was even possible to track them twenty-four hours prior—everything was recorded, but the city budget allowed for only one day's worth of data storage.

Tracking a vehicle was especially easy when the vehicle license plate was known. The DAS even provided a windshield shot of both Clark and Ryan in the front seat of their generic sedan. Exactly the kind of confirmation Kyle liked.

Clark had, indeed, driven aggressively to either avoid or shake any kind of tail. Kyle hoped it was the former. Dixon had been quite specific about not getting caught in the act. The final picture in Merriweather's text was of the car passing through the general aviation gate toward the FBO terminal.

But why Dulles? Reagan National was far closer to the Hendley Associates building. Then Kyle remembered: Reagan was good only for domestic flights for private charters. A private charter had to go through either Baltimore or Dulles for international flights. Reagan National didn't have the U.S. Customs and Border Protection facilities needed for international travel on private planes.

So Ryan was flying out of the country. But to where?

No way to tell from these photos. But Kyle had an idea. She jumped on her laptop and started digging into her favorite databases. Within an hour she had pieced it all together. Hendley Associates owned a Gulfstream G550. After procuring its tail number, it was a short jump to the FAA database to find the filed flight plan.

Bingo.

Jack Junior was heading for Warsaw, Poland.

She called Dixon with the intel.

Strangely, the senator didn't seem surprised.

26

NEAR RIVAK, TAJIKISTAN, CLOSE TO THE BORDER OF AFGHANISTAN

The big Chinese-built JAC diesel tractor-trailer rumbled down the narrow asphalt road at the foot of the gray-and-rust-colored Pamir Mountains, rising higher the farther west they traveled.

Giant sandstone boulders crowded the road shoulder. The driver, Lin, imagined the rocks crashing down from high above centuries ago—or maybe even this morning. Any one of them was big enough to catapult his big red diesel rig into the pale green Gunt River on the other side of the two-lane.

Despite his cushioned air-suspension seat, Lin's rear end and lower back were trashed after sitting for so many kilometers from Kashgar in Xinjiang, China's westernmost province, where the three-truck convoy had loaded up. His mouth was dry from the bitter tobacco he'd been forced to smoke for the last three days, but his screaming bladder told him not to drink any more warm soda.

The three-truck convoy was due at its destination in three hours, but Lin doubted they would arrive on time. The narrow road twisted and turned as it followed the river wending its way through the anticline mountains, snowcapped in the far distance.

The forty-year-old driver lit another cigarette as he began a long turn around the next bend.

"Another smoke?" the man in the next seat asked, smiling. He was staring up at the mountains through a monocular pressed against his eye.

"Nervous habit," Lin responded, snapping his lighter shut.

"Yes. Nervous."

Lin thought the Frenchman looked a little like the American movie star Matt Damon, in part because he heard one of the other **laowai** call him Mathieu. His last name was Cluzet. He looked to be thirty years old, if that, and wore his dirty-blond hair short. Cluzet was clean-shaven, unlike his friends, and built like a runner. He seemed unremarkable in most regards, but he was a pleasant fellow and his Mandarin was good. He wore Levi's, running shoes, and a University of American Samoa Law School sweatshirt.

He carried no weapons. Not even a knife.

And he was in charge.

"The mountains are beautiful, and the air is

crystal clear," Cluzet said. "You can see forever." He lowered the monocular.

They rounded the sharp corner and Lin slammed his brakes. The truck shuddered to a halt in a whoosh of air brakes.

A roadblock. Two battered, open-aired Soviet-era UAZ jeeps stood bumper-to-bumper in the middle of the highway. Both drivers flashed AK-47s, and the men in back of each held RPGs on their shoulders. Each bearded man wore the distinctive woolen Afghan **pakol** cap, including the tallest, a scowling giant standing over six feet five inches in the middle of the road, a short-barreled AKS-74U rifle draped by his side, held in one hand by the pistol grip. His face was dark and leathered from years in the mountains, his woolly beard shot through with flecks of gray.

Cluzet winked at Lin. "I bet now you're really nervous, eh?"

Lin tossed his cigarette out the window, mute with fear. He glanced in his sideview mirrors and saw the two other trucks lunging to a halt behind him, rocking on their shocks. It was lucky they didn't crash into him or each other.

"Kill the engine," Cluzet ordered as he dropped down out of the high truck cab and approached the giant Afghan.

"**Salaam alaykum**," Cluzet offered cheerfully.

The grim Afghan leader nodded. "**Wa alaykumu salam.**"

"What do you want?" Cluzet asked in passable Dari, one of the two major languages here and across the border in Afghanistan.

The tall Afghan did a poor job of hiding his surprise that the infidel spoke his language. His wide eyes narrowed. "How long were you in my country?"

"Three years."

"You fought?"

Cluzet nodded at the Russian military-issue watch on his wrist. "You did as well, but not Russians. Too young."

The giant smiled broadly, showing a few missing teeth. "My father killed many Russians. He took this from an officer. 103rd Guards Airborne Division."

Cluzet smiled in return and held up his arm. A big Casio G-Shock was on his wrist. He tapped it hopefully. "Let's trade! Mine is much better."

The Afghan dismissed the smaller, younger man with a shrug. "I don't want your watch. I want your trucks. Or at least what is inside of them."

Cluzet laughed. "You must be joking. They're full of nothing but DVD players, portable radios, and children's toys." He nodded toward his armed friends. "They don't look like children to me."

The Afghan leader shook his head. "Indeed, they are not. They are men who do what I command."

Cluzet held up his left hand in a peaceful gesture. "I'm reaching into my back pocket to show you something. Don't get nervous, okay?" He flashed a friendly smile, then slowly reached into the back pocket of his jeans and extracted a thick wallet.

The Afghan leader's dark eyes were fixed on the billfold. Cluzet opened it and pulled out a wad of American twenty-dollar bills. U.S. currency was more valuable in this part of the world than local paper. Cluzet held the cash out and the Afghan slung his weapon. Cluzet handed the stack of bills over as he scanned the rocks above. The metallic click of rifles grabbed Cluzet's attention. The nervous Afghan drivers raised their AKs as two more Europeans stepped forward, one on each side of Cluzet. Unlike Cluzet, these two men were armed with pistols holstered on their legs.

"These men are my friends. They mean you no harm," Cluzet said.

Without looking up, the Afghan leader shouted back at his men, "Put your rifles down."

The rifles lowered, but the hard stares didn't.

"Everything okay, boss?" the man on Cluzet's left, a German, asked in English.

"Kein Problem," Cluzet said. "We're just about done here."

The other man, a short, barrel-chested Spaniard, smiled broadly, speaking in a near whisper through clenched teeth, like a ventriloquist. "These guys speak English?"

"Not a word."

The Spaniard raised his voice but kept staring at the armed fighters in the jeeps. "I counted ten men up top."

"Thirteen," Cluzet said. "Including a sniper on the other side of the river."

The Spaniard nodded. "Good eye."

"Four hundred American dollars," the Afghan finally said. "Not enough."

"But that is all I'm going to give you." Cluzet smiled even more broadly than before. "Take it. Please."

"Do you think I am an idiot? Do foreign devils with guns travel in these mountains to deliver children's toys?"

"Look, I admire you. I really do. You picked a terrific blocking point. A narrow part of the road just around a blind curve. That is very expert. And your men above on both sides with long-range weapons and RPGs."

"Then you realize I can kill you all and just take what I want."

"Of course I do. And I understand you. I really do. You are a businessman, just like me. We can be friends. No need for violence. Just take the money."

The Afghan nodded thoughtfully as he pocketed the money. "Yes. I will take the money." His fierce scowl broke into a wide grin. "And your trucks."

Cluzet shook his head as he ran his fingers

through his hair. "That is truly unfortunate, my friend."

The Afghan suddenly noticed the tattoo on the Frenchman's forearm. A wing with an arm and a sword. He didn't recognize it for what it was: the arm of the Archangel Michael, the patron saint of the 2e Régiment Étranger de Parachutistes of the French Foreign Legion.

"Fortunate or not, I am taking what I want. Stand aside or I will kill you and take it anyway." He raised his weapon. "I don't fear a man with a woman's smooth face."

Cluzet rubbed his beardless face. "Yes, smooth, like Setara's, I imagine. She's your youngest wife, right? The prettiest, at least. I should think she would like my face."

The Afghan chieftain scowled with confusion. "You know my wife's name?"

Cluzet's boyish charm suddenly vanished, his face hardening like the limestone looming above their heads. "Pull out your phone, Behzad Khatloni, and call her now."

"How do you know these things? You are a devil!"

"My job is to know everything. Call now. Or you will regret it."

Khatloni marched over to his jeep and his driver handed him his phone. He dialed. A moment later, a panicked woman's voice answered.

"Our sons! Behzad! Please!" a woman's voice shouted over the speaker. Everyone could hear it.

"What is happening?"

"Foreigners. Infidels. Rifles, machine guns. Vehicles. They have rounded us all up. They said they will kill us."

"How many?"

"I don't know," she cried. "Many."

Khatloni's eyes widened with rage. He turned toward the Frenchman. "What is this?"

"All of your fighters are here. If you don't leave in the next sixty seconds, my men will burn your village, kill your elderly, rape your women—and your sons."

The Afghan whipped a long **choora** knife from its sheath and lunged at Cluzet, landing the blade millimeters from Cluzet's neck before the other two mercenaries could react.

"Call them off!"

Cluzet didn't flinch. He could smell the stink of Khatloni's breath. "My men have their orders. They will slit your children's throats, drop the bodies into the dung trench, and piss on them."

He pressed the t-shaped blade against Cluzet's throat. "Have you no fear?"

"Yes. Of boredom."

The Afghan's men stirred anxiously, worried about their own families. Cluzet's men stayed frozen in place, ready to pounce on command.

The giant Afghan searched Cluzet's unblinking eyes.

"You are the spawn of Satan!"

"Probably. Thirty seconds."

Khatloni cursed, sheathing his blade. He barked orders to his men. The jeep engines fired up and he turned to leave.

"Not yet," Cluzet said.

The Afghan spun around. "What?"

"Your watch."

Khatloni stiffened. "Are you insane?"

"Your watch, now. Or I don't call."

"You would kill my children for a cursed watch?"

Cluzet shrugged, puzzled. "Yes. I would."

The Afghan clawed at the watch's wristband, grunting with frustration.

"I hate you devils! You curse my land."

"Yes, I suppose we do. But it's an interesting way to pass the time."

The Afghan flung the freed watch at Cluzet, who caught it with a laugh.

"Make the damn call, infidel!"

The Spaniard reached behind his back and handed Cluzet a sat phone as Khatloni piled into his jeep. The engines roared and the two UAZs sped away in a screech of smoking tires burning on the asphalt.

Cluzet punched numbers on the sat phone, catching the puzzled gaze of his two men. He turned around and saw Lin in the cab of the truck, his white-knuckled hands welded to the steering wheel in abject terror.

Cluzet turned to the German, grinning. "I think that went very well, don't you?"

27

BADAKHSHAN PROVINCE, NORTHEASTERN AFGHANISTAN

It was a clear, cool morning, the sky a blue so brilliant it hurt Cluzet's eyes as he stared at it, sipping a hot tea.

His three tractor-trailers stood beneath tents of heavy camouflage netting to mask the heat signatures of the big diesel engines and to avoid the prying eyes of the school-bus-sized KH-11 Keyhole satellite passing over Afghanistan nearly fifteen times per day at a mean altitude of four hundred kilometers.

The satellite's optical sensors were capable of seeing objects just four inches across in broad daylight, but it also possessed thermal and infrared capabilities. Deployed primarily to assist U.S. and ISAF coalition military operations, it was sometimes tasked with drug interdiction assignments for the ISAF and the Afghan Army. Given their remote location, unless the KH-11 satellite was tasked with a mission specifically directed at them, they were likely safe. Still, as far as Cluzet was concerned, it never hurt to be too careful.

The first items that had been unloaded and restacked overnight from the trailers were pallets of BEGO-brand "Star Battles" toys—Chinese knockoffs of the famous LEGO **Star Wars** building-block sets. The rest were, as Cluzet told Khatloni, pallets of Chinese-manufactured DVD players and portable radios.

Once the cheap Chinese goods were unloaded, it was possible to remove the dozens of two-hundred-liter plastic drums of chemical precursors for the manufacture of heroin. Despite decades of American and European interdiction efforts, Afghan heroin production was at an all-time high at nearly 500,000 acres of poppies—the equivalent of 500,000 American football fields, not including end zones—producing an estimated 9,000 metric tons of refined product, the vast majority of global heroin sourcing.

While there was no shortage of poppies to produce the raw opium latex typically harvested by Afghan children, the largely agrarian and dysfunctional Afghan economy was incapable of producing the hydrochloric acid, acetic anhydride, and other chemical precursors required in the otherwise simple heroin manufacturing process.

European governments had successfully monitored legal shipments of these important chemicals used in many industrial and pharmaceutical applications, and had even managed to clamp down on the illegal distribution of them.

Chinese government officials who were secretly part of the global criminal enterprise known as the Iron Syndicate were more than happy to fill in the gap. The Iron Syndicate rerouted the heroin precursor chemicals into Afghanistan under official cover with all necessary documentation out of Kashgar, an ancient city along the original Silk Road of Marco Polo fame in China's far-western Xinjiang Province. The city had enjoyed a great deal of German foreign investment of late, including with development of the largest and most sophisticated chemical plants in Central Asia, with managers on the Iron Syndicate payroll.

Cluzet and his team were hired to provide security for the illicit chemical shipment needed in the process to transform raw opium into a morphine base, then into brown tar heroin, and finally grade 4 "pure" white heroin.

Delivering the four tons of precursors was only half of Cluzet's dangerous assignment. The second half was even more treacherous: delivering one metric ton of processed heroin to the shipyards in Gdańsk. The distribution and sale of the final heroin product would generate just over **two hundred million dollars** of profit for his employer and their Afghan producers.

The Afghans unloaded the pallets of radio cases with the aid of a rusted 1964 Massey Ferguson forklift–tractor conversion and stacked them inside a cinder-block storage shed, where young village women began their work. They first opened the cases of radios, then pulled out individual units, carefully opened the boxes, and removed the specially designed digital radios, mindful not to damage the packaging or lose the instructions.

Individual radios were pried open and a package of heroin was placed inside a storage compartment. Once a radio was loaded with heroin, it was placed back in its packaging box and the box was resealed. Then the box was marked with a small brown sticker, round and innocuous. The "heroin radio" was then put back in the case of "clean radios" and the process repeated. Only one in four of the radios carried the illicit drug. Once finished with the pallets of radios, the women moved on to the DVD players and finally the children's toys.

While the women continued stashing heroin packets, men unloaded the heavy barrels of dangerous chemical precursors and transported them gingerly to the heroin-processing lab with the help of the wheezing tractor.

The Afghan in charge of the mobile heroin-processing station, Ahktar Hayat, was a twenty-four-year-old gray-eyed Pashtun with a chemistry degree from a university in Peshawar, Pakistan. He and Cluzet had worked together before.

Cluzet's team was spread out around the camp,

cleaning weapons, eating food, or catching up on sleep, including the Ingush mercs he'd hired for the job—murderous Caucasian cousins of the Chechens. Two of his men he kept on sentry duty. His walkie-talkie crackled with chatter in Pashtun. One of Hayat's sentries called in over the radio:

"A Devil's Chariot! Ten kilometers out!"

A Devil's Chariot—the Afghan term for the hated Mi-35 Hind helicopters flown by the Afghan Air Force—was bad news for Hayat, Cluzet knew. His wasn't a Taliban combat unit, per se. Hayat's job was to cook heroin, bag it, and ship it on. His small band had only AKs and RPG-7s for defense against bandits or rival gangs. The forty-millimeter rocket-propelled grenades were powerful enough to blast away a rotor assembly even on the heavily armored Russian helicopter, but the RPG-7 had an effective range of only two hundred meters. Every helicopter pilot who had ever flown in Afghanistan over the last forty years knew to stay high off the deck, especially in the mountains.

Cluzet didn't wait for Hayat's panicked call. An attack by the heavily armed machine—called the "Flying Tank" by the Russians who built them— would be catastrophic.

A lone Hind, though, likely wasn't on a combat mission. Quite possibly it was on a surveillance run, or even just a training exercise. But discovery of their operation or his convoy when it pulled out in the morning would be equally disastrous.

Either outcome would interrupt his assignment, something both he and the Iron Syndicate took very seriously. Failure was not an option.

The Hind had to be destroyed.

The lookout called in the incoming direction of the Hind as Cluzet whistled up his number two and designated spotter, the German, an ex-KSK (Kommando Spezialkräfte) sergeant named Manstein. The two of them jogged over to the back of a Range Rover. Cluzet grabbed the FIM-92B Stinger MANPADS from its locker in the back of the vehicle and Manstein fetched range-finding binoculars.

The two of them scrambled to higher ground as the mountains began to echo with the whirring doom of the Hind's rotors beating the thin, cool air.

"Got him," Manstein said, pointing toward the southwest. "I'd say one thousand meters elevation above our position."

With the five-foot-long launcher balanced on his shoulder, Cluzet slammed home the battery cooling unit into the stock's pistol grip and twisted it, powering up the missile with a thermal battery and cooling the seeker to operating temperature with argon gas.

He lifted the launcher in the direction Manstein was pointing and glanced over the top of the sight.

"Yes, I see him. About four kilometers out and one kilometer altitude." Well within range of the fearsome Stinger.

"Confirmed." Manstein kept his binoculars fixed on the Hind.

Cluzet raised the launcher even higher and put his eye to the sight. In order to set the UV/IR tracker, he lined up the sight above the helicopter against the clear blue sky as he pressed down and in on the safety and actuator switch. This immediately initiated a howling tone over the small speaker that also shot through his skull, thanks to the vibration of the small transducer pressed against his cheekbone.

He lined up the Hind in the "canoe" between the forward range ring and the rear reticle. Once the tracker locked in the "negative UV"—the light blocked out by the chopper—the tone changed sharply, telling Cluzet his missile was also locked in.

Cluzet uncaged the missile with the press of his left index finger, releasing the missile's seeker eye to follow the Hind independently. He superelevated the launcher at an exaggerated angle and depressed the trigger, holding it until—

WHOOSH!

The missile's small ejection motor fired, spitting

the twenty-two-pound missile out of the tube, just far enough to clear away safely from Cluzet before falling away. The now powerless missile dropped a few inches before the second, more powerful two-stage solid-fuel flight motor engaged, driving the missile toward the Hind at nearly 2,400 feet per second, almost ten times faster than its target. A plume of white rocket exhaust trailed behind the speeding Stinger.

The Hind instantly fired countermeasure flares and chaff, but the Stinger's UV/IR homing system was impervious to them. In just over five seconds after launch, the missile's 6.6-pound high-explosive fragmentation warhead ripped into the airframe. A secondary explosion erupted in the fuel tank, and the flaming nine-ton wreckage plummeted toward the earth.

Cluzet lowered the launcher, a smile plastered across his boyish face. His green eyes tracked the falling wreckage until it crashed in a fiery heap on the valley floor far down below.

The irony wasn't lost on him that he'd just shot down a Russian helicopter flown by an Afghan pilot. It used to be Afghans that shot down Russian pilots.

But always, it was the Stinger that was the victor. **Plus ça change, plus c'est la même chose.**

"Nice shot," Manstein said, clapping him on the back.

"Hard to miss a flying brick."

Cluzet checked his recently acquired Russian airborne watch. "Let's get all hands on deck and help these mountain goats to finish up. We need to get this shipment loaded up fast and get out of here and on the road before another helicopter comes looking for their dead friends."

"The Ingush won't like it," Manstein said. "They're fighters, not stevedores."

"They'll like getting eighty-millimeter Russian rockets up the ass even less," Cluzet said. "Now go!"

28

Jack wasn't embarrassed to admit that flying in the Hendley Associates Gulfstream G550 was better than first-class commercial any day. No TSA lines at the terminal, no waiting to board, no coughing kids throwing snot and bacteria into the air, and no snoring seatmates—well, unless Ding Chavez was sacked out somewhere in the cabin.

It was expensive for Gerry to fly him over in an empty plane, but it was his call to make and Jack was grateful. It was a great time-saver on an assignment he really hadn't wanted to take. He had an obligation to fulfill on the other side of the planet, and it bothered him like hell to put it off a single day longer than necessary.

The G550 executive jet kissed the tarmac under the steady hand of Captain Helen Reid and her first officer copilot, Chester "Country" Hicks, at Warsaw Chopin, the capital city's principal airport and the largest one in Poland. Captain Reid taxied to a small private terminal of a local fixed-based operator that Lisanne Robertson, the director of transportation for Hendley Associates and The Campus, had contracted with for refueling and scheduled maintenance services in addition to landing rights.

Jack yawned as he pulled on his sport coat. The overnight flight had taken just over ten hours, nonstop, well within the range of the Gulfstream's twin Rolls-Royce engines. He originally planned to sleep on the way over, but decided instead to dig a little deeper into the few files he had on Gage Capital Partners and the two dozen shell companies he'd found connected with Aaron and his son, Christopher. He finally managed to squeeze in a power nap an hour before they landed, and Lisanne had whipped up a couple of cups of strong black coffee and a spicy turkey-sausage-and-egg breakfast sandwich for him to wolf down before landing.

It was too bad Midas—Bartosz Jankowski— was stuck in the Philippines on a Campus assignment. He'd never heard the former Ranger talk about his parents' native homeland, nor did he ever mention spending time in Poland. But Midas spoke the language fluently, as well as Russian. The former Delta recce was damned handy to have in a gunfight, too, though the only wounds Jack anticipated receiving on this trip were paper cuts from an accounts receivable ledger if he could ever lay his hands on one.

"We're wheels up in eight hours. Any chance you'll be done by then? Happy to give you a lift back if you don't mind an overnight in London."

Jack tried to hide his disappointment. Ysabel was still in London, staying with her parents. It would be a convenient excuse to visit her without actually being invited and try to figure out what was going on between the two of them.

If anything, Jack thought. He was beginning to wonder if her radio silence was more than just rest and recuperation. Their time together in Afghanistan proved they both still cared for each other. On the other hand, it also proved they still had unresolved issues. Right now, he wasn't sure which side would win out in the end.

"Sadly, no. Could be eight hours or eight months before I get to the bottom of this thing."

"What can I do to help?"

Jack smiled. Lisanne knew how to handle weapons, how to clear a room, and how to kick ass, generally, besides being fluent in Arabic. However, as far as he knew, she had no forensic accounting skills, so there wasn't much she could do to help, and even if she could, she hadn't been read in to his assignment. But it was her nature to be helpful, no matter the circumstances. It was just one of the many reasons she'd been the perfect person to replace Adara Sherman as the director of transportation.

"Maybe a short prayer for patience. I'll be

pushing on a string, uphill, in the dark until I can figure this thing out."

"Beats shoveling shit in Louisiana, to borrow a phrase."

"Couldn't say. I've never been to Louisiana."

Jack poked his head in the cockpit to shake hands with Reid and Hicks and thank them for the great flying before Lisanne handed him his leather satchel and laptop case.

"Safe travels," she said.

"You, too."

Jack descended the cabin stairs to the tarmac. The darkening sky threatened rain and a slight breeze tousled his dark hair. The gloomy weather didn't particularly bother him, but neither did it help his mood. He proceeded into the private hangar and offices of the FBO, where he passed through customs quickly and without incident— another check mark in the private-charter column. With his two bags and a freshly stamped passport, he headed out the front door of the mini-terminal in search of his Polish contact, Jerzy Krychowiak, the fifty-seven-year-old ABW agent Gerry had arranged for him to meet.

Jack approached the curb. Scanned the street. Where the hell was he?

Jack Ryan?" A woman's voice.

Jack turned around. He was greeted by the

confident but exhausted gaze of a striking blond, blue-eyed woman about his age. She stood in front of a silver Audi A5 coupe parked at the curb behind her. A shoulder holster printed beneath her loose-fitting blue blazer.

Not what he was expecting. **But better than a kick in the head.**

"Yeah. That's me."

She thrust out her hand. "Hello, Mr. Ryan. My name is Liliana Pilecki. I'm with the ABW."

Jack hesitated. This was highly unusual. "Where is Mr. Krychowiak?"

"I'm sorry, he can't be here. He was struck by a car in a hit-and-run last night. He was put into a medically induced coma just an hour ago."

"I'm really sorry to hear that. My grandfather was a cop. Is he going to pull through?"

"Jerzy is a strong man. I pray he will survive this."

No wonder she looks exhausted, Jack thought. "You look like you've been through the wringer. He must be your partner."

"I sat with his wife during surgery. It was a long night."

"Was it an accident or intentional?"

"We're still investigating. The car was found three kilometers away from the crime scene, burned to the ground."

"How did you identify the car?"

"We tracked it through CCTV traffic cameras.

The car was stolen. We couldn't identify the driver."

"I hate to ask, but how about you show me your credentials?"

"Yes, of course." She reached into her coat pocket and pulled out a small leather billfold and handed it to Jack. It was all in Polish, naturally. He had a little Russian under his belt, but it didn't help.

"Thanks." He handed it back to her. "Look, you've got a lot going on. I can catch an Uber to my hotel and—"

"Don't be ridiculous. My supervisor briefed me on the assignment and forwarded me Gerry Hendley's e-mail request. I'm just driving you around and translating when necessary. It's not a problem for me. Honestly." She frowned. "Didn't you get Mr. Hendley's text?"

Crap.

Jack hadn't checked his phone since landing. He powered it up. There it was. With her name in the address next to his.

Change of plans. Agent Liliana Pilecki will be taking care of you over there. Call me if there's a problem.

Jack rubbed his tired eyes. "Sorry about that, Ms. Pilecki. I'm a little off my game this morning. I appreciate you picking me up and dragging my sorry butt around."

"Can I help you with your bags?"

"No, I'm fine, thanks." Jack stifled a jagged yawn with the back of his hand.

"You look jet-lagged. I'll drop you off at your hotel and we can get started later this afternoon perhaps."

"No, I'm fine. I want to get after it right away."

"As you wish."

Liliana popped the trunk of her Audi and Jack dropped in his bags. Minutes later they were on a tree-lined four-lane road crowded with commuters, heading for the city center, where modern skyscrapers loomed in the distance.

"Have you ever been to Warszawa before, Mr. Ryan? Or Poland?"

"Please, call me Jack. And no. It's my first time."

Jack glanced out the rain-spattered passenger window. A lot of greenery and clean streets. The storm was picking up. "It's a nice city."

The first few drops of rain hit the windshield. The automatic wipers kicked on.

"It's big for me. I originally came from a smaller town just outside of Kraków in the south, but I love it here."

"Your English is superb, by the way."

"Thank you. I have family in Chicago. I did a year-abroad program there in high school, and another two years in college at Loyola, where I majored in piano and minored in accounting."

"Interesting combination."

"Accounting was my father's idea. He was a very practical person."

"He's passed away?"

"Last year. Prostate cancer. He was a good man."

"I'm sorry."

"Thank you."

"So how long have you been in the ABW?"

"Five years."

"Do they need a lot of piano players in your department?"

She laughed. A pleasant surprise for them both.

"Not many, no. It was my accounting degree that got me in, how do you say, by the skin of my teeth?"

And such pretty teeth they were, Jack noticed. Also, no wedding ring. But Bosnia had taught him a few more lessons about women, so he told himself to throttle back.

"So, how did you go from piano recitals to packing heat?"

"My sister overdosed on heroin the year I graduated."

"That's terrible. I'm so sorry."

"Death is not such a stranger in Poland. But thank you. After she died, I felt so helpless, so angry. The ABW was a place where I thought I might be able to do some good. Perhaps save someone else's sister. It was the least I could do."

"Drugs are a poison killing the entire West," Jack said. "Over seventy thousand Americans died from drug overdoses last year. More Americans than died in the Vietnam War."

"It's a big problem all over Europe, too, and getting worse here every day. My casework is focused on organized crime, so drugs and drug money play a big part in my investigations."

"And then you got stuck with me."

"I would hardly say 'stuck.' I'm happy to assist you in any way that I can."

"I appreciate it."

But how can you help me? Jack wondered. **I can't exactly tell you I'm hunting for dirt on an American senator.** Besides the fact that he was under strict orders from Gerry to keep it quiet, Jack didn't much like the idea of showing America's dirty underwear to an agent of a foreign security service, even an allied one.

"If you don't mind my saying, I am a big fan of your President," Liliana said. "He had the guts to stand up to the Russians when most NATO leaders didn't want to."

"I'm a big fan, too. And no, I don't mind you saying it."

"You are a financial analyst with Hendley Associates, correct?"

"Yes."

"Interesting that your boss, Mr. Hendley, is close friends with the head of the ABW."

"Gerry was formerly a U.S. senator. He knows a lot of people everywhere."

"I understand he is a close personal friend with President Ryan."

"Yes, he is."

"So tell me, Jack, where do you want to start?"

"I'm not entirely sure."

"Perhaps if you can tell me what you're looking for?"

"I'm investigating the business relationships of a corporation registered in Poland as Baltic General Services LLC. It's wholly owned by two parties, one of which is an American named Christopher Gage. Have you heard of him?"

"I'm afraid not. And why are you investigating him?"

Jack hated to lie, but she wasn't read in to any of this.

"Poor choice of words. It's not really an investigation. My firm is working on behalf of a client that wants to do business with Gage, but they want more details about his financial affairs before they proceed further in the relationship. Does that make sense?"

"For now, yes. And what is this Baltic General Services company doing in Poland?"

"That's partly what I'm trying to figure out. They seem to be partnering with other companies in Poland."

"What kind of companies?"

"I'm not sure. They are privately held, just like Baltic General Services and, for that matter,

Gage's parent company, Gage Group International. That's one of the reasons why I came. I can't exactly figure out what those companies are doing—my resources for Polish companies back home are limited. Besides the fact Gage's company has invested in them, the only common denominator between them is that Gage has done so through a German regional bank, which seems like an odd thing to do."

"What is the name of the bank?"

"OstBank."

Liliana frowned. "Are you sure?"

"Yes. Why?"

"I'm not at liberty to be specific, but I can say that my office is familiar with OstBank."

"Dirty?"

Liliana drummed her fingers on the steering wheel, weighing a decision. Finally, "A German BKA agent—a sister agency to mine—was killed last week in Berlin."

"And he was working the OstBank angle."

"Exactly so."

"Then that's the place to start. What time do the banks open here?"

"Not for another hour."

"Then maybe I will let you run me by my hotel for a quick shower and shave before we head out."

"Very well. I'll wait in the lobby."

29

Jack's hotel was in the city center, convenient to everywhere by foot, which most of Warsaw seemed to be. The hotel lobby was bright and modern, in muted grays and blues, with white leather couches and Danish-style furniture. The young desk clerk, a cheerful Ukrainian woman, spoke fluent English. She informed him with a bright smile that his room was ready and the corporate tab opened in case he wanted room service or anything else.

"The bank opens in a few minutes," Liliana said. "Would you like me to call and make an appointment for you?"

"For us, I think."

"And what do you want me to say the appointment is for?"

"Tell him I'm with Hendley Associates, we're a large American financial firm, and we want to do business in Poland." He was quick to add, "All of which is technically true. If there are any business opportunities here, Gerry will want to know about it."

Liliana smiled. "You have a hard time lying, don't you?"

"It wasn't exactly encouraged at home."

"You'd make a terrible spy."

"I can't cook, either."

"And how should I introduce myself?"

"Are you okay saying that you're my personal assistant, locally based?"

"Makes perfect sense. I'll call him while you take care of business."

"Back in thirty."

Liliana took a seat on one of the white couches and pulled out her phone.

Jack took the stairs with his two bags to boost his energy. What he really craved was another cup of coffee. Actually, a whole pot.

Twenty-five minutes later he was back in the lobby, showered and shaved and in clean clothes, with a leather folio in hand and his laptop bag slung over one shoulder. He found Liliana on the same leather sofa, texting.

"Ready?"

"Yes." Liliana stood, pocketing her phone. "The bank manager's name is Stanislaus Zbyszko and he's expecting us."

"Great. Lead the way."

A constant stream of city trams and cars shuttled passengers everywhere, but the sidewalks were also crowded, even in the rain.

Liliana skillfully navigated the crowded six-lane boulevard, keeping pace with the bright yellow electric tram rolling down the middle seventh lane. Warsaw was a modern, bustling European city. Office buildings crowded the main thoroughfares, along with high-rise apartments and gleaming skyscrapers.

"Almost there," Liliana said.

"The buildings in Warsaw seem brand-new, or at least most of them do." The Audi stopped at a red light. Jack pointed at a tall building across the street. "I don't know what that thing is. Looks like a wedding cake from hell."

"That's the Palace of Science and Culture. It was built by Soviet Communists in the fifties. For decades, it was the second-tallest building in all of Europe."

"I can't quite make it out. It sort of looks like the Empire State Building, but then it has those weird other features. It's damn tall, for sure."

"We locals call it Stalin's Penis."

Jack laughed. He wasn't expecting that one. "Yikes. It does seem rather imposing."

"The Russians were definitely sending a message. We were, after all, a Soviet colony at the time."

"It really stands out from the rest of the architecture."

"Most of what you see is relatively new. What you need to understand is that Warsaw was almost completely destroyed—flattened, just like those pictures you've seen of Hiroshima and Nagasaki after the bombing."

"The Nazis?"

"Yes, and the Russians, who allowed it to happen. Have you heard of the Warsaw Uprising?"

"Yes, but only in passing. We didn't study it in detail."

"It is one of our most heroic moments. Thousands of Poles rose up against the Nazi occupiers in 1944, using handmade or stolen Nazi weapons, and guns supplied by the Brits from the air. The Soviets were on the other side of the Vistula, urging us to rise up. But our forces were slaughtered—the very best of the Polish underground—because the Russians refused to intervene. Stalin allowed the Germans to butcher sixteen thousand Polish fighters because he didn't want any Polish national patriots to survive the war."

"If it were me, I'd blow that wedding cake up and use the bricks to build outhouses."

"We prefer to leave it there as a reminder of Russian treachery. Do you know history very well?"

"I studied history in college."

"That's good. Most Americans don't seem to care about the subject. I've noticed that

Americans seem to think that World War Two started when the Germans invaded Poland on the first of September, 1939, but I think you forget that Hitler only did so because he signed a treaty with Stalin, who also invaded us three weeks later, dividing us in two, like a Christmas goose. The Germans were defeated, but the Russians kept all of Poland for themselves after the war anyway. Ironic, isn't it? The British appeased Hitler before the war, and then they appeased Stalin after the war. In both cases, Poland paid the price. The Allies declared war on behalf of Poland, but in the end betrayed us by giving our country to the Communists as a gift. For you, the war ended in 1945. But for us? Not until 1989, when Communism finally fell. We suffered fifty years of occupation, and in the end, we had to save ourselves."

"I never thought of it that way."

"I'm sorry to talk so much. History isn't just a school subject for us. It's our daily reality."

The red light turned green and Liliana hit the gas. "By the way, the reason why so many buildings are new is because almost ninety percent of the original ones were destroyed by the Germans throughout the war. When the Uprising ended, they razed what was left of the city to the ground in their retreat, and slaughtered two hundred thousand civilians in mass executions."

Jack hardly knew what to say. He couldn't

imagine the utter devastation, let alone the collective anguish of brutality and betrayal by friends and foes alike.

Liliana offered him a polite smile. "Welcome to Poland."

They rode along in silence. A few minutes later, Liliana turned onto another busy boulevard near the city center and pulled into a parking lot across the street from a towering building still under partial construction. She killed the engine and set the parking brake.

"We're here."

Jack stuffed his laptop underneath his seat. "Let's go."

30

Liliana and Jack rode the swift elevator up to the seventh floor in silence, standing opposite three well-dressed Chinese businessmen, smiling and quiet.

The elevator doors opened and Jack and Liliana exited directly into the receptionist's lobby. The OstBank corporate offices occupied the entire seventh floor of the twenty-two-story building. The three Chinese businessmen continued to a higher floor.

The receptionist was a young man in a trim, dark suit and steel-rimmed glasses sitting behind a marble-and-steel half-round desk.

Before Liliana said a word, Jack approached the desk.

"Dzień dobry"—Good morning—Jack said, hoping his terrible accent wouldn't cause an international incident.

"Dzień dobry. How may I help you?"

"We have an appointment with Mr. Zbyszko. The name's Ryan. He's expecting us."

"I'll call him. Please, have a seat."

Jack stepped away from the desk. Liliana cocked an eyebrow. "I thought you didn't speak Polish?"

"I don't, but my Uncle Google taught me a few words on the flight over. I can ask where the bathroom is and apologize profusely for being an American idiot. But that's about it."

"Mr. Zbyszko will be right out," the receptionist said.

"Thank you."

"Would you like a coffee? A water?"

"We're fine, thanks."

A moment later, a trim, middle-aged man came through the glass door. Tailored suit, French cuffs with gold links, and a matching tie pin. Very old-school, Jack noted, compared to his own sport coat and slacks. He thrust out a firm but manicured hand. Jack shook it.

"**Dzień dobry**, Mr. Ryan. So nice to meet you. My name is Stanislaus Zbyszko. I am the bank manager." He handed Jack his business card.

"Pleased to meet you, sir. This is my assistant, Ms. Pilecki."

The manager took her hand as well.

"Please, both of you, come to my office. Did my receptionist offer you something to drink?"

"Yes, thank you. We're fine."

"Good, then please, come with me."

The manager led them through a wide floor crammed with cubicles and busy brokers working the phones, to his office on the far side of the room. The actual bank—tellers and the like—was located on the first floor on street level. Liliana had brought them to the business offices of the regional headquarters of OstBank.

Zbyszko opened his door and ushered them in. "Please, please. Have a seat."

Jack and Liliana sat in short-backed teak-and-leather chairs on the other side of the manager's wide, modern desk, also in teak.

"I hope you don't mind, but I did a quick Internet search of your company, Mr. Ryan. Quite impressive, as is your list of clients."

"We're a small boutique firm, but we have a very special clientele. We provide wealth management and investment services. We're always looking for new and interesting opportunities."

"A very wise decision to come here. Poland is rapidly becoming an economic powerhouse. Certainly, the most important economy in Central Europe. In fact, just last week the FTSE announced we are the first Soviet-bloc country to achieve 'developed' status."

Jack nodded. "Believe me, our firm is very impressed with your country's commitment to free-market reforms. We're also impressed with the fact you're part of the European Union and yet you avoided the Maastricht Treaty and kept your own currency rather than adopting the euro."

"Keeping our own currency means we control our own monetary destiny, avoiding the struggles that economies like Italy now face. But being part of the EU grants us access to the world's largest trading zone. Poland is the place to be, and Warsaw is the heart of Poland. So, how can OstBank be of service to you?"

"We certainly need local expertise and guidance, and your bank's reputation is stellar. You have the kinds of relationships we seek, and we're hoping you can help make introductions for us."

"Thank you for the kind words. Banking is all about relationships. I hope that ours will be long and profitable. So, what is it I can do for you today?"

Jack opened his folio and removed a notarized letter with Hendley Associates letterhead authorizing Jack Ryan, Jr., to wire-transfer $10 million into any bank account of his choosing. He set it on Zbyszko's desk. He then pulled out a black ballpoint pen from his pocket, clicked it, and prepared to take notes on the pad inside his folio.

"If you'll notice, that ten million dollars is the first of three tranches I'm authorized to invest over the next twelve months."

The manager read the letter casually, registering no response.

The best damn poker face Jack had ever seen.

"If I were to deposit a ten-million-dollar check in your bank today, Mr. Zbyszko, how would you recommend I invest it?"

Zbyszko set the letter down on his immaculately clean desk. "I can think of several opportunities, Mr. Ryan. Of course, that all depends upon your appetite for risk, as well as for reward."

"No risk, no reward, right?" Jack smiled. "However, we take the safety of our clients' money very seriously. The least amount of risk possible with a reasonable rate of return is our standard."

"Quite admirable. We are similarly conservative in our approach to our clients' assets. At the moment, real estate is an excellent investment opportunity here in Warsaw. Office rents per square meter have increased six percent year over year, and residential rates approximately nine percent. As I'm sure you've seen, construction is booming here in the capital. Besides the favorable foreign investment climate, we have over a million Ukrainian refugees in Poland, most of them in and around Warsaw. The housing shortage is a problem—and a great opportunity."

"Interesting. I was led to understand that Poland was hostile to immigrants."

"EU propaganda. In Poland, we believe that a man should not eat if he does not work. Far too many so-called refugees showed up in Poland only to find our welfare payments were too small. Most of them picked up and moved on to Germany, where the benefits are more generous and the work requirements quite relaxed, if nonexistent.

"Besides the fact that Ukrainians are fellow Slavs and our languages are similar, they have proven themselves to be eager workers—better workers than many Poles, as it turns out. So you see, Poland welcomes anybody who wants to integrate into our society, speak our language, and work instead of collecting government benefits."

Must have touched a sore spot, Jack thought. Changing the subject, he said, "Real estate is a definite possibility," jotting the note down. "We also like construction."

"There are many construction possibilities in residential and commercial real estate, but also in manufacturing and both public and private infrastructure. Take your pick."

"And then there's the risk."

"Not much risk in this booming economy." Zbyszko smiled.

"Still, there's always some risk. And we have found that one way to mitigate risk is to partner with other companies. We find that investing, like banking, is all about long-term relationships."

Zbyszko stole another glance at the letter on his desk. The American dollar was extraordinarily strong against the Polish zloty these days.

"Our legal team can help you with partnership contracts, and we have a department that specializes in mergers and acquisitions."

"Perfect. There is, in fact, one relationship we

want to explore. There is a company by the name of Baltic General Services. Are you familiar with it?"

"I'm not certain."

"Christopher Gage is one of the owners and the CEO."

The manager's eyes narrowed.

"Christopher Gage is the CEO of Gage Group International and he's a senior vice president of Gage Capital Partners, a twenty-seven-billion-dollar equity firm."

"Oh, yes. I do recall now. Baltic General Services is a fine, reputable company."

"I believe they arranged for a sizable loan from your bank to purchase at least one other business here in Warsaw."

"Which one?"

"I'm not sure. That's why I'm here. I'd like to know before I make any offers to partner with them. I'm not interested in their financials or any other privileged information. I'm only interested in the companies they've purchased or partnered with, and what financial condition those firms are in."

"I'm sorry, but I don't believe that will be possible. We take a great deal of pride in protecting our customers' privacy."

"You must have done due diligence before you agreed to loan Baltic General Services the money to make their purchases. What kind of company it is, where they do business, are they profitable, and so forth. Just generalities. That's the only information I'm asking for."

"Why don't you contact Baltic General Services directly?"

"I would prefer that they not know we're making inquiries. If they know my firm is interested in a partnership, they might decide to raise the cost of doing business with them. If I know their financial condition before I make an offer, I'm in a better negotiating position. I'm sure you understand."

"I'm sorry, it just isn't possible."

"Can you at least provide me with the name of the company that BGS just acquired here in Warsaw?"

Zbyszko leaned back in his chair, tapping the tips of his fingers together, thinking. Finally, "Let me speak with the regional vice president. Would you excuse me for just a moment?"

"We'll be in the lobby."

Jack left his folio and pen on the chair, then stood with Liliana and left the office as Zbyszko reached for his phone.

Jack and Liliana sat on one of the two lobby couches, out of earshot of the receptionist. Jack was working on his phone. Without looking up, he asked Liliana, "How do you think it went?"

"Putting that ten-million-dollar letter of intent on his desk was like setting a hook in a fish's mouth." She stifled a laugh. "It hardly seemed fair."

Jack tucked his phone into his coat pocket. "Let's hope it set deep enough that he can't swim away."

Liliana's phone buzzed in her purse.

"Excuse me, Jack. I need to check my messages."

"Sure. Go for it."

Jack decided to do the same, but nothing new pulled up. He saw the receptionist answer the phone. A moment later, he called them over.

"Excuse me, Mr. Ryan? Mr. Zbyszko would like to see you now."

The manager came out from behind his desk before the two of them could sit down.

"I'm sorry, Mr. Ryan, but I spoke with my vice president and I'm afraid we won't be able to help you with your query regarding Baltic General Services' financial statements. Trust and privacy are our two most important assets."

"I understand."

"However, I have been authorized to give you the name of the companies that Baltic General Services has invested in through our bank branches."

"'Companies'? More than one?"

"Yes. One here, in Warsaw, one in Kraków, and

one in Gdańsk. I will e-mail their particulars to you within the hour."

"That is very kind of you."

"Not at all. It's the sort of thing we do for our friends."

Jack picked the folio up off the chair, along with his pen. He left the letter on Zbyszko's desk as a reminder and handed him his own business card. "I'm looking forward to working together in the very near future."

"As am I." Zbyszko beamed. They shook hands vigorously. "The card I gave you earlier has my direct office line and also my personal cell phone. Please don't hesitate to call me if I can be of service."

"Thank you. I certainly will."

"Ms. Pilecki," Zbyszko said, shaking her hand. "A pleasure."

"And you."

Jack and Liliana headed for the elevator under Zbyszko's watchful eye.

31

KLATOVY DISTRICT, PLZEŇ REGION, CZECHIA (FORMERLY KNOWN AS THE CZECH REPUBLIC)

The hunting lodge stood on the banks of the lake on a few hundred privately owned acres of the Šumava, called the Böhmerwald by those living just over the border in Germany, and known by most other foreigners as the Bohemian Forest.

The fall air was already chill, but the leaves had yet to turn their full brilliant colors. "Still a good day for a stroll, eh, Rexi?" the old man said, patting his favorite hunting dog on the head, a bearded wirehaired Bohemian pointer.

The old man was tall and gaunt, his skin yellowed like parchment from decades of smoking dark, unfiltered Turkish tobaccos. Despite his age and near cadaverous appearance, his strong back remained ramrod straight and his grip like a blacksmith's vise. He stood in the dark wooden hallway in a pair of well-worn leather hiking boots, oiled and soft, pulling on a heavy woolen hunting coat and felted Tyrolean hat.

His real name, Petr Hašek, was lost to history when he burned his own secret files as the last head of the assassination bureau of the ŠtB—State Security—of Communist Czechoslovakia. His mother was a Sudeten German, killed in the ethnic cleansing following the war, a fact hidden from the world by his Slavic father, an ardent Communist functionary, to protect his son.

Hašek was now known simply as The Czech, the head of the world's most dangerous and influential criminal organization, the Iron Syndicate. Formed by himself and several other comrades from other security services of former Soviet republics after the fall of the Iron Curtain, they transformed their skill sets in killing, intimidation, and intelligence into a vast criminal network spanning the globe. Among their number, they now also included many Western colleagues in active service.

Global crime was big business, and no criminal organization was bigger than the Iron Syndicate. Translated to GDP—gross domestic product— organized transnational crime would be the ninth-largest economy on the planet. Illicit drugs comprised nearly one-fifth of that total.

If the Iron Syndicate were a legitimate corporation—as many of its operations were—it would have been listed on the Fortune Global 500 somewhere between General Electric and the Bank of China. Its illicit operations centered primarily on the dirty business of heroin and methamphetamine production and distribution, as well as the cleaner and faster-growing area of cybercrimes, including cybertheft and cyberespionage.

The Czech was in a fine spirit this morning. The news from Berlin was excellent. The BKA had few resources to combat all of the European and Slavic Mafias, global terror networks, and industrial espionage operations targeting Germany, the richest country in Europe. The recent death of the BKA's only undercover agent on the case against his organization in an apparent robbery would set the BKA's investigation back for months if not indefinitely.

More important than the intel was its source, and the promise of virtually unlimited access to more.

But only under CHIBI's terms. The Czech did not like being dictated to. His own technical department failed to locate this CHIBI fellow or determine his identity. He was invisible. But he was also omniscient, or so it seemed. It would be worth the price to acquire what he was selling, whatever that price might be. The Czech decided to send a representative to the London auction, as per CHIBI's demands.

The Czech snatched up his favorite bird gun from its rack, a Merkel 303-E Luxus 12-gauge shotgun. Manufactured in the East German city of Suhl throughout the Cold War, the finely crafted weapon was highly sought after, even in the West, for its outstanding qualities as a firearm. This particular shotgun was also a piece of art, featuring deep-chiseled hunting scenes engraved on all of the metalwork and a finely checkered European walnut stock inlaid with ivory oak leaves and acorns.

The gun dog whined with anticipation at the sight of the Merkel, wagging its short, docked tail.

"Now, now. Patience, old friend." The Czech laughed until the cell phone in his pants pocket vibrated. Frowning, he leaned his gun against the wall and pulled out his phone. He read the text:

Priority Target Alert: Subject #11281961

The Czech tapped the hyperlink. It took him to a series of CCTV surveillance videos of Jack Ryan, Jr., at Warsaw Chopin Airport and later in a silver Audi sedan as it navigated through Warsaw city streets. Each video was date- and time-stamped.

The Czech swore under his breath.

The Iron Syndicate tapped into government surveillance cameras all over the world, but it also maintained its own vast network of them. All images were captured, stored, and run through dedicated Iron Syndicate servers featuring facial-recognition software that was vastly superior to any commercially available system and rivaled those of the major security services. The Iron Syndicate deployed the ubiquitous surveillance capabilities as a means of gathering intelligence on potential targets and competitors and, more important, tracking threats to its criminal operations.

Threats such as Jack Ryan, Jr.

The Czech speed-dialed his number three, the director of operations. A Cambridge accent answered.

"Sir?"

"I just received your text. Why wasn't I notified earlier?" The first time stamp was just over two hours old.

"The subject is difficult to identify."

The Czech knew this to be true. All facial-recognition software was based on comparing existing facial records against new captures. Ryan's image had been carefully scrubbed from social media by the American government, no doubt to protect the son of the President. Few photos of Ryan were publicly available, and the ones that were came from years past, when he was clean-shaven, thinner, and younger.

"Is the target still in Warsaw?"

"He is, indeed. However, I noticed on his file that he is a priority target but there is no kill or capture order. How would you like me to proceed?"

"Continue camera surveillance until otherwise notified. Understood?"

"Sir."

The Czech rang off. Ryan's sudden appearance on the Continent was troublesome. Because of young Ryan, The Czech had the unpleasant experience of meeting John Clark in the early morning a year prior, waking up in his own bed to the cold steel of Clark's pistol barrel sticking into his ear. The Iron Syndicate had put out a hit on Jack Junior in order to satisfy the vengeance of the Iron Syndicate's previous boss, Vladimir Vasilev. Young Ryan had killed Vasilev's nephew, and Vasilev wanted his head in exchange.

Literally.

Clark offered him a deal. In exchange for Clark taking out Vasilev, The Czech would cancel the hit on Jack. "Not only will it make you the head honcho," Clark had said, "you can avoid the .45-caliber headache waiting for you on the other end of my pistol."

The Czech agreed.

But Clark further warned that if any harm ever came to Jack, he'd be back, and there would be hell to pay. The Czech had known of Clark's reputation prior to meeting him that fateful morning— the former Navy SEAL and CIA operator was well known in Soviet bloc intelligence circles.

To his credit, Clark had lived up to his end of their bargain.

But loyalty was a virtue. The Czech prized it above all things, save his own self-preservation. Vasilev had been his boss, but also a brother-in-arms from the old days. Egomaniacal and murderous at the end, Vasilev's death was necessary for the health of the Syndicate and personally advantageous for Hašek. But the idea that an American cowboy like Clark could murder a Syndicate colleague and escape without punishment was galling in the extreme.

So The Czech held to his bargain with Clark, at least for now. He wanted to keep track of Ryan because Clark would never be far behind him. Killing young Ryan would satisfy his old friend's last wishes, and killing Clark would be scratching an itch that never left his mind. For now, tracking Ryan would be enough. In time, he was certain an opportunity to kill both men would present itself.

And The Czech was, if nothing else, a patient man.

He pushed his simmering rage out of his mind and turned his thoughts to the day ahead. He broke open a fresh box of shotgun shells and pocketed them, then retrieved his shotgun.

Nothing brightened his mood like the prospect of a good kill.

32

WARSAW, POLAND

"Now where?" Liliana asked as she pressed the Audi's start button.

Jack yawned like a hippo. "I could use a cup of coffee while we wait for Zbyszko's e-mail."

"I know just the place. It isn't far from here. Fantastic coffee. And maybe you'd like a **pączki** or two."

"If it's sweet, I'm in."

They entered the small, crowded café on the first floor of a remodeled building, shaking the rain off. The air smelled of roasted coffee and sweet baking bread. Jack's mouth watered.

He noticed mostly young people, fashionably dressed and professional, much like Liliana. Bright laughter and animated Polish voices bounced off the tiled floors. A very social scene. The rain spattered the big picture window as new patrons came in behind them, shaking out their raincoats and umbrellas as they entered the tiny foyer.

"There's a table," Liliana said, threading her way across the jam-packed floor.

Jack pointed at a door near the front counter. "I gotta make a pit stop." He pulled a credit card out of his wallet. "Go ahead and order for us."

Liliana waved off the card with a friendly grimace. "It's on me. You're my guest."

"The next one's mine, or else."

"Or else what?"

"A crisis in Polish–American relations," Jack said with a wink.

Liliana set her things down at the table, then headed for the counter, while Jack hit the door with a circle and a triangle.

Inside the unisex bathroom was a single toilet, brand-new, along with the sink, tiles, and everything else. Very clean and tidy. But Jack wasn't here for a remodeling tour.

He reached into his pocket and pulled out a short cable with a lightning connector on one end and a 3.5-millimeter audio jack on the other. He fetched out his smartphone and his ballpoint pen and connected them via the cable, then tapped on the audio software app on his phone. Written by Gavin Biery, Hendley Associates' IT director and The Campus's electronics hacker wizard, the audio program instantly detected the file stored on the digital recorder pen he'd used in Zbyszko's office and began downloading it.

The progress bar reported five minutes

remaining. After the audio file downloaded, the program would automatically run through a voice-to-text program and then, if a language other than English was detected, the document would be automatically translated.

The whole setup was Gavin's idea, and he told Jack in the office just before he left for the airport, "Sometimes old-school is best." But the tech guru smiled, handing him some other equipment. "On the other hand, the new stuff is pretty cool, too."

A sharp knock on the door told him his alone time was up.

Jack pocketed everything and let Gavin's magic do its stuff automatically. He flushed the toilet and washed his hands with the minty soap just to keep the ruse up.

"Przepraszam"—sorry—Jack offered over the rushing sink water, hoping that Google hadn't let him down. He added, "One second."

A moment later he unlocked the door and pulled it open. A short young woman with bright maroon hair and John Lennon glasses stood at the door. Her frown bled into a wry smile at the sight of the handsome young American.

"Dzień dobry," Jack said as he slipped past her.
"Dzień dobry."

Jack saw a small plate standing on the counter right next to the bathroom door littered with one- and two-zloty coins. He suddenly remembered it was common throughout Europe to pay for bathroom services, usually collected by the attendant who kept the facilities sparkling clean. He flashed a memory of an elderly lady with an apron and broom wandering past him doing his business in a line of occupied public urinals at the Berlin Zoo train station years ago.

He tipped her pretty well, as he recalled.

The bathroom door locked behind him as Jack reached into his pocket, but he didn't have any Polish coins—he chastised himself for not exchanging money while they were at the bank earlier. Two zlotys—about fifty cents—was a good bathroom tip, from what he'd read earlier. Unfortunately, all he had was an American dollar in his wallet, so he dropped that onto the plate. He probably looked like an idiot doing it, but not tipping was even worse.

Jack searched the boisterous room for Liliana. He spotted her in the far corner. She saw him and waved him over with a smile.

How did you like your **pączki**?" Liliana said, taking a sip of hot tea.

Jack swallowed the last bite and washed it down with strong black coffee. "Best jelly doughnut I ever had. Especially the jelly. It's not too sweet and a little tangy."

"In English it's called rose hip. It's the most traditional flavor, but you can get **pączki** stuffed with just about anything."

"I couldn't believe all of the stuff I saw at the counter."

"Polish pastries are the best in the world—as good as anything you'd ever find in a French patisserie. Are you still hungry?"

Jack's sweet tooth was screaming, and a sugar rush wouldn't hurt his jet lag. But he knew how many miles per **pączki** he'd have to run to work them back off.

"I'm fine, thanks. You come here a lot?"

"Yes, but there's no shortage of great places to eat in Warsaw. Trust me, we Poles know how to eat. Our cuisine is a unique blend of Austrian, German, Russian, and even Turkish traditions, but all with a unique **polski** twist."

"I can't wait to try it."

His phone vibrated in his pocket. He pulled it out. The translated text stood on the screen.

Gavin Biery, you magnificent bastard, Jack thought as he glanced at the document. The program was smart enough to differentiate between the manager and the vice president, designated A and B, respectively, by the pauses between each speech. The good news was that the manager had inquired about Baltic General Services after all. The bad news was that even though the high-gain microphone was able to pick up pieces of the vice president's conversation—he was practically shouting on the other end—the translation had suffered as a result.

Jack frowned as he read. The sentences weren't making a ton of sense. But at least the program was able to pick out the most important reference: Christopher Gage.

"Is that Zbyszko's e-mail?"

Jack kept reading. "Huh? Uh, no. It's a message from work."

"May I ask you a question?"

"Sure."

"It seems to me there is more to your investigation than you are telling me."

Jack glanced up at her. **Bright woman,** Jack thought. **It won't be easy keeping her in the dark**. "Why do you say that?"

"I'm a federal agent currently working two different active criminal cases, but for some reason my job for the next week is to drive you around Poland in order to help you and your firm to make an investment decision. That makes no sense to me."

"What did your boss say?"

"You don't speak any Polish, so you need me for translation and, if necessary, personal protection."

"Sounds about right."

"My uncle in Chicago always used to say, 'Never kid a kidder.'"

"My dad says the same thing, only he uses a

different word than 'kid.' So here's the straight
dope: Mr. Gage might be weaving a very tangled
financial web. I'm just trying to figure out how big
and bad that web is. Okay?"

"Okay."

They sat in silence for a moment, finishing their
tea and coffee, retreating to neutral corners.

Jack watched a Polish nun march past the plate-
glass window beneath a bright umbrella. She
couldn't have been more than thirty years old.
He'd seen several young nuns and priests already.
Not at all like home.

Just then, the e-mail from Zbyszko they'd been
waiting for slid across his screen.

"Speak of the devil. Zbyszko's e-mail just arrived. I'll send it to you." Jack forwarded it to her
phone.

She opened it. "With traffic, this location is
twenty, maybe thirty, minutes from here."

"I'd like to check it out." Jack pocketed his
phone. "Are we good?"

Liliana's eyes narrowed. He could see the wheels
turning behind them.

"Yes, we're good." She added, "For now."

"Then how about we go find this place?"

33

Jack tracked their progress on his smartphone. He liked to know where he was and where he was headed at all times, not just out of his abundant natural curiosity, but for tactical reasons. He could still hear Clark's voice hammering in his head from training early on: "Kid, the best way I know to avoid eating a shit sandwich with all the fixins is to avoid the shit sandwich shop altogether."

The morning rush-hour traffic had thinned but not entirely ended. They were heading in the opposite direction, out of the city center and back toward Warsaw Chopin Airport, south and west of the city proper.

Jack's only concern at the moment was the tension filling the car. Liliana's suspicions had clearly been raised. He almost wondered if it would be better to ditch her and try to figure this all out by himself. He couldn't afford to have her find out what he was really up to. But then again, she was proving to be a real asset.

She was also darn easy on the eyes.

He needed to break the ice.

"On the ride to the hotel you said you went to Loyola Chicago. That's a big Jesuit school."

"Yes, it is. But, of course, I'm Catholic."

"Poland is the most Catholic country in Europe, isn't it?"

"Yes," she said proudly. "Are you Catholic?"

"Yes, I am," though he didn't say it with much conviction. It wasn't like he was practicing much these days, but it was still part of his heritage, just like the guilt he now felt for falling short in that area of his life. "My whole family."

"Then you will understand the constant references to Pope John Paul the Second you will find here. Especially in Kraków. We are very proud of him and what he did for our country and the whole world."

"I was just a toddler when he was around, but my folks talked about him all the time. He was a great man. One of the brightest lights of the twentieth century."

"Yes, he was. The first Polish pope. He helped end Communism in Europe by supporting the Solidarity movement in Poland, where the first free elections behind the Iron Curtain were held. It wasn't long after until the Berlin Wall fell and the Soviet Union finally collapsed."

"We could use a few more like him."

"I was told to keep our conversations to a minimum, but I just wanted to say I greatly appreciate your President trying to establish a permanent American base in Poland."

"Too bad Congress dropped the ball." He wanted to say "Dixon dropped the ball," but he didn't want to tip his hand.

"Yes. It seems only your President understands Poland's strategic significance." She slowed the car, hit the turn signal, and pulled into a parking lot fronting a large, gray concrete warehouse. Chain-link fence separated the front of the property from the side where the loading docks stood—at least twelve by Jack's count, with trucks parked at each.

"We're here," she said as she yanked on the parking brake.

The single-wide glass door read STAPINSKY TRANSPORTOWE in small white sticker letters, faded but uniform. Liliana pushed through, followed by Jack.

They stood in front of a modest desk. A middle-aged woman with badly bleached hair sat behind it, staring at a computer screen, a pair of thick glasses perched on the end of her bulbous nose. The air smelled of stale cigarettes.

"Dzień dobry," Liliana said with a musical lilt.

"Dzień dobry," the woman replied halfheartedly, glancing over the top of her glasses with the sad, brown eyes of a basset hound.

Liliana launched into a cheerful but pointed

discussion Jack couldn't exactly follow, but the meaning was clear enough. He heard his name mentioned along with a few cognates, including "investor," so he knew she was introducing him as they had arranged previously at the bank.

Finally, the woman pushed her glasses back up to the bridge of her nose, but the wide lenses only served to magnify her already enormous eyes. She turned in her rolling chair with a squeak and leaned in to a microphone, depressing the call button.

"Pan Kierownik!"—Mr. Manager!—thundered over the loudspeakers in the small waiting area and beyond.

The woman returned to her work on the computer and Liliana turned to Jack. "It shouldn't be long."

She'd hardly finished speaking when a steel door flung open and an older broad-shouldered man stormed into the room. His neck was too thick for the cheap, wide necktie and polyester shirt he wore, and his gut looked as hard as a beer barrel. Jack could tell by the way he moved that the man knew how to handle himself in a fight, which explained the large, veiny nose, clearly broken at least once before. He even stood like a boxer, leaning slightly forward, legs bent, ready to take a swing at whatever life might throw at him.

The man barked at the woman behind the desk, who only pointed a nicotine-stained finger in Liliana's direction and muttered something without looking up. The man turned his steely blue eyes toward Liliana and barked another question.

She didn't flinch, but in the same smiling, soft-spoken way, largely repeated what she had already explained to the woman behind the desk.

The manager turned toward Jack. His thickly accented voice sounded like he gargled with vinegar and steel wool.

"We don't need no investors, so thank you and good-bye."

Jack stepped toward the older, heavier man and extended his hand to shake. The manager stiffened at Jack's first step, his eyes narrowing as he sized up the big American.

"My name is Jack Ryan. It's a pleasure to meet you, sir."

Jack's display of respect softened the man, and he reluctantly took Jack's hand. Poles were, if nothing else, ferociously polite and respectful of others, especially those they considered to be of a higher social status, which Jack clearly was, being both an obviously rich investor and an American.

The thick, callused hand closed around Jack's. Mutual respect in a firm, solid grip.

"Are you Mr. Stapinsky?" Jack asked.

"No. My name is Wilczek. Pavel Wilczek. I am the manager here. Mr. Stapinsky is the owner. What is it you want, exactly?"

"As my assistant, Ms. Pilecki, suggested, I work for a financial firm that—"

"Pilecki, did you say?" He turned toward Liliana. "Any relation to—"

"My great-uncle."

The man's broad shoulders slumped as if in surrender. Jack swore he saw the hint of a smile creep across the leathery face. He raised a thick arm and pointed a catcher's mitt–sized hand toward the steel door.

"Please, won't you both step into my office?"

34

Jack, Liliana, and Wilczek sat in his cramped office, the shelves of the steel bookcases stuffed with decades' worth of transportation and shipping records. His desk was littered with stacks of stained manila folders, shipping reports, and a hubcap-turned-ashtray overstuffed with butts. Wilczek clasped his thick hands across his wide, stiff belly as he leaned back in his chair behind the battered steel desk.

"I have no idea, Mr. Ryan. I never heard of this Christopher Gage person. Perhaps the owner, but not me."

"Can you at least tell me what the relationship is with Baltic General Services? What do you do for them?"

The big man shrugged. "What do we do for them? Nothing that I know of. But they have done a lot for us. A small pay raise for my employees, a new computer system that Mrs. Lewandowska is still trying to learn. A new soda machine in the break room."

"And how is business?" Jack asked. "I noticed trucks in all the docking bays when we pulled up."

"Business is good. Very good. But I don't keep the financial records. That is information that only Mr. Stapinsky has."

"Is he available to speak with?"

"Mr. Stapinsky lives in Kraków. His family is from that area. He owns businesses down there, and property."

"Regarding business here, are there more trucks coming in? More shipments?"

Wilczek scratched the top of his head, thinking. "Yes. More trucks, more shipments. But different than before."

"Different how?"

The springs in his chair squeaked like a rusted hinge as he stood. He snatched an industrial-sized folding box cutter from off his cluttered desk.

Jack imagined Wilczek lunging at him with that blade, a great slashing arc with his gorilla-length arm aimed right at his throat.

It was how Jack's brain worked these days—or, more precisely, how it was trained by Ding and Clark. **Always anticipate.** Wilczek wouldn't be an easy man to take down in any case, but with a blade he knew how to use? It would be hard to do without getting hurt.

Or, more likely, killed.

"Follow me, Mr. Ryan."

The warehouse floor was stacked with pallets, neat and orderly, aligned with the loading bays. Forklifts ran in and out of the long trailers, carefully stacking the pallets. Other dockworkers rolled hand trucks filled with unpalletized boxes. The air stank of natural gas from the forklift engines and burnt hard rubber from their tires. The big steel forks rattled and clanged as they sped, empty, out of the trailers.

"You see?" Wilczek said, casting a wide arm at the floor. "All we get now is cheap Chinese crap. It is all part of this 'New Silk Road' business they keep talking about."

Wilczek slashed away the plastic wrapping from a pallet with his razor-sharp box cutter, pulled off one of the boxes marked as radios and cut the tape on it, then pulled out a boxed radio. He pointed at the radio box with his razor blade. "See? Made in China. All of it. All of it!"

Wilczek barked an order to one of his men to repackage the radio, then led Jack and Liliana over to one of the open pallets close to the nearest door. The boxes were marked in combinations of English and Chinese, and sometimes Polish, French, or German. Two young men were stacking boxes from it onto heavy-duty hand trucks. They seemed to move a little faster as Wilczek approached. He growled something at them and the taller one answered back in a deferential tone as the other one sped off with his loaded hand truck toward the open maw of the forty-plus-foot-long trailer. The tall one loaded the last of his boxes onto his hand truck and sped away after his friend.

When they were out of earshot, Wilczek chuckled. "Ukrainians. Good boys. Hard workers." He winked at Jack. "But you can't tell them that or they won't work as hard, eh?"

Jack glanced around the warehouse floor. He couldn't read Chinese, but in English he read the contents: stacks of boom boxes, children's bicycles, glassware, women's shoes, hand tools, roofing nails.

A phone rang over the loudspeakers attached to the ceiling, and a moment later the receptionist's voice barked over the warehouse speakers. Jack caught only the words **Pan Kierownik!**

"Excuse me, please. I must take a call. But please stop by my office on your way out."

"We will," Jack said.

As soon as Wilczek disappeared behind his office door, Jack said to Liliana, "You're awfully quiet."

"Are you finding what you're looking for?"

Jack nodded toward one of the pallets still wrapped in plastic. "If I needed two hundred cordless jigsaws, then yeah, I've found it. Other than that? I'm confused."

The two young Ukrainians were grunting and chatting as they stacked boxes in the back of the truck.

"I'm going to look around a little more," Jack said. "I'll talk to the boys when they come back."

Jack approached the back of the half-full trailer as the last boxes were stacked. The Ukrainians sped past him with their empty hand trucks, the hard rubber wheels rattling on the steel loading gate.

Jack stepped deeper into the trailer to the neatly stacked boxes that ran from floor to ceiling and wall to wall. Near as he could tell, the boys were doing a good job of putting the heavy stuff such as floor jacks and roofing nails on the bottom, and lighter stuff toward the top. He didn't touch anything. Didn't need to.

He headed back out of the trailer and dropped down to the bottom of the loading bay. The trailer itself was of Chinese manufacture, and so was the big red JAC tractor that hauled it. A quick glance down the loading dock revealed several more Chinese-made tractor-trailer rigs, mixed in with a few Volvos and Mercedes.

Not wanting to get his sport coat and slacks dirty, Jack used the steel staircase to ascend back onto the warehouse floor.

Jack grinned as he watched the two Ukrainian boys doing their best to stack boxes onto their hand trucks while trying to flirt with the pretty Polish woman who was clearly interested in talking to them. They finished stacking their trucks and heaved them away toward the trailer as Jack approached.

"Looks like you might have a date lined up tonight."

"Two, if I play my cards right." She laughed. "See anything interesting?"

"Nothing much. What did you find out?"

"The best pub around here is owned by the tall boy's uncle. Says he can get us beers at half price after he gets off work."

"Sounds like an investable proposition. Anything else?"

"They just load and unload trucks. Paid in cash, probably to avoid taxes. They said the trucks mostly travel to Polish and German cities, but sometimes as far as Spain, Italy, and France."

"Ready to go?"

"If you are."

"Let's say good-bye to Mr. Wilczek."

"Then what?"

"That depends."

"On what?" Liliana asked.

"Your dating plans."

She smiled. "My Ukrainian boyfriends can wait a few days, I think."

——

ilczek hung up the phone and lit a cigarette just as Jack and Liliana stepped back into his office.

He yanked open a desk drawer and fished out a crumpled business card. He handed it to Jack.

"Mr. Stapinsky's main office is located in Kraków. You can usually find him there."

"Thanks for this." Jack pocketed the card.

"Better still, let me call him for you." Wilczek reached for his phone.

"You don't have to bother—"

"No bother at all," the big man said, punching numbers on the dial with his middle finger. The end of his index finger was cut off and healed over like melted wax.

The phone rang twice before a female voice answered in Polish on the other end. Wilczek growled a few questions, then took a long drag as he waited impatiently for the woman's voice to come back on the line. Wilczek frowned, thanked her—or so Jack assumed—and hung up the phone.

"I am sorry to inform you that Mr. Stapinsky is out of town and not interested in any investment opportunities you might have." He stabbed the butt out in the hubcap.

"That's too bad," Jack said.

"Thank you for trying," Liliana added.

The three of them shook hands. Wilczek picked

up the phone and dialed another number as Jack
and Liliana cleared the office.

Liliana beeped open the car doors and the two
of them fell in.

"Now where?" Liliana said, punching the start
button.

"Kraków, of course."

"Stapinsky isn't there. Unless you think
Wilczek lied to us."

"Not Wilczek. Stapinsky. And I want to find
out why."

"What if he really isn't there?"

"We can still check out his stuff. If that's okay."

Liliana searched his eyes. "You are a stubborn
man, aren't you?"

"Only when it counts."

She shrugged. "Makes no difference. My assignment is to take you where you want to go,
so we go."

35

Liliana pulled into a gas station and called her supervisor while topping off the Audi.

Jack knew it was too early in the morning in Alexandria to call in to Gerry and give him an update. They were six hours behind on the East Coast, and it wasn't as if he had any hard data to pass along. He wasn't convinced the trip to Kraków was going to be any more productive. It was a thin lead, but it was all he had.

Liliana returned the nozzle to the gas pump, slapped the gas door shut, and slipped into her seat.

"Ready?"

"I love me a road trip."

"Me, too. And I think you'll love Kraków."

She fired up the car and stomped the gas, burning rubber and turning a few heads.

Jack and Liliana rode along in silence.

Liliana felt she might have crossed a line with her impassioned history lessons, and Jack was still fighting jet lag; his eyelids felt like lead weights. She focused on the road while he buried his nose in his smartphone, researching about Stapinsky and his business.

Other than a few advertisements for firms that he thought Stapinsky might have owned, or, at least, someone named Stapinsky did own, he didn't come across much. He couldn't even make a connection between Baltic General Services and Stapinsky Transportowe, let alone with Stapinsky and Christopher Gage or, for that matter, Senator Dixon, the true target of his investigation.

He wished Gavin was available for a search. He could ferret out anything if it had a digital footprint. But Gerry said Gavin was off-limits for this assignment, so no point walking down that road.

It was starting to feel like a wild-goose chase, and he had better things to do than waste time chasing his tail. He had an obligation to Cory to fulfill. The sooner, the better.

Hitting yet another dead end, Jack yawned and set his phone between his legs. His eyes wandered to the scenery sliding past his window. The roadside businesses, strip malls, warehouses, and billboards—some of them in Chinese—diminished the farther they got from Warsaw, giving way to tractor dealerships, greenhouses, and nurseries.

Liliana pointed at the radio. "Music?"

"Sure."

She punched the Bluetooth button on her audio

console. Piano music poured through the Bang &
Olufsen sound system.

"Chopin?" Jack asked.

Liliana smiled, delighted. "You know him?"

"Not well enough. I know he's Poland's most
famous composer."

"I hope you don't mind. This piece is Piano
Concerto Number One in E minor. That's Martha
Argerich on the piano. Just brilliant."

The music was a perfect accompaniment to
the pastoral landscape emerging outside his window. The gray clouds were shot through with blue
sky and sunlight that illuminated the variegated
greens all around them.

"What are you thinking about?" she asked.

Jack sat up straighter; slumping in the plush
leather seat wasn't helping him to stay awake.

"What else can you tell me about OstBank?"

"What I am allowed to tell you is that OstBank
is a German financial institution headquartered
in Berlin, with branches in the Federal Republic,
Italy, Spain, and Poland."

"And off the record?"

"There is no such thing as off the record. But I
suppose you can read a newspaper? Especially the
financial section?"

"Not without moving my lips."

"Did you ever read about the 'Russian Laundromat'? From a few years ago?"

"Refresh my memory."

"Because of the Russian invasion of Ukraine, your government and mine and several other Western countries levied harsh economic sanctions not only on the country but on the individual oligarchs that empowered President Yermilov. But the last thing a Russian wants to do if he wants to remain rich is keep his money in Russia. He needs to get his rubles converted into dollars and out of the country before the currency collapses entirely."

"Otherwise, all that ill-gotten cash turns to Monopoly money."

"The Russian Laundromat was an ingenious scheme that moved out over twenty billion dollars from inside Russia to fake shell companies the Russians set up. Those fake companies secured fake loans secured by Russian 'investors.' Then the fake companies declared bankruptcy and the 'investors' were forced to pay back the fake loans by the Western bankruptcy courts."

"You mean they figured out a way for our judges to force them to send their money out of the country? That's freaking slick."

"In the reports I read, laundered money was found in seven hundred and thirty-two Western banks, everything from small regional institutions to the biggest international giants. Many of them are accused by their respective governments of being complicit."

"And would one of those banks happen to be OstBank?"

"Funny you should ask."

"I'll take that as a yes."

"That would be a mistake."

Jack frowned, confused. What was she trying to tell him?

Oh. Okay. Yeah.

"But that doesn't mean OstBank couldn't be involved in some other kind of money-laundering scheme, though. Right?"

"As a financial analyst, I leave you to draw your own conclusions."

"And you think the German agent was killed because he was getting close to whatever scheme was going on inside of OstBank?"

"That's our assumption, but the German government isn't confirming or denying at this point. OstBank has powerful friends in the Bundestag."

"Banks have powerful friends in every legislature, and they're seldom held accountable for the issues that really matter. Even Thomas Jefferson said that private banks are more dangerous than standing armies."

"Strange that a financial analyst for a private equity firm would hold such an opinion."

"I work with money, I don't worship it. It's a means to an end, or should be. For too many people, money becomes the purpose for their existence."

"You sound like a Communist."

"I sound like my old parish priest. It's in the

Bible, I think. The love of money being the root of all evil or something like that."

"It sounds like you missed your calling."

"I'm just tired of politicians and corporations always doing what's best for themselves instead of doing what's right for the country."

"You're quite passionate on the subject. Have you ever thought about running for office?"

"The only way I'd run is in the opposite direction."

She laughed.

Jack was smitten. Liliana was lovely and intelligent and had a good sense of humor. But he nearly got his head shot off last year by falling for another beauty back in Bosnia-Herzegovina.

And then there was Ysabel.

"So tell me, Mr. Ryan. How do you plan on looking into Mr. Stapinsky's businesses if he's not around?"

"Well, we can just show up in Kraków and start asking around and try to find out what we can. We might get lucky right away. Or it might take several hours, or even days. Hell, weeks."

Jack searched Liliana's face for a reaction, but there wasn't one.

"Or . . ." he offered.

"Or?"

"If you want to get back to your case assignments and get me out of your hair, maybe you can access your public tax records and get us some addresses."

"Who says I want you out of my hair?"

Her blond hair danced in the wind rushing in from the cracked window, and her eyes locked with his. A familiar tingle ran up and down Jack's spine.

Flirting? Maybe.

Or maybe a test.

"Nice deflection. How about it?"

"We're not on official ABW business."

"You don't know that. We already have a tie into OstBank, which is operating on Polish soil and is already suspected of something that might have gotten a German BKA agent killed. I'm not asking for anything that isn't publicly available or that requires a warrant. I just don't have access to Polish tax records, and my Polish is about as good as my Martian."

That cracked another smile. "Okay. I'll call my boss and get approval."

"Might go faster if you didn't."

She glanced over at him. "Never kid a kidder, Mr. Ryan."

He flashed a boyish smile. "Wouldn't dare try."

"Charming, witty, manipulative. Are you quite sure you're not a politician?"

"Me? Oh, hell no."

Liliana shook her head, hardly believing she

had fallen for Jack's blarney. She spoke to the Audi's MMI—multimedia interface—and a number pulled up.

Jack pretended not to listen, but he was, since the two women were chatting it up in Polish over the Audi's amazing sound system. He didn't understand a word.

But so far, so good.

36

Twenty minutes later, Liliana's phone chirped with a text message and a file from a friend in the Polish Tax Office. She opened up the file and read it.

"We have a list of places to visit," she said.

"Perfect. How many?"

"Four, not counting his house."

"Hopefully we can knock them out quickly."

"You're in a hurry to get back home?"

"I have a lot going on." He wasn't in the mood to tell her about Cory's promise.

"A woman?"

Jack shook his head, smiling. "Hardly."

"Oh. More than one?"

"Are you kidding? I don't have time for a pet goldfish."

"Never married? No kids?"

"Someday, on both counts, I hope."

"Family is important."

"The most important," Jack said. "Everything comes from that."

"Your father was good to you, growing up?"

"Yeah. The best. Yours?"

"The finest man I ever knew."

"Then you are a lucky woman."

Jack felt something stirring inside him. He admired her loyalty. She was a very impressive woman.

Time to change the subject.

"Can I ask you a question?"

"Sure."

"Mr. Wilczek wasn't exactly a warm and cuddly teddy bear, especially when we first met him. But after you mentioned your great-uncle, he softened up. What was that all about?"

"Do you know World War Two history very well?"

"Mostly the American version of it. My grandfather fought the Germans as a paratrooper with the 101st Airborne Division."

"My great-uncle's name was Witold Pilecki. His story is really the story of Poland. If you understand him and what kind of a man he was, then you understand the heart of the Polish people." She stopped herself. "I don't want to bore you."

"No, please. Tell me about him."

"His active military career began after World War One, when he started fighting the invading Bolshevik armies charging west."

"Wait. Remind me again. I'm a little fuzzy on that period."

"After the Bolsheviks defeated the counter-revolutionary White Armies in the Russian Civil War, Lenin and the other Bolsheviks saw their opportunity to invade Europe. The Allied armies were exhausted, and the Axis armies defeated. Lenin ordered Trotsky and Stalin to conquer the West with a Red Army of eight hundred thousand men and thirty thousand horses. They could have swept away every Western government and created a Red Communist empire from the Pacific to the Atlantic. Except for one problem. An army of barefoot Poles under Marshal Piłsudski stopped them at the gates of Warsaw in 1920. We call it the Miracle on the Vistula. It is the greatest battle of the twentieth century that no one outside of Poland has ever heard of."

Jack didn't remember reading about any of that in his history courses.

"And that wasn't the first time Poland saved Western civilization, either," Liliana said.

"Enlighten me."

"In 1683, the Ottoman Empire was marching across Europe undefeated and driving toward Vienna, which they surrounded and besieged with two hundred thousand troops. But the Polish king Sobieski amassed a relief force, and though greatly outnumbered, he led the Winged Hussars in a charge that smashed the Turks and saved Vienna."

"Wait. I remember now. The Winged Hussars

were badasses. Heavy armor polished bright, nineteen-foot-long lances and poles strapped on their backs with eagle feathers that whistled like Stukas when they rode into battle."

"Were it not for King Sobieski and the Polish Hussars, all of Europe might well have fallen to the Muslim invasion. The Ottoman Empire was never a threat to the Christian West again."

"I suppose as a Westerner and a Christian, I should thank you."

"Twice. Or perhaps three times."

"Three?"

"Polish mathematicians broke the German Enigma code just before World War Two and passed it along to the British, with instructions to Turing on how to build the electromechanical components of his code-breaking machine."

"I had no idea. So finish the story about your great-uncle."

"He fought very bravely both at the front and also behind enemy lines during the Polish–Soviet war and was twice awarded the Cross of Valor."

"He sounds like a stud."

"He was only just getting started. Between the two world wars he established a cavalry training school and later commanded a cavalry squadron. He fought the Germans when they invaded on the first of September, 1939, and then turned around and fought the Soviets, who invaded on the seventeenth of September. His unit was defeated by the Communists, so he fled to Warsaw and co-founded the Secret Polish Army under German occupation."

"Did he survive the war?"

"While still one of the commanders of the Polish underground, he heard rumors there was something horrible taking place in a camp called Auschwitz, near Kraków. You know it, of course."

"Horrific. Inhuman."

"At the time, most people thought it was just another POW camp. My uncle knew the only way to find out the truth was to get himself arrested and imprisoned there."

"Wait. Are you saying he intentionally broke **into** a Nazi concentration camp?"

"Yes."

"Was he Jewish?"

"No, he was a Christian. But he was a human being, wasn't he?"

"And he died in the camp?"

"No. Once he got inside the camp, he organized the resistance movement, and also began writing reports that made their way back to London, detailing the atrocities and trying to convince the Allies to join forces with the Polish underground to liberate the camp. But Churchill and the others didn't believe him and refused to do it."

"That sucks. What was Pilecki's response?"

"He escaped in order to help organize the Polish underground forces to liberate it, but they were too weak to do so, and even though the Russians were close enough to offer military support, they refused to help as well."

"How long had he been in Auschwitz?"

"Just under three years. Most people didn't survive six months."

"And after his escape?"

"He fought in the Warsaw Uprising. Remember, Stalin refused to cross the Vistula to help them, and sixteen thousand Polish fighters were massacred by the Germans so that Russians could take control of Poland after the war."

"Sounds like the Russians have never been friends to the Polish people, either."

"My great-uncle would have agreed. He was finally captured by the Germans after the uprising but was liberated from his POW camp by the American Army. He returned home after the war, only to find that the West had given Poland to Russia, and now the Russians were the occupiers. Naturally, my great-uncle had to join the resistance movement against the Soviet Communists, especially after he began to investigate the Katyn Forest massacre."

"That was during the Phony War, wasn't it?"

"Yes. In 1940, the Russians murdered twenty-five thousand Polish soldiers and intellectuals in the Katyn Forest and buried them there. Stalin lied about it, and blamed the Nazis.

"The Russians eventually captured my great-uncle for his efforts. They tortured and then murdered him after a show trial in 1948, then buried him in an unmarked grave. It wasn't until the fall of Communism in Poland that Witold Pilecki's story was finally told to the whole world, though people who knew him personally knew it well."

"Like Mr. Wilczek?"

"He told me his grandfather fought alongside my great-uncle against the Germans and even saved his grandfather's life."

Jack shook his head. "I understand now when you say that history isn't just a school subject for you, but a daily reality."

"Which is perhaps why I talk too much about it. Sorry."

"Nothing to apologize for. It's fascinating and painful all at the same time. You must be very proud of your family."

"A family's name and a family's honor is everything, don't you think?"

"No question."

They were tooling along a southbound two-lane now. The road was fairly busy, mostly with passenger vehicles, but quite a few commercial ones as well, traveling in both directions.

"You mentioned before that you appreciated the fact my country wants to put a military base in Poland outside of NATO commitments. Is that because you don't trust France and Germany to come to your aid against another Russian invasion? Sort of like the Phony War?"

"Would you? When have they ever lived up to their NATO commitments? The French and the Germans couldn't save us from a Russian invasion, even if they wanted to."

"But you trust us to come to your aid?"

"I trust President Ryan, yes." She smiled. "Your Congress? Not so much."

"I'm sorry you feel that way."

"Am I wrong to do so?"

Jack shook his head. "I'm even sorrier you're right."

Liliana slapped him on the shoulder. "Hey, don't think we Poles don't love America. We do! You know our country disappeared from all of the European maps for over one hundred and twenty-three years, right? We were divided up and absorbed by the Austro-Hungarian, Russian, and German empires until 1918. But it was President Wilson who insisted after World War One that Poland be allowed to be a country again. That's why we're celebrating our hundredth anniversary this year. We love America, and we know we can rely on you whenever it really counts."

"So long as President Ryan has anything to say about it, yeah, you can count on us, for sure."

37

KRAKÓW, POLAND

Jack and Liliana hit traffic on the two-lane road on the north side of the city. Traffic was heavy in both directions.

It was hard to believe that a city of nearly eight hundred thousand residents had such small roads, but then again, Poland appeared to have a lot more public transportation than the United States did. On this side of town, at least, there weren't any skyscrapers. Mostly low apartment buildings, homes, and businesses. Everything was neat and clean, as it had been in Warsaw. Maybe more so. The architecture had changed somewhat. Jack knew he was about as close to Budapest in the south and Vienna in the southwest as he was to Warsaw in the north. So perhaps it was the influence of the Austro-Hungarian Empire he was feeling.

"Everything looks neat and clean here. I take it Kraków was destroyed during the war, too, and then rebuilt?"

"The city was last destroyed during the Mongol

invasion in the thirteenth century. The Nazis felt Kraków was the most Germanlike city in Poland, so they preserved it. They even ran their wartime administration from here, instead of Warsaw. There is a great deal of history here, including German history, which the Germans admire most of all."

There were just five addresses and income tax statements on the list sent by Liliana's friend at the tax office, and Liliana had already marked them on Google Maps.

"So where do you want to start?" Liliana asked.

"The most interesting place. His house."

"I was hoping you'd say that."

Liliana followed the ring road west, then south, avoiding the city center. They crossed the wide Vistula River and headed farther south. Without the onboard navigation, Liliana admitted, she would have had a hard time finding Stapinsky's neighborhood, located on the edge of a protected forest. The homes here were larger than most, with distinctly alpine features and situated on large, heavily wooded private lots. From an American perspective, it had a middle-class feel, but Liliana assured him that the average working person could never afford these properties.

The woman's voice in the Audi's MMI console directed them onto a gravel road cutting through a stand of trees, which they followed around an S-curve.

A two-story house stood on the crest of a small hill. New construction, to judge from the remnants of fresh lumber and paint buckets stacked neatly to one side.

A tallish man, balding and bearded, tossed Tumi luggage into the back of a brand-new grape-colored Mercedes G-Class, a square-shaped SUV that Jack's dad referred to as a high-dollar Tonka truck. The man's round gut bulged beneath an Adidas-branded turquoise-and-black tracksuit, with the famous three white stripes running the length of his sleeves.

But it was the two big black-and-tan Rottweilers in the yard that caught their attention.

Or was it the other way around?

The two thickly muscled guard dogs barked as they charged in a flash of snarling teeth toward the Audi at full speed.

The man set his bags down in the grass, squinting behind his glasses at the silver Audi rolling up his driveway.

Liliana hit the brakes and slammed the car into park just as the enormous forepaws of the black-and-tan monsters slammed onto the driver-side glass, their massive jaws snapping and snarling, fogging the window with their hot breath and saliva.

Liliana reached into her coat pocket to grab

her pistol, but a sharp whistle from the man outside yanked them away as if they had been jerked
by leashes. Their stubby tails wagged furiously
as they charged back toward their master and
dropped to a sitting position on either side of him
in perfect synchronicity.

The man smiled.

Liliana turned to Jack. "Shall we?"

"So long as you've got that pistol, I'm good."

She hit the unlock button and the two of them
emerged from the Audi, opening the doors slowly.
They approached, careful not to make any sudden
or threatening moves. The two male Rotties were
each easily one hundred pounds of raw muscle
and slashing teeth, descended from a breed of dog
first brought to the region by Roman legions two
millennia earlier.

"Mr. Ryan, I assume?" the man said.

"Mr. Stapinsky," Jack said. The man didn't offer
a hand. Neither did Jack.

Stapinsky turned to Liliana. "And you must be
Ms. Pilecki?"

"I am."

"Pavel was quite impressed with you, according
to my secretary. I can see why."

"He is a nice man."

Stapinsky laughed. "Nice? I've heard him called
a lot of things, but never 'nice.' One evening not
so long ago, we went out to a pub and he got roaring drunk. A young idiot insulted his wife and

a minute later Pavel threw him against a plate-glass window. Fortunately, the glass didn't break, or else the man would have been shredded like a cabbage."

"That sounds very gallant," Liliana said.

"It might have been, except that Pavel has never been married. So, how can I help the two of you? Something about an investment?"

Jack shot a quick glance at the panting dogs, their eyes fixed on him. He handed Stapinsky his business card, hoping his arm wouldn't be snapped in two by a pair of anxious jaws.

"I'm an analyst with Hendley Associates, a private equity firm. We're looking for investment opportunities in Poland, and, more importantly, partnerships with well-managed local businesses."

Stapinsky held the card with two hands, pinched between his thumbs and index fingers, straining to read it through his thick lenses.

"I've not heard of your firm, I'm sorry." He handed the card back to Jack.

"Keep it, please."

Stapinsky shoved the card into his pocket as if it were a dirty Kleenex.

Jack continued. "We're one of the most successful private equity and investment firms in the United States. We're looking to expand overseas."

"You were wise to pick Poland. Our economy is booming, and we are in the heart of Europe. But I'd like to know: Of all of the thousands of companies in Poland, how did you happen to pick mine as a target of opportunity?"

"Research, Mr. Stapinsky. That's what I do."

"As a skilled researcher, you must have discovered that I have no need of any investors."

"You mean any **new** investors, don't you?"

"To whom are you referring?"

"I believe Baltic General Services has recently partnered with you, providing cash and other services to bolster your enterprise."

"What of it?"

"Did they buy you out? Fifty-fifty ownership?"

"I'm not inclined to discuss my arrangements. But tell me, what is it about my company that interests you so?"

"That's what we'd like to talk to you about, if you have a few minutes."

"As you can see, I'm packing to leave for a long vacation."

"Somewhere fun, I hope."

"It's really none of your business, is it?" Stapinsky lifted another bag into the trunk.

"It will only take a few minutes of your time, and I think you'll be glad you did."

"You assume a lot."

"I assume ten million dollars is worth your time."

Stapinsky's eyes widened at the number.

"And that's how much I have to invest. Today, if possible."

"I suppose I can spare a few minutes. Please, won't you come inside?"
Gotcha.

They sat on a green leather couch in Stapinsky's library, its newly built shelves bulging with books, mostly paperbacks. The covers were pristine, as if the books were unread. The English-language titles were business texts and literary classics. The same with the Russian. The Polish book titles he couldn't read, but he assumed they were the same.

"May I?" Jack asked, pointing at one of the shelves near his desk.

"If you must," Stapinsky said, annoyed, as he tamped sweet-smelling tobacco into the bowl of his Italian briarwood pipe.

Jack lifted a copy of Hemingway's **For Whom the Bell Tolls** off the shelf.

"Great book. Love the movie. Have you seen it?"

"Many times. Bergman is a dream," Stapinsky said, lighting his pipe.

"But the actress who played Pilar stole the show. What was her name?"

"I haven't the slightest."

Stapinsky's attention turned to his young live-in maid as she entered the room with a tray. The Ukrainian girl brought in cups of instant coffee and Biscoff cookies, still in their plastic wrappers.

Jack returned the book to its shelf as Stapinsky dismissed the girl with a flick of his hand.

"I love these cookies," Liliana said. "They usually serve these on airplanes."

Stapinsky released a cloud of blue smoke, then offered an oily smile. "We are the exclusive Biscoff distributors in Poland."

"Impressive."

Jack took a seat next to Liliana. Stapinsky pointed at the coffee and cookies. "Please, help yourselves."

"Thank you." Jack took a sip of the weak coffee.

Stapinsky folded his long fingers together and leaned forward on his desk, his pipe clenched firmly between his yellowed teeth.

"So, Mr. Ryan, what is it exactly you are proposing?"

38

"Did that go as you expected?" Liliana asked as she pulled out of Stapinsky's curving driveway.

"One second," Jack said, putting AirPods in his ears. "I need to check something." He punched a speed-dial number, careful to hide the screen from Liliana's peripheral vision.

A ring later, the call connected to the listening device Jack had planted on Stapinsky's bookshelf. He'd likely never find it, because Jack placed it behind a book the man had clearly never read. In fact, most of the books on his shelf looked unread. They were probably all for show to impress any visitors.

Jack listened for a moment, smiled. **That didn't take long,** he told himself.

Stapinsky was already on the phone with someone, and speaking in English, so no translation was needed. The call was being recorded on his phone in case he wanted to listen to it again later.

"Something funny?" Liliana asked as she turned onto the narrow asphalt road heading back toward Kraków.

Jack hit the pause button. "Just a voice mail from work. I'll be with you in a second." He hit play and listened to the rest of the message.

"He wanted to know if I was seeking an investment partner . . . Of course I told him I wasn't, but he insisted on making his case . . . Of course . . . Of course not . . . I will let you know if he contacts me again. Yes. Right away . . . Good-bye, Mr. Gage."

"Gotcha again," Jack said. At least that was a confirmation that Gage and Stapinsky knew each other. Not that it meant anything substantial, and it certainly didn't connect any dots to Senator Dixon. But who knows? Maybe they would have a more interesting conversation later. If so, the automated bug would pick it up and transmit it to Jack's phone.

"What?" Liliana asked.

Whoops.

Jack closed the app and pulled out his AirPods, saying, "Oh, nothing important. Just something from work."

"So did your meeting with Stapinsky go the way you planned?"

"Absolutely."

"But he didn't say or offer you anything."

"Which is exactly what I expected."

Of course, the meeting had pissed him off. He couldn't stand Stapinsky's smug nouveau-riche arrogance, which was a real tell. Most people crumbled when they came into a lot of money quickly, especially money that wasn't earned. The problem wasn't the money; fast cash only amplified existing character faults. Stapinsky was probably always an arrogant, self-interested son of a bitch, but now he could afford to not hide it. Nor his obvious greed. Just waving the possibility of an easy $10 million was enough to get Jack and Liliana past the Baskerville hounds and into the Baskerville house.

"Then what was the purpose of the meeting?" Liliana drove through a stand of trees on either side of the narrow lane. It looked like some kind of a park or nature preserve.

"That's a great question." It really was. Jack knew that his answer would determine his immediate future. Either a chance at cracking open whatever nut Christopher Gage had put together, or a stint of jail time in a Polish prison cell. It all depended on how far he could trust Liliana.

Or if he could trust her at all.

His dad taught him years ago that reading people was one of life's most important skills. His dad claimed he could assess someone's character within sixty seconds of meeting them. Until Bosnia, Jack might have thought he possessed the same skill. Now he wasn't so sure. And now he found himself in yet another vehicle in another foreign country with another beautiful woman who also possessed a pistol that could blow his brains out. Aida had given it her best shot. Would Liliana?

"Are you asking me as a friend or as an agent of the ABW?"

"Oh." She smiled. "I didn't realize we were friends."

"Aren't we?"

"We've only known each other for a few hours."

"Is there some sort of minimum number of hours required for Polish friendship? Maybe a certificate I need to acquire?"

"How about lunch and we'll discuss the details?"

"You read my mind."

"Perfect. I know just the place."

KRAKÓW, POLAND

Kuchnia u Doroty exuded both Old World charm and modern sensibility, with its exposed-brick walls, terrazzo tile floors, and white linen tablecloths. It was definitely a place for locals and served food family style.

The hostess greeted Liliana with a kiss and the two caught up on recent history in a flurry of words Jack couldn't possibly follow even if he spoke Polish. Liliana introduced him to her friend and she greeted him with classroom-perfect English, but not without shooting a quick conspiratorial glance at her friend, which Liliana quickly dismissed with a curt shake of her head.

Women.

The hostess ushered them downstairs to a private table away from the other lunchtime guests and left menus with them.

"Hungry?" Liliana asked.

Jack picked up a menu. "Starved. I'm not really into airplane cookies."

"Me neither. What a penny-pinching asshole."

"Have I mentioned how good your English is?"

"Have you ever had Polish food before?"

"Besides **pączki**? No."

"Then you're in for a real treat. Do you mind if I order for you?"

"Please."

Fifteen minutes later, plates of food began landing on the white linen tablecloth like F/A-18F Super Hornets on a carrier deck. They split each plate; Liliana narrated as Jack tucked in.

"Buraczki," Liliana said, pointing at a plate of shredded beet salad. "A good place to start."

Jack agreed. The salad was cold and refreshing, and not sweetly pickled after the American fashion.

"Next, **gołąbki**." Liliana smiled as Jack dove into the cabbage rolls—rectangles, really—the leaves as thin and translucent as parchment paper, stuffed with minced chicken, pork, and rice, and topped with a tomato gravy.

"Unbelievable." Jack took another sip of a strong local porter, smooth and potent at 9.8 percent alcohol content.

Outstanding.

The next plate arrived. "**Bigos.** Very traditional." She explained it was a stew made with sauerkraut— "Not bitter, like the German kind"—and meat: sausage, pork, and bacon, all sautéed together with onions, garlic, paprika, and other spices.

She was right. The flavor of the sauerkraut was more tangy than sour, and paired perfectly with the protein. His only concern was that he was already starting to fill up.

"Now, for my favorite here. **Placki ziemniaczane z gulaszem**."

"Easy for you to say," Jack said, enjoying his porter. It was so good he seriously considered ordering a second one, but knew if he did that Liliana would have to fireman-carry him up the stairs and pour him into the backseat of her Audi.

Liliana pushed the plate toward him. "Potato pancakes and goulash, though not goulash the way the Hungarians do it."

The fried potato pancakes were large and thick, and smothered in chunks of buttery-soft pork bathed in yet another rich tomato sauce and topped with a dollop of fresh sour cream. His stomach told him he was topping off, but his taste buds begged him to keep shoveling until the plate was clean.

His taste buds won the argument.

Another wash of dark porter almost emptied the glass and took up the last remaining centimeters of available space in his gullet. There was no more room at the inn.

Until the dessert arrived.

"Racuchy," Liliana said. "Apple pancakes." Thick and hearty and dusted with powdered sugar. Jack dipped each savory bite into a ramekin spilling over with raspberry-and-cream sauce.

Jack forked the last bite into his mouth and lifted his white napkin in surrender. He did a quick calculation. He would need to do approximately thirty thousand crunches to match the caloric content of this meal.

And it would be worth it.

"Check, please."

How do you do it?" Jack asked, standing on the sidewalk of the narrow, tree-lined street outside the restaurant.

"Do what?"

"Eat what you eat and look like you do."

"I'll take that as a compliment."

Jack felt the heat rush to his face. "I mean, you must have one heck of a metabolism."

"The trick is to not eat like that every meal, like most Americans do. And exercise, of course."

"I could use a gym right about now."

"How about a walk instead? Two of Stapinsky's properties are within twenty minutes of here."

"Let's do it."

"Good. It will be a chance to show you some of the Old Town."

Liliana led them north toward the center of Old Town. The air was damp and cool but pleasant. Jack was grateful to stretch his legs. He'd spent the better part of the last sixteen hours on his rear end.

"The part of the city you're in now is called Kazimierz. It's the old Jewish Quarter. King Kazimierz the Great reigned in the four-teenth century during another time in Europe when Jews were being persecuted. He offered them sanctuary in Poland, where they prospered for cen-turies, until the Second World War. Sadly, there are few Jews here now. In recent years, Kazimierz has revitalized. There are many art galleries, res-taurants, craft beer brewers, and hipsters. It's my favorite part of the city."

The streets became more crowded with pedes-trians and especially tourists the closer they got to old city center. When they finally reached the Main Square, one of the largest medieval squares in Europe, the place was packed with milling tourists admiring the soaring steeple of St. Mary's

Basilica dominating the center, and across from it, the Cloth Hall, a hub of international trade since the time of the Renaissance, Liliana informed him.

"Promise me you'll hire a local guide next time you're here, Jack—Wawel Castle is a short distance away, but it is the heart of Poland, our Westminster Cathedral, where our great kings and queens are buried."

Colorful horse-drawn carriages stood in line, waiting for passengers near the cathedral, and the cafés and coffeehouses surrounding the square were packed with gawking tourists, many of them Chinese, judging by the conversations Jack heard walking past them.

Ten minutes later, they stood on a narrow side street north of the Main Square, facing a small two-story building. The first floor was gray and was occupied by a grocery store; the second floor was beige.

"Stapinsky owns the entire building, according to the property tax records. He collects rent from two residential units on the second level, and from the grocery on the first, according to his income tax statements."

"He doesn't own the grocery?"

"No."

"Is the rent money substantial?"

"Decent."

"Enough to buy a brand-new six-figure Mercedes? That G-class still had paper plates on the bumper."

"Perhaps he is frugal in other areas of his life."

"Like coffee and dessert?"

Liliana snorted. "You are too funny."

Jack stepped inside the modest grocery. Its plain white tile floors, bare fluorescent bulbs, and two cash registers didn't impress. It was minuscule by American standards. A few aisles, a half-dozen patrons. The two long walls were well stocked with a wide variety of local and imported beers and wine, as well as vodkas and whiskeys.

"Anything else you need to see, Jack?"

"No. Let's check out the next place."

39

From the grocery store, Jack and Liliana headed east on foot, crossing through a narrow band of urban park and walkways that circled most of the Old Town. They headed south down a busy four-lane street, Westerplatte, passing, among other things, a Dominican convent. They eventually arrived in front of a formal neoclassical four-story residential building on a very quiet and pleasant tree-lined street. An electronic passkey was required to gain entrance, but an elderly couple exited and took no notice of Jack and Liliana passing through the half-open door.

The building was quiet, save for the sound of an energetic but well-played violin on one of the top floors and the happy laughter of small children behind the nearest of two doors on the first floor. The names on the mailboxes were all Polish; the ancient marble floors were clean, the dark wood doors and fixtures polished, and the air tobacco-free.

"Four floors, two apartments each. Stapinsky

owns the entire building," Liliana offered in a soft voice.

"Doesn't look like a drug den or a terrorist training camp, does it?"

"Is that what you're looking for?"

"Not exactly."

Liliana frowned. "Are you sure you're a financial analyst?"

"I wouldn't want my investors to get caught up in anything illegal."

"Of course not. Anything else to see here?"

"No."

A fifteen-minute walk led back to Liliana's Audi. She drove them to the last two stops.

The first was a cubbyhole of a liquor store— "Alkohole," the sign read—not much bigger than a phone booth, attached to a chain grocery store ten minutes from the apartment building. There was barely room for Jack to poke his head in and look around, trying to avoid the hard stare of the disheveled man behind the tiny glass counter. Every nook and cranny was crammed with hard liquors and spirits, especially flavored vodkas, and Irish and American whiskeys, and most of those in bottles small enough to fit in a pocket or purse.

The last stop was equally unremarkable, Kraków Kandy, a small shop offering a wide variety of boxed and packaged candies, imported and domestic.

"Stapinsky owns the shop. My guess is that he would make more money renting the place out, judging by the net income he declared," Liliana said.

"Now what?" Liliana said as she unlocked the car.

"Back to Warsaw."

"Any place in particular?"

"Drop me off at my hotel, if you don't mind. I'll try and pull something together tonight and we'll hit it again tomorrow."

"As you wish."

They headed back north toward Warsaw on the S7, the way they had arrived. The sky darkened about the time they left the city limits, and twenty minutes later rain spattered the windshield, the wipers completely out of sync with the Dave Brubeck album Liliana had pulled up on her audio system.

Jack stifled his third yawn in as many miles.

"I have a hard time with jet lag, too," Liliana said. "Grab a nap if you want."

"Thanks, but I'll push through it. Otherwise, I'll be fighting it the whole time." The traffic had thinned out quite a bit heading in this direction.

"How long do you think you'll be in Poland?"

"A week. A month. No telling."

"So, what do you think of my country?"

"So far, I'm impressed. Your economy is doing much better than I realized."

"It is. We're trying to grow in every area, especially manufactured goods, and trying to expand our exports."

"What do you think about the Belt and Road Initiative?"

Liliana shook her head. "I'm worried about it. The idea sounds good on paper—opening trade routes between China and Europe should benefit everyone. But in reality, what we see is a lot of Chinese manufactured goods being dumped into our markets, and what we're mostly exporting to them is pork and dairy products."

"And the Chinese don't exactly play fair, do they?"

"You should know. Look at the massive trade deficits your country runs with them."

"I'm surprised you follow international trade patterns."

"Why? Because I'm in law enforcement? Trust me, we talk about these things all the time in our department."

"Why?"

"Have you kept up with the news? There are riots and demonstrations all over Europe these days. Youth unemployment is over forty percent in Greece, more than thirty percent in Italy and Spain, and nearly twenty percent in Portugal.

Their manufacturing sectors were crushed in the last recession and they've never fully recovered, and they won't, if Chinese imports keep flooding in."

"You're saying that subsidized Chinese imports are contributing to European instability?"

"Absolutely. Without jobs, what will young people do? What kind of a future will they have? And look at how Europe is dividing right now. The countries with the worst youth unemployment— Greece, Spain, and Portugal—have radical socialist governments. That's the wrong direction for Europe to take."

"So how do you feel about foreign investment in your country?"

"You mean like Hendley Associates?" Liliana smiled.

"To name one outstanding financial firm, yes."

"Investments that grow my economy I can support. Anything that creates jobs and wealth in Poland is good for Poland. But the purpose of so-called free trade seems to be to make a few individuals and corporations rich at the expense of the rest of the country. Importing cheap foreign goods means exporting Polish jobs, and that isn't sustainable in the long run."

"I agree. But the world is running in the opposite direction. Globalism is the trend."

"Yes, it is. But we are at a critical crossroads, don't you think?"

"How so?"

"Ironically, in the name of free trade, government power is becoming more centralized in order to erase borders and eliminate national sovereignty. But if we lose our national identity, what good does it do to belong to the European Union?"

"If Polish people become more prosperous, wouldn't it be worth it?"

"But will they? What happens when power is centralized? Do you think the largest German and French corporations will allow Brussels to let Polish corporations grow at their expense? Or do you think it will be the other way around? Not in theory—tell me, you studied history. What happens when big corporations partner with big government?"

"The rich get richer, and the politicians get more power."

"Fascism and socialism are the same things." Liliana cursed herself under her breath. "I'm sorry to keep talking this way. It's not polite."

"I don't mind, really. It's fascinating."

"You must remember, my country disappeared from the map for one hundred and twenty-three years. Occupiers wouldn't allow Polish to be taught in our schools, or for our children to learn their own history. Same with the Nazis. We had to fight to keep our identity and our culture and our language. We don't want to give it all away for the sake of cheap toaster ovens and Chinese takeout, even though I happen to love kung pao chicken."

Jack pointed at a pair of flashing lights on the road up ahead. An elderly woman stood in the rain without an umbrella, trying—and failing—to pull out a spare tire from her trunk.

"Poor thing. I'll call for help," Liliana said.

"Pull over. I can handle it."

"But it's raining."

"What if nobody shows up?"

"Okay."

Liliana pulled in behind the woman's rusted sedan, a Volkswagen Jetta. She turned around, squinting against the thick drops pelting her concerned face.

Liliana and Jack jumped out and dashed over to the woman. Liliana identified herself as an agent of the Polish government and that Jack was her American friend—or so Jack assumed. He didn't wait around for the formalities. He was getting soaked, too.

The old woman insisted on showing Jack what to do, and Liliana kept trying to wrestle her under the mini umbrella she had. She finally convinced the woman to come sit in the Audi while Jack finished the job. Fifteen minutes after they'd pulled over, the woman's spare tire was attached and Jack was soaked from head to foot, slathered in mud but satisfied with his work.

The rain had stopped. The old woman thanked Jack profusely in a spate of Polish that Liliana hastily translated, then climbed back into her car. She stomped the gas and sped away, throwing a rooster tail of mud that splattered all over the two of them.

All they could do was laugh.

Liliana opened the trunk of the Audi and fished out an emergency blanket. The two of them toweled off as best they could, climbed back into the Audi, and headed for Warsaw. Liliana cranked up the heat. Twenty minutes later, Jack was sound asleep, snoring his head off.

40

SAN FRANCISCO, CALIFORNIA

Watson put her desk phone on speaker as it rang. Four rings in, Elias Dahm finally picked up.

"Hello, Amanda. To what do I owe the pleasure?"

"I was checking my calendar and I saw that I hadn't received the text for your speech yet so I can review it." The sound of gusting wind battered the phone speaker.

"My speech?"

"The TechWorld conference, remember? It's two weeks away."

"Oh, yes. Sure. Sorry. My mind is somewhere else."

"By the sound of it, so is your body. Where are you?"

"I'm standing in front of the Wickenburg Chamber of Commerce building. It's quite charming. The whole town is charming. Straight out of an episode of **Lassie**. Do you know what I'm looking at?"

"Wickenburg where?"

"Wickenburg, Arizona. So can you guess what I'm looking at?"

Watson wanted to scream obscenities at him. He was a genius and a great lay, but mostly he was a precocious, self-centered man-child.

"I haven't a clue."

"A Texas longhorn. It's standing on top of the building across the street. It's plastic, I'm sure."

"Fascinating. Is that why you're in Whackaburg—"

"Wickenburg."

"Wickenburg, Arizona? To look at cows standing on buildings?"

"Didn't I tell you I was flying out here today?"

Of course not. "It's not on your calendar."

"There's a tract of land I've had my eye on not too far from here. Thirty-two thousand acres. Perfect for a solar farm."

"Solar farm? I thought we weren't walking down that road again."

Like many of Elias Dahm's brilliant ideas, solar farming was both the wave of the future and an economic boondoggle. CloudServe had previously owned two other solar farms, and both had nearly bankrupted the company.

Elias's idea was to power all of the company's vast server farms with solar energy and sell the excess electricity produced back to the utility companies, making both a profit and effectively providing free electricity to CloudServe.

Unfortunately, the cost of solar energy per kilowatt hour was prohibitively high, even when subsidized, and a poor price alternative to fossil fuels, particularly oil, which had plummeted in price in recent years, thanks to technological advances in oil sands and shale production. Worse, the Ryan administration had successfully lobbied to end subsidies for the solar industry. The CloudServe board liquidated both money-losing solar projects over Dahm's objections.

"Things change, Amanda. Board members change. Markets change. The climate changes. But the sun never changes. It's the perfect energy source, and it's free. We need to be part of the solar revolution."

Her jaw clenched. She had neither the time nor the energy to rehash the debate. It was just another goose in the flock of wild geese Elias Dahm endlessly chased. All of their feasibility studies indicated that another solar-energy investment would be a net-net loser for the company, even with federal subsidies that no longer existed. But Elias Dahm was an obstinate, relentless dreamer. She wasn't going to win this argument.

"Can't wait to hear all about it when you get back. But in the meantime, I need you to remember that we have a lot riding on this London conference. It's the most important media event of the year for us."

"I shouldn't think we'd have much trouble generating media attention." Elias had appeared on both the cover of **Fast Company** and the Joe Rogan podcast in the last week.

"I'm talking about the good kind. You know, the kind that makes us money? These are industry people I'm talking about. People who sign contracts. That means we have a lot of hands to shake and a lot of egos to stroke."

"You're really good at that stuff, Amanda. I'm confident you'll handle it."

Of course I'll handle it, she told herself. **Like I handle every other goddamn thing around here while you're banging interns and artificially inseminating Argentine polo ponies.**

"Elias, I really need your full attention on this."

"I'm totally focused."

"So where's the speech? You're the keynote speaker, remember?"

"It's dynamite. I can't wait for you to see it."

By which you mean you haven't written a damn thing.

"When are you coming back?"

"We're four-wheeling out to the property in about twenty minutes. Oh—there's an In-N-Out Burger just forty minutes up the road. We should grab a Double-Double sometime together."

"I'm vegan, remember?"

"Since when?"

Go to hell, Elias. "Just don't get bit by any Gila monsters or whatever is crawling around out there. And call me when you land in California."

"Will do."

"Safe travels."

She ended the call, her blood boiling.

CloudServe was her company, too. She was one of the largest stockholders—on paper, she was filthy rich. Unfortunately, she wasn't allowed to cash any of those stocks anytime soon. There was every chance Elias would crash the company before she had the chance to cash in.

Dahm was one of those new financial geniuses who didn't see any particular value in the concept of corporate profits. That was just one of the reasons the price-to-earnings ratio on CloudServe stocks ran in the triple digits, thanks to aggressive accounting practices. In reality, it should have been zero.

Rather than profits and earnings, Dahm measured success by cash flow. CloudServe computing services was a high-margin business with heavy capital expenditures, but, as a separate division, it still ran at a profit. It was all of the other adventures Dahm dreamed up, including his passion project, his space company, SpaceServe, that were draining the coffers. Dahm simply didn't understand the word **no**, and his handpicked board of directors didn't want to buy him a dictionary.

They were having too much fun going along for the wild ride.

Watson yanked open a desk drawer and snatched up a small bottle of essential oil. She put a couple drops on her palms, rubbed them together, and cupped her hands over her mouth and nose. She closed her eyes and took several slow, deep, lavender-infused breaths, imagining herself standing all alone on a sugary white-sand beach beneath an achingly blue sky. Her breath slowed. So did her pulse. Her conscious mind collapsed to the singular point of her breathing.

In. Out. In. Out.

Slowly, imperceptibly, the rage ebbed away.

A soft knock on her doorjamb snapped her out of her trance. She opened her eyes.

It was her new assistant. An Indonesian on an H-1B visa, her head covered.

"What do you need, Masayu?"

"You have a call on line two, Ms. Watson."

Watson glanced at her silenced desk phone. "Who is it?"

"Mr. Dahm. He said he forgot to tell you something."

Watson forced a smile.

"Thank you."

She took it. A joke he'd heard. Wanted to tell her before he forgot it. She faked a laugh and hung up.

She tried the lavender oil again.

It didn't help.

41

WARSAW, POLAND

W e're here, Jack," Liliana said, gently shaking him.

Jack jolted awake, startled, not sure for a second where he was. His right arm instinctively drew back for a punch, but Liliana's smiling face short-circuited his instincts.

"Having a bad dream?"

Jack wiped his face. He was groggy as hell. The day all came flooding back.

"How long was I asleep?"

"About two hours. I tried to wake you a couple of times, but you wouldn't budge."

Jack sat up and glanced out the window. They were in the forecourt of his urban hotel.

He glanced down at himself. The smeared mud on his coat, shirt, and slacks had at least dried.

"Now that you're awake, do you want to go inside and get cleaned up, and we can head out again?"

Jack shook his head, as much to clear the cobwebs as to communicate anything. "I think we played out all of our options today. I'll put a plan together tonight. We'll regroup tomorrow morning."

"Sounds good."

"Well, thanks for everything." Jack stuck out his hand. They shook.

"See you tomorrow. Say, eight o'clock?"

"Eight o'clock."

Jack watched Liliana pull away before heading through the hotel's sliding glass door. A fashionably dressed young couple was coming out. The man shot him a dirty look and the woman giggled as they passed by.

The clerk behind the desk frowned at the sight of Jack. At first, he wasn't sure why, but it suddenly occurred to him that he must look like a homeless guy with a laptop bag who had been sleeping under a bridge.

Jack pulled out his electronic room key from his wallet and flashed his best used-car-salesman smile. "Ryan, room three-eleven."

The man took the card but was skeptical.

"Helped change a tire in the rain. Got a little messy," Jack said as the man typed on his keyboard.

Jack's unsoiled check-in photo appeared on the clerk's screen. "Yes. Mr. Ryan. Very good. Will you be requiring a dry-cleaning service, then?"

Gee, Einstein, how could you tell?

"That would be great."

"Please put your dirty clothes in the dry-cleaning bag provided in your room and hang it on the door latch tonight. Everything will be available tomorrow by seven a.m."

"Thanks."

The clerk peeked over the top of the desk at Jack's feet. "Shoes, too?"

Jack's brown oxfords were trashed.

"Please."

"Leave them outside the door as well."

"Just bill it to my room number."

"Already taken care of."

Jack nodded his thanks and headed for the stairs. He was wide awake this time, but he didn't relish the idea of riding up the elevator with anyone right now.

Before he did anything else, Jack locked the hotel room door and crossed over to the far wall fronting the entire space. He reached down and pulled out the square wall charger he used to power up his laptop from the European-style plug adapter and brought it over to the desk.

He powered up his laptop and connected the wall charger to it with the dual-use USB connector. He opened a program that accessed the motion-activated digital camera embedded in the wall charger unit that doubled as his computer's power source. The camera's tiny fish-eye lens had a one-hundred-and-eighty-degree angle, wide enough to capture any movement in the room's single living-sleeping area. If anyone had entered, the camera would have captured it. The unit could even detect if it had been tampered with.

Jack deployed a similar power/camera unit for an electric razor in the bathroom. But no point in pulling that one up if this one didn't capture somebody breaking into his room in the first place.

The program indicated that nothing recorded except Jack leaving earlier that morning and returning just now, the final image showing his lens-distorted hand enveloping the unit as he unplugged it.

"Good ol' Gav," Jack whispered to himself, grateful for the bag full of electronic tricks Biery had given him to deploy on this trip. None of them had actually paid off yet, but it was nice to have something to do besides ask questions that nobody intended to answer honestly.

Next Jack treated himself to a hot, steaming shower. It had been a long day, most of it spent on his keister, either in the Hendley Associates Gulfstream or in Liliana's Audi. The bottom line was that he hadn't come up with squat regarding Dixon or any dirty deals she might have cooking with her stepson, Christopher Gage. Gage himself appeared to be moving and grooving on business deals here in Poland, at least with Stapinsky, who seemed harmless enough, even if he was a pretentious ass.

The steamy bathroom air felt good as he brushed his teeth, trying to decide his next course of action. The best he could come up with was to call Gerry.

"Hey, kid. How's it going over there?"

Jack gave a brief overview of the day's events, concluding with "And nothing to show for it."

"Look, I didn't send you over there to prove anything. I sent you over there to see if there was anything to find. If there's nothing, then there's nothing. And after all, it's still only your first day. Give yourself a little credit."

"I still have a few long shots to run down. I'll check back with you tomorrow with what I have—or don't have. If nothing else, I'll have a list of leads to chase on the computer when I get back."

"What's your gut telling you?"

"You know, everybody dances on the margins these days. Companies allocate big budgets to their accounting departments to push the absolute limits of legality to avoid paying taxes, which is smart, I suppose. It may be that Christopher Gage is just playing by the rules others have made, and the fact that I don't like it doesn't mean he or his stepmother are necessarily guilty of anything."

"That's a fair assessment. But keep digging anyway."

"Will do."

Jack pulled on a pair of athletic pants and a sweatshirt before dropping down in front of his laptop and composing a text message for Liliana.

> **Any chance we can get Baltic General Services info from their last quarterly VAT tax filings? I'm thinking: other businesses they might have purchased or partnered with? Also, any chance we can find out if Christopher S. Gage has formed any other corporations in Poland or that operate in Poland? I know it's a big ask, but I'm running out of ideas. Thanks again for the terrific lunch and the excellent driving services. Can't wait–**

Jack caught himself. He deleted "Can't wait" and wrote instead,

> **See you tomorrow at 8.**

He drummed his fingers on the desk. He knew he was really missing something. But what?

What about generating a list of every Chinese company operating in Poland, and cross-referencing that with any Christopher Gage–related corporation? Then what? He'd have to dig into those as well. But without a warrant or some other legal authority to crack open their books—and that wasn't possible without probable cause—he wasn't likely to get very far. After all, if someone walked in Gerry's door and asked him to show Hendley Associates' business accounts, Gerry's likely response would be a swift kick in the ass and a quick call to security to escort the idiot out the front door.

As far as Gage's American tax records, those weren't public documents, and if Gage owned less than ten percent in a foreign company he wasn't obligated to report it to the IRS anyway.

Jack brainstormed for another twenty minutes but wasn't coming up with anything. Despite the shower, his mind was still a little fogged.

His phone dinged. It was Liliana.

One step ahead of you. I had been thinking along the same lines. I called ahead while you were sleeping. We should have a list of possibilities first thing tomorrow morning. Shall I bring you coffee?

Interesting. Why would she be willing to dig further unless she was now interested in Gage as well? As a favor to him? Not likely. She was a pro—and a patriot. If she were interested in Gage, it meant she thought he might be into something that worked against her country's interests. If that were true, that meant he was working against the interests of one of America's best allies. And that was worth digging into.

> **One step ahead? Sounds like two or three. Thanks for doing that. I'll grab coffee and breakfast at the hotel before you get here, but thanks. Have a great evening.**

The offer was nice and, no doubt, perfectly innocent. But it was his own wicked heart that Jack was worried about.

He pulled up Ysabel's contact info. **Might as well drop her a line and see how she's doing**. He did a quick check of the message conversation history. He last wrote her two weeks ago, asking how she was doing.

She never replied.

What few conversations they were able to have in between dodging bullets and bad guys in Afghanistan and Iran weren't exactly pleasant. She was angry, and had a right to be. He thought maybe they could patch things up.

Looks like he thought wrong.

Jack shut his computer. Might as well take advantage of the downtime and see the city. He started to pull up TripAdvisor on his phone to get a list of ideas of places to check out at night, but it suddenly struck him that he just wasn't in the mood. He sure as hell didn't want to hit the bar scene, and any museums he'd want to see would be closed by now. Besides, he still had a shit-ton of work to do on the Dubai deal that was still sitting on his virtual desk. He'd feel better about himself if he actually accomplished something for the good money the firm paid him.

He decided to put in three good hours of work, and if that didn't settle his brain down, he'd pop an allergy pill and knock himself out so that his brain clock would reset itself for the task at hand tomorrow and maybe, just maybe, he could get the hell back home and reschedule his trip for Cory.

42

LUANDA, ANGOLA

It was the newest and most exclusive luxury hotel in the capital city—surprisingly, one of the most expensive cities in the world now, thanks to all of the oil money—built by a Chinese firm for Chinese investors. Expat Europeans and Americans loved it, though there were fewer of them these days, thanks to the regime change. Mostly it was Chinese executives. It was the place to be seen for business and social contacts. Few Angolans could afford it.

The young, mixed-race Angolan woman turned nearly every head as she crossed the expansive lobby. Green eyes, caramel skin, thick blond curls, and a hard, curvaceous body flowed with effortless grace toward the private express elevator serving the penthouse floors.

She waved a key card in front of the buttonless call device, and moments later the mirrored elevator doors opened.

She was a regular now.

The hard, familiar face of the rock-jawed

Chinese security officer greeted her with a curt nod as she stepped inside. Once the doors closed, he pressed a button holding the elevator. He wanded the perfectly proportioned physique with a hand-held metal detector. His cold eyes searched hers for any sign of deception or fear, but found none.

She flashed a teasing "come hither" smile for her own amusement but elicited no reaction from the iron-hard security man. He checked her small handbag. Key card, lipstick, breath mints, and three condoms in gold foil packets.

He spoke into the mic attached to his wrist.

The elevator rose swiftly.

The doors opened on the fifteenth floor. Another unsmiling security officer with an earpiece greeted her with a nod. He stepped aside.

She brushed past him toward the double mahogany doors. A third guard opened one of them, and she passed through.

She stood on the polished Carrara marble floor of the vast living area, feeling the suck of air as the heavy door closed behind her. The last rays of the setting sun were swallowed by the blue-black Atlantic Ocean filling the wide picture window.

Fan Min, the CEO of Sino-Angola Energy, rose from the circular red leather couch in the center of the room, a wide, toothy smile on his face. The fifty-nine-year-old man wore a black smoking jacket, black silk trousers, and red velvet slippers. His poorly dyed jet-black hair was combed back and greased, Pat Riley style.

He asked her in his thickly accented Portuguese what she wanted to drink. She told him rum and Coke. He poured one for each of them. She thanked him. He took his blue pill. She smiled. His dark eyes raked over her body as she drank.

She said she had a surprise for him. He lit up like a child at Christmas. She showed him the new condoms she brought him. Three of them, wrapped in gold foil. Very special.

He smiled, eyes crinkling at the corners.

Extra, extra pleasure, she promised.

Like she was supposed to say.

"Lindo maravilhoso," he said, pouring her another drink.

They sat on the red leather couch together. Ships' lights like stars floated in the black Atlantic beyond.

She finished her second rum and Coke while he stroked her smooth skin with his long, delicate fingers, whispering **"Belezhina"** over and over like an incantation.

She smiled at him between sips of her third drink. When his eager face finally darkened, she excused herself to use the restroom.

He retreated to the bedroom, his manhood tenting his silken trousers. He played Céline Dion. Turned the volume up.

She heard it through the bathroom wall. She flushed the toilet. Crossed herself before opening the door. She tried to put the image of her young husband out of her mind.

He wouldn't understand. He was just a boy.

It was good money.

LOBITO, ANGOLA

The port city five hundred kilometers north of Luanda was asleep at this late hour, save for the three Chinese guards—civilian-clad PLA soldiers—patrolling the perimeter of the construction site against thieves. The Lobito-1 refinery was scheduled to come online within seven months. It would be only the second refinery in sub-Saharan Africa's second-largest oil-producing country, which, ironically, imported eighty percent of its refined petroleum needs. The Lobito-1 project would go a long way to correct that imbalance while lining the pockets of Angola's corrupt political class.

Funded by exports of Angolan crude oil and diamonds, Chinese engineering and construction firms were in charge of the entire project. Despite the crushing unemployment and bitter poverty of a country where nearly forty percent of the population survived on less than $1.25 a day, Angolan politicians in the capital were eager to allow China to import its own labor force for the Lobito-1 refinery project, adding three hundred more construction workers to the thirty thousand Chinese already employed in the country, and nearly a million across the African continent.

China was Angola's number-one foreign investment and export partner in Africa, thanks to the seemingly bottomless seas of crude oil on- and offshore the former Portuguese colony.

Angolan oil reserves were so valued that even the Cold War took a backseat. During the vicious twenty-seven-year Angolan Civil War, American oil companies pumping socialist Angola crude were protected by Communist Cuban forces from attacks by antisocialist rebels backed by the American government.

Money was its own loyalty.

The Lobito-1 project was a significant step forward for both Chinese strategic planners and the Angolan kleptocracy in Luanda. Besides the generous development funds that mostly found their way into the regime's hand-tailored pockets, the new Angolan president preferred Chinese investments because of China's "noninterference" policy toward local governments. Western politicians asked too many questions about income inequality, bribery, money laundering, nepotism, pollution, and other meddlesome issues toward which the Chinese happily turned a blind eye.

Repulsed by the predatory greed of the Angolan

government, the rapacious neocolonialism of China, and the resulting exploitation of the suffering Angolan masses, a new rebel group arose, the NFLA—Nova Frente de Libertação de Angola in Portuguese.

The NFLA had focused all of its previous attacks in the far-north exclave of Cabinda, where the movement originated, its efforts directed at intimidating corrupt Angolan civil servants and the nonviolent disruption of government operations.

Until now.

The wooden skiff was worn but sturdy, like the old fisherman running the sputtering Honda outboard. His sinewy arms were corded like rope, still capable of rowing the fifteen-foot-long fishing boat on the open Atlantic, but with the load he was carrying beneath the oiled canvas tonight, the two-stroke motor was necessary.

A Coleman lantern swung lazily behind the stern, an irresistible lure to the fish lurking in the oily waters of Lobito Bay. His gap-toothed smile and silver-stubbled face was a familiar sight in the port, selling fresh fish from his nightly catches to the construction crews in the morning. Few knew his ragged shirt hid bullet scars he carried from the civil war. Even fewer had seen the Makarov pistol hidden beneath an oily rag in the bottom of his boat, a prize he'd taken from the young Cuban lieutenant he'd hacked to death with a machete twenty years before.

His callused fingers killed the engine as the boat eased behind the rusted hulk of an ancient trawler lying on its side in the shallow water in the early-morning darkness. He tied off to the hulk and killed the light before throwing back the tarp.

Five black-skinned NFLA commandos slipped noiselessly from the boat into the chill water with their AKs held chest high. Balaclavas hid their faces, despite the warm air. The last of them laid a hand on the old man's shoulder and whispered in his ear, **"Obrigado, vovô."**

Thanks, Grandpa.

They made their way to the base of a low concrete wall topped by cyclone fencing as the Honda engine puttered away into the dark. They pressed low and hard against it, waiting.

The team leader hand-signaled a silent command, then whispered another on his throat mic.

Thirty seconds later, the crunch of Chinese-made boots passed by overhead. A second after that, the subsonic rush of hot lead from a sniper rifle snapped above them, thudding into the guard's chest like a cinder block, dropping him in the butt-strewn dirt.

The team leader signaled again and his number two stood up with long-handled bolt cutters, snipping a neat hole in the fence. The leader climbed up and dashed through it in a low crouch, followed by the others.

Careful to keep low behind the steel pipes and girders stacked in the brightly lit yard, the team made its way fifty meters north to the row of single-story trailers crammed with nearly a hundred mainland Chinese steelworkers. Lights in the trailers were off.

The team leader raised his silenced pistol. The nine-millimeter slug ripped through the brainpan of the half-asleep guard, spattering blood and bone against the steel door.

The suppressed shot was the go signal for the others. They dashed forward, tossing grenades and satchel charges through the windows. They sped past the buildings at a dead run before the first explosions erupted, and headed for the north fence.

The last screams of the survivors burning alive in the flaming wreckage echoed in the warm night air as the men disappeared between the cinderblock shanties of the squalid favela in the low, barren hills above the city.

43

LUANDA, ANGOLA

He needed to pee.

Fan Min threw off the bedcovers. He was sweaty. In the other bed, knocked out cold by her sleeping pills, his fat wife snored like a ripsaw cutting through sheet metal.

The oil executive sat up and pulled on his glasses, then shuffled toward the bathroom, limping on a cramping leg. He wiped his runny nose with the back of his hand, then wiped his hand on his pajama top as he pushed his way through the door and shut it behind him.

The motion-sensor light popped on but the bulb was dim. He made a mental note to get an assistant to replace it. He had a hard time breathing. He leaned over and lifted the toilet seat. It made him dizzy.

Am I catching the flu? he wondered.

He fumbled with the slit in his pajama bottoms and fished out his flaccid manhood. He pushed, waiting for the flow to begin. Sweat trickled down his back and his nose ran faster. He wiped his face again with one trembling hand as urine finally began dribbling into the bowl. His other shaking hand splattered the yellow liquid.

He farted. The squawk of air turned into a short gush of runny goo as the room began to spin—

Sharp pain stabbed his chest. Fan Min screamed, but nothing came out. He had no air. He grabbed for the over-the-toilet shelving to catch himself. It gave way. He crashed to the floor, smashing his skull on the corner of the marble sink, spraying blood from his broken scalp. Mirrors and perfume bottles shattered on the tile floor.

Clutching his dying heart, he thrashed in agony in the widening puddle of urine and blood. His narrowing pupils dimmed the light as his foaming mouth sucked for a last, gasping breath that never came.

Crashing glass and metal woke Fan Min's wife from her pill-induced sleep.

She rolled out of bed, cursing her idiot husband as she hobbled to the bathroom on arthritic knees.

She called his name through the door. No answer.

She turned the knob. It was unlocked. She pushed on it. It wouldn't budge.

She panicked, calling out his name as she shoved feebly against the door. It nudged open.

She saw Fan Min lying on the floor, his back to

her. Adrenaline fueled her flabby arms. The door pushed open further. She squeezed her round belly against the crack and wedged a thick leg through the opening. Her bare foot slapped onto the tile floor, splashing urine and blood. But it was the shards of broken glass stabbing her tender sole that made her scream.

44

WARSAW, POLAND

Liliana arrived at the forecourt exactly at eight a.m., as promised, and didn't bring Jack coffee, as he requested.

Jack was disappointed to discover that the hotel restaurant served only dinner, but TripAdvisor found him a great little place nearby with a walk-up window where locals queued for hubcap-sized **pączki** and steaming-hot Illy coffee in sturdy paper cups. The allergy pill had knocked him out, which was good, but he woke up in a chemical fog that took two cups of the caffeinated brew to clear away.

Jack yanked open the Audi's passenger door and fell in.

"Dzień dobry."

Liliana smiled. **"Dzień dobry.** Did you sleep well?"

"Like a rock."

"Then we'll get started."

"Great. Where to first?"

"My office."

———

Twenty-five minutes later, Jack sat in Liliana's modest office on the fourth floor of the non-descript and unmarked six-floor building on Rakowiecka Street that housed the ABW. It had all the charm of a Communist-era police head-quarters building, which, in fact, it had been.

Jack was greeted at the front door by internal security and issued a temporary visitor's pass after his passport was scanned.

They spent the next four hours poring over computerized tax records, business licenses and applications, corporate filings, and even bank-ruptcies.

Jack's Polish was nil, but the search function on Liliana's computer was fluent enough to search for word combinations and variants of "Christopher Gage," "Baltic General Services," "Gage Group International," and even "Gage Capital Partners." Jack wanted to add "Dixon" to the search but didn't dare drag the senator's name into this—certainly not at Polish ABW headquarters—and besides, if she were up to something illegal, she'd hardly put her name on it.

Property tax records showed the location of a BGS holding in Gdańsk. "Looks like this build-ing is down by the port." Jack pointed it out on the computer screen.

"Most likely a warehouse of some kind. Could be a repair or maintenance facility as well. Or some combination of the three."

Well, that was something, at least.

Liliana checked her watch. "How about some lunch? I know a great restaurant. Best pierogi in town."

Jack was afraid to count the number of carbs he'd socked away yesterday, but it was so damn worth it.

What's another five thousand calories at this point?

"Sounds great."

"You've had them before?"

"Never. But I saw the way your eyes lit up when you said 'pierogi,' so I know it's gonna be good."

Liliana pulled her shoulder holster off the coatrack and slipped it back on. Jack looked away as the straps cinched around her shoulders, emphasizing the curves of her upper torso.

"Nine-mil?" Jack asked as she holstered her weapon.

"You know guns?"

"A little."

"Are you any good?"

"Haven't shot myself in the foot yet. So not bad, I guess."

"Perhaps I can get permission to take you down to the shooting range later. Would you like that?"

"Yes, I would, actually."

"And to answer your question, yes, it's a nine-millimeter WIST-94, a Polish-designed and -manufactured pistol."

She unholstered the weapon, dropped the mag, and racked the slide to clear the chamber, launching a bullet that Jack snatched in midair.

"Nice catch. Here." She handed him the gun, butt first.

He felt the weight in his hand. Polymer and steel, like the Glock 19, which he personally favored. This one was bigger, like a Glock 17. And like the Glock, the safety was in the trigger. John Clark still preferred an all-steel Colt .45 1911. "Old-school," Clark said. "It's how I survived long enough to get old."

Jack wanted to sight the pistol, maybe even break it down. But he had a cover to maintain, so he played it cool.

"How many rounds?"

"Sixteen in the mag, one in the chamber—well, one in the hand, eh?" She held out her open palm.

"Oh, yeah." Jack dropped the brass into her hand.

They locked eyes. Jack felt a tingling in the back of his neck. Somewhere else, too. Was she checking him out?

Or just testing him?

He smiled and handed her the gun back, butt first.

She slammed the mag home and racked the slide, putting one in the chamber, then dropped the mag and loaded the last bullet into it, then reloaded the mag and holstered her weapon.

Jack knew she'd keep count of the number of shots fired in a gun battle. Seventeen was her number, and she wasn't going to screw that up.

"Ready."

"Lead the way, Officer."

The Warsaw air was cool but delightful, and the sky clear. A perfect day to walk anywhere, but especially to lunch.

"I can't thank you enough for all of the help you've given me today," Jack said.

"You're welcome. It's a nice change of pace from what I normally do."

"That's right, I forgot. You're an undercover piano player for the Polish security services. What's your latest case? Let me guess. The Austrian Mafia is smuggling unlicensed harpsichords into the country."

She laughed. "I wish. I'm working on a very nasty drug case at the moment, and with a vile human trafficking ring. Young Eastern European girls who were promised the moon, only to be dumped into Dante's Inferno."

Jack wanted to commiserate with her. The child-trafficking case in Texas that The Campus had worked on a couple years ago had shocked him to his core. But Liliana had no idea he was working for The Campus or even that it existed. He needed to guard his words carefully.

"Sounds terrible."

A priest was across the street, walking in the opposite direction. He looked like a freshman in college.

Liliana frowned. "It's worse than you can imagine."

"Now you're making me feel guilty."

"Why?"

"You've been pulled off of two important cases to help me look into what is probably going to be a whole lot of nothing."

"Trust me, there will be plenty of filth and tragedy to get back to when you leave."

"Seriously, though. Why are you helping me?"

"I'm not helping you. You're helping me."

"How so?"

"We're investigating a questionable American businessman and his possible dealings with Polish national citizens that you brought to our attention. Our government is grateful."

"I seem to recall an old Polish proverb about not kidding a kidder?"

"Except we use a different word than **kid**," Liliana fired back.

Nothing was more attractive in a woman than

a great sense of humor, Jack thought, and Liliana was funny as heck.

"Seriously. It seems like you're going the extra mile for me."

"Because I am."

"I'd like to say it's because of my winning personality, but I suspect it has more to do with Gerry Hendley."

"To be honest, sure. My boss is a big fan of the senator's. And so is his boss, the president of Poland."

"And they want you to make a good impression on me so that I will report back to Gerry and twist his arm and make him get Congress to pass that forward base treaty, right?"

"Something like that. I'm told they want to call it Fort Ryan."

"Are you kidding? That's the fastest way to get the President to back off. Better to name it Fort Pulaski, after the Polish general who died fighting in the American Revolution. He was the founder of the American cavalry, and I think the First Cavalry Division might even be the unit that would be stationed there, so that's a slam dunk."

"So you do know your Polish history."

"Sadly, only as it relates to my own."

"I'll pass your suggestion along."

They arrived at the restaurant, hardly more

than a hole in the wall. Jack opened the door for her. The tiny place was jammed with locals. The place buzzed with lunchtime conversation and the tink of silverware and ceramic plates.

A young waitress lit up when she saw Liliana. Her eyes drifted to Jack for a second, then a smile flashed across her round, Slavic face. She shouted something and motioned for them to come to the back of the small dining area.

"She's making a place for us," Liliana said as the two of them wedged between crowded tables. Jack kept muttering **"Przepraszam"** as they worked their way back, but nobody seemed to mind the intrusion.

The woman cleared a small table used for holding silverware and napkins, then pulled two unused chairs from adjoining tables just as they arrived.

Liliana thanked her profusely and gave her their order. Ten minutes later, a heaping plate of pierogi arrived. Liliana pointed them out—each plump little dumpling stuffed with sweet plums, minced mushrooms, and beef or pork. They drank bubbling mineral water served at room temperature. Not uncommon in this part of the world. Only America seemed fixated with ice in its water.

Halfway through their meal, Liliana asked, "So, have I made a good impression?"

"Yes, actually. The whole country has."

"Poland is a great country. A country worth dying for."

"Do all Poles feel that way?"

"It's increasingly rare these days, I'm sorry to say. Especially among young people."

"Same in my country."

"Their allegiances are shifting to the EU or to globalism or climate change or a hundred other things they wouldn't die for, either."

"I know you're not big on the EU, but it was meant to defeat nationalism and prevent another world war, wasn't it?"

"If national borders were the cause of wars, then there would never be a civil war, would there?"

Jack thought about his travels in Bosnia and Herzegovina last year and its horrific civil war that still haunted the people there.

Liliana shook her head. "And there I go again. Sorry."

"Don't apologize for loving your country. I sure as hell won't."

She waved at their waitress, signaling for a check.

Jack paid this time, over Liliana's protests, and they headed back to her office in reflective silence.

They spent the next four hours combing through the last records they could access. A summary of the day's findings was crystal clear. Altogether they had discovered exactly nothing beyond the business relationship Gage had with Stapinsky, which they already knew about, and as far as Jack could tell, there wasn't anything illegal about it or the business transactions they were engaged in.

Even Liliana's constant cross-checking with another ABW database—which Jack wasn't allowed to see—pulled up nothing.

"All I am authorized to tell you is that I can't find any legal associations BGS has with any known criminal elements or enterprises."

"Well, that's something. Do we have anything else to look at? Something I'm not seeing?"

"That's the last of what we have been authorized to examine. I'm sorry, Jack. What's next for you?"

"The only thing I can think of is checking out the properties Baltic General Services owns in Gdynia and Gdańsk. Exactly three, by my count."

"We can go there tomorrow if you like."

"I would, actually."

Liliana's cell phone rang. "Excuse me, that's my mother calling. Do you mind?"

"No, not all. Moms always come first." He glanced at his watch. It was just after five-thirty local.

She spoke with her mother in Polish. Jack wasn't trying to listen—what was the point, since he couldn't understand them anyway? But he noticed her voice dropped to a near whisper as she turned her back and stepped away from the desk, her vocal inflections more intense. Finally, she turned around with her hand covering the receiver. Her face flushed with embarrassment.

"Excuse me, Jack. I have a question for you."

"Sure. What's up?"

"It's my mother. She wants to know if you would come over for dinner tonight. She is a great fan of your country and would like to meet you."

Jack was conflicted. It was very kind of her mother to extend the invitation. On the other hand, he couldn't help but feel this might be another test.

"I can see it in your face. It's too much to ask. I apologize." Liliana lifted her hand from the receiver to tell her mother the bad news.

"No, wait."

Liliana paused.

Jack smiled. "What's for dinner?"

45

Liliana parked the Audi at the curb of a modest two-story home north of the city center, across the street from a greenbelt or perhaps a park. The recent rains had slicked the heavily treed street with leaves that were just beginning to riot with fall colors.

She led them through a wrought-iron gate and up a few stone steps to a magnificent wooden door. Jack carried a small bouquet of flowers and a bottle of merlot. He insisted they stop on the way. His mother taught him long ago the power of flowers. Liliana opened the door and the sweet, peppery aroma of grilled steak came wafting out. Jack's mouth began to water.

While they were still standing in the foyer, a handsome, middle-aged woman came out of the kitchen, a flowery apron wrapped around her well-kept figure. Jack saw instantly where Liliana got her good looks. Apart from a few strands of gray in her light brown hair and laugh lines around her eyes, the two women almost looked like sisters. He remembered a line his mother told him years ago. "If you want to see your wife in the future, meet her mother." It wasn't always true, but this looked like a sure bet.

Jack held out the bouquet of flowers. Liliana's mother lit up like a candle.

"Oh, you shouldn't have."

Oh, but I'm so glad I did.

Thanks, Mom.

The woman extended her hand. "Mr. Ryan, it is such a pleasure to meet you."

Jack shook hers. A warm, firm grip, wet from washing dishes. "It's very nice to meet you, Mrs. Pilecki. And please, call me Jack."

"And I'm Maria."

"Like Madame Curie?"

"Very good. Yes, like me, born in Poland. But I never left, except to go to school at Oxford."

Yikes. A brainiac.

"Please, make yourself comfortable. I hope you came hungry."

Jack sniffed the air. "I am now."

"Mother is the best cook in Warsaw."

"Can I get you something to drink? Wine? Beer? An aperitif?"

"I'm fine right now, but thanks." He handed her the wine. "Almost forgot. For you as well."

"You shouldn't have."

"I told him not to, Mother. But he's persistent."

A door slammed toward the back of the house. Stockinged feet thundered down the hallway.

Liliana knelt down just as a greased ball of blond lightning crashed into her, wrapping his little arms around her neck.

"Tomasz!" She kissed him as she stood.

Jack grinned ear to ear as he stepped toward them. "And who's this little fellow?"

"This is Tomasz. He's my son."

Clinging to his mother's neck, the boy's large, luminous blue eyes searched Jack for some sign of evil intent.

Jack smiled at him. "Hello, Tomasz."

Tomasz locked eyes with him fearlessly.

"Tomasz, be a good boy and say hello to Mr. Ryan," Liliana urged.

"You can call me Jack."

"Jack is having dinner with us tonight. Are you hungry?"

The boy nodded furiously.

His grandmother spoke to him in Polish. He reached for her and she took him.

"He's, what, two, two and a half?"

"Two and a half next week," Liliana said.

"He's a beautiful boy."

"Thank you."

"And he's obviously bright if he speaks English and Polish already."

"Mother only speaks to him in Polish, and I only speak to him in English."

"That's brilliant. I studied languages in college. They didn't stick so well."

"It's always better to learn them when you're young. The brain is wired for it."

"Let's get you washed up for dinner," Maria said in Polish, and carried Tomasz off to the bathroom.

"I apologize for my son's rudeness," Liliana said.

"He wasn't rude at all. He was just checking out the stranger. He's the man of the house. It's his job. How long will his father be deployed?"

Liliana's eyes narrowed, curious. "Why do you ask that?"

Jack nodded toward the fireplace mantel on the far wall. A handsome soldier in a Polish uniform stood inside a silver frame.

"He's a good-looking fellow. I see where Tomasz gets it from."

"Yes. Tadeusz was a very handsome man . . ." Her voice trailed off, nearly cracking.

"I'm so sorry. How did it happen?"

"Six months after Tomasz was born. He was a lieutenant with Task Force White Eagle, attached to the American First Cavalry Division in Ghazni Province, Afghanistan. A roadside IED took out his vehicle."

"It's a shitty war that never ends."

"He served his country faithfully and bravely. I would rather be the widow to a brave man than a wife to a coward."

When she said death wasn't a stranger, she wasn't kidding.

Now Jack felt like a pile of shit. She was a grieving widow and a single working mom and he had allowed his mind to go places it shouldn't have gone. All he wanted to do was leave.

"I need to secure my weapon and wash up a bit. Please, make yourself comfortable. I'm sure dinner will be ready soon."

Jack turned toward the front door.

"Jack?" It was Maria.

He turned back around. Tomasz was in her arms, staring at him. They approached.

"Come, let's get you something to drink."

"I hate to be a bother—"

"Nonsense." She sniffed the air. "My steaks!" She set Tomasz down and pointed at a box of toys in the living room, urging the boy in Polish to go play with them. Tomasz scampered off with a squeal while she dashed to the kitchen, shouting, "Excuse me, Jack—" over her shoulder as she went.

Jack watched Tomasz attack the toy box, yanking out each piece one at a time, obviously searching for something. He leaned over into the box and emerged with a triumphant grin on his face, with a plastic giraffe in one hand and a lion in the other.

He glanced up at Jack and then the animals in

his hands, and then held up the giraffe toward Jack. "Play?"

"Me? Heck, yeah, bud. Let's play."

Jack dropped down on the floor with him and the two began their plastic safari adventure.

Fifteen minutes passed before Liliana came back out into the front room in a fresh change of clothes and with her face washed.

"What are you two up to?" she asked.

Jack sat cross-legged on the ground and proudly pointed at his giraffe standing in the back of a dump truck that Tomasz was pushing around with the help of the lion. There was also a plastic hammer, a Thomas the Tank Engine figure, and a green plastic knight with a broadsword held high over his helmeted head.

"Seems we're on some kind of construction-related safari."

"He loves to play. He'd rather play than watch TV any day."

She reached out her hand toward her son. "Come, it's time for dinner."

"Nie," Tomasz said, half pouting.

"Put your toys away right now, Son. You can play later, after Mr. Ryan leaves."

"Nie."

"Can we play some more after dinner?" Jack

pleaded with Liliana, like a trial attorney on behalf of his young client.

Liliana shrugged. "Only if Tomasz eats all of his dinner."

Jack turned to Tomasz. He nodded. "Hey, bud. That sounds like a pretty good deal. Okay?"

Tomasz grinned and bobbled his head exactly like Jack, nod for nod.

"Great!"

Jack stood up.

Tomasz reached up.

To Jack.

Jack picked him up. "Here we go!"

Jack tossed him up in the air a little. The toddler giggled.

"Again!"

Jack tossed him one more time.

"Again!"

"After dinner, okay?"

"Okay."

"If you two are done fooling around, dinner is served."

46

Jack and Liliana feasted, raving about Maria's steaks and the side dishes as they ate, especially the sour rye soup with sausage and bacon. Tomasz sat next to Jack, who cut up his steak into little boy-sized bites.

Maria instructed Alexa to play Spanish guitar instrumental music during dinner. The conversation flowed from favorite music to movies, then to history, and finally politics, which Jack quickly deflected, feigning ignorance and disdain for the subject to avoid conjuring up any possible connections with his famous father, to whom he still bore a strong resemblance despite the beard. When the subject finally turned to economics, Maria's professional expertise, Liliana threw her hands up.

"Oh, no. When we start talking about inverted yield curves and Smoot–Hawley, I know it's my turn to wash the dishes." Liliana stood and gathered plates.

Jack stood as well. "Here, let me help you."

"Nonsense. You're our guest," Maria said, laying a hand on his arm. "As soon as she clears the table, we'll have dessert." She turned to Tomasz and told him the name of the dessert in Polish. The boy laughed and repeated it. **"Szarlotka!"**

Maria quizzed Jack about the American stock market—he was a financial analyst, after all—and what direction he thought the market would take after the recent announcement by the Fed to hike interest rates a half-point. He gave his opinion and fired back at her about the European Central Bank and its latest round of quantitative easing. And so it went for the next twenty minutes.

Somewhere in that conversation, Tomasz had managed to slip out of his chair and into Jack's lap, his bright eyes flitting back and forth between Jack and Maria as if he were following the conversation word for word.

Liliana fell into her chair. "Okay, Mother. Where's that **szarlotka** you promised?"

Jack sniffed the air. "Oh, I'd say it's right around the corner." A timer went off a second later.

"Coming right up." Maria stood. "Coffee?"

"Please." He said this as Tomasz was rubbing Jack's beard with his stubby little fingers, slick with steak grease.

"Tomasz! What are you doing?" Liliana pointed at her son. "Do you want me to take him?"

"Nah. He's fine. I used to hold my younger brother and sister like this, a million years ago. I kinda miss it."

Maria arrived, setting bowls on the table heaping with **szarlotka**—steaming-hot apple pie, along with big scoops of vanilla ice cream that was already starting to melt.

"Oh, Mother. This is too much."

"Ridiculous. You're skinny as a rail. And Jack packs so much muscle he'll burn it off just sitting there."

She returned with a small bowl of the same confectionary concoction for Tomasz and set it down on his place mat in front of his chair.

"Leave Mr. Ryan alone to eat his dessert in peace," she said in Polish, or so Jack assumed.

"Nie" was the boy's familiar reply. He leaned over the table and reached for the corner of the place mat, which he seized with his little fingers, and gently pulled the apple pie over to himself. He picked up the spoon and jabbed it into the pie and lifted it to his mouth.

"Careful, bucko. It's hot." Jack blew on his spoon to demonstrate.

Tomasz gave him a quizzical look, then did the same to his before taking a bite.

"You're ruining my son," Liliana said. "Or is it the other way around?"

Jack shrugged and smiled, and kept eating. "Man, this pie is awesome."

———

They finally finished dinner, and while Maria and Liliana cleaned up the rest of the kitchen, Jack and Tomasz finished their plastic safari adventures.

Twenty minutes later, Liliana reappeared and told her son in no uncertain terms, "It's time for bed."

Tomasz shot a worried look at Jack. **Back me up, dude.**

Jack shrugged. "Sorry, buddy. When the boss says it's time, it's time."

He stood, and Liliana reached down to pick up her son. The boy laughed and squirmed. She finally got ahold of him and lifted him up like a sack of potatoes, holding him upside down, to his squealing delight.

"Oh, such a big boy. Too big for Mommy to carry much longer." She looked at Jack. "Give me a few minutes and I'll take you back to your hotel."

"Oh, don't bother. I can catch an Uber."

"No, please. Happy to do it. Just fifteen minutes or so."

"Okay."

Jack sat on the comfortable couch, pulled out his cell phone, and checked for messages. He grinned when he heard Liliana fussing to get Tomasz to wash his face and brush his teeth.

A text from Gerry caught his eye. He'd sent it about an hour ago.

Everything okay over there?

Jack texted back.

All good but nothing to show for it. Heading to the coast tomorrow. Will check in after I get there.

He heard Maria, Liliana, and Tomasz at the end of the hallway. The door was open to Tomasz's bedroom. They were praying in Polish. He wondered if it was the same prayer his folks prayed with him at bedtime when he was a little boy. He was glad he wasn't asked to join them—he hadn't prayed like that in years.

But then again, why would they?

They finished up about the time Jack had cleaned out his inbox. Liliana and Maria came into the living room. Jack stood.

"Something else to drink, Jack? A brandy? A vodka?"

Jack patted his stomach. "I don't have another ounce of room in me. Dinner was fantastic. Thank you so very much for inviting me into your home and for the wonderful evening."

Maria hugged him. "It was a pleasure meeting you as well. Take care of yourself, Jack, and I hope you find whatever it is you're looking for."

"Maybe we will."

"And, please, you must come by again if you're ever in Warsaw. Our home is always open to you."

"Tomasz says good-bye, too," Liliana said. "He doesn't want you to leave."

Maria leaned in close and whispered to Jack. "I think you remind him of his father a little. Or at least, his picture."

Jack wasn't sure what to do with that. But he had to admit, the kid really got to him.

"I'm so sorry for his loss, Maria. But at least he has the two of you, and that makes him one fortunate young man."

Liliana buttoned her topcoat. "Ready?"

"Yeah."

47

BEIJING, CHINA

Chen Xing was a devoted Party man. All power came from the Party, and if one wanted power, one belonged to the Party. It wasn't an ideological conviction; Mao's commitment to the world Marxist revolution died with him. All that mattered now was furthering the national interests of China. If Chen had a religion, it was this.

The Great Chairman himself taught that all power flowed from the barrel of the gun, and the gun in the hand of the Party was the Ministry of State Security, where Chen flourished.

His uncle taught him the rules of the Party game as a child: "Mandarins in peasants' jackets," he called it. Petty egos, group consensus, deferred responsibilities. He played the game well but rose above the inevitable inefficiencies of any large bureaucracy. Unlike most Party hacks, Chen was supremely talented. Dogged efficiency and ruthless execution of his assignments within the ultrasecretive International Counterterrorism Division led to swift promotions, a division he now led. His underlings feared and admired him.

So did his superiors.

Few men or women in China had his power or influence. Some of the ones who had more of both were on the other side of the conference room door.

He'd been waiting for more than an hour. A flurry of encrypted text messages with his staff filled in a few needed details. The last was a toxicology report.

The security man held a finger to his earpiece, then nodded toward Chen but dared not look him in the eye. Chen stood and buttoned his suit coat. The guard opened the wide door leading to the conference room and Chen marched in.

Chen was not invited to sit, nor was he offered a bottle of water.

A hi-def color photo was displayed on the wide-screen on the far side of the room. It was the close-up image of the charred remains of one of the workers killed in the NFLA attack. The blackened corpse lay on its back in the smoking ashes, its shrunken arms clawing at the air.

The men and women comprising the Lobito Working Group sat around the long mahogany table stone-faced and silent. Chen knew them all, at least by name. The room was choked with clouds of cigarette smoke, as acrid and foul as the hazy air outside the seventh-story window of the green-glass-and-steel tower.

Chen stood before them, his guts knotted. There were moments in every life that changed everything in an instant. A car crash, a winning lottery ticket, the birth of a child. Today's meeting was one of those moments. Chen's career hung in the balance.

So did his life.

He surveyed the room. Empty bottled waters and butt-choked ashtrays stood on the table. It had been a long meeting, apparently. The chairwoman of the Silk Road Fund sat at the head of the table. The deputy foreign minister, the CEO of the state-owned China National Offshore Oil Corporation (CNOOC)—the parent company of Sino-Angola Energy—and the personal secretary of President Zhao all sat to her right. To her left were various Party and ministerial deputies from the most powerful state-owned enterprises and government bureaucracies in Beijing.

Chen did not speak. He knew his place. The picture on the screen told him why he had been summoned, as if he didn't already know. Seventy-eight Chinese nationals slaughtered in Lobito, along with dozens more critically wounded or burned, many of whom weren't expected to survive.

The questions regarding the Lobito-1 attack came hard and fast from around the table.

"Who is responsible for this atrocity?"

"The NFLA claimed responsibility in social media fifteen minutes after the attack."

"Who are these bandits?"

"Unknown."

"Where are they based?"

"Unknown."

"How many are there?"

"Unknown."

"How do you plan to find them?"

"I am working all available sources at the moment, and reaching out to new ones as well."

The oil executive leaned forward, folding his liver-spotted hands.

"The NFLA also claimed credit for my nephew's death. How did they do it?"

"One of the Novichok 'Newcomer' nerve agents the Russians developed."

"Nerve agent? Like the American VX?"

"Yes, but five to ten times more powerful. Completely disrupts the connection between the brain and muscle tissues, causing, among other symptoms, cardiac arrhythmia and respiratory paralysis. Likely one of the A, B, or C variants. The D is a powder, and no powder was found."

"How was it administered?"

"Specially treated condoms."

"Condoms? Nonsense. His wife was infertile."

"He had been with a woman earlier."

"A woman? Or a whore?" The CEO of CNOOC turned beet red. Family honor was at stake.

"She was a regular visitor. Quite extraordinary, I'm told. And expensive. Fan Min's personal security team had checked her out. She carried no weapons that evening. There was no reason to suspect her."

"Obviously, there was," the chairwoman said.

Chen dared not shoulder that responsibility. Even a hint of guilt would chum these shark-infested waters. He needed to proceed with extreme caution.

"That is a matter for Fan Min's security team to evaluate, Madame Chairwoman. We are happy to assist in that evaluation."

Chen didn't need to mention that Fan Min's security team was employed by Sino-Angola Energy, not the Ministry of State Security.

"How do you know it was a poisoned condom?"

"We found an unused one in her purse. Unfortunately, the technician that opened it is now in a coma."

"You have the whore in custody?"

"We have her corpse at the morgue."

"You killed her? That was stupid!" the oil-man said.

"She was struck and killed in a hit-and-run by a cement truck thirteen minutes after she left Fan Min's hotel, according to traffic-camera footage we secured."

"An accident?"

"Highly unlikely."

The deputy foreign minister interrupted. "If you have traffic-camera footage, you surely have found the truck."

"The truck was reported stolen eighteen hours earlier. It was found three kilometers north of the city, abandoned and torched. We assume the charred corpse inside is, or was, the driver."

The oil executive continued. "Why would this whore want to kill my nephew?"

"I doubt that she did."

"Why do you say that?"

"Too dangerous. Had she not been killed by the truck, she would have died from the toxin that must have secreted through the condoms, according to her toxicology report."

"You believe she used them without the knowledge they were poisonous?"

"Correct."

"How would she acquire such murderous devices?"

"We believe someone she trusted—or feared—gave them to her. Logically, that would be her pimp."

"Who is he?"

"An Australian national. Nothing in our databases indicates he is with any kind of foreign service."

"He must have a criminal record."

"Not according to local police records. He paid well for police protection, we surmise."

"Where is he now?"

"Unknown."

"Best guess?"

"A shallow grave. But we are checking our sources in Australia." He turned to the PLA general on his right. "We are formally requesting assistance from Unit 61398 in order to access airline, train, and other foreign travel databases."

The general smiled broadly and addressed the room. "The Army stands ready to help your ministry clean up this mess."

Chen stiffened. Another challenge.

"We regret the death of the three PLA soldiers killed **before** the refinery assault where no security cameras were deployed. In spite of this, we believe our meager efforts will result in the swift capture of their murderers—with your generous assistance."

The general's eyes narrowed with Chen's deftly struck insult. The PLA guards were, in fact, derelict in their duties.

"Why would an Australian pimp want to murder a Chinese oilman?"

"He was likely a cutout for the person or persons who wanted Fan Min dead. He was probably paid a great deal of money to pass the poisoned condoms along, no questions asked."

The president's secretary added, "And now the cutout has been cut out."

"Exactly my thoughts, sir."

The questions stopped.

So far, so good, Chen thought. His team in Luanda had done spectacular work in such a short period of time. He hoped it would be enough.

The most important heads in the room conferred in sharp whispers. Chen was known for his brutal honesty, another rare trait for a man in his position. That honesty was a temporary shield, at best.

The chairwoman of the Silk Road Fund spoke next.

"I'm not sure you fully appreciate the significance of this attack."

"I'm sure I do not, Madame Chairwoman. Please enlighten me."

What else could he say?

The chairwoman launched into a long lecture regarding the nature and scope of the Belt and Road Initiative and its vital significance for China's future economic and military development.

Then came a brief review of Angola's strategic role in the BRI from the deputy foreign minister.

The CEO of CNOOC detailed at length the repercussions of the resulting workers' strike in Lobito and the catastrophic effect of halted construction for the refinery and potentially every other Angolan project.

A warning of President Zhao's **personal** interest in this heinous attack was given by his secretary,

along with the urgent need to punish the perpe-
trators of the national humiliation that reflected
poorly on the president and, ultimately, the Party.

And finally, the nature of Chen's penalty for
failing to resolve the issue was made crystal clear.

"Thank you" was all he said.

It was all he could say.

The chairwoman delivered his single instruction: "Pull every string, turn over every rock, tear
apart every nest. Do whatever you must do to find
the criminal bandits who murdered our people
and wipe them off the face of the earth immediately."

He bowed slightly, in the old manner.

"It shall be done."

48

What do these bastards expect?

Chen fumed silently as he turned on his heel and headed for the conference room door. The refinery attack had happened less than four hours earlier. There wasn't a security service on the planet that could have provided the answers his team did in that period of time.

Fortunately, the MSS had human and technical assets on the ground all over Africa.

Chen began running his extensive list of Angola assets through his mind as he crossed the threshold. By the time he stepped into the elevator, he had already exhausted it.

There was no question in his mind that Fan Min's death and the refinery attack were connected; after all, it was Fan Min's company that was building the refinery. More important, the two events combined sent a very powerful political message. To be certain, however, he had tasked his best operator to explore Fan Min's private life to determine if the assassination was the result of a personal vendetta, which Chen deemed highly unlikely.

The chief problem Chen faced was that the NFLA was a new group, and until yesterday had committed no acts of lethal violence. There had been neither time nor opportunity to infiltrate the organization, let alone identify members, funding sources, and weapons suppliers.

The more immediate difficulty preventing him from identifying the killers was that all of his potential leads—the prostitute, the pimp, the truck driver, and, of course, Fan Min and the PLA security guards—were all dead.

Whoever staged the attack on the refinery and the assassination of Fan Min had been exceedingly thorough in their planning and execution. Every possible lead had been cut down or burned away. The NFLA must be very well organized and disciplined.

"Bullshit," he said as the elevator doors slid open. It wasn't possible. Most indigenous revolutionary movements were hardly more than criminal gangs coalesced around a political or religious ideology. First attempts at kinetic assaults by such groups were always problematic and faltering, at best. But the NFLA's operational efficiencies suggested advanced tactical training and intelligence gathering, capacities far beyond an indigenous rebel gang.

Chen's bodyguard-driver opened the rear door

to the black Hongqi (Red Flag) H7 government limousine parked in the basement lot opposite the VIP elevator.

"My office," Chen barked as he climbed in, his thoughts barely interrupted.

These sophisticated abilities could have been provided only by an advanced intelligence service—the Americans, the French, the British, the Israelis, the Russians—the usual suspects with the usual motives.

Who else? Perhaps the South Africans. They had invaded Angola during the civil war to protect their interests there. Highly unlikely, though. After the radical regime change in Johannesburg, their intelligence capacities had degraded enormously, especially of late.

The North Koreans? **Always a pain in the ass,** Chen thought, but hard to believe they'd range this far and deploy scarce resources just to annoy their Chinese older brothers with no discernible benefit to themselves.

Perhaps the Cuban DI—Dirección de Inteligencia—was behind this disaster. At one point, thirty-seven thousand Cuban soldiers were fighting in Angola, and ten thousand were killed during the civil war. China had since displaced Cuba as a force in Angola. Were the Cubans laying the groundwork for a resurgence in the region?

As the limo sped along Beijing Financial Street, Chen began to panic. The MSS certainly had sources within the Western intelligence service, and bribes could be offered to other amenable bureaucrats. But that would all take time, and time was the one commodity he was short of.

Chen lit a cigarette. He was missing something. What was it? He searched his mind.

A place? A name?

Yes. Both.

"CHIBI," he said aloud.

"Sir?"

"Nothing. Drive."

Chen pressed a button. The security glass rose, separating him from the driver's compartment.

He cursed himself. How could he have forgotten? CHIBI was one of the strangest experiences of his professional life. His brain must have buried it like a traumatic memory.

As his Red Flag limo pulled up to the Stalinist marble edifice of the Ministry of State Security, Chen made a decision.

He would reach out to CHIBI one more time. It was fortunate the enigmatic source had left instructions for just such an occasion.

Chen would express his concern that the information provided previously was well appreciated but likely a fluke. In order to participate in the London auction, he would need another proof-of-concept demonstration of his own choosing— finding actionable intelligence on the Lobito assault. Five soldiers who led the attack would be easier to locate than an unknown number of invisible assassins who murdered Fan Min. Chen was certain that finding the NFLA attackers would lead to the assassins eventually.

It was a long shot. Perhaps CHIBI was no longer interested in his proposed quid pro quo. Perhaps he couldn't acquire the intel needed. Perhaps CHIBI was, in fact, a digital honey trap.

But if CHIBI could help crack this case, it would save Chen's career—and, more important, his life.

49

WASHINGTON, D.C. AMERICAN POLICY AND SECURITY INSTITUTE (APSI)

Senator Dixon rose to a round of enthusiastic applause and approached the podium, flanked by teleprompters.

She shook hands with a beaming Senator Blair, the retired former chairman of the Senate Intelligence Committee. His impassioned introduction of her—some would call it a hagiography—was his blatant and rather ham-fisted attempt at securing the directorship of the ODNI in her administration after she was elected President.

Fat chance, she told herself. **But let him dream.**

The smiling faces of the American Policy and Security Institute board members in the front row were equally committed to a Dixon presidency, though for different reasons. Over the last three years, she had elevated the status and reputation of the think tank, opening doors to Chinese military, political, and ministerial elites that few others could enter. Because of this access, APSI now held private meetings with the most important players in Congress, in the Pentagon, and on Wall Street.

Thanks to its pivot from European to Asian security and economic matters, APSI was now the most influential think tank in D.C.

Best of all, they were exceedingly well funded. The Center for East-West Progress and Advancement (CEWPA), a Hong Kong nonprofit, had selflessly underwritten all of the institute's administrative and personnel costs, provided generous salary increases for senior fellows, added five new administrative staff positions, and fully funded two additional endowed chairs for the study of Chinese-American relations and East-West peace studies. The director of CEWPA, Dr. Lixia Yang, was in attendance tonight, along with her husband and two beautiful daughters.

Senator Dixon's speech tonight would further solidify the institute's reputation when she announced her presidential campaign. It would also burnish Dr. Yang's status with CEWPA's board of directors and, more important, with the head of the United Front Work Department, an organ of the Central Committee of the Chinese Communist Party, which secretly funded CEWPA's operations.

———

L adies and gentlemen," Dixon began, "I want to thank you for your warm welcome, and especially to Dr. Lixia Yang and CEWPA for your friendship and generosity, and in particular to Senator Blair for his years of service to our great nation and his kind introduction.

"It has been my pleasure and privilege to work with APSI over the last several years, and I've come to rely on both the brilliant scholarship and the practical insights of its incomparable contributors and fellows.

"More important, ASPI's commitment to the safety, peace, prosperity, and progress of our great republic is unquestioned and unfailing. It takes a special kind of moral and intellectual courage to stand against the tide of popular trends, rooted in familiar ideas and old habits."

Dixon paused for effect.

"But as all of us who are gathered here tonight know, what is popular isn't always right, and what's right isn't always popular."

Applause rippled throughout the packed auditorium.

"NATO was formed in the aftermath of World War Two, when Europe was in ruins and a vast Soviet Army stood poised to sweep across the Continent. NATO was designed to be a bulwark against the Soviet empire and its stated desire to spread Soviet-style Communism across the globe.

NATO's mission was right, noble, and good. Best of all, it worked. Containing Soviet expansion not only saved the world from Soviet domination, it amplified the fatally flawed contradictions of its command economy, leading to its collapse from within.

"But containing Soviet aggression also bought enough time for Western Europe to recover from the devastation of the war. The European Union is now the largest economic entity on the planet, larger even than the United States, let alone China, Russia, or Japan.

"In short, NATO won the Cold War, and the Cold War is over because the Soviet Union no longer exists. The purpose of NATO died with the death of the Soviet Union. Now, does that mean Russia is no longer a threat? Hardly. Russian aggression is real. I would even argue that Russian aggression is still pointed west. The question now is, how do we address it?

"The purpose of NATO is to defend Europe, and we defend Europe not by fighting wars, but by preventing them. But in the last few years under the Ryan administration, we have fought not once but twice with the Russians. Clearly, the Ryan administration has failed to prevent war.

"To be fair, I give him credit for standing up to the Russians once hostilities began. But to be equally candid, I also fault him for allowing it to happen in the first place. And why did it happen? There are three answers to this question.

"First, the largest European NATO members—France and Germany, to be specific—have not lived up to their treaty commitments to NATO, particularly in regard to finances. We have footed the bill for NATO far too long.

"Second, NATO is supposed to be a defensive organization. But NATO keeps expanding its membership to include members of the former Communist bloc. NATO continues advancing eastward toward the Russian border. It's understandable how even a reasonable Russian administration might view this as an aggressive posture. But more to the point: How is NATO better defended by making treaty commitments to go to war on behalf of Montenegro, Latvia, or Iceland?

"The recent attempt by the Ryan administration to unilaterally commit the United States to a permanent forward base in Poland was the height of folly. Such a base would prove to be an unnecessary provocation of the Russians, and that is why I opposed it."

This elicited a strong round of applause.

"Third, the United States itself, for all of its inflated defense spending—equal to the spending of the next eight countries combined—is still woefully unprepared to actually defend the European continent. We need at least twenty brigade combat teams to fight and win a war in Europe; we currently only have fifteen in total for all of our global defense commitments, and only three of those BCTs are in Europe. But of the fifteen we have, only five are in full readiness. How can this be? In a different administration . . ."

She paused, a wide smile brightening her handsome face.

"Or should I say in a **Dixon** administration, this would not stand."

Thunderous applause erupted around the room. It quickly rose to a standing ovation. Dixon beamed, obviously pleased. She let it ride for a while, finally lifting one well-manicured hand to quiet the crowd.

"My legislative record regarding national security is without peer on Capitol Hill. I believe in a strong and vigorous national defense, with the latest weapons and best-trained soldiers, sailors, airmen, and Marines. I have also supported our strategic alliances around the globe. But I also believe in everyone paying their fair share. After seventy years of American leadership, American treasure, and, yes, American blood, isn't it time for Europe to defend itself?"

She paused again. Another explosion of approval.

"Let us remind ourselves: NATO is a mutual defense pact, and Article Five of the NATO treaty states that an attack on one member state shall be treated as if an attack has been made against all.

In the age of nuclear weapons, the next world war may well prove to be a holocaust. If the Russians decide to invade Montenegro or Iceland or Poland, we are legally bound to declare war against the Russians. I, for one, am not willing to shed one American life for the sake of Montenegro— let alone risk the destruction of our entire nation because of an antiquated and outmoded treaty obligation from seventy years ago. If Europeans won't fight and die to defend Europe, why should Americans?"

This was **the** question. The one that would differentiate her from Ryan and the neocons in his administration, who would throw their weight behind another candidate who fell in line with them, including some people sitting in this room tonight. She had to make her point.

"Some might argue that we have to defend Europe even if Europe won't do the job because it's in our national interest. It reminds me of the Domino Theory. Remember? Eisenhower, Kennedy, and Johnson all told us we had to fight in Vietnam to prevent the rest of Southeast Asia from falling to Communism. And fight we did! American armed forces fought valiantly and brilliantly against the North and South Vietnamese Communists. We never lost a single battle. And yet, having won every battle, we lost the war, at the cost of over fifty thousand American lives.

"What was the result? Southeast Asia—Vietnam,

Laos, and Cambodia—all fell to the Communists. Was our country subsequently threatened by these events? Did our way of life change? No. In fact, all of those countries are now falling all over themselves to do business with us. The Domino Theory was right—and it didn't matter.

"As I said before, what is right isn't always popular. NATO was a brilliant success, but its time has passed. The purpose of American foreign policy should be to serve the interests of the American people, not the interests of the Europeans.

"We need new partnerships, new alliances, new ways of thinking. The Ryan doctrine of expanding our military commitments in Europe has turned NATO into a mutual suicide pact. We need a new kind of leadership. We need a new kind of world that guarantees peace and freedom for the United States through strength and cooperation. China is the natural bulwark against Russian expansion into Europe. The future belongs to America and China, the two strongest national economies and the two strongest militaries on the planet.

"What NATO did for Europe in the last century, a Sino-American partnership will do for the entire world this century and the one to come. Thank you, and good night."

50

FRENCH GUIANA CENTRE SPATIAL GUYANAIS (CSG)

The SpaceServe heavy-payload G-series ("Goddard") rocket stood on the recently constructed SS-1 launchpad. The scheduled night launch would put not one but three of the latest Malaysian MEASAT communications satellite payloads into a geosynchronous transfer orbit (GTO) at 91.5 degrees east. Launch was just thirty seconds away.

Tonight's G-series launch was the first at the Centre Spatial Guyanais facility. The first had been fired at Cape Canaveral eight months ago, successfully placing the Azerbaijani Intelsat 39 into orbit at 45 degrees east.

The second G-rocket launched out of Vandenberg AFB two months later and successfully placed one of the new Advanced Extremely High Frequency (AEHF) communications satellites into orbit for the Air Force. The satellite also carried a secret CIA comms package operated by the National Reconnaissance Office and tied into the IC Cloud.

Tonight's launch was critical. The Malaysian government had committed to four more launches if tonight's proved successful. Singapore and Thailand were equally interested in this highly successful second generation of SpaceServe rockets. SpaceServe's smaller N-series ("Newton") had been successful, but far too many private and public contractors were nailing the low-to-mid-payload range, often with tax-subsidized funding. SpaceServe's future depended entirely on the G-series heavy-lifters.

The G-series was currently the most powerful rocket deployed in the world. The first stage, comprising two boosters and a central core, deployed thirty engines that generated well over five million pounds of thrust at launch—the equivalent of sixteen Airbus A380 aircraft.

Its nearest competitor was the future European Ariane 6 A64 heavy-lift rocket, but it was experiencing severe development delays and wouldn't be available for launch for at least two more years.

The best news of all, though, was the phone call Elias Dahm received from the head of NASA yesterday. The Ryan administration was actively seeking alternatives to the ultradependable Atlas V rocket because of its reliance upon the Russian RD-180 main engine. The American-built G-series was the obvious first choice for a replacement.

Dahm hated the Ryan administration's policies, but he was happy to cash their checks.

Many governments were watching tonight's launch. Billions in future contracts for SpaceServe, including ones with the U.S. government, were at stake. Tonight's successful launch would secure them all.

SpaceServe, a subsidiary of CloudServe, was Elias Dahm's greatest dream: a platform that would allow him to build a rocket fleet to rival those of the spacefaring nations and their private contractors. His goal was to put the first manned rocket on Mars and inaugurate the colonization of the Red Planet. Unknown to most, Dahm had founded CloudServe only as a means to achieve his SpaceServe vision.

The G-series was designed for heavy payloads and, ultimately, manned spaceflight. He had staked CloudServe's future on SpaceServe and the G-series in particular, borrowing heavily against CloudServe assets to finance the capital-intensive operations. SpaceServe had invested more than $1 billion developing the new SS-1 integration and launch facilities at CSG, and designing the "SpaceCloud" for all CSG operations.

The CSG facility location in French Guiana was ideal for tonight's launch. Established in 1964 by the French space agency (CNES), it had been continuously upgraded by the French, European, and even Russian space agencies for a variety of commercial, scientific, and military satellite launches. Because it was closer to the equator than any American spaceport at 5.3 degrees north latitude, less energy and fuel were required to place a satellite into geostationary equatorial orbit than a pad located in California or Florida. An infantry regiment of the French Foreign Legion provided base security.

Elias Dahm stood in the SpaceServe remote mission control center in Fremont, California, which was jointly monitoring the liftoff with the CSG launch control facility. His eyes were fixed on the eighty-five-inch monitor with a live feed from the Guiana SS-1 launchpad and the 232-foot rocket standing on it. Forty-five smaller displays at the fifteen stations around him in Fremont monitored every technical aspect of the launch, from hardware to software. Live audio from French Guiana launch control was full of chatter from the mission management team, including the range control officer and finally the launch director, who each gave their "go for launch" commands.

Flight computers had already taken control of the launch sequence. The countdown advanced by digital numbers on the screen and also in audio: a woman's voice speaking in heavily accented English. The audio countdown was pure PR for the live Internet feed, a nod to the melodramatics of Fritz Lang's 1929 film **Woman in the Moon**.

"Three, two, one, zero, ignition . . ."

Thirty roaring launch engines fired, lighting up the night sky. The vehicle rose majestically as the hold-down arms and the service structure umbilicals fell away.

The two launch centers erupted with cheers and applause. Dahm high-fived the technicians seated around him, a victorious grin plastered on his handsome face.

A graphic superimposed on the video image displayed telemetry stats of speed and distance. Seventy seconds into the flight, the G-rocket reached a height of 10.5 kilometers and a speed of 1,234.8 kilometers per hour—the speed of sound.

With applause still ringing in his ears, Dahm watched a ball of flame erupt from one of the booster nozzles, and in less than a second the entire second stage was enveloped in explosive fire.

The room quieted, as if a volume knob had been turned down.

The range safety officer calmly announced he was initiating the remote destruct sequence.

A moment later, the night sky erupted with the resulting supernova of burning liquid oxygen and RP-1 rocket fuel propellant. Most of the rocket's fiery wreckage rained down harmlessly over the Atlantic Ocean, while some engine components crashed on infamous Devil's Island, evacuated during each launch in case of just such an occasion.

An explosion of technical and emergency chatter flooded the audio and the room Dahm stood in. No one dared look at him. Everybody involved understood the magnitude of this catastrophe, none better than Dahm.

He stared ashen-faced at the image on the wide-screen.

Flaming embers trailed through the night sky like falling stars, dying out as they splashed into the cold, dark Atlantic.

51

THIRTY KILOMETERS NORTH OF BEYNEU, KAZAKHSTAN

Cluzet's three-truck convoy of blood-red JAC tractor-trailer rigs had been rolling along at a good speed since descending from the jagged, snowcapped mountains of Afghanistan down into the verdant greenery of Tajikistan. But the farther north and west they drove, the drier it got, finally hitting the desiccated edges of the borderless Kyzylkum Desert, a wild, hellish expanse of dehydrated moonscape stretching from Uzbekistan through Kazakhstan along the E40. As they traveled at night, it felt like they were moving through the belly of the sea, surrounded on all sides by the suffocating dark.

The convoy had fueled up at Beyneu and was making good time. They were on a tight schedule to arrive in just under forty-eight hours. Part of the payment bonus to his crew depended on arriving on time; earlier was better, but certainly not possible at this point. Late would prove difficult. **Too** late would prove fatal.

The endless miles, the constant thrumming of the big diesel engines, and the warmth of the cab lulled the former paratrooper into a waking dream of a Senegalese woman he once knew. The Chinese driver was similarly hypnotized, apparently. Neither man saw the spike strip draped across the narrow two-lane asphalt, but they sure as hell heard it when the big front tires first blew, followed by the next six. The driver stomped on the air brakes instinctively when the front tires erupted on the sharpened steel. The trailer fishtailed behind him as the entire rig skidded to a thundering halt.

Shouts from his men in the two other trucks crackled in his earpiece, asking what happened.

Before Cluzet could speak, a bar of bright lights flashed on a quarter-mile ahead.

Cluzet lifted a pair of binoculars to his eyes. Through the blinding glare of the lights he made out what appeared to be the outline of a "technical"—a small pickup truck with a machine gun mounted in the open bed. He assumed at least one man on the machine gun and one driving, and likely a third in the vehicle.

Another bar of lights lit up at Cluzet's three o'clock a moment later, and then one at nine o'clock, both also a quarter-mile away. Cluzet swung his binoculars in both directions. Same setup.

Cluzet began to issue an order, but he was cut off by the German in the rear truck. "There's one behind me."

Surrounded.

All four technicals eased forward until they came to a stop some two hundred feet away.

"What do you want to do, **jefe**?" the Spaniard asked in Cluzet's earpiece. Their trucks had braked to a halt, but with their tires intact.

The contract with the Ingush mercs he'd hired to escort them from Kashgar ended at the Uzbek border. They'd served him well in the mountains of Tajikistan, but out here on the desert flats he was all alone on the ground. He had two good men in the Spaniard and the German riding shotgun in the other trucks. Unfortunately, like him, they were armed only with nine-millimeter pistols. Three pistols against four machine guns plus whatever automatic weapons the opposition would be carrying and, most likely, an RPG or two made for bad odds.

Cluzet turned to his driver, trying to light his cigarette with a Zippo lighter trembling in his hand. Cluzet asked, "What do you want to do, boss?" in Mandarin, but the Chinese man was too scared to say anything.

"Yes, you're right. We're quite fucked." He whispered into his mic, "Hold tight. Nobody get excited."

A man exited the technical directly in front, his features draped in shadow beneath the glare of the truck lights. But in the outline of the lights, Cluzet saw the man pull a pistol out of his waistband

and hold it at his side. The bandit's easy gait told Cluzet he was an experienced if not arrogant man, his pride no doubt fueled by the success of previous hijackings.

Cluzet turned to the driver. "Me, or you?"

"You," the driver managed to whisper between nervous puffs.

"Okay. Me." Cluzet nodded dramatically, as if there were any question to begin with. He opened the passenger door and climbed down from the big rig.

Cluzet stepped into the lights of his own truck as he approached the lead hijacker, a smile plastered on his face and his open hands extended forward, more like a push-up than a surrender. He wanted to show the man he wasn't armed or dangerous.

They met about halfway between vehicles. This close, the hijacker's features were clearly visible. The empires that collided here over the centuries were etched in his round, dark face and almond-shaped eyes. His long hair and mustache were brown rather than black. A typical Eurasian of mixed Slavic and Mongol ancestry.

"What do you want?" Cluzet asked in passable Russian.

"What do you think, asshole?" the man answered in American-television English.

He raised the pistol and pointed it at Cluzet's face.

Cluzet raised his hands higher. "Whoa, hold on there, cowboy. You can take what you want."

"I want all of it."

"That will be kind of a problem."

"Not for me." He grinned. He snicked the safety release to "fire" with his thumb. "I kill you all, then I take everything."

"Yeah, that makes sense. But before you kill me, can I pray?"

The man grinned, flashing a golden tooth. "Of course. I'm a religious man myself. But hurry."

Cluzet dropped to his knees and raised his outstretched hands even higher, shut his eyes, and shouted in English, "Oh, Michael! Thou Great Archangel high above in the sky! If you can hear me, do as I say and bring down your vengeance on these godless heathens now, while I'm still talking, before I finish my prayer, you stupid son of a bitch—"

The ground shook as the four technicals erupted in flames simultaneously, struck by Chinese laser-guided/infrared homing HJ-10 Red Arrow missiles fired from a remotely operated CH-4 Rainbow drone, a Chinese knockoff of the iconic American Predator.

The bandit flinched at the explosions, whipping around just in time to see the wreckage of his flaming vehicle tossed into the desert like a burning tumbleweed.

He spun back around, raising his pistol to fire, but Cluzet shot before the man could raise his gun, putting a nine-millimeter hollow-point round into the bridge of his wide nose, dropping him to the asphalt.

The Spaniard jogged up, a pistol in his hand.

"You okay, **jefe**?"

"Never better."

Cluzet stood, turned aside, and spoke into his mic. "Nice shooting."

The Frenchman was speaking to the lead drone pilot for Star Surveillance, a legitimate security contractor that was also silent-partnered with the Iron Syndicate, who deployed them for operations such as Cluzet's.

"Thank you, sir."

"So tell me, how was your nap?"

"Sir?"

"Surely you were sleeping. How else could those bastards have surprised us?"

"They must have taken up position before our cameras were in range. Advance reconnaissance wasn't in our mission profile. My apologies."

"Well, we're stuck here for a while now. Keep your eyes open and alert me if anyone approaches. Understood?"

"Loud and clear, sir."

Cluzet checked his Russian paratrooper watch. Time was not his friend. He needed eight truck tires right away, but he was out in the middle of nowhere in the middle of the night.

The German approached. He must have been

reading Cluzet's mind. "Where are we going to find tires for your rig?"

"I'll put in a call back to Beyneu. Perhaps they can bring some out."

"We could unload your cargo. Reshuffle the load on the other two trucks."

"That would take hours. And if the police arrive when we're in the middle of it?"

A wounded cry echoed in the darkness.

"Do you want me to stay with your truck and you take the others and drive ahead? At least most of the load will arrive on time if we push on."

"And leave you out here to defend yourself? I doubt those bastards work alone."

Cluzet held up his still-smoking pistol, a PAMAS G1 nine-millimeter. The all-steel gun was a French-manufactured Beretta 92 issued to him in the Légion Etrangère. He never missed with it. "Three pistols are better than one, **n'est-ce pas**?"

"Natürlich," the German said.

"Grab the extinguishers from the trucks and put out those fires. No point in drawing attention to ourselves," Cluzet said.

"And the wounded?" the Spaniard asked.

"Put them out of their misery." Cluzet laid a hand on the shorter man's shoulder. "But don't waste any bullets on them. We might need them later."

52

Liliana's Audi coupe pulled into the hotel's little courtyard at precisely ten a.m., as per their arrangement. She said she wanted to avoid morning rush-hour traffic. Their four-hour trip to Gdańsk would be long enough already. She hadn't offered to bring him breakfast and he was grateful for that, partly because he woke up still full from dinner and dessert; mostly because he needed to kill the craving for something sweet. "Metaphor alert," he told himself as he headed to the small hotel gym on the first floor at six a.m., banging out enough burpees to leave him gasping for air and wanting to puke.

And then he did twenty more.

All he really needed was strong, black coffee and he knew exactly where to get it. After his three **S**'s, he did exactly that, then came back to his room and checked his e-mail and text messages, and even managed to knock out some more of the Dubai project.

But standing there and watching her car pull up created just a little dread in him. He thought about calling her earlier and canceling their trip to Gdańsk, and then just grabbing the train there on his own.

The truth was he had a hard time falling asleep. He was really taken by little Tomasz. They'd become fast friends in a few short hours. He liked kids well enough, but the two of them bonded very quickly. Tomasz was a remarkable little boy.

But Jack also felt really sorry for him. The poor kid was dealt a bad hand early on, losing the two most important men in his life so young. Jack hoped that God would turn over a few aces for him soon, starting with a good man to raise him and to love his mother.

Last night was something special. Maria was both charming and engaging, and Liliana was particularly attractive. It had been only a couple days, but they had spent a lot of time together. She was bright, hardworking, and fiercely patriotic. Jack had little patience for lukewarm souls, especially when it came to the important things. "Dead skunks and yellow lines," his Grandpa Em used to say.

The three of them had invited him not just into their home but into their lives. He was surprised how easy it was to enter into that. "Instant family," it seemed. And it felt good. Too good.

He felt guilty. It wasn't going to happen. There wasn't going to be any magical ending to their tragic story, at least not one that he would be part of. He had no intention of staying in Poland or changing his life for the sake of a woman he'd just met or her amazing son.

He didn't care that she hadn't mentioned Tomasz before. Why would she? Field operatives kept their personal lives hidden. Married undercover guys—even the good ones who didn't fool around—didn't wear wedding rings on the job. You couldn't hand your enemy any leverage or, worse, put your family at risk by advertising their existence. No, Liliana had played it straight.

But what about him? Had he led her on last night? He hoped not. He was just being social, right? Enjoying himself and being a good guest, the way he'd been raised.

But last night bothered him. Had he crossed a line? Was he playacting like a dad? A potential husband? He didn't think so. God knows he wanted to be both someday. But he wasn't auditioning for those roles last night. He was certain.

So why the guilt? Maybe because he hadn't fully resolved things with Ysabel yet.

Hell, he just wasn't good at any of this people stuff.

Liliana's car stopped and the trunk popped open. Jack tossed his leather satchel and his laptop bag into the back. There was a distinct possibility that Jack could get everything he needed in Gdańsk in a few hours and they could make it back to Warsaw late that evening. Better to be prepared than not.

"**Dzień dobry,**" Jack said, climbing into the front seat.

"**Dzień dobry.** Sleep well?"

"Yeah, great. You?"

"Yes, fine. Thank you."

She seemed a little distant herself. That was good, right? Or just a confirmation that he screwed something up last night.

She pulled out of the little courtyard and maneuvered onto the main boulevard. Traffic was light.

"About four hours, you said?"

"Yes. Do you have the addresses you need?"

"On my phone."

"Perfect. Mind if I play a little music?"

"Not at all." A reason to not talk.

Fine with him.

Jack and Liliana had ridden along in silence for the better part of an hour. Jack used the time to check for new e-mails and texts and to explore some travel options for his Cory trip.

"You haven't spoken much this morning," Liliana finally said.

Jack glanced up from his phone. "Just a little tired, that's all."

"I thought you said you slept well."

"Yeah, well, I lied."

She grinned. "Me, too."

"Did I do something wrong last night?"

"What? No." She popped off the music. "I was thinking we had offended you somehow."

"Me? Not at all. I had a great time. My head is just in a weird place these days."

Liliana smiled knowingly. "So you **do** have a woman."

That was the question, wasn't it?

"I don't think so."

"I understand. Relationships can be complicated."

"So, you and I are square?"

"Square? Yes. Better than that. Friends, I hope."

"Yeah. For sure."

They rode along for a few more minutes, Jack relieved that he hadn't ruined their friendship, and Liliana was clearly thinking about something.

"This woman, Jack. Is she smart?"

"Brilliant."

"Then don't worry about her. Give her time. I doubt she's foolish enough to let you go."

Jack grinned and shrugged. "Like you said, relationships can be complicated."

"Friendships are easier."

Cory came to Jack's mind. Despite everything, they'd never lost their friendship. "Yeah, you're right about that."

"Sometimes a friend is better than a brother."

Clark, Dom, Midas, Ding, Adara. Brothers-in-arms, for sure. Friends for life. Lisanne, too.

"Agreed."

"I can't thank you enough for spending time with Tomasz last night."

"He's a great little kid. You're lucky to have him."

"You made quite an impression on him. He woke up this morning asking, 'Where's Uncle Jack?' He wanted to go on safari again."

"What did you tell him?"

"That Mommy and Uncle Jack were going to work. He asked to come along, naturally."

"Well, it is kind of a safari, isn't it?"

"Yes, maybe so."

"I imagine Tomasz was close to your dad, as well as your husband."

"I should tell you that Tadeusz was my fiancé, not my husband. We were to be married after his deployment."

"You sound like you're apologizing for something."

"The Church teaches we should be married before having children, does it not?"

Jack smiled. "You know the expression 'glass houses'? Besides, you wouldn't be the first to get it turned around. What matters is that you loved each other and your son. Tomasz must really miss his dad."

"He knew my father better, and his death hit

Tomasz harder. We keep a photo of Tadeusz by his bedside and pray for him every night, but I don't think Tomasz really remembers him." She said it matter-of-factly, without emotion.

"That's tough. You and your mom are doing a great job with him."

"Thank you. We try. You will make a great father someday."

"I have a great role model."

"It must be hard for a son to live up to the image he has of his father."

You have no idea.

Jack changed the subject. "Have you been to Gdańsk often?"

"Yes. It's one of my favorite places in Poland. It's quite different than either Warsaw or Kraków. You can feel the Prussian influence in the region. We'll also be passing Malbork Castle on the way, just outside of Gdańsk. It was the home of the Teutonic Knights in this region."

"The Teutonic Knights? How cool is that?"

53

GDAŃSK, POLAND

A ll stop," Captain Voroshilov ordered.

Wu, his chief mate, eased the twin handles of the engine order telegraph to the stop position with one hand. On a modern ship like the **Baltic Princess**, the EOT was really a remote control, though there was an identical unit in the engine room: two handles for two engines. The EOT looked more like a small adding machine; no more of the big, polished brass units like those on the great old ships such as the **Titanic**.

They were ten miles northeast of Gdańsk in the Gulf of Danzig, clear of the shipping lanes and well away from the route of the Gdańsk–Stockholm (Nynäshamn) ferry, which ran seven days a week. Every commercial vessel of any size was required to broadcast an automatic identification system (AIS) signal, providing position, navigation, and timing (PNT), including his own. The class-A device aboard his vessel was the latest design—hardly the size of a loaf of bread—and sent and received

PNT signals via the American GPS global navigational satellite system. According to the ECDIS display, which included his maritime radar inputs, no ships were within five nautical miles of his vessel at the moment.

His cargo was due to be unloaded in Gdańsk this evening. But he had received word that the truck convoy from Afghanistan was running twenty-four hours late. This was a problem for Cluzet, but even more so for him. The port was busy and the pier where they were scheduled to dock was heavily trafficked. He couldn't just tie up and wait there for Cluzet to show his face.

Voroshilov also couldn't unload and leave fourteen metric tons of methamphetamine in the warehouse, for fear of discovery and seizure. The plan was for the convoy to arrive at the same time as the **Baltic Princess**, rapidly exchange cargoes, and depart. The other concern was that the trucks themselves might never arrive, which meant the transaction was null and void.

Until the trucks arrived, his orders were clear: Don't unload the cargo. So he parked his boat offshore and waited. He hoped an overly zealous Coast Guard captain wouldn't view his vessel as suspicious and ask to board her for an inspection.

If he did, there would be hell to pay for both of them.

Where is Cluzet?

54

BELVEDERE, MARIN COUNTY, CALIFORNIA

Elias Dahm stood on the aft cockpit of his custom-built HH6 "Flash" catamaran, a high-tech carbon-fiber boat from the mast to the heads. Sumptuously appointed above- and belowdecks, its most attractive feature was the automated, centerline helm in the 360-degree-view saloon. The automated helm allowed Elias to pilot the globe-spanning vessel singlehandedly with push-button remotes controlling the mainsheet and sails, as well as all navigation, engine, electronics, thrusters, pumps, and other sailing controls, from the comfort of his captain's chair.

It was even possible to sail the boat by the long-handled rudder in the aft cockpit, where he now stood, sitting in the bucket seat featuring push-button winch controls for the sails.

Built for luxury, speed, and convenience, the HH6 was painted in the custom blue-and-white

CloudServe colors, and the Mylar/carbon fiber mainsail featured the company logo.

The boat's clean, sharp lines turned heads every time he took it out, much like the leggy brunette stretched out on the cushions before him. She was a series lead on one of the most popular network dramas, currently hiding her face beneath over-sized sunglasses and a floppy hat but displaying more dangerous curves than Lombard Street just a few miles across the Bay. The morning sun was bright and warm. The cockpit sheltered her from the chill, gusting wind.

"Elias!" A woman's voice called from the dock.

Dahm turned around. It was Dorothy Stamps, his CFO. The forty-two-year-old African American woman appeared years younger, thanks to her handsome face and athletically trim body. The former captain of the U.S. women's Olympic volleyball team stayed fit these days by running ultramarathons, but her mind was even faster than her run times. She had earned a full-ride athletic scholarship to Pepperdine, where she double-majored in English lit and accounting, graduating summa cum laude, and later earned her MBA from Stanford.

"Oh, Dorothy. Hello! What brings you here?" His eyes were red-rimmed and glazed.

The curvy actress didn't budge. AirPods were jammed in her ears and she was gently rocking out to an old Guns N' Roses song blaring inside of her skull. A tall glass of white wine was on the table nearby.

"I've left you seven messages. We were supposed to meet two hours ago." She stood on the dock, towering over him. Alcatraz Island squatted in the middle of the white-capped bay churning beyond the harbor.

"Oh, God. I totally forgot. I'm sorry. I woke up this morning and decided I needed some time on the water today. Real stress-reliever."

"I'm sorry about last night."

"Which is why you're here, I'm sure."

Stamps had watched the live launch feed along with ten million other people, including several Wall Street analysts.

The loss of the revenue from the launch alone cost the company nearly nine figures. Double that sum when material losses were factored in, net of insurance. But the lost opportunity costs from canceled future and potential contracts was in the billions. No wonder he looked like he hadn't slept in twenty-four hours, she thought.

Dahm raised a hand to shield his eyes from the sun's glare. "Won't you come aboard?"

She nodded at the brunette. "You look like you're busy. This will only take a minute."

He flashed his famously boyish grin. A grin that had once charmed her panties down to her ankles on a Learjet to Vail on a ski vacation/ business trip.

She never made that mistake again.

"So how can I help you?" Elias asked. "Or should I just listen to your messages?"

"You already know what I'm going to say."

"Yes, I know. Our debt load is crushing us. We have four billion in short-term loans coming due in thirty days and we don't have the cash flow to cover it. We've already discussed all of this at the last board meeting. We can issue more preferred stock to raise capital."

"But the board didn't approve that move, re-member? It dilutes the value of existing shares and, as far as my accounting practices are concerned, only adds to the debt load, even though preferred shares are technically equity."

"Then we borrow more money to cover the loans coming due."

"After last night, S&P Global downgraded us to junk-bond status. We'd have to pay far higher in-terest rates on the new money to pay off the lower interest rates on the old money."

"I can go back to my venture capital sources. This new solar farm has amazing potential—"

"Elias, you're not hearing me. Not only do we need to stop borrowing more money to acquire more assets, it's time you faced the music. It's time to start **liquidating** assets. Starting with Space-Serve."

The infectiously affable and charismatic man suddenly darkened like a storm cloud.

"That's not going to happen."

"You don't have any choice. All of your money-losing assets will suck CloudServe into a black hole of bankruptcy. CloudServe is your only viable enterprise. You can't afford to lose it. Everything else must go."

Dahm sprang onto the dock in a single leap. Stamps instinctively flinched as he brushed against her and headed toward the ship's bow. She could smell the savory-sweet tang of dope on him even in the slightly gusting breeze.

"The JP Morgan analyst following us gave me a heads-up this morning," she shouted.

He was fifty feet away now and kneeling down to untie the dock line from its davit. He didn't respond.

She continued. "They plan to issue a major downgrade in the next week if we can't demonstrate some kind of a plan to rectify this situation."

He tossed the freed nylon line onto the deck and headed back her way, his face flint-hard and determined.

"That's really for the board to decide, isn't it?" he said as he stomped over to the davit at her feet and knelt down. "And when push comes to shove, the board will do as I say." He struggled to untie the knot.

"One of the board members called me as well. They've all decided they want to address this crisis head-on before it's too late. They want to teleconference this afternoon at four p.m."

Dahm finally worked the line free and tossed it onto the deck, then leaped back on board.

He turned around. "I'll be on the conference call, but I'm not selling any assets. That's the old way of doing things."

"It's the right way of doing things, Elias."

"Forget it. I'm not selling!" Dahm stormed toward the saloon and his automated helm.

"Then I resign," she whispered to the back of his head as he disappeared into the cabin.

She turned and marched away to the sound of the boat's diesel engines turning over. She wiped away the tears clouding her fierce eyes, saddened for her friend. He was a sailor heading into a storm he refused to see. Like "The Wreck of the **Hesperus**," she thought.

A line from another Longfellow poem swept across her mind.

Whom the gods would destroy they first make mad.

What was the poem? Oh, of course. But who said it? A chill ran down her spine.

She turned around to see his yacht pulling away from the dock and into the harbor.

The answer was written on the stern.

Prometheus.

55

GDYNIA, POLAND

A re you sure?" Liliana asked. "It seems like a waste of time."

"Why not?" Jack shrugged. "You work undercover. Sometimes people tell you things without meaning to."

"Oh. So this really is a criminal investigation? I thought it was a business trip."

"Just sayin'."

They sat parked in front of the Citi Handlowy building, Liliana's Audi still idling. Christopher Gage's office was on the tenth floor, according to his website. The bank building, like so many others in Gdynia, was modern steel and glass. Jack had called ahead for an appointment with Gage's secretary, who booked him for this afternoon.

Gdynia was just a few minutes' drive from Gdańsk. Like Gdańsk, Gdynia was a port city, one of three (Gdańsk, Gdynia, and Sopot) making up the Trójmiasto lying on Gdańsk Bay, an area of more than one million people. The tricity Trójmiasto was expanding rapidly, thanks to Scandinavian tourists, who favored the much cheaper housing and cost of living, as well as to a recent influx of Chinese investments. Gage had located his headquarters in the middle of the action.

"You coming?"

"If you like." Liliana killed the engine. "But I doubt he's going to tell you anything you don't already know."

Jack Ryan?"

Christopher Gage stood up from behind his desk. He was Jack's height and weight, but he was more flab than muscle stuffed inside a tailored gray Armani suit. His well-groomed hair was flecked with gray, like his neatly trimmed beard.

Jack smiled. "Yes."

"Christopher Gage."

Jack didn't detect any hint of recognition in the eyes of Dixon's stepson, which was fortunate. Despite the fact that they were both children of D.C. politicians, Gage was several years older than Jack, they had attended different schools, and the Gage family fortune put them in a vastly different social circle from the Ryans'. To the best of Jack's recollection, they had never met before.

They shook hands. Jack noted the soft, uncallused hands. On the wall behind Gage were a dozen framed photos of Dixon-Gage charity projects featuring Christopher with smiling Africans in front of schools, water wells, bicycles, and farm equipment paid for by the trust. Jack gestured toward Liliana. "This is my assistant, Ms. Pilecki."

Gage's eyes were a little too eager, but she shook his hand anyway. "A real pleasure, Ms. Pilecki."

"For me as well, Mr. Gage."

"Please, both of you, have a seat."

Gage waved at the two leather club chairs in front of his Danish-minimalist desk. "Can I get you anything to drink? Coffee? Tea? Something stronger?"

"We're fine, thanks."

"So, according to my appointment book, I understand you're looking at investment opportunities here in Poland. How can I help?"

"I know you've been on the ground here for a while. I just wanted your CliffsNotes on the lay of the land."

"Mine? My God, you're with Hendley Associates. That's one of the best financial firms around. Why would you need my advice? How's Gerry, by the way?"

"He's great. Still the sharpest knife in the drawer. And thanks for the compliment, but we're not in Poland, and Google is a poor substitute for hands-on experience."

"Well, my first advice would be to meet with my personal banker, Stanislaus Zbyszko." A thin smile creased Gage's mouth. "But then, you've already met him, haven't you?"

Jack didn't pretend to be surprised. They both knew that Zbyszko had reached out to one of his most important American clients regarding his visit, especially after Jack flashed the $10 million letter of intent.

"Very nice guy, but a little short on details. He suggested real estate, generally."

"I agree. They're not making any more land, are they?"

Just assholes, Jack thought. "Real estate is a great investment, but not very liquid, and the European situation is, well, how to put it? Fluid. We were hoping for something with a little more flexibility, in case things went sideways."

Gage waved a dismissive hand. "Europe is a real mixed bag these days. A few productive nations like Germany are subsidizing the shirkers, like the Greeks. I think the euro is doomed, and when it collapses, chaos will follow. Might be some interesting opportunities then."

"You picked Poland. Why?"

"We liked the idea that they kept their own currency, which is good for us because the zloty is very weak against the dollar. And the government is very pro-business."

"Sounds ideal."

"Well, we've put a few chits down. Nothing spectacular has happened, to be honest with you."

"Transportation bets, right? Trucking. Shipping."

"That's right. You met Stapinsky. Quite a character, isn't he?"

"Nice fellow, if you like your cookies in a plastic wrapper."

Gage laughed. "He's a cheap bastard, for sure—pardon my French, Ms. Pilecki—but he's a smart one, too."

"So, if you don't mind my asking, what's your overall goal?"

"We wanted to start slow. A distribution warehouse in Warsaw—Stapinsky's, the one you visited—and one in Gdańsk. We thought we'd start with setting up a regional distribution base and then expand into manufacturing. But the Chinese and the Germans are crowding everybody out around here."

"Looks like there's a heck of a building boom going on."

"We were a day late and a dollar short in this market. Prices are out of line now, according to our valuation metrics. If I were starting over today, I'd think about Portugal. A lot of bargains over there right now, especially in real estate. Buy low, sell high, right?"

"Aren't the Chinese moving there, too? I just read something about Portugal wanting to get on board with the BRI."

"Yeah, but it's still early. Strike while the iron is

hot is my advice. The best deals to be had in Poland have already been struck."

"Hu Peng is your partner here at BGS, right?"

"You have done your research."

"What's his background?"

Jack kept pushing the questions, trying to rattle Gage. But Gage was playing it very cool.

"He comes from banking. I wish he was here. He's the big-picture man. I'm just the smile-and-dial guy."

"I'd say you're more than that. You've built up a great portfolio for yourself, and for your dad's company as well."

"Thanks. I try."

"I was thinking that maybe we could come up with some kind of partnership. Your expertise, our cash."

"Zbyszko said you had some serious money in your wallet. Thirty million?"

"Well, that's what the letter of intent says." Jack leaned slightly forward and winked. "Between you and me? Gerry will double that if the deal's right."

Gage made a long face, nodded. "Wow. Impressive."

"You know Gerry. He's a serious man," Jack added. "A good man to be in business with."

"He must have a lot of faith in you to give you that kind of walking-around money."

"Thanks. I try," Jack said. "So, interested?"

Gage rubbed his face. The money clearly tempted him. But something was holding him back.

"Man, I wish you would have come to me six months ago. Right now, we're tied up in several contracts that don't give me much wiggle room. And you're right, there's no substitute for being here on the ground. You've got to pick your targets very carefully, and know when to pull the trigger. The worst thing you can do is just start throwing money around this place. The people around here have been separating fools from their cash since the Hanseatic League in the fourteenth century. I'm sorry."

"Yeah, me too."

"How long are you in town? I'd love to take you to lunch next week." Gage shifted his gaze to Liliana and smiled. "Both of you, of course. We can talk more business, and I can introduce you to a few folks. I'd offer to show you around but I'm betting Ms. Pilecki is a better tour guide than I am."

"I'm leaving tomorrow, but I hope to be coming back next month. Let's definitely set something up for next time."

"Sounds like a plan." Gage stood, ending the meeting. He handed Jack a card. "Don't hesitate to call me if you have any questions before then. But like I said, Portugal is a better bet right now. You're wasting your time in Poland, and maybe even your clients' money."

"Thanks for the advice. I'll check it out."

Gage handed his card to Liliana as well. "And if I can be of any service, please call that number, anytime."

"Thank you, Mr. Gage. I appreciate it."

Gage's phone rang.

Jack shot out his hand. So did Liliana. They shook.

"We'll see ourselves out. Thanks again for your time."

Gage picked up the phone receiver. "Good to see you again, Jack. Ms. Pilecki." He punched the button to speak, smiling and nodding at Jack as he shut the door behind them.

Jack and Liliana thanked the receptionist and headed out of the office and into an empty elevator.

On the way down, Liliana said, "I don't like that man."

"Why not?"

"He kept undressing me with his eyes."

"There's something about that meeting that doesn't add up."

"Why? Because he turned down your sixty-million-dollar offer?"

"If business is so bad for him here, you'd think he'd welcome the chance to offload some of it onto a sucker with cash burning a hole in his pocket."

"At least he acknowledged the fact he knew you met with Zbyszko and Stapinsky."

"Gage isn't stupid, and he knows I'm not, either."

The elevator dinged and the doors slid open to a busy lobby.

"What do you want to do about it?"

"I'd like to take a look around Gdańsk, if you don't mind, and check out his other two properties."

"Shouldn't be difficult. I know the area. They aren't far from here."

"Good. With any luck, we might be heading back to Warsaw tonight."

Gage stood at his window, his phone stuck to his ear, watching Jack and Liliana pull away from the curb in her silver Audi coupe.

"They just left. This can't be good."

"Are you sure he isn't just looking for an investment opportunity like he said?" Hu Peng asked. Gage had had his phone on conference mode during the meeting so Hu could listen in.

"I didn't just fall off the turnip truck. With all of the opportunities available to a firm like Hendley Associates all over the world, what are the chances he would show up in my two-bit office looking for a deal? Or, for that matter, that penny-ante douche Stapinsky's?"

"You're panicking."

"I'm being realistic. We have to do something."

"I already have."

Gage blanched. "What have you done?" Junior was an arrogant prick, but he was still the son of the President of the United States. He never would have recognized young Ryan, but his father called him a few days ago informing him of Jack's arrival in Warsaw, thanks to a PI firm employed by his stepmother. He reassured his father that the "vacation" plans were still canceled, but that was a lie. Ryan was also working for Gerry Hendley, and Christopher's father had warned him to never cross the ex-senator, a man of incredible resourcefulness with a vengeful memory to match.

"Nothing drastic," Hu said. "Just surveillance. I made arrangements after Ryan set his appointment with you."

"Is that necessary?" Gage didn't tell Hu about Junior's true identity, fearful that his Chinese partner might panic and do something stupid.

For his part, Hu didn't tell Gage that for unknown reasons Jack Ryan, Jr., was on a high-priority watch list set by The Czech personally, along with strict orders to track him but not to harm him. Gage was Hu's partner but not yet a full member of the Iron Syndicate, which held a higher loyalty for the Chinese princeling.

"Ryan's been talking to people we know and asking a lot of questions," Hu said. "We just want to make sure he gets on that airplane tomorrow, and then we won't worry about him anymore."

"Yeah. Sure. Makes sense, I guess." Gage slid open a desk drawer and pulled out a bottle of antacid pills, popped the lid with one hand, and tipped a few into his mouth, crunching them like Pez candies.

"Of course it does. Just don't shit your silk suit in the meantime and everything will be fine."

56

SAN FRANCISCO, CALIFORNIA

Watson sat in her office, staring at her computer, then glanced briefly toward Fung's glass-walled office on the other side of the room. She sighed, frustrated.

Fung was the best hacker on the Red Team, her handpicked group of cyberwarfare specialists tasked with attacking the IC Cloud, probing for any weaknesses or vulnerabilities before America's enemies found them.

But weaknesses and vulnerabilities within systems were more often wet than electrical. People were the weak link, she'd found. Whether they implanted back doors out of malintent or accidentally created vulnerabilities from fatigue or carelessness, the results were the same. She was confident her CloudServe team hadn't been careless and any available exploits in the software running the cloud for the intelligence community wouldn't be there for lack of skill or oversight.

If there was a problem, it would be because of a bad actor.

And from where she sat, Fung had all of the markings of a bad actor. MICE was the acronym they'd drilled into her during her security training: money, ideology, compromise, and ego.

Fung's money problems were well known; he wore them like stigmata, the sacred wounds of a saint, or, in his case, a self-styled martyr to the needy souls he seemed to collect, including his boyfriend in transition. Somehow, Fung never equated his money problems with his own extravagant lifestyle. But then again, he was hardly alone. Millions of American families owed trillions of dollars in student loans, auto loans, credit cards, and mortgage debts. Did that make them all spies? Hardly.

Perhaps Fung was compromised. Nobody paying close attention to the prickly personality and arrogant demeanor would believe he was tied to anybody's leash. True, he lived an alternative lifestyle. Thirty years ago, that would have been trouble, but not anymore. And he was hardly a candidate for a #MeToo moment. But who knew what troubles anybody faced behind closed doors?

Fung's ideology? Again, to the casual observer, he would have passed as politically neutral. He just didn't talk about politics in the office, and he was certainly too smart to speak openly against the U.S. government. But anyone who knew him outside the office would have known about his staunchly progressive views and strong support for progressive candidates. It wouldn't be a stretch to say he wasn't President Ryan's biggest fan, nor, presumably, a fan of Ryan's pro-America, pro-defense policies. But that was probably true of eighty percent of the people in the building, and likely ninety percent within a twenty-mile radius. Patriotism was as fashionable as a pair of Crocs in this town, and nationalism as popular as cancer.

Ego? That was a slam dunk, Watson had to admit. A first-semester criminal justice freshman could smell the pride on Fung like the Creed Aventus cologne he splashed on too liberally each morning. If ego were the motivator, then Fung was surely motivated. But then again, why wouldn't he think as highly of himself as she did? He really was a software virtuoso. Did Michael Jordan or Tiger Woods have an ego? She was sure they did. But it was a safe bet they weren't FSB operatives.

Watson and Fung had struck up a kind of strained friendship. It wasn't easy, but it was certainly possible to excuse his character flaws and personal foibles as anything other than motivators for espionage.

But her job wasn't to explain those things away.

She needed to track him. Document any irregularities, even if it meant sacrificing him to the greater good. But she needed proof, not innuendo.

Watson turned her attention back to her screen. She tapped a few keys on her keyboard. Fung's desktop appeared in a picture window on her screen. With this hidden mirroring capacity, she could follow his every keystroke, every screen grab, every Web page visit, without him ever knowing.

If Fung did anything stupid, she'd see and record it in real time.

Fung sat in his office staring at his computer, then glanced briefly toward Watson's glass-walled corner office on the other side of the room. She was hard at work in front of her monitor as well. He could have sworn she was watching him, but he ascribed that feeling to his growing sense of paranoia. At this rate, his nerves would be shot before he managed to visit Torré in Thailand next month.

Fung was writing a software program for a wire-less camera and audio device the Red Team wanted to install throughout the LED lighting systems at the U.S. Coast Guard Intelligence (CG-2) office in Washington, D.C. The USCG's intelligence office was one of the sixteen intelligence agencies making up the IC, and, by some accounts, might prove the most vulnerable to hacking. The headquarters office was tasked with supporting the forward-facing intelligence activities of subordinate units around the world as well as interfacing with the

IC. Anyone breaking into the CG-2 office would have access to the entire IC and the IC Cloud.

Knee-deep in an interface command problem he couldn't fully resolve, his cell phone vibrated inside his pocket. That was quite unusual. Few people outside of his parents and Torré had access to this particular private number. His parents seldom called during his work hours, and Torré hadn't called this number in weeks.

He pulled the phone out of his pocket. He saw a phone number he didn't recognize, along with a text message.

Hello, Lawrence. I have a favor to ask.

Fung glanced around the room. He wasn't sure why. It wouldn't be anyone on the floor—they'd just walk over or call him on the office phone. A cold chill shook him. He typed a question, already guessing the answer.

Who is this?

Your old friend. CHIBI.

The cold chill turned to a full-body dip into a liquid nitrogen bath. He never gave CHIBI his private, unlisted cell phone number. And using this unsecured phone was a catastrophic breach of their security protocols. His adrenals kicked in. He wanted to run. This breach was practically an invitation to the FBI to come and kick the doors down. His terror turned to rage.

WTF?!

Sorry. But I have an emergency situation and I need your help ASAP.

We're done, remember?

Yes, well, things have changed. I need one last favor.

That's what you said last time.

Fung scanned the floor again. Watson glanced up from her work. Their eyes met. She smiled.

Fung nearly pissed his pants. He forced a smile back at her, then turned to his monitor, lowering the phone into his lap as casually as he could and killing the transmission.

Did she know something was up? Had she seen him texting? Any kind of private cell phone activity on the job was strongly frowned upon. Beyond the obvious security concerns, everybody had way too much work to do to spend time screwing around on personal business.

Fung's heart hammered in his thin chest. He focused his mind on the string of text commands on his monitor, willing CHIBI to go away—

His phone vibrated again. He was afraid of what might happen if he didn't pick up. He leaned over his keyboard as if studying his monitor closely, but he secretly manipulated his phone to access it. The message on the screen from the unknown phone number read:

> **That was not very friendly. We are still friends, are we not?**

Shit. Now what? Was that an implied threat? What would CHIBI do if they were no longer "friends"? Fung wondered. **Yeah, fucking friends.**

> **Of course we are. Sorry about that. I'm being watched and I had to hang up.**

> **Watched by whom?**

> **Watson. She's in her office and she keeps watching me. She's ALWAYS watching me.**

> **Maybe she is in love. ☺**

> **I don't think Gaysian is her thing.**

Then let us keep this short. I need you to
dive in immediately on a search. I cannot
tell you how important this is to me
and it is extremely time-sensitive. I will
compensate you accordingly.

This is not a good time. I'm right in the
middle of a major project with a hard
deadline and everybody is on the floor and
Watson is practically sitting in my lap.

I do not think you understand.

YOU don't understand. I can't go to jail.
I won't go to jail! I'd rather kill myself. It
would destroy my parents, shame Torré.

You will not go to jail. How will anyone
find out?

Watson. I'm telling you, she suspects
something. I can feel it. The bitch is a pit
bull.

Do not worry about Watson.

Easy for you to say.

Yes, it is. Watch.

Fung kept staring at his screen but strained his peripheral vision. With the slightest turn of his head, he caught sight of Watson standing up, then leaving her office and marching toward his.

Fung's heart started galloping again. What should he do? Confess everything? Smash her in the face and run? He wished he had a knife somewhere close. He'd slit his own throat and—

"Lawrence?"

Fung feigned surprise. Her phone was in her hand, and her face was troubled.

"Oh, Amanda. Hi. What's up?"

"Sorry to bother you, but something's come up. I gotta leave the office for a while. Do you mind holding down the fort while I'm gone?"

"Oh, sure. No problem. I'm here for the duration. This coding is kicking my ass."

She smiled. "I'm sure you'll work it out. You always do. And thanks."

"Everything okay? Anything I can do?"

"No, just something going on with my bank account. I just got a text. I think I've been hacked."

"Oh, shit. Really? That sucks big-time."

"I'm sure it will be fine. But I need to get over there right now."

"Yeah, sure. Go. I'm here, no worries. Call me if you need anything."

Watson turned and marched toward the elevators. After the doors closed, his phone vibrated again.

Shit. Did CHIBI have video access around here? And how did he . . . ?

Fung suddenly felt utterly and completely trapped. If CHIBI could manipulate Watson like that, he surely could do the same to him. And that was the point of that little demonstration, wasn't it?

Despair fell on him like a cold, wet blanket.

He read CHIBI's text.

So here is what I need.

Fung memorized the details. He'd never heard of the NFLA before, or Lobito-1, and Angola was only a crossword puzzle answer to him. But the task was clear and he thought he might have a way to grab the data quickly. He hoped so. He'd never seen CHIBI so anxious.

And that made CHIBI extremely dangerous.

57

GDYNIA, POLAND

Jack and Liliana pulled away from the curb and headed for Gdańsk. Liliana stole a glance at her rearview mirror.

"Problem?" Jack asked.

"A man in a black Mercedes sedan has followed us since we left Gage's office."

Jack checked the passenger sideview mirror. "Can't see it."

"About eight cars back now, right lane. I think I know the man."

"Not in a good way, I take it."

"His name is Goralski. Ex-ABW. A real bone-breaker. Tossed out for taking bribes from a local Mafioso, or at least, suspected of doing so. It was never proven. My partner, Jerzy, always suspected him of being connected to our case, but he could never prove how."

"And now he's following us. Interesting. What can you tell me about the case you and Jerzy were working?"

"Our informants told us that a new heroin

pipeline has opened up from China to Afghanistan and then to Poland, where it gets redistributed around the rest of Europe. We still don't know who or how or where, but the Germans were chasing a possible tie-in to OstBank."

"What kind of tie-in?"

"OstBank might have been part of an investment group building chemical factories in China."

"And the German BKA agent got knocked off chasing that tie-in. And now Jerzy—"

"It wasn't an accident. I'm sure of it now."

"And this clown in the Mercedes starts following us from the meeting with Gage, and Gage is connected to OstBank, and he's investing in warehouses and distribution."

Liliana shot Jack a look, as if seeing him for the first time. "You're not a financial analyst, are you?"

"What are you talking about? Of course I am. Call Hendley Associates if you don't believe me."

She slammed the turn signal, preparing to cut across two lanes of traffic to get to the next turn.

"What are you doing?" Jack asked.

"I'm going to grab this bastard and kick him in the balls until he tells me why he tried to kill Jerzy."

"Whoa, wait a second. Let's think this through."

"There's nothing to think through."

"Sure there is. You don't have any actual proof, and wrecking him might feel good in the moment, but it might kill our chance to blow this whole thing up."

"I'll take my chances."

"What would Jerzy want you to do? Get revenge or solve his case?"

She shot Jack a withering glance. But behind the furious blue eyes, Jack saw something click.

"Fine. His balls are safe, for now."

"Give me a second." Jack pulled out his phone and did a map search.

They rode along the three-lane road in silence for a few minutes. Liliana decided to take the slower, more direct route toward the center of Gdańsk, near where Gage's port warehouse was located. Near the Baltic, the air was colder but still pleasant. The closer they got to Gdańsk, Jack noticed, the more traditional the buildings became, even the brand-new ones. More brick, for sure, and brick-and-timber construction—the kinds of homes you might see on a German postcard.

Liliana checked her rearview again and swore in Polish. "I lost him."

"Perfect."

"Why 'perfect'?"

Jack scanned the road up ahead. He pointed. "Take the next exit."

She did, and Jack steered her toward a giant shopping mall, the Galeria Metropolia, and specifically toward the parking lot of a huge movie cineplex.

"Slow down, please, but keep moving," Jack said, scanning the rows of cars.

"What are we doing?"

"I always wanted to see **Deadpool Two** dubbed in Polish."

"What?"

Jack pointed at an open spot. "Pull in there."

Liliana swung into it. "Now what?"

"Keep your eyes open for Goralski."

Jack got out of the car, scanned the lot. Nobody was around. Liliana got out as well and searched for the black Mercedes. It was nowhere to be seen.

Jack bent over and ran his hand beneath the perimeter of the Audi. Just behind the left rear bumper he muttered, "Got it."

He showed Liliana the small magnetic object.

"A GPS tracker," Liliana said. "That's why he fell back. He doesn't need to maintain visual contact."

"Exactly. Now watch this."

Jack crouched low and dashed across the lot toward a silver Audi with German license plates. Checking around one more time to make sure he wasn't being spotted by any mall cops, he slapped the tracker underneath the German Audi's right front fender, then dashed back to Liliana and climbed into her car.

"Let's hope the German is watching a double feature and then gets homesick."

"Nice trick. They taught you that in business school?"

"No, the Boy Scouts. Let's go—and head out the opposite exit on the far end over there, just in case our friend is close."

Jack and Liliana drove to the first property on her tax list, both of them keeping a careful watch on the mirrors to make sure Goralski hadn't figured out Jack's sleight of hand. As an extra precaution, Liliana called in Goralski's plate numbers to the ABW automated surveillance supervisor and asked for a trace of the vehicle's whereabouts. When she mentioned it could be linked to the Jerzy Krychowiak hit-and-run, it was flagged as high priority. If the Mercedes drove past any of the CCTV traffic cams the ABW had access to, an automated text would be forwarded to her phone.

The first property they visited was just south of the city center off highway 91. It checked out as described in the tax records: a gas- and diesel-fueling station for both cars and big rigs. They did a quick drive around the property and saw nothing unusual. They parked and popped inside the clean and well-stocked minimart/restaurant. Nothing and nobody stood out.

Back in the Audi, they headed toward the center of Gdańsk, not far from the European Solidarity Centre, where the last property was located.

"Yeah, I know. Next time," Jack promised before

Liliana said a word, as they rolled past the famous museum.

The museum was located on the property of the famous Gdańsk shipyards where Lech Wałęsa and the Solidarity union led the strikes culminating ultimately in the downfall of the Communist government. Though much smaller than in its heyday under the Communists, the shipyard was still in operation. Giant cranes that lifted the multi-ton sheets of steel used in ship construction dominated the skyline. Machine shops, engine repair facilities, and every other construction and maintenance facility required to build or service ships were also present, along with docking facilities and equipment for loading and unloading ships' cargoes. The entire facility was built along the Martwa Wisła River, a tributary of the Vistula that gave easy access to the nearby Baltic Sea.

The shipyard area was surprisingly open, Jack thought, with no security he could determine. Not even surveillance cameras. Forklifts and other utility vehicles rumbled along the well-worn asphalt roads between semi-dilapidated buildings, mostly brick and iron.

"The ones in the best shape were built by the Prussians, before the First World War," as most of the city had been, Liliana explained. "The ones falling apart were built by the Communists."

They turned onto one of the service roads,

alternately passing around or crawling behind slow-moving forklifts and other service vehicles. Many of the shop and warehouse doors were open. Pallets were loaded and unloaded, cutting torches threw sparks, welding rods flashed. Clanging, banging, and shouting punctuated the air.

Liliana had to dodge one forklift racing out of a workshop with a load of pipe, and was nearly hit by a delivery truck loaded with acetylene and oxygen tanks that demanded right of way on the tight-fitting road.

"Gage's property is just up here," she said, though Jack saw it clearly marked on the Audi's map display.

"It's the warehouse on the end," Jack said.

A truck horn blasted behind them. Jack turned around. A hundred feet back, a red JAC tractor-trailer rig was honking at a forklift blocking the road. It looked a lot like the one he saw being loaded up at the Warsaw warehouse, but there was no way this was the same one. Through the windshield glare he barely made out the driver, a Chinese man, and his passenger, a white guy, with his booted feet splayed up on the dashboard. It appeared as if two more tractor-trailer rigs were inching along behind the first one.

Just as Liliana pulled up to the Gage warehouse, two huge green sliding steel doors were pushed open by a couple of beefy Poles. They glowered at the Audi beneath their yellow hard hats. One of them shouted over his shoulder. Jack caught a glimpse inside of the cavernous warehouse. Forklifts raced around, stacking palletized loads, but what really caught Jack's attention was the docked ship unloading its cargo just outside the warehouse in the fading sunlight.

A mountain of a man stepped out of the shadows and into the open doorway. His brush-cut blond hair and broad shoulders made him look like Dolph Lundgren's younger brother, only bigger and uglier. His mallet-sized fists were perched on his hips and his elbows splayed out-ward like steel joists in physical challenge to the strangers in the Audi. The glare in his cold, blue eyes told them to keep moving. So did the pistol printing on his hip beneath his work shirt.

"Friend of yours?" Jack asked.

"I should ask to see his carry permit. I doubt he has one."

"Might not solve our bigger problem. We need to find out what's going on in that warehouse. And I wouldn't mind a look around on that ship unloading, either."

"Won't be dark for another two hours. Hard to do any surveillance undetected in this alley."

"We'll come back when it's dark and see if we can get a better look."

The truck that was behind them came barrel-ing up, blaring its horn. Jack turned around again. The scowling Chinese driver didn't try to hide his disgust. The other man's boots still rested on the dashboard.

The driver gave the horn a long, hard blast.

"Osioł," Liliana swore as she stomped the gas, throwing rocks and debris.

The goon and his buddies shouted and cursed as the Audi sped away.

"I hope you're hungry, Jack. I know a place. It's not far from here."

"Starving. We can eat and talk at the same time."

Jack knew he would love the food, and Liliana would hate his plan.

Cluzet's boots were on the dashboard of the JAC truck he'd ridden across most of Central Asia. His back ached and a hammer pounded the inside of his skull. He had no patience for anything now, especially lost tourists. They were less than three meters from ending an ass-breaking journey of more than six thousand kilometers. He was a day late already, which cost him and his men their bonus. They were just a few hours short of a bullet to the back of the head.

"Hit the horn again," he told his driver. Lin gave it a long, hard blast. The silver Audi sped away, throwing debris from the pitted road.

The Chinese man laughed. "I scared them good!"

Cluzet sat up, staring at the Audi.

The Chinese shifted into low gear and the truck lurched forward.

Something wasn't right about that Audi. But the throbbing migraine torturing his brain wouldn't let him think about it. He snatched a bottle of Tylenol from the glove box as the air brakes **whoosh**ed. He dropped three white tablets into his mouth and started chewing them as the truck shuddered to a final stop in front of the open warehouse doors. His advance man, a towering slab of Scandinavian meat by the name of Hult, was still staring daggers at the fleeing Audi.

Cluzet climbed down out of the cab, stretched, and yawned. He shook hands with Hult, and the two briefed each other over recent events. Hult agreed to supervise the unloading and reloading of the trucks while Cluzet set out in search of a good meal, a clean bed, and a pair of enthusiastic whores before the convoy headed back out in the morning.

58

Jack and Liliana parked in a paid parking structure adjacent to the Motława River, which snaked its way through the old town and the heart of the tourism district.

Liliana's phone buzzed. "Looks like Goralski is headed out of town, south on the E75. He could be headed to Warsaw. It's too early to tell."

"So long as he's not here in Gdańsk, I don't give a rat's."

They made their way by foot to her favorite restaurant in the city, Machina, housed on the first floor of a soaring Gothic-style building. "Best pasta in the city," Liliana promised.

They opted for inside dining to stay out of view instead of enjoying the festive ambience on the porch and people-watching beneath the warm flame towers. Jack's pesto gnocchi topped with smoked bacon and fresh mozzarella was the best he had ever eaten, and the chocolate-and-quince tiramisu was perfection. He passed on the craft beer selection and opted for bottled water. Liliana had finished her spinach-and-ricotta ravioli and was working on a house merlot instead of dessert.

They reviewed the facts as they knew them and tried connecting a few more dots as they ate. Jack gave her as many details about Christopher Gage and BGS as he could recall. Mostly, he was stalling. But it was clear that Liliana wasn't really paying attention.

"What are you thinking?" They didn't have to whisper. The place was lively. Locals and tourists having a good time. The four women seated at the table next to them had killed off three bottles of wine already, gossiping and laughing like schoolgirls.

"I shouldn't be sitting here. I should have Goralski picked up and questioned. Tonight." She checked her phone. "He's definitely heading for Warsaw."

"And if he doesn't talk?"

She took the last sip of merlot. "Believe me, he'll talk by the time I get through with him."

"Maybe, maybe not. Or maybe he lies. But if he's a pro, he's on a check-in schedule. You pull him in, his handlers will know he's blown. There's a bigger picture here."

Liliana let out a long, frustrated breath. "Yes, you're right. I should call in for a warrant for the warehouse right now."

"Do you think a judge will issue one just because

you thought that big dude was carrying illegally? That wouldn't cut it with any judge I know of in the States."

"No, probably not."

"So, I have this idea," Jack began. "More wine?"

"I can tell already I'm not going to like it."

"It's a good one. You've got to trust me on this."

"You want to go in there tonight, don't you?"

"Have to. You don't have any compelling legal reason for a warrant to search the place. I can get you something."

"I can't let you break the law. My boss would have my head if you got caught."

"I won't get caught. And I'm not going in there to commit felony armed robbery. Just a little trespassing. I'll get you your evidence, you get your warrant, and we'll crack this nut wide open. My guess is that ship is as dirty as anything in that warehouse. It's a twofer."

"Then I'm going in with you."

"No way. If we found anything and word got out that you broke in there illegally, any evidence we found would get tossed."

Liliana leaned forward. The candle flames were dancing catchlights in her eyes, but she was stone-cold serious.

"Tell me the truth, Jack. You're CIA? Military?"

Jack laced his fingers together and leaned forward on the table, matching her intensity. He lowered his voice.

"If you're asking me if I can play the piano, the answer is no."

Liliana's expression darkened, and then suddenly she caught the joke and burst out laughing. Loud enough that the four women at the next table glanced over, smiling, wondering what all the fun was about at their table.

Jack raised a bottled water in a mock toast to them. "She said 'yes.'"

The table of four women looked at one another, then cheered and clapped and raised their glasses to them, congratulating them in English and Polish.

Liliana blushed seven shades of red before turning toward Jack. She lowered her voice, staring daggers at him despite the fake smile. "I didn't say 'yes' to anything."

"They think you did. They just don't know to what." Jack stood. "We should go."

He helped Liliana with her coat and threw a wave to the table of smiling ladies, who cheered them on one last time.

59

After dinner, Jack and Liliana grabbed their bags from the Audi and walked toward a hotel on the other side of the river near where they had parked.

The harbor area of the city was busy with tourists even though it wasn't high season. The waterfront restaurants were packed and the lights were just coming on. It was a picture-postcard image that on any other night Jack would have called beautiful, but tonight they were still too involved in formulating their plans for ingress into the warehouse and tomorrow's follow-up actions.

They passed by a garishly ornate theme-cruise "pirate ship" that had just docked and was unloading its last tourists. The familiar sea shanty "What Do You Do with a Drunken Sailor?" was blasting on the ship's loudspeakers in Polish and the pirate crew was securing the boat for the evening. Liliana explained that it ran daily tours past the Westerplatte—the place where World War II started when German forces opened fire on Polish defenders.

Construction cranes dotted the sky on the other side of the river behind the ship on one of the two islands formed by the splitting of the Motława River. Brand-new buildings designed to mimic seventeenth-century architecture were going up, shoulder to shoulder.

Jack picked the hotel off a TripAdvisor recommendation, an authentic, renovated seventeenth-century, four-story royal granary. Photos showed a double-sized bed for her and an extra-long couch that could accommodate his six-foot-one, two-hundred-pound frame.

She agreed with Jack that there was no telling if her organization was compromised, given the fact that an ex-ABW agent was now working for the other side. She also reluctantly agreed to his idea to rent the room for the night with cash and his Gavin-generated passport under an alias. He would bring her in later that evening as a "guest" with a nod and wink to the desk clerk—along with a twenty-zloty tip—so she didn't have to show her credentials or reveal her identity.

He paid his bill and dropped their bags off in the fourth-story suite after pocketing a couple of Gavin's devices and headed back down to meet Liliana. The good news, Liliana reported, was that Goralski's car was still on the move and tracking toward Łodź rather than Warsaw. She said that tourists traveling to either Prague or Vienna would take the same route, but it was too early to tell which one.

With any luck, Goralski was out of the picture for the rest of the evening. That was good. There was too much else to worry about without the ex-ABW agent charging through the back door when they least expected it.

Liliana was an officer of the law and a patriot. When she and Jack finally got back to the hotel room, she started to get cold feet.

Jack rightly pointed out that she couldn't break into the warehouse and gather any information that wouldn't automatically be compromised for lack of a warrant. Worse, she'd lose her job, which to her was more than a source of employment—it was her life's calling. How better to serve the nation she loved so dearly?

But Jack's offer to break in instead was equally problematic. He was a foreigner threatening to trespass on private Polish property, though Jack reminded her that Gage was an American like he was, and Hu Peng a Chinese national, and they were the property owners, technically.

"Look, I promise not to steal anything. Only plant these." Jack showed her two small cellular video cameras with both optical and night-vision capabilities. With their own SIM cards and transmitters, they could broadcast live video and audio signals to Jack's cell phone or store them on The Campus's cloud, which Gavin managed. The Campus's cloud was, of course, just a data-storage facility, i.e., racks and racks of bare metal servers built and designed by the world's premier company for that sort of thing:

CloudServe.

Still in the hotel room, Jack set up the two camera units to record when the motion-detection sensors were activated. At any point he could manually fire the cameras, turn them off, or program them to record on a set schedule of his choosing. The lithium-ion batteries and supplemental solar cells would provide a minimum of one hundred hours of continuous recording. More than enough time to identify any possible criminal activities that might occur inside the warehouse.

"I put these in, and then I'm out of there. Twenty, thirty minutes, tops," Jack promised.

"You're putting me in a very awkward position."

"That's what friends do." Jack smiled, packing up the cameras. "Trust me. In and out."

Given the possible connections to the international drug syndicate she and Jerzy had been investigating, as well as Jerzy's likely attempted murder, and given the relatively minor criminal infraction that Jack was about to commit, she reluctantly agreed.

Liliana called Tomasz and wished him good night and, at the boy's request, so did Jack. "Mommy will be home tomorrow, sweetheart," she said. She struggled to hang up, but finally did when her mother said good night and whisked Tomasz away for his bath.

The two of them set their alarms for midnight and grabbed some fitful shut-eye in their separate beds, giving themselves some rest and the warehouse district time to empty out.

Gdańsk was a very safe city, particularly in this part of town, even at this late hour. Rather than walk back to the car, drive it, and park it at a safe distance, it was easier and even faster to just make the brisk twenty-two-minute walk from their hotel to the port facilities and the Baltic General Services warehouse.

The port itself was mostly shut down from its hectic daytime activities of shipbuilding and repair, but a number of ships tied up at pier were well lit, and a few still loading or unloading.

The line of workshops along the narrow street where Gage's warehouse was located was dark and quiet, and the street itself poorly lit, but a half-moon shone enough to keep them from stumbling over their own feet. A cloudless sky chilled the air, but at least it was dry. The weather app on Jack's phone promised rain later, but for now they were fine.

They stayed in the shadows wherever possible. Jack didn't see any surveillance cameras, and the one police vehicle that passed through did so at a speed as if taking a shortcut rather than actually patrolling.

They took a position behind a long blue dumpster across the street opposite the giant green doors of the BGS warehouse, now shut tight. The lights inside were off and there wasn't any noise coming from within. The truck that had honked them out of the way was nowhere to be seen, nor were any others.

Jack inserted his wireless earbuds and put his phone on silent mode. "Call me if anyone shows up. Otherwise, I won't be long, twenty minutes at most, once I get inside."

"I'm still not crazy about this."

"The sooner I leave, the sooner I get back."

"Promise me you won't attempt to get on board that ship."

Jack held up two closed fingers. "Scout's honor."

A flickering sodium lamp high up on the weathered brick building behind them strobed her worried face in a ghostly yellow cast.

"Please be careful, Jack."

"Always."

Triple-checking that no one was in sight, Jack dashed from behind the dumpster and over to the corner of the warehouse building. In the dim light he saw that the green doors were padlocked shut. He had lockpicks—a lesson learned after Singapore—but the size and weight of just one of those doors was problematic and would make a helluva racket when opened. If locked, they were probably also alarmed.

He tried the small entrance door to his left. The door handle was locked, and the door itself was also padlocked shut with a heavy-duty hasp.

Crap.

He glanced up. One of the twelve cantilevered glass windows thirty feet above his head was open, but all of them, including the open one, were iron-barred against thieves. Even if he could find a ladder or some other means to scale the wall, he wouldn't be able to get in. Worst-case scenario, he could set a camera in the window—but again, only if he could reach it. On the other hand, whoever had opened it in the first place might decide to close it tomorrow and find the camera, so that wasn't a good option.

His last shot lay on the other side of the warehouse, facing the water. Jack made his way through the low, leafy branches of a fallen tree wedged against the building, then picked his way through the rest of the vacant lot strewn with old pipes, fittings, scaffolding, and bricks.

Moving as quickly and quietly as he could, he finally reached the rear of the building, his back pressed against the brick. He listened for a moment. The cold river water chucked against the steel hull of the ship he'd seen earlier. The acrid tang of cigarette smoke bit his nose, but he didn't hear any footsteps or voices.

He crouched low and ducked his head around the corner. The stern of the ship was twenty feet away, and at least that high in the air. BALTIC PRINCESS and ST. PETERSBURG were painted on the hull. A mast light shone overhead, and a dim lamp glowed inside the bridge.

He also saw the faint red tip of a burning cigarette on the fantail. He pulled out his night-vision monocular and took a look. In the dim mast light, a smallish man in a dark woolen coat and watch cap leaned on the rail, staring out at nothing. If he was the night watch, then Jack wouldn't have much of a problem getting on board later, his promise to Liliana notwithstanding. First, though, he needed to get inside the warehouse.

Jack scanned the rest of the ship's deck but didn't see anybody else. He took a long look down the length of the pier that fronted this side of the river. He saw one other ship with a few lights on but no human movement anywhere. He turned his attention back to the man on the stern just in time to see him toss his cigarette over the side, turn around, and disappear back into the ship.

Seeing his chance, Jack dashed around the corner. He couldn't believe his luck. One of the two warehouse doors on this side of the building had been left open about four feet—just wide enough to walk in and out. Someone had been either too lazy or too careless to shut it entirely.

Jack slipped silently up to the entrance and crouched down low again. He listened. Nothing. His nose didn't detect any sweat or smoke.

"Better to be lucky than good," he reminded himself with a smile as he ducked in through the opening.

The warehouse floor, which he felt more than saw, contained a few rows of stacked pallets, but otherwise was mostly empty. The faint light from the mast outside barely reached into the dark, cavernous space. Still hearing nothing, Jack pulled out his smartphone and activated the flashlight feature, then advanced toward the far wall to place his first camera.

Passing the first row of pallets of bagged cement, he felt the faint rush of swiftly moving air. He ducked the swinging fist just enough that it only grazed the top of his head, but the heft and speed of the arm throwing it carried enough energy to spin him slightly clockwise.

Jack used that momentum to accelerate a driving left hook that landed with a punishing thud into the muscled chest of the monster he'd seen standing in the doorway earlier that day.

The big man had his own left jab, and Jack suffered mightily for it as the rock-hard fist crashed into his right ear, driving the earbud deeper into the ear canal, its hard plastic stabbing the soft, sensitive tissues.

Jack yelped at the sharp pain but used its energy and the adrenaline dump to drive an openhanded punch at the man's meaty throat. He aimed for the larynx but missed, hitting the much taller man at the base of his neck, where it met the collarbone instead. The hulking giant gasped for breath but didn't slow his attack until—

Crack! A pistol fired from the doorway, the sharp report ringing daggers in Jack's ears as a nine-millimeter round slammed into the cement bag just above the taller man's head.

"Stop! **Policja!**" Liliana shouted from the doorway. She was a black shadow behind the blinding glare of her pistol's tac light.

Both men turned. Liliana approached slowly.

"Jack? Are you—"

But before she could finish her sentence, another shadow lunged from behind her, his hand held high, holding a truncheon. The force of the blow against her skull knocked the pistol out of her hand and sent it tumbling to the concrete floor, spinning the light like a strobe.

Her unconscious body slammed into the pavement as Jack shouted, "Lil!" and ran toward her, but two steps in, his own skull exploded in searing pain, blinding his mind an instant before he crashed into the oil-stained concrete.

60

BALTIC SEA

Each beat of Jack's heart stabbed his brain.

His eyes fluttered open with the stench of solvents. He saw nothing in the darkness save random, jagged patches of dim light. His aching hands were bound with zip ties. He reached forward and felt the curve of the cold, oily steel wall.

He was inside a drum. His eyes widened with panic and his senses flared. He was suddenly aware of a slight undulation tossing his inner ear. He was moving.

A ship at sea.

The chemical smell became overpowering. His eyes watered and his nose ran as his breathing accelerated with panic. Voices outside laughed and shouted.

A sudden clang against the punctured lid startled him out of his stupor. Steel grinding on steel led to a metallic crunch, and suddenly the barrel lid flew away.

Cluzet's smiling, farm-boy face peered down at

Jack, the harsh sodium mast light forming a filthy halo around his head.

"Get him out," Cluzet said to someone out of sight.

Moments later, rough hands seized him by the arms, nearly dislocating his shoulders as he was heaved up with cursing grunts. The weighted barrel hardly budged as Jack's limp legs slammed against the rim; he was too tall to lift out completely. They dropped his feet to the steel plating, but his numbed legs gave way. Jack crashed to the deck.

"Help him up!" Cluzet shouted.

Jack shook his head, trying to clear it, but that was a mistake. He swore he felt his brain rattle against his skull as the Spaniard and the German hauled him upright and held him in place. Jack felt the cool sea breeze on his skin and smelled the tang of salt air. His numb legs suddenly ached and tingled as blood flowed back into them, but he could hardly open his eyes for the light.

"Jack? Can you hear me?" Cluzet asked.

A hand seized Jack by the hair on the crown of his head and jerked his face upward. "**Jefe** is talking to you," the Spaniard said.

"Who the hell is Jack?" the younger Ryan asked as he forced his eyes open.

As near as Jack could tell, they stood on the stern of a ship—the **Baltic Princess**, he assumed. A cloudless sky shone with a million bright stars, and the gleaming half-moon fluoresced the dark ocean. But it was the other barrel with air holes next to Cluzet that Jack's eyes focused on. It stood on the edge of the deck, where there wasn't any rail.

Cluzet grinned. He held a small pry bar in one hand and scratched his beardless face with the claw, as if thinking. Jack saw the tattoo on the Frenchman's forearm. A wing with an arm and a sword. The man was a Foreign Legion paratrooper. Or used to be.

A rough customer.

"Jack? Jack!" Liliana's muffled voice echoed in the barrel, the steel thudding with her impotent punches.

"You see? She keeps calling for Jack. But you? You registered under the name of Paul Gray at the hotel, and your passport photo matches your face. I'm so confused."

"Don't worry about me. Do you know who she is?"

"**Ah, oui, certainement.** Her name is Liliana Pilecki and she's with the Polish ABW. Correct?"

Jack didn't bother to answer. His blurry eyes caught sight of a big, bearded man standing off to the side. He wore beige maritime coveralls with captain's epaulets on the shoulders of his jacket.

Cluzet grinned like a horse. "And she is your woman, yes, Jack? A very beautiful woman."

The German and the Spaniard chuckled.

"So who are you, Jack?"

"What the fuck do you want?"

Cluzet smashed the pry bar into the barrel lid, his eyes raging.

"I ask the questions here, **friendo**. Not you."

The strong fingers meshed in Jack's hair tightened, almost ripping it out.

"Tell me she's safe, and I'll tell you who I am."

Cluzet dropped the pry bar. It clattered to the deck as he whipped around and put both hands on the top of the barrel and began tipping it over the side.

Liliana screamed.

"ALL RIGHT! I'LL TELL YOU WHO I AM!"

Cluzet let the barrel fall back into place with a clang and snatched up the pry bar again.

"Tell me your name, Jack. Your **full** name. And don't lie. I'll know it."

"My name is John Patrick Ryan . . . Junior. Jack is short for John."

Cluzet shrugged slightly. "See, Jack? That wasn't so hard, was it?"

"And who are you?"

"Oh, there you go, asking questions again." Cluzet turned toward Liliana's barrel.

"Stop! Please. Won't happen again."

Cluzet grinned. "I'm just playing with you, John Patrick Ryan, Jr. But what am I to do with her? Or with you?"

"She's a federal agent of the Polish government. If you kill her, they will hunt you down."

Cluzet turned to the captain, still standing in the back, and said to him, "You see? Now, that's impressive!"

Captain Voroshilov answered with a smiling nod.

The ex-paratrooper whipped back around and pointed at Jack.

"Any other man in your position would have said anything to save themselves. But not you. You could have said you are an American citizen or that you have powerful friends like Senator Hendley to protect you. But you didn't. Why not, I wonder?"

Another binary grin flashed across the boyish face. "CIA, perhaps? Or DEA?"

Jack didn't bother to answer.

"No, I think not, Jack. Security types work in teams. But you work alone, or, should I say, work alone with the girl? No, there is something else that keeps you from trying to save yourself. I wonder what it is?" Cluzet paced for a moment, thinking. "You know, Jack, it is our loyalties that bind us to our fates. Don't you agree?"

Jack answered with a withering stare.

"Of course you do. Most men are loyal only to themselves. Oh, sure, some claim to be loyal to friends or family, but in my experience, when pressed hard enough, those loyalties are quickly abandoned. Most people love their own skins more than anything else in the world."

Cluzet stepped closer. "But you, Jack? I'm not so sure. Liliana said you were a money man—an analyst with some bourgeois financial firm, yes?"

"Yeah."

"Some men like you are devoted to money. But money is really about power, and power is about the self. Is that you, Jack?"

Jack knew the man wasn't really looking for an answer.

"The noble few have no loyalties at all, not even to themselves. They are the divine ones, Jack. Men who don't cling to the absurdity of this life and hold no delusions about the next. Only such men are truly free."

Cluzet stepped even closer. "Is that you, Jack?" Cluzet sniffed the harsh chemical aroma on Jack's clothing. His face soured. He shook his head. "I think not."

Cluzet returned to his pacing. "Liliana told us everything. We've already changed our routes and distributors. What little you think you know is now utterly meaningless."

Cluzet tapped the pry bar in his palm like a weapon.

"You can't hurt us, Jack, but we can still hurt you."

61

Hurt me?" Jack said. "Maybe. Maybe not. How about you tell these guys to back off and the two of us have a go at it? Or don't you have the balls?"

"Oh! Balls! Yes, balls. I've got balls, Jack. Big, brassy ones."

Cluzet charged forward, whipping out a spring-loaded blade. He flicked it open and pressed its razor-sharp edge against Jack's left cheek just below the eye.

Jack didn't flinch.

Cluzet grinned, then slashed down, slicing the plastic cuffs binding Jack's wrists without touching his flesh.

"Better?"

Cluzet reholstered his blade as Jack flexed his numb hands, tingling as the blood flowed back into them.

"And don't worry yourself about my balls, Jack. I think Liliana will quite enjoy them after I get through with her—"

Jack shouted and lunged at Cluzet, but Cluzet's men yanked him back at the last second.

Cluzet grinned. "Oh, Jack. I've hit a nerve!"

Cluzet's men laughed.

"How frustrated you must feel," Cluzet said, stabbing the air with the pry bar. "Here you are, a rich, young American, obviously strong and, I would guess, possessing some level of combat skills, judging by the way you attacked my man Hult. And yet here you stand, helpless as a mewling kitten, your woman locked in a barrel, and your privileged life in the palm"—he tapped his palm with the pry bar for emphasis—"of my hand. There's nothing anyone can do for you. Only me." He laughed at his own joke. "I guess that makes me your savior now, eh, Jack?"

"What the fuck do you want?"

"What do I want? I want to atone for my sins."

Jack frowned with confusion. "You're mixing up your metaphors, Ace."

"Come over here. I want to show you a little trick."

Cluzet nodded at his two men. They kept a firm grip on Jack as they walked him over to the barrel.

The French paratrooper held up the pry bar. "Here, watch how I do this—are you paying attention, Jack? It's very important."

"I'm watching."

"Good. Now, see here."

Cluzet laid the claw of the pry bar against

the release clamp that held the lid in place by a metal band.

"See this? The clamp is far too tight to be opened with a human hand. It's a chemical barrel—no spills allowed, yes? So all we do is put the claw right here and—"

The release clamp popped open, the metal band slackened, and Cluzet pulled the lid off.

"Why, hello, there, beautiful. Did you miss me?"

Liliana spit like a cobra into his smirking face.

Jack stiffened. Her hair was matted with blood, as was her upper lip from her broken nose, purpled and twisted out of joint. Her eyes, however, were still bright with defiance. "Lil!" Jack charged forward again to help her, but the two thugs held him tight. Jack struggled, but in his weakened condition he couldn't free himself.

"Jack—"

Liliana was cut off in mid-sentence as Cluzet slammed the barrel lid back into place and clamped it shut. Her muffled, angry curses were punctuated by her fists pounding on the lid.

"Quite a fighter, that one," Cluzet said, wiping her spit off his face.

"You must be one hell of a coward to beat up an unarmed woman. Or maybe you just have mommy issues?"

Jack's head snapped sideways at the force of Cluzet's backhand. He raised the pry bar high over his head to drop a killing blow onto Jack's skull, but hesitated.

"Oh, Jack. I must say, nicely played. It's been a long time since I lost my temper." Cluzet grinned again. "You amuse me. Now, it seems to me you asked me a question—What the fuck do I want?"

Cluzet returned to pacing. "On the one hand, the thing I really want is to watch my friend Hult kick you to death. Now, that would be **very** entertaining. On the other hand, there are people who are very interested in you and don't want to see you harmed. But the truth is, I don't give a shit about them. If I let you live, it will be because I desire it. The question is, what would give me the most pleasure?"

"Is this the point where I'm supposed to beg for mercy? Cuz that ain't happening."

"Not even for Liliana?"

Jack darkened. "I'm worth more to you alive than dead."

"But is **she**?"

"Whatever deal we strike, she's part of the bargain, or else no deal, and that means no money for you."

"Yes, without question she is part of the deal. And you're right, you would be worth quite a bit of money to your rich senator friend, I'm sure. And in exchange for not killing you, he must agree to not come hunting after us. I believe your friend

John Clark has already made such an arrangement on your behalf."

It was Jack's turn to smile. **You're Iron Syndicate.** How else could Cluzet know about the deal Clark cut with the Czech last year? "I'm sure that won't be a problem."

"Excellent. Now come over here." Cluzet nodded toward the rail.

Jack stepped over to the rail as instructed, Cluzet's men close at hand. He looked over the side. The ship was making an easy nine knots or so, judging by its small, luminous wake in the coal-black water.

"Are you a strong swimmer, Jack?"

"Good enough."

"But here's the problem. That water is five degrees Celsius. Even a strong swimmer can't last more than ten minutes at that temperature. Your muscles would seize up, you'd start to feel numb, and your waterlogged clothes would begin to weigh you down. It's also quite likely a jump from this high up will knock the breath out of you, and you'll wind up dying with a belly full of seawater before you make your first stroke."

"Or I could die of boredom listening to you run your pie hole all night."

The German lunged toward Jack with a cocked fist, but one look from Cluzet stopped him in his tracks.

"You are worth quite a bit of money to me, so perhaps we will make our deal. But I need a promise from you first—that you won't try to escape before we reach port, so that I can turn you over to Senator Hendley at a place and time of my choosing. So don't even think about jumping overboard. I wouldn't want anything to happen to you."

"I'm not an idiot. Why would I do that?"

Cluzet frowned. "Yes, that would be stupid, wouldn't it?"

"What about Liliana?"

"Oh, yes. Poor Liliana. We mustn't forget about her."

Cluzet marched over to her barrel and laid the pry bar on the lid. He stopped and glanced up at Jack with a puzzled look on his face.

"Liliana can live, too. But first you must choose."

Cluzet tossed the pry bar to Jack in a high arc like a baton.

As the pry bar reached its apogee, Cluzet turned and shoved Liliana's barrel over the side, her fading screams echoing inside.

62

BALTIC SEA

"IL!"

Jack surged forward on wobbly legs. He snagged the falling pry bar out of the air with one hand and charged toward the empty space where the barrel had been.

And jumped.

"Good luck, Jack! I mean it!" Cluzet called after him, but Jack didn't hear a word as he plummeted toward the water.

His long fall through the cold air felt like a HALO jump, feet first. He pulled his arms in tight, locked his knees, pointed his toes down, and prayed he'd be able to keep his grip on the pry bar when he hit.

His feet hit so hard he thought he'd fallen through a plate-glass window. The momentum of weight and speed shot him beneath the surface like an arrow, blasting salt water into his nose and battering his already fragile skull. The pry bar loosened in his grip, but sheer will kept his fingers wrapped around it.

As soon as he felt his downward plunge begin to slow, he started crawling furiously toward the surface and broke it several strokes later, blowing out snot and seawater before gasping for air.

He turned his head just in time to see all of the lights of the **Baltic Princess** snap off. She was now a giant steel shadow slipping away into the dark, only the luminescent ribbon of churning water behind her twin screws to mark her way.

Jack whipped back around and spotted the barrel a hundred yards distant, upright in the water but already half submerged. He clawed through the water like a man possessed, the pry bar retarding the stroke of his right hand. He couldn't drop it to speed his pace, or even take the time to pull off his jacket or kick off his shoes. He kicked furiously, churning the cold water all around him, numbing his skin, especially his face.

Over the splashing of his strokes he suddenly heard Liliana's anguished cries up ahead.

"LIL! I'm coming!" he shouted as he swam, her desperate voice ramping up his already furious sprint. Digging even harder with each stroke, salt stinging his eyes, lungs gasping for air, he pushed beyond his agony until his left hand suddenly crashed into the barrel, which was already three-quarters submerged and sinking fast, air bubbles frothing the water.

"LIL! HOLD ON!"

"JACK? JACK!"

Only seconds left.

"HOLD YOUR BREATH!" he shouted, as his left hand seized the latch and his right hand jammed the pry bar claw under it.

But the barrel kept sinking, and the claw slipped out as the lid breached just below the surface, pulling Jack under with it. He grabbed a half-breath just before the cold water slapped his face, the last air bubbles from the barrel sweeping past his ears.

The rising momentum pushed the pry bar away from the latch. Jack's iron grip welded him to the barrel, but in the growing dark it gave him his main point of reference. He jammed the pry bar claw beneath the latch again as the barrel plummeted deeper, the pressure stabbing his eardrums like jagged ice picks. His lungs burned as he worked the pry bar against the latch, but it didn't catch and the claw slipped out again.

The cold water turned to freezing as he shoved the claw back under the latch a third time, his aching skull crushed like a vise by the water pressure. He strained his exhausted arm, trying to work enough leverage against the steel-tight latch, but the effort was stealing away his last oxygen until—

A sharp, metallic pop rang in the water and the lid gave way.

Liliana shoved it aside with bleeding fingers.

Jack dropped the pry bar and grabbed her hands, his lungs straining to hold their last, stale breath, her wide eyes hopeful in the moonlit gloom.

Suddenly her body jerked in his hands and her face spasmed with terror.

Jack's salt-burned eyes could barely see the weighted barrel far below her and the glimmering chain stretching from its black mouth to her ankle.

Her left hand slipped out of his, but he held the other one tight. The two of them plunged deeper into the abyss. He didn't care.

He would never let go.

But in a desperate burst of strength, she did, with a sharp yank of her small, slippery hand.

He panicked. His hand grabbed back out at hers, but she was already too far below him.

The triumph in her eyes turned to horror.

She screamed a word at Jack.

He couldn't understand it.

She reached up to him with both hands like a grasping prayer, the billowing halo of her blond hair shrouding her pleading eyes as she vanished into the eternal black.

63

It was Jack's turn to die.

He hung suspended in the bone-chilling waters beneath the surface of the Baltic Sea. His oxygen-starved mind began to dim and his burning lungs begged for a last, watery breath.

But he refused.

The shimmering half-moon beckoned him like an angel. Jack began clawing at the black water. His heavy clothes were body weights pulling him back and his cramping legs could hardly move, but he dug and pulled and kicked, still twenty feet below the surface.

Straining with every fiber, he thrashed his way upward, but the effort robbed him of his last ounce of oxygen. His mouth spasmed open, causing him to inhale a gulp of salt water just as he broke the surface. His coughed out the vile liquid, choking and spewing. He rolled onto his back for relief, gasping for air.

He scanned the black horizon, his teeth chattering. Nothing, save a light in the distance. How big? How far? It didn't matter. His only choice was to shiver in the dark and drown right here or swim a little and die.

Might as well swim.

He shouted once, then twice, and finally a third time. No telling if he was heard. His voice carried over water, but without someone to hear him, it didn't really matter.

He coughed up more water; his sinuses burned with salt. He started to pull off his coat but couldn't do it. Taking off his shoes wasn't going to be any easier, and as he thought about it, exposing more flesh to the freezing water wasn't a good idea.

"How fast can you run?" he said out loud in a bad Australian accent as he began his first labored strokes toward the distant light. "Fast as a leopard," he replied in a bare whisper. "Then let's see ya do it." His favorite lines from **Gallipoli**, the first movie that ever made him weep.

A few strokes later his dim spirits faded. He had exhausted himself in the sprint toward Liliana's barrel and was now completely spent. The only thing that kept his aching arms and cramping legs moving at all was the sheer force of his will.

He shouted hoarsely a few more times between weakening strokes, and cupped his hands to make more noise even though it slowed him down. He could hardly feel his hands anyway now, and he hoped his numbed feet were still attached to the bottom of his legs, heavy as lead weights pulling on his torso.

He lifted his left arm in the air but dropped it—it was too heavy to even try now. He switched to a pathetic breaststroke, but he couldn't raise his head up high enough between strokes to keep his mouth out of the water. A few frog kicks brought on cramps that seized his legs like a roped calf.

He rolled onto his back one last time, stretching his arms out wide as if crucified, rotating his wrists to generate enough momentum to keep him barely afloat.

His shivering torso ached, spasming the muscles across his back and chest. The pain didn't matter now. His blurred eyes filled with the infinite sky of endless stars. He wasn't afraid of death, now that it was inevitable.

His numbing mind began to race. A life flashed before his eyes—but not his.

Liliana.

He saw her face as it fell away into the darkness. She shouted a word.

What was it?

He began to despair.

What was it?

His hands barely turned in the water. It wasn't enough. The sea lapped at his chin.

Any minute now.

Please, God. I've got to know.

A word.
A word.
A word . . .

And then he knew.
    Of course.
The only word that mattered.
His salt-burned eyes began to weep.
Tomasz.
He smiled.
So tired.
He closed his eyes.
Time to sleep.

64

CABINDA PROVINCE, ANGOLA

The NFLA compound near the shore of Lagoa de Massabi was only a cluster of three simple cinder-block buildings hidden beneath a thick canopy of dense palm trees. The local farmers and lagoon fishermen they lived among in the remote wilderness provided both protection and an early warning system.

In recent years, inhospitable and insular Chinese workers had flooded the poor province, especially along the coast, where the offshore oil rigs were located. The NFLA fighters, including an ex-Portuguese foreign intelligence (SIED) operator who coordinated their assaults, were already local heroes for their efforts to "liberate Angola from the corruption of the state and Chinese hegemony here and throughout the continent," as their hand-printed flyers stated.

But the assault four days earlier on the Chinese compound at Lobito had raised the status of the NFLA even further as a genuine liberation movement fully committed to the advancement of democratic ideals, income equality, and the over-throw of the thieving politicians in Luanda.

The small commando unit had been on high alert since the attack, but yesterday their informants in the capital reported that the hopelessly corrupt and incompetent Angolan security bureaucracies knew nothing about the identities of NFLA personnel or its location.

Their sources also gleefully described the Chinese alternately throwing cash or threats at whoever they thought might provide them with a lead to the "butchers, killers, and murderers" they sought in vain.

It was understandable, then, that the NFLA unit allowed themselves the smallest of celebrations that evening, amounting to no more than a few beers and a plate of roasted pig before turning in.

The twenty-four men of the PLA "Swift Sword" special operations group came in by foot, guided by satellite images provided by Chinese intelligence and their night-vision goggles. Dropped off ten kilometers back by a single, French-designed Harbin Z-9 transport helicopter, each of the superbly conditioned fighters sped effortlessly through the trees toward the NFLA compound, eager for enemy contact.

Not even the lake fishermen were awake at this hour. The one dog they encountered was dispatched with a single shot to the skull by a suppressed .22-caliber pistol before he could bark.

Otherwise, they arrived undetected, bypassing the primitive dwellings of the other villagers, making their way to the three designated buildings.

Flash-bangs through the windows tossed on a single command instantly disabled the eleven NFLA fighters and the women who were bedded with them. Well-placed 5.8×42-millimeter rounds fired by suppressed QBZ-95B-1 carbines tore into unprotected flesh and shattered brainpans. Digital photos and fingerprints were recorded; personal effects and other artifacts with potential intelligence value were bagged.

The entire operation from flash-bang to exfil was under seven minutes, in exact accordance with their training drills. An hour and thirty-one minutes later, the Z-9 touched down at the Luanda Air Base, home to the Angolan 23rd Air Transportation Regiment.

Proof of concept number four, by request.

BEIJING, CHINA

Chen's encrypted Huawei ("To Serve China") smartphone rang. It was a direct call from the Swift Sword unit commander calling on his satellite phone. The noise of the Z-9 turbines whirred in the background as the commander shouted his report.

Chen was relieved to hear that all eleven identified NFLA fighters, including the five that participated in the Lobito-1 slaughter, were killed in the attack, with no Chinese casualties. The captured Portuguese operative would be interrogated with prejudice in Luanda regarding the murder of Fan Min, and his participation in the slaughter of Chinese nationals used as leverage against Lisbon to negotiate better terms in a trade summit next week.

Altogether, it was a textbook operation—one that would be taught at the Special Forces training academy soon enough. He thanked the commander and his team profusely and hung up, privately thanking the gods in whom he did not believe for not needing to use the Z-19 Black Whirlwind attack/recon helicopters that had also been deployed for cover. The bird's Red Arrow missiles were as effective as the American Hellfire but hardly a surgical instrument. He needed boots on the ground to confirm both the NFLA kills and their identities for his report to his superiors in the Lobito Working Group.

Most important, the intelligence provided by CHIBI had proven both accurate and invaluable to both China and, more significantly, his own career. Clearly he had misjudged the potential of

CHIBI's original offer. He would rectify that immediately.

Chen dialed the number of the woman who headed his elite cloud-hacking unit APT15, aka JADE SMOKE, a "privately owned" Hong Kong–based company secretly funded by his department. She picked up on the first ring.

"Sir?"

Chen asked, "Have you ever been to London?"

65

WASHINGTON, D.C.

Foley read over the last report again. Something wasn't adding up. The numbers were there, but she couldn't make the algebra work.

She spoke Russian fluently. Mary Patricia Kaminsky Foley had learned the elegant form of the language at her grandfather's knee, and was a field agent in Moscow while her husband, Ed, served as Moscow chief of station. She knew the language, the people, and the politics as well as any outsider could ever understand the place Churchill described as "a riddle, wrapped in a mystery, inside an enigma."

As a Russia expert during the Cold War, she knew its operational history in Africa. Angola had fallen to the indigenous Communists with Moscow's support, but the country—a former Portuguese colony—was Castro's play on the continent, a massive Cuban military intervention. At the time, America feared the Domino Theory in Africa. The worry seemed frivolous now, in hindsight. She'd never heard of Lobito, or the NFLA.

But dead Chinese nationals in Angola were a red flag. Her intuition was flashing DEFCON 3.

Ten days earlier, an Argentinian special operations team had been shot out of the sky by Iranian-backed Hezbollah operatives. That had been a head scratcher, too. So was the killing of the Turkish Maroon Berets in Syria—a hell of a provocation by the Russians.

And then the NFLA, discovered, located, and utterly wiped out in a single, surgical strike in a matter of days. Chinese intel in Africa couldn't be that good, could it? Hell, the CIA didn't even know anything about the NFLA until Portuguese foreign intelligence reached out for a NATO consult just a few days ago.

Unlike the spy movies, the real Game wasn't usually played for keeps. In peacetime, killing the opposition was a serious escalation of the stakes and an open invitation for a retaliatory strike, usually disproportional in its violence and damage, to discourage future incivility. That's why the killing of the German BKA agent by an unknown agency was so disturbing. But the three other attacks were equally problematic.

The four attacks were geographically separated—South America, the Middle East, Africa, and Europe. The three military operations by Iran, Russia, and China were against a state police force, the Turkish military, and an indigenous rebel group, respectively. The fourth

attack—technically, the first on the calendar—
was a street murder of an undercover agent working on a drug case by knifing him in the back.

They all seemed so different. What was the connection? She couldn't see it, but she could damn
well feel it.

What was the same about them? Not the
weapons, not the victims, not the objectives. They
were all so different in so many ways. And yet
something connected them. She was sure of it.
But what?

Think, damn it!

Her husband, Ed, now retired, was the cerebral
one in the family. Poker-faced and taciturn even as
a young man, he remained detached and analytical when challenged. She was the one who wanted
to go over the wall or through the window with
a pistol in her hand—the one they nicknamed
Cowboy, until she put a stop to it.

But she knew even back then that intelligence
work, like science, was first and foremost an act of
observation. From observation came comparisons,
and from comparisons, conclusions. How were
things the same? How different? The ability to
categorize was an exercise as old as Genesis, when
God told Adam to name the animals.

She had sketched out all of the differences
among these events in her mind. What was the
same among them? The Argentines were blasted
out of the sky after they were lured into a trap.

The Turks were blown away by a long-range missile strike. The NFLA were killed while they slept in a surprise ground assault. The undercover BKA agent was ambushed in a faked robbery.

If there was any similarity among the four attacks, it was that each mission required a piece of intelligence.

Well, duh. Doesn't every operation?

But the quality of intel each of these operations required was both specific and significant.

What was the source? Could all four attacks be related to a single source?

No. How could they be?

It just didn't add up.

"You're getting too old for this stuff, Mary Pat," she told herself. Maybe Ed was right. Time to take up golf and start playing with him and his buddies at the club.

She shook her head at the idea.

Not yet, kiddo.

Not yet.

She picked up her phone and dialed Jesse Benson, the CIA's national counterintelligence executive (NCIX), the best number-cruncher in the business and an old friend. He was still in PT for a double knee replacement, but he was already back at the job. She briefed him and sent him a link to the four reports.

"Jesse, I can smell the smoke but I can't see the fire."

"What priority?"

"Yesterday would be preferable. But ASAP will have to do. I've got a bad feeling about this."

"Then I'll handle it personally, Mary Pat."

"I was hoping you'd say that. Say, when are you and Melinda coming over for dinner next? It's been too long."

"Let me get this done for you and then we'll check our calendars."

"Thanks, Jesse."

She ended the call. If anyone could pull a rabbit out of a hat in record time, it was Jesse.

She just hoped the rabbit wasn't stuffed with C-4 on a timer and set to blow before Jesse worked his magic.

66

SAN FRANCISCO, CALIFORNIA

Lawrence Fung checked the radar. All clear.

He stomped the gas pedal and the Porsche 911 Targa's 370-horsepower engine responded in kind, rocketing past the speed limit.

Racing the car on the winding Pacific Coast Highway was dangerous and thrilling: exactly where Fung loved to be every moment of his life. The phone call from Elias Dahm he'd received a few hours earlier felt exactly the same way. Fung wasn't sure if he was speeding toward a brilliant future or a fiery crash.

Dahm's invitation to a private dinner with him at his pleasure palace in Marin County was a stunning development. It was tantamount to being asked to sing a duet with Mariah Carey or play one-on-one with LeBron James. Dahm was the brightest star in the Silicon Valley firmament. It was an invitation to Mount Olympus to dine with Apollo, the god of light and beauty.

Fung had been to his house before, but always

as part of a large social event. Dahm was famous for his bacchanalian parties disguised as perfectly orchestrated networking events lubricated with copious amounts of expensive liquor and premium weed. The last time he'd been to one of Dahm's parties was with Torré several months ago. A pang of longing shot through him, but he pushed it aside. He needed to focus.

Being invited to Dahm's place alone was a singular honor. But it made no sense. Why invite him now? Why on such short notice? For all of his physical beauty and charisma, Dahm was nobody's fool—a true genius in his own right. His scores of sexual conquests were a careful camouflage, Fung suspected. Portraying himself to be a libertine and hedonistic playboy, Dahm was, in fact, a cunning and controlling intellect whose lifelong love was only himself and the company he had built. Anyone threatening him or his kingdom would be ruthlessly destroyed. Dahm had ruined careers, no doubt. But Fung knew of at least one competitor who simply disappeared; whether he was bought off or knocked off, no one knew for sure.

If Dahm suspected that Fung was leaking IC Cloud intel, he was doomed, one way or another. But then again, how could Dahm know?

With Dahm's cliffside mansion coming into view, he couldn't help but wonder if tonight was a seduction or an execution.

Dahm's personal chef and sommelier did not disappoint. The two of them feasted like kings on grilled Wagyu tenderloin, fresh-cut organic greens, garlic and thyme fondant potatoes, and a fine Napa Valley reserve Cabernet Sauvignon. They dined near the infinity pool overlooking the Pacific Ocean, warmed against the slight chill breeze by a limestone fire pit.

The conversation had been light and witty as they discussed their favorite local indie bands, Italian neorealist films, pop-up restaurants, and vacation destinations. With the sumptuous meal consumed and the mood lightened by a second bottle of wine, Dahm's radiant smile suddenly softened. A single gesture of his finger sent the lovely young server scurrying away. They were alone now.

"So glad we finally did this," Dahm began. "I can't believe it's taken us this long to get together."

"It's been a fabulous evening. I can't thank you enough."

"Nonsense. It's me who should be thanking you. You're one of my most important people doing one of the most important jobs. CloudServe wouldn't be where it is today without you."

"I'm just following in Amanda's wake. She's the real rock star."

Dahm huffed. "Yes, well, Amanda. Brilliant, no doubt. But I imagine she'd be difficult to work under." He took another sip of wine.

"She has taught me a lot, but yes, Amanda is . . . uniquely herself."

"You're far too smart and, I suspect, ambitious to remain a number two. What are your long-term plans?"

"I love my job at CloudServe. The opportunity to keep rising in the ranks is my immediate goal."

"And after that?"

"You know what they say about rock stars? You either want to be them or to fuck them."

Fung instantly regretted the comment. The wine had loosened his tongue. But it was true. Dahm really was the ultimate rock star. He wanted to be just like him.

And he really wanted to—

"Careful what you ask for." Dahm smiled. "It's lonely at the top, and there's only one way to go from there." He refilled Fung's wineglass and his own.

"It's a risk I'm willing to take."

"I'm glad to hear it. Because, to be honest, you worry me."

Fung panicked. "How is that?"

"You're too smart to stay inside of any organization, even one as dynamic as mine." Dahm leaned closer. "The reason I invited you here is because I see you as a threat."

"Me? Why?"

"Because I see myself in you. The same hungry look, the same fire in the belly. You're willing to risk everything just to test the boundaries other, lesser minds want to impose upon you. You know your own greatness and the chains of mediocrity that others would bind you with."

Fung took a sip of wine, evaluating Dahm's face over the rim of his glass. The compliments Dahm threw at him were an endorphin rush he'd hardly felt before. Better than a first kiss. Better than . . .

Where was this going?

"Society has rules, governments have rules. It's all bullshit," Dahm said. "To reach one's potential, one must live beyond these conventions. National- ism, patriotism, progressivism—all these isms are just shackles the midwits impose upon us to keep us away from the sun. Don't you agree?"

Fung suspected maximum danger here. But also, maybe, an opportunity.

"I'm grateful for America and what it has done for my family and for me."

"As am I. You know, I was born in Holland, but my parents immigrated to this country when I was only two. You and I are both hungry because we are immigrants, or the children of immigrants."

"That's what makes America great, isn't it? The constant influx of hungry, ambitious immigrants."

"Chinese and other Asian communities, es- pecially. By the way, most people don't know this, but my father was born in what used to be called the Dutch East Indies but is now known as Indonesia. He was half Dutch and half Chinese."

"Oh, really? Fascinating."

"And while I'm as grateful as you are for the opportunities this country has given me, it's clear as day that the future belongs to China, don't you agree?"

Fung studied the handsome face across the table. The clear blue eyes seemed to devour him, like a lover or a killer. Fung wasn't sure which.

"Yes," Fung agreed. "Western liberal democracies seem to be standing on their last legs. The China model appears to be more stable and dynamic."

"Exactly. And to hell with all governments, by the way, including China's. Laws are only the tools of the powerful few, to keep the rest of us in line."

"It certainly feels that way at times."

"And so now you know why my focus is on China. CloudServe needs to expand aggressively there before it's too late, and I think you are the man to help us get there."

"Why? Because I'm ethnic Chinese?"

"Yes. But a brilliant and driven ethnic Chinese with language and cultural skills, along with the perfect hacker skill sets needed for the task at hand."

Fung's blood pressure rose. **Where is this going?**

"You're the head of IC Cloud Red Team, which means you have management skills, and most important of all, you think like a hacker." Dahm laughed. "I sure as hell wouldn't want you coming after me!"

Now Fung's alarm bells were screaming.

"What are you proposing, exactly?"

"I want you to start your own China-focused cybersecurity company. Build it from the ground up. It will be your company, your vision, your baby, but tethered to CloudServe for protection and support."

"For what purpose? To hack the Chinese—or the U.S.?"

"Both, certainly. But legally. You'd be offering the Chinese and American governments a safe and secure way to check for vulnerabilities in any system anywhere. The money potential is limitless."

"I'm stunned. I don't know what to say."

Dahm sat back. "Look, let me be perfectly honest. If you went out and started your own company, which eventually you would, at some point we'd be going to war, and I'd do everything I could to destroy you—I'm speaking businesswise, of course. We're not actual killers, are we?" He smiled mischievously.

Fung's eyes widened. "I sure hope not."

"I prefer instead that we form an alliance, here and now. I want you to achieve your wildest dreams, but I want you to do it as my partner, not my competitor. What do you think?"

"It's a dream come true. I just don't know how to wrap my mind fully around it."

"Of course, with the CloudServe board and the SEC breathing down my neck, it's going to be up to you to raise the capital. It will take millions. But that won't be hard for you, will it?"

Again, Fung was confused, thrilled, and panicked. What was Dahm suggesting?

Fung was like CloudServe itself—fantastic cash flow but always on the verge of bankruptcy. If Dahm knew that, they wouldn't be having this conversation. Or would they? CHIBI knew all about it and played on his vulnerabilities. Was Dahm doing the same thing as CHIBI?

Wait. What? No. It couldn't be. Could it?

"I'm not exactly a venture capitalist myself, Elias. I'm not sure how I could be your point man for raising that kind of money."

"You helped start a couple of unicorns—yeah, they went belly-up, but they were good bets. I even had a little money on one of them. You just need to go back to the VC people that funded those projects with a virtual letter of intent from me, and raising the money shouldn't be a problem. What do you think?"

"I'm beyond flattered. Everything in me tells me to jump at this. Do you mind if I take twenty-four hours to give you an answer?"

"No, not at all," Dahm said. He stood and stretched his six-four athletic frame. "Are you ready for dessert?"

"Sure."

"Great. I'll be right back."

Dahm then disappeared into the house.

Fung was sipping his wine when Roberto suddenly appeared, ripped like a swimmer and wearing nothing but a Speedo and a smile.

"Roberto?" Fung was confused.

The tall Brazilian laid a familiar hand on Fung's shoulder. "I hope you're hungry, because I'm the dessert."

Fung set his wineglass down.

Roberto stepped toward the edge of the infinity pool just a few feet away.

"Care to join me?" He pulled off his swimsuit.

Fung leered at the marbled Adonis standing in front of him. His confusion melted into lust.

How could Dahm possibly know about Roberto, his favorite?

He couldn't, could he?

No.

But CHIBI could.

"Yeah. A swim sounds delicious."

67

ALEXANDRIA, VIRGINIA

Jack sat on his couch, staring into space, a half-finished beer warm in his hand. What had happened in the Baltic a few days ago still gripped him like a waking nightmare.

Lying on his back in the frigid sea, numb from the cold and exhausted, he had closed his eyes and surrendered to the sleep overwhelming him, knowing he'd never wake again in this life.

But here he was now, very much awake and alive. His nerves were frayed and his heart shattered. Rage, grief, and guilt were numbing him as badly as the Baltic had that night. Liliana's terrified face disappearing into the merciless gloom looped endlessly in his mind's eye. For a moment in the hospital bed at the Polish clinic, he imagined he really had died and the image repeating in his mind was his own personal Hell.

A knock on his front door broke the loop and got him off the couch.

"Hey, kid. Mind if I come in?"

John Clark stood in the doorway. Just slightly

taller than Jack but with a leaner frame, the former SEAL was his boss at The Campus and also a close friend. The seventy-something-year-old man still trained with the team he led, which explained why he looked twenty years younger than he actually was.

Jack's body language said **Go away.** He motioned him in with his bottle anyway.

"Yeah. Sure. Come in."

Clark saw the beer. "I'll have what you're having."

Jack shuffled toward the kitchen. He pulled a bottle out of the fridge and handed it to Clark.

Clark popped the top and clinked his bottle against Jack's bottle. "I heard you checked out fine on your physical." He took a swig.

"That's what the doctor said."

"You look good. Tired, maybe."

"Didn't sleep much last night. Otherwise, I'm good to go."

"You mind telling that to your old man? He called me today."

Jack's eyes narrowed. "I sent him a text."

"Not the same thing. In fact, your folks were hoping you'd stop by. They'd love to put their arms around your neck and see for themselves."

Jack headed back toward the front room and fell onto the couch. Clark took a chair and another swig of beer.

"It's one thing to not call your dad, but you really should call your mom. Trust me on this."

Jack shook his head, frustrated. *The President of the United States dispatched one of the finest warriors this country has ever produced just to get him to call his mommy?*

"They know I'm okay. I'm just not ready to talk." He looked Clark straight in the eye. "To anybody."

Clark ignored him. "I get it, kid. I read the report Lisanne put together. You're lucky to be alive."

Lisanne's debrief chilled Clark to the bone when he read it. Jack should be dead. If that Polish fisherman had repaired his motor ten minutes earlier and headed back to port, he would have missed Jack entirely. Covering him in blankets, the fisherman got Jack to a clinic on shore just in time. They pumped him with warm saline solution and got his body temperature back to normal before any permanent damage was sustained.

"You should be grateful to the Man Upstairs, Jack. Not sulking around the apartment feeling sorry for yourself."

Jack's jaw clenched. "You don't know what happened that night."

"Enlighten me."

"The only reason I'm alive isn't luck. It's the fact that the bastard knew I worked for Gerry Hendley."

"How'd they find out?"

"Liliana must have told them to save my life."

"It worked."

"But it didn't save hers."

"That's not on you. You did everything you could, including risking your own life to save hers."

"You don't understand—"

"The hell I don't."

During the war, Clark had been forced to stand by and watch a Vietnamese family get slaughtered one by one before he finally decided to act against his orders. He stopped the killing but got shot for the effort and nearly died.

"All you can do is give it your best effort. You can't control the outcome."

"She got caught trying to protect me."

"That was her job, and I'd say she did it well, judging by the fact you're sitting here breathing and feeling sorry for yourself."

"I should've kept her out of the op. Should've gone in all by myself without her knowing."

"So why didn't you?"

"She was a professional. I didn't really think there would be a problem. I liked working with her. And it was her case, too."

"Did you force her to go? Lie to her or bribe her or threaten her in any way to get her to go?"

"No, of course not."

"Then I don't see the problem. She was doing her job and you were doing yours. You know by now, kid, what we do ain't all sunshine and rainbows. And the worst damn enemy we ever face isn't out there, it's the guy staring back at you in the mirror every morning. You need to get a handle on this, Jack."

"She had a kid. A little boy. Tomasz."

The image of her screaming out his name as she sank into the gloom flashed across his mind again. He drowned it with a long pull of beer, draining the bottle.

"His dad was killed a few years back in Afghanistan, and now this. It's so damn unfair."

"I know it is. And I don't know how to sort it all out on this side of Heaven. That's why I let the priests handle all of that metaphysical stuff. I can't control what I can't control. And by the way, thanks to your call from that clinic, the boy and his grandmother are sequestered in a Polish safe house right now, so quit kicking yourself in the ass."

"Yeah. A phone call. Big hero."

"For what it's worth, your dad pulled a few strings. The Brits are sending over a deep-water submersible to the location that Polish fisherman gave us. He wasn't too specific, but with any luck, they might be able to find your friend and maybe even get her back to her family for a decent burial."

Jack darkened. "Yeah, that would be something, at least."

They sat in silence for a while. Clark watched Jack falling deeper into his hole.

"That guy you sent on a wild-goose chase? What was his name?"

"Goralski."

"Yeah. That's right. He wound up in Dusseldorf. They picked him up, but he didn't tell the cops anything. A high-dollar attorney bailed him out a few hours ago. They couldn't hold him for anything because he had all of his legal permits to do whatever it was he was doing, and apparently it's not against the law over there to tail somebody." He chuckled. "That was a pretty slick move you pulled on him, kid."

"What about Christopher Gage?"

"He was questioned, gently, because of his stepmom the senator. But he has an alibi for that night and he said he had no idea what was going on at the warehouse—he just leased it out. According to the embassy guys, he seemed genuinely surprised and upset to hear what happened to you and the girl. And unless he threatened you or you saw him at the warehouse or on that boat, there's nothing else to be done—innocent until proven guilty, right?"

"I know who's guilty."

"You mean the foreign legion paratrooper?"

"I'm gonna cut his fucking heart out."

"Gotta find him first."

"Can't be too hard. I was thinking about it on the flight over, even did a little research between naps. That tattoo I saw was Second Parachute Regiment of the French Foreign Legion. They have thirteen hundred enlisted officers and men at any given time. Can't be that many blond guys aged eighteen to thirty-five over the last seventeen years in an elite unit like that."

"That's a good start. I'll back your play, any way I can."

"I need Gavin to do his hack magic. Is he available yet?"

"Gerry told me that Gavin is back in the saddle starting tomorrow morning. I'll be sure he gets right on it."

Jack rose to fetch another beer. "You want another one?"

"Still working on this one."

Jack yanked open the refrigerator door. "They find the **Baltic Princess** yet?"

"Yeah. She's somewhere in the middle of the Gobi desert."

Jack frowned as he unscrewed the cap. "What are you talking about?"

"That ship spoofed itself. Our people did a search of her AIS signal but they must have turned it off, because she wasn't showing up on anybody's radar. But about an hour ago, the ship's signal popped up in the Gobi desert. Some joker must have pulled the box, put it on a plane, and then shipped it by camel out there just to shoot us a big middle finger."

"That's just great." Jack took a long pull of his beer, lost in thought.

Clark saw the wheels grinding behind the younger man's eyes. "So, what's the plan now?"

"I've got something I've got to do. I gotta prove to myself I can keep a promise and not fuck it up."

"Does Gerry know about this?"

"He knows I was planning on this trip before he sent me to Poland."

"When do you plan on leaving?"

"Tomorrow."

"How long will you be gone?"

"A day down. A day there at most. A day back. Three days, tops."

"You need any of us for backup?"

"No. This isn't an op. It's a favor for an old friend who died just two weeks ago. But I need to do it."

"So you'll do a friend a favor but you won't do the right thing by your mom?"

"I just can't talk about anything right now. I need to process it."

"Makes sense. But you can still call her and tell her you're okay and will see her in a few days."

Clark had a way of making a suggestion into an order without seeming to.

Besides, he was right, Jack admitted to himself.

He would call his mom, then finalize his trip plans. A visit to the "Parsonage"—his dad's name for the free public housing known as the White House—would have to wait until he settled his account with Cory and got his head screwed back on straight.

After that, he'd go hunting.

68

It was late. Ed was fast asleep, and Mary Pat Foley's raging headache only worsened as she reread Jesse Benson's report freshly arrived over the digital transom fifteen minutes earlier.

She took no comfort in the realization that her instincts were spot on, but it had taken a CIA supercomputer with AI analytical software to confirm her gut sense with hard data.

Benson's report took it one step further. He believed a fifth incident preceding the other four was part of the mix—the liquidation of a Chinese asset working in the quantum satellite program at Hefei.

The statistical analysis of the five attacks revealed a nearly imperceptible pattern. All five were connected to a single CIA comms satellite managed by the NRO. Access to this satellite was, in effect, access to the entire Western intelligence community—or at least, any communication that transmitted through this particular bird.

Equally disturbing was the company that put it into orbit: Elias Dahm's SpaceServe. Even more troubling was the fact that its parent company, CloudServe, had secured the satellite's connection to the IC Cloud. Clearly, they had dropped the ball.

But what to do about it?

The IC had moved all of its data and communications into the cloud in order to improve its cybersecurity. Now the cloud was proving to be the avenue of this particular security breach. Sounding the general alarm would put the entire IC Cloud program in jeopardy or, worse, put the IC itself into a general state of paralysis. The only way to prevent a flooding ship from sinking was to dog the doors between compartments in order to contain the damage to the smallest possible location and stop the flow of water.

The same would apply here. IC departments would want to lock down to prevent further data leakage, but that would defeat the purpose of the cloud—namely, to increase the flow of information throughout the community.

The other challenge was the lack of specific data. Benson's analysis had strongly suggested—but not proved—that the comms satellite was the common link and therefore the "leak" in the system. But who was accessing the satellite? How did they do it? How long had it been going on? Did others have access? Were other satellites at risk? Was the Cloud/SpaceServe connection a coincidence? Was the satellite breached or the cloud itself?

A hundred other questions flooded her mind, but without specifics there was nothing actionable. If there was a leak in the boat, they had to find its exact location and determine its size in order to plug it.

Foley needed more information, and the best person to provide it was the head of the IC Cloud security team, Amanda Watson. Watson had made a hell of an impression on Foley: a smart, patriotic young woman who was succeeding brilliantly in a largely male and progressive culture that wasn't exactly known for waving American flags. More to the point, Watson had designed much of the cloud software to begin with, and designed the IC Cloud security program. If anyone would be able to answer the questions she now had, it would be Amanda.

Foley shot an e-mail to her executive assistant to arrange an immediate and secure face-to-face with Ms. Watson ASAP.

69

ALEXANDRIA, VIRGINIA

Jack packed light.

It was going to be only three days and, worst-case scenario, he could wash his clothes in a river or something. Or, better yet, pull a Jack Reacher and just buy some cheap local stuff and not bother with doing any laundry.

The Uber driver, a polite and soft-spoken young Afghan immigrant named Mohammad—a former translator for the U.S. Army—picked him up in front of his apartment and headed for Dulles International in heavy rush-hour traffic. It was just after five.

Neither man noticed the battered blue Toyota Corolla following in the distance, nor the man driving it, an acne-scarred, ex–Pinkerton man by the name of Tyler. Hiding his bloodshot eyes behind a pair of Oakleys, Tyler was determined not to lose sight of Jack Ryan, Jr. He wanted to impress his new employer, Sandra Kyle, after losing

John Clark on a previous tail a few days back. Reassigned to Junior, this was his chance to prove his worth.

The Uber driver dropped Jack off with his carry-on backpack at arrival door 6 at Dulles International Airport and sped away. Tyler managed to snap a photo of Jack as well as the Uber license plate before pulling back into traffic.

Tyler texted his photos to Kyle before calling her. She rang back immediately.

He couldn't tell her what airline Jack was heading for or where he was going. Following Jack in wasn't an option unless Jack was planning on buying a ticket at the counter, which was highly unlikely. He would simply pass through ticketed security and disappear into one of the two insanely long Dulles terminal buildings, where nobody could follow without a ticket.

Since Ryan had only a single piece of carry-on luggage, he was no doubt grabbing a domestic flight taking off within the hour, if not two. Tyler agreed that this information didn't help narrow much of anything down. Several hundred flights were taking off in that two-hour window to all points of the compass connecting to the rest of the planet.

To prove his mettle, he requested and received permission to question the Afghan later that night, preferably in the man's home with a gun to his young wife's head. "Something a tribal man will understand," he assured her.

Kyle agreed, and promised to forward the Afghan's address within the hour.

In the meantime, the paunchy ex–Pinkerton man was feeling a powerful thirst. D.C. metro traffic was snarled at this time of day, but twenty minutes later he managed to shuffle into a busy strip-mall Irish pub he frequented.

Tyler climbed onto his favorite stool just as a shot glass of Jameson and a draft PBR were set on the bar in front of him. Two failed marriages cost him his house and wiped out his pension. At least the shitty per diem Kyle paid was in cash so he could avoid paying taxes and, more important, wage garnishments from his ex-wives' blood-sucking attorneys. A couple of trips to O'Hare's each week was his one solace, and the guy behind the bar—an ex-cop—charged him only half-price, thanks to some nasty PI photos of the man's wife he'd provided in a vicious custody battle.

The second round arrived as a dark-eyed Mexican about his age took the stool next to him. They nodded a silent greeting before the bartender asked, "What'll ya have?" The Mexican ordered a club soda.

Tyler fought back a grin as he tossed back the whiskey. What was the point of ordering a club soda? He chugged his beer and wiped the foam from his mouth with his hand, relishing the familiar burn in the back of his throat.

He pulled a ten from his wallet as he stood, tossing it onto the bar.

"Sit down." The Mexican was talking to his club soda.

Tyler couldn't believe his ears. "Excuse me?"

"You deaf? I said sit the hell down."

The Mexican turned to him. Ding Chavez was a half-head shorter than Tyler, but the soul-snatching eyes boring into him suggested the smaller man was not to be trifled with.

"I won't say it again."

Tyler wobbled uneasily in place, weighing the options in his booze-addled brain.

"You buying?"

"Sure."

The fat man sat and waved for another round for himself.

"What do you want to know?" Tyler asked.

"Why you're tailing people from Hendley Associates."

"What does it matter to you?"

"The shovel in the trunk of my car thinks it's important."

Tyler nearly shat himself. This sumbitch wasn't kidding. "I need to take a piss."

Ding took a sip of club soda. "Talk first, then piss."

"I really gotta piss."

"Then talk fast or piss yourself. I don't care which, but you ain't moving."

Tyler talked, his tongue loosened by two more rounds of boilermakers and the vision of ending the evening lying on his back in the cold ground with his face covered in freshly spaded earth.

WASHINGTON, D.C.

Amanda Watson's face paled like she was about to vomit.

Mary Pat Foley was on a secure, encrypted video chat line with the senior CloudServe executive in her San Francisco office.

"I don't know what to say, Madame Director."

"First of all, my friends call me Mary Pat." The DNI needed Watson to gather her wits and calm herself down. Foley could only imagine the guilt and embarrassment she must be feeling at the moment.

"Well, Mary Pat, if you hadn't sent me your analysis, my first response would have been to say it isn't possible. But the numbers are pretty damn convincing. It would be easy for me to pass this off as a satellite and hardware problem, but my instinct is that the report is onto something."

"You and me both. That's why I reached out to you. I think you see my dilemma. Without specifics, I can't find the bastard behind these leaks, let alone nail his scalp to the wall."

Watson leaned back in her chair, her eyes narrowing in thought.

"The reason why your report bugs me so much is that I thought I had discovered a problem with part of that very same satellite uplink code a few months ago. You know, we're always searching for vulnerabilities in our systems, and I put my best man on it. He said the vulnerability was there, but it was minimal and, to the best of his knowledge, had never been exploited. He patched it and we moved on."

"Is it possible he missed something—another vulnerability, perhaps?"

"No, we ran diagnostics up and down after he patched. It was bulletproof."

Foley sighed. The worst American spy scandals in history weren't perpetrated by foreign agents but by American traitors. Aldrich Ames was CIA, as Edward Snowden had been before he began working for an NSA private contractor. Robert Hanssen was FBI; Pollard and Walker were both Navy. It was as likely as not that this breach was an inside job as well. "I hate to ask, but do you trust your man on this?"

Watson frowned. "Funny you should ask. Larry Fung is one of the smartest guys I've ever worked with. Up until recently, I would have pounded the desk in his defense."

"What's changed your mind?"

Watson shook her head, obviously disgusted with herself.

"He's passed every in-house security audit and his TS clearance is active, so there's no reason to suspect him, right? But in my counterintel briefings I was told to watch for certain behavioral signs—and that whole MICE thing. The guy likes to play martyr, and he's bleeding cash, as near as I can tell."

"I thought you Silicon Valley types were all rolling in dough."

"We get paid very well, but not the kind of money you think—and between federal and state taxes, we lose almost half of that. The big payoff is in stock options, and Elias has been very generous with those for me and Larry in particular. The problem is, the way he guarantees the NDAs and noncompetes we sign is that he holds our stocks in escrow for five years after the last date of our employment."

"Is that legal?"

"Legal? Yes, but not ethical. Certainly effective. So Larry's gotta wait quite a while to cash in his CloudServe lottery ticket."

"Money is a powerful motivator. So are the other incentives: ideology, coercion, and ego."

"That's why I started nosing around a little a few days ago. Never found anything, and never caught him doing something he shouldn't be doing. But then again, he's so damn smart he could hide his tracks, and he would, wouldn't he, if he were up to no good? I know the man. He's careful, methodical, and precise."

"You almost sound as if you're saying the fact you couldn't find any evidence against him is the best proof he's guilty."

"I know, it's ridiculous, and that's why I ultimately dismissed my concerns out of hand. But the coincidence between your report and the fact he worked on this very problem sent chills down my spine. And in that nosing around I told you about, I discovered that my computer had been searching the NRO workstation you identified in your report. The problem is, I never accessed that workstation. I checked the date and time in question and thought I was losing my mind until I pulled up my Uber receipt for that night. Bottom line is someone accessed my computer to check out the NRO workstation without my knowledge."

"And you suspect Fung?"

"Your report practically confirms it. He was the last person in the office after me that night. If I didn't know any better, it's almost as if he wanted to leave my digital fingerprints on that machine to point at me if some problem were ever discovered."

"Isn't your computer biometrically passcoded?"

"Yes, but the Red Team has developed a device called PassPrint to overcome that kind of security and—"

Watson shut her eyes. "I'm such an idiot."

"What?"

"Larry was the point person heading that up."

"How do you want to proceed?"

"Let me start by first rechecking the satellite software all over again and running a new diagnostic. I think it's important we find tangible evidence that this really is a problem. Not taking anything away from your people, but correlation isn't proof. I'd like to nail that down, and if I can do that, it might yield more clues."

"How long? Time is not our friend here."

"I can have something to you by EOB today at the latest."

"Good. While you're banging away on that, I'll have some of my people begin a discreet inquiry into Mr. Fung."

"Yes, please do, and **discreet** is the operative word. He's innocent until proven guilty, and if we're wrong about him and he finds out what we're doing, he'll be outraged and I'll lose one of my best people for no good reason. Worse, he'd blab about this thing all over town just to ruin our reputation. Maybe even sue us."

"I understand completely. We'll keep everything under wraps. I look forward to hearing from you by end of business today."

"Will do. And please keep me posted on anything you find out about Larry."

"You have my word on that," Foley promised.

The video call ended and Mary Pat texted the director of the NSA's counterintel outfit, referred to in the media as the Q Group, requesting assistance on the Fung matter.

CHIBI read the text exchanges between Foley and Q Group a few hours later, highly amused.

70

CIELO SANTO, PERU

The overnight flight from Dulles to Jorge Chávez in Lima was the fastest Jack could find, but it still had a layover in Dallas. His only luggage was a carry-on Osprey Farpoint 40 backpack toting the bare essentials.

Arriving a little after five in the morning, he splashed his face with cold water in the men's restroom after he deplaned. He grabbed a venti drip, dark roast, no-room Starbucks coffee, waiting until seven before boarding a one-hour puddle jumper to the regional airstrip near Anta in Carhuaz Province north of Lima.

In the colorful and scrupulously clean little town of a few thousand, Jack found the store he'd located on the Internet, where he purchased a flimsy but serviceable folding knife and a disposable lighter, two items he couldn't carry on a plane. They were already over eight thousand feet, the air cooling considerably from Lima's. A snowcapped peak loomed in the distance beyond the low hills surrounding the town.

From Anta he caught a brightly painted GMC school bus that made the long and winding climb high into the Andes. The bus was crowded with locals, mostly working-class men, to judge from their callused hands, worn clothes, and meager belongings. Short-statured, with dark, almond-shaped eyes and sharp, broad noses, the indigenous Quechua rode shoulder to shoulder in grim silence. The man next to Jack on the bench seat sat silent as a stone the entire trip, staring wordlessly out of the windows. Jack didn't mind. He didn't feel like talking anyway.

Two hours into the four-hour trip, the blue skies darkened and rain fell like Noah's flood. The unexpected torrent surprised Jack; this wasn't the rainy season, according to his brief weather research. This far south of the equator, the weather was flipped from Virginia's. It was supposed to be approaching Peruvian summer, but the chill air suggested the mountains hadn't checked their calendars yet.

The steepening climb slowed the straining engine, and the bus rumbled through the mud and rocks washing over the pavement. The wipers slapped furiously at the sheets of water blinding the windshield, and the low clouds shrouded the stunning beauty of the Andes.

Just after noon, the bus screeched to a halt at its terminus in Cielo Santo, Jack's destination. The driver killed the noisy V-8. No one spoke.

Jack stood a head and a half taller than the men in front of and behind him, the rain drumming the roof just inches above his ball cap. He pulled on his disposable emergency poncho and followed the others into the storm as they shuffled off the bus and into one of Dante's circles of Hell.

Cielo Santo wasn't on any map Jack could find, but Cory told him he wouldn't. Originally, it was a quaint, alpine village nestled at the foot and midway between the looming twin peaks of La Hermana Alta and El Hermano Gordo. It stood approximately thirteen thousand feet above the Pacific Ocean, which was less than a hundred miles to the west, typical of Peru's dramatic topography.

According to Cory, a gold rush in the forties had exploded the population to a few thousand and expanded the number of buildings to include at least one hotel, La Vicuña Roja. When the gold ran out in the sixties and the government made further mining in the region illegal in the nineties, the miners left but the adventure tourists came, including Cory's father, who had climbed La Hermana as a young man.

Standing beneath the thundering steel roof at the bus terminal—a gas station—Jack surveyed the rain-soaked gloom around him. Unlike the clean and neatly ordered villages like Anta he'd seen previously, Cielo Santo was the Peruvian version of Deadwood.

The street he surveyed was lined by rusted, faded, and crumbling two- and three-story buildings, with skeins of improvised power lines webbing the sky overhead. The rain hadn't quite washed away the stench of diesel where he stood, or the garbage and urine from an alley behind him.

Dozens of dark-faced Quechua in ponchos and rain gear stood in knots beneath leaking awnings or hustled up and down the muddy, trash-strewn street. Others wore construction helmets and heavy rubber boots, carrying tools or plastic buckets, like miners. Jack had read that with the economy tanking, desperate Peruvians—mostly Quechua and mestizos—engaged in illegal mining operations that had popped up all over the Andes, rummaging through the tailings or attempting to revive abandoned gold and silver mines like the ones in the mountains above the town.

Cory's instructions told Jack where to find La Vicuña Roja, the hotel-bar where his father had stayed decades before. Cory had written everything down for Jack, but the tone in his deathbed voice carried the weight of the unfulfilled promise he had made to his father to climb La Hermana together. The two of them had hiked a dozen mountains together in America before his father died when Cory was still in college. His tragic death had cut short their plans to travel to

Peru together for a trekking adventure, including La Hermana near Cielo Santo, where his dad lived for a time.

Jack touched the hollow wooden amulet hanging around his neck for the thousandth time, an unconscious check to make sure Cory's ashes were still in place, but also to connect once again with his dead friend. Jack also carried a faded Polaroid of Cory's dad standing on the peak. Jack's mission was to carry the picture, along with a small portion of Cory's ashes, to the top of La Hermana and scatter them so that Cory could keep his promise to his father to one day climb it together, and then to bury the photo on the spot where his dad had stood.

Jack's promise was to keep Cory's promise to his father, and he was determined to keep it no matter what.

Cory estimated Jack could make the trek up the steep incline in five hours, most of it walking a rugged trail with the last hundred meters being an easy hand climb over granite boulders.

The plan was to hit the trail by one o'clock and arrive at the peak just as the sun was setting, then make his way back down with a flashlight and grab the noon bus back to Anta the next day, reversing his trip and winding up back in D.C. by three p.m. the day after tomorrow.

It was a good plan.

Until the rain killed it.

71

Jack worked his way from the gas station toward the hotel, past makeshift shanties of plastic and tin, splashing in puddles and stepping over a few drunks passed out in the alleys. There weren't any sidewalks in the shitty Shangri-La.

The Vicuña Roja sign showed just that—a hand-painted red animal that looked a lot like a llama, its larger, domesticated cousin. Jack's original schedule precluded a visit here, but with the rain knocking down his plans for the day, he figured it might be the only place in town to find a room for the night. He headed inside. Heavy chopper blades beat the air in the distance.

The hotel's first floor was a run-down little bar, dark and depressing, and stinking of cigar smoke. Waylon Jennings twanged on the jukebox speakers. Dusty trophies of stuffed rainbow trout, geese, and ducks hung on the smoke-stained walls.

The Anglo man behind the bar was leaning on the counter, fixated on a newspaper and nursing a whiskey. A cigar smoldered in an ashtray near his elbow.

Jack had shaken off as much rain as he could outside, but he was still dripping onto the faded vinyl flooring.

A mestizo woman with bad makeup, a too-small dress, and the figure of a Christmas ham sat in the back corner with a brooding Quechua man seated next to her, his arms folded across his round belly, staring bleary-eyed at the wall. Tall bottles of Peruvian beer stood on the table in front of them. She flashed Jack a propositional smile through heavy red lipstick, but he declined with his own polite smile and a slight shake of his head.

Another patron in a cheap suit and cowboy boots was passed out in the other corner, snoring on his folded arms. A half-empty bottle of sweet, clear pisco sat on the table near his head.

Jack approached the barkeep, still bent over his newspaper. His long dark hair and beard were shot through with gray. He closed the paper and rose up, his keen brown eyes drawing a quick assessment.

"American?" It wasn't really a question.

"That obvious, eh?" Jack extended his hand. "Name's Jack."

"Sands." They shook. A firm grip. He was an inch taller than Jack and leaner, but not in a good way. The crow's-feet around his eyes were deeper than they should have been. Busted capillaries around his nose and rosacea on his forehead told the rest of the story. Sands was an alcoholic.

"Where you from, Jack?"

"Virginia." Jack avoided references to D.C. whenever possible, especially with strangers.

"Whereabouts in Virginia?"

"Alexandria."

"Never been. So what the hell brings you to this shithole corner of the world?"

"You talking about the bar or the town?"

Despite the alcoholism, Sands looked like he could still handle himself in a fight. But Jack was beyond caring what anybody thought about him.

Luckily, Sands laughed. "Same difference." He eyed Jack again. "Nobody ever comes here unless they got a story."

"Maybe so." Jack's eyes narrowed. There was something weighing on Sands like a lead blanket. "But the people who **stay** here have got the best ones."

That earned Jack a begrudging smile. His eyes searched Jack's for a moment, but for what, Jack couldn't tell.

"Pull up a stool. I've got cold beer and warm whiskey and all the time in the world. What's your poison?"

Jack normally didn't drink this early, but he was angry and depressed at the prospect of the climb delayed.

"Beer."

"Dark or light?"

"Wet."

"Coming right up, pardner."

Sands reached down and pulled a beer out of the ice and popped the top as Jack grabbed a stool.

The distant helicopter now roared overhead, its staccato thunder hammering the air and rattling windows. It passed by quickly.

"What the hell was that?"

"A Halo," Sands said. "Big Russian bird. Mi-26. A real heavy hauler."

"What's it doing up here?"

"Haulin' heavy shit would be my guess."

"For who?"

"Whoever needs heavy shit."

Jack started to push back but decided he really didn't care.

"I think I'm gonna need a room."

"Hourly or nightly?"

"Nightly. You got one?"

Sands set the Cusqueña Dorada in front of Jack. "Depends. You got cash?"

"Yeah."

Sands grinned, flashing tobacco-stained teeth. "Then I've got a room. How long are you staying?"

"Depends on the rain."

"Supposed to stop tonight."

Jack did a quick calculation. If he could hike tomorrow, he could pull out on the noon bus the day after. His return ticket out of Lima was open-ended. He just needed to change the reservation.

"Two nights."

"That'll be . . . fifty, American."

"Each night?"

"Total."

Jack lifted his beer. "Deal."

Sands clinked his whiskey glass against the bottle. **"Skol."**

Jack took a long pull as Sands tossed his off in a single slug.

"Carlita back in the corner will take care of you right nice, but you gotta pay her husband five dollars American if you want a throw."

"I'm good, thanks."

As Sands poured himself another, he asked, "So, what's your story, Jack?"

"No big deal. I'm heading up to La Hermana to scatter the ashes of a friend."

"Must have been some friend to come all the way out to this dump."

Jack snorted. "Yeah, well, he didn't quite describe the town like this. I guess back in the day it was a nice little part of the world."

"It was as pretty as a postcard until five years ago. Illegal gold mining on El Gordo is what brought the shitstains you see around here now. Poor bastards go swarming down into the mine like carpenter ants. No training, no gear, except maybe a helmet and a hand pick. If they're lucky they'll scrape out a few ounces in a week or two, but most of them aren't that lucky. The few that do get lucky are as likely to get a shiv between the ribs topside by a desperado too lazy or scared to brave the tunnels."

"Why don't the authorities stop it?"

"People busy digging for gold are too tired to riot and too distracted to start a revolution." He took a sip of whiskey.

"Too bad. It's beautiful country around here."

"I used to run a little tour-guide service back in the day. There's a lake that had the most gorgeous trout you've ever seen, but the mercury and other chemicals leaching into the water killed them off. I haven't seen a tourist here in years, especially an American one. Kinda nice to hear a familiar accent."

Jack's eyes darted around the bar. He spotted a shot glass on a shelf behind Sands. It bore a familiar crest and a motto.

"**Sua sponte,**'" Jack said. "'Of their own accord.'"

Sands frowned, surprised. "You were in the Seventy-fifth?"

"Me? No. I did my tour of duty in expensive private schools with Jesuits beating Latin into us like we were rented mules."

That earned another chuckle from Sands.

"But **you** were a Ranger," Jack said.

Sands's eyes narrowed. "Why do you say that?"

"Because you don't look like a Shriner." Jack nodded toward the shot glass.

"HUA," Sands said. He eyed Jack again. "You weren't in the Rangers, but you look like you served."

"No, but I have friends who did, and my dad was a Marine. Where were you deployed?"

"Wherever they fuckin' sent me." Sands's face clouded over, lost in a memory.

"I've got a friend who's a retired Ranger. A real stand-up dude by the name of Bartowski."

"Midas Bartowski?" Sands asked, incredulous.

Jack smiled, equally surprised. "Yeah."

Sands ran a hand through his long hair. "Man, that young hoss pulled my bacon out of the fire more than once. How the hell is he?"

"Tough as ever, like every other Ranger I ever met."

Well, except maybe you, Jack thought. He finished his beer.

Sands turned around and grabbed the Ranger shot glass from the shelf, wiped it out with a bar rag, and splashed whiskey into it. He pushed it over to Jack and lifted his own glass.

"To Midas."

"To Midas."

They tapped glasses and tossed back their whiskeys.

"Next time you see him, tell him . . ." Sands's eyes glassed over.

"Tell him what?"

"Nothin'. Not a goddamn thing."

Sands poured himself another one and downed it in one throw, slamming the shot glass back onto the bar, his mind lost in another time.

The beer and whiskey were hitting Jack pretty good on his empty stomach. Maybe it was the booze that made him sorry as hell for the broken-down Ranger standing in front of him. Something was eating Sands alive besides the liquor he was using to try and drown it. Some kind of sleepless guilt, Jack suspected, judging by the rings around his large, sad eyes.

A chill ran down Jack's spine. For a fleeting moment, he wondered if he was staring in a mirror at his future self.

"Another whiskey," Jack said.

Sands snapped out of his stupor and poured him another one, then refilled his glass.

"So, I told you my story. What's yours?" Jack asked.

"You didn't tell me shit. Besides, the law of bartenders is sacrosanct. We listen, we don't talk." Sands tossed back his whiskey.

Jack glanced around the bar. "So, if tourism business is bad, why are you still hanging around this place?"

Sands shrugged. "Where else would I go? I ain't

got no people. Besides, one place is the same as another."

Which was another way of saying you can't run away from yourself, Jack thought.

Sands added, "Besides, I own the place, and a man's place is his castle."

"What'd you pay for it?"

"I won it in a poker game a while back." Sands grinned. "Or maybe I lost."

"So, a tour guide. That's what brought you here originally?" Jack asked, putting the glass to his mouth.

Sands darkened for a moment, then gathered himself. "Something like that."

"If you were a tour guide, maybe you have a map I can look at? I need to find the trailhead for La Hermana."

"Sorry, pal. That mountain is closed. Rock slides and bad chemicals from the mining up there. Dangerous as hell."

"I'll take my chances."

"No, you won't. There's no way up. Trust me, your friend won't know the difference if you scatter him on some other hill around here."

"He won't, but I will." Jack finished off his whiskey.

Sands's eyes flashed grudging approval. But then he said, "Farts are like promises. Everybody makes 'em but nobody can keep 'em."

Jack stiffened. "Not in my family."

"Look, Jack. I got an old four by four Jeep Willys out back that runs like a top. There's a mountain about ten klicks from here that'll knock your socks off and your friend will love it. I'll run you up there tomorrow."

"Thanks, but I'll pass."

"Seriously, kid. There's evil shit up on Hermana that you don't want any part of. I'm telling you, stay the hell away."

Jack stretched and yawned. He was stiff from sitting way too long on the bus ride up and now on a barstool. He needed to get up and move around a little. "What do I owe you for the beer and whiskey?"

"That round was on the house. Otherwise, beer's a buck and whiskey shots are two, American."

"Thanks."

"Give me thirty minutes and I'll get that room ready for you. There's a not-too-shitty place to eat around the corner if you're hungry. The guinea pig is outstanding if you're into grilled rodents. Me, I prefer the **bisteca con huevos**."

The drunk at the table suddenly roared a Spanish obscenity, rising up out of a nightmare, swinging his arms in an imaginary fight. His balled fist knocked the pisco bottle to the floor, shattering it, startling the hooker and her pimp husband.

"Ah, fuck me," Sands growled, marching out

from behind the bar, towel in hand. He swore a blue streak in Spanish as he approached the man, who was protesting his drunken innocence.

Jack took that as his cue to step outside for a breath of fresh air and to clear his head.

72

WASHINGTON, D.C.

Gerry Hendley hadn't served as a U.S. senator for nearly two decades, but he was still a legend on the Hill. His close friendship with President Ryan also gave him the kind of influence and respect that everyone in the swamp craved but seldom achieved.

Hendley's own impeccable credentials as an honest political broker and his legitimately acquired wealth in the cutthroat world of finance proved his judgment and worth as an ally, especially in a presidential race, which was why Senator Dixon readily agreed to meet with him in her office on short notice.

"Gerry, it's so good to see you," Dixon said, coming out from behind her desk as her assistant shut the door behind him. She extended her hand and Gerry took it in both of his. He squeezed gently. His smile faded.

"Something wrong?" Dixon asked.

"Sandra Kyle. Tell me about her."

"An old friend. Ex–Capitol Police. She owns a gun range I frequent."

"Why is she having my people followed?"

"How should I know?"

"Because you're the one who arranged it." He released her. She stepped back, heading for the comfort of her desk.

"I don't know what the hell you're talking about."

"A man named Tyler works for her, and he was tailing Jack. Tyler told a friend of mine that he was under orders from Kyle, and that Kyle had suggested she was working with someone 'very powerful' in D.C."

"That could be a lot of people," Dixon said, sitting behind her desk. "That could even be you."

"But it wasn't me, was it? What's going on?"

"Honestly, I don't know. Sandra is someone I use every now and then to do a little opposition research. Showing a potential opponent pictures of him screwing his Jamaican au pair has an amazing effect on his campaign plans. C'mon, Gerry. You know how the game is played."

"What does that have to do with Jack Junior? He's not running for anything."

"Like I said, I'm not sure. Something must have led her in that direction."

Gerry glanced around the office. All of the typical photos, plaques, and honorifics hung on her walls, much like they had in his office years ago. "I love the game, Deb, just as much as you do.

Sometimes I even miss it. It might shock you to know that I think you have the potential to be a very effective President."

Gerry came and sat on the corner of her desk and leaned over. "I can help you, Deb, or I can break you. And so help me God, if you do anything to hurt Jack Junior in any way, shape, or form, I will break you so badly you will wish you had never been born."

"Is that a threat from you or President Ryan?"

Gerry stood. "He doesn't know I'm here. But you sure as hell do. If you can find any dirt on President Ryan, go for it. All's fair in politics. But you don't touch a man's family, especially his kids."

The pathos in Gerry's voice struck a chord in her childless heart. The man had lost his entire family, and she knew he considered the Ryans as his own now.

Dixon lifted her phone receiver. "I'll call Kyle immediately and get her to stand down."

"You do that."

Gerry's face suddenly took a pleasant turn, affecting the down-home smile of a country politician.

"And good luck on your campaign, Senator. I'll be watching."

CIELO SANTO, PERU

Jack stood beneath the covered awning in front of La Vicuña Roja, his pack slung over his shoulders, listening to the rain pounding the sheet metal and watching the rivers of mud and human misery wash past. Sands's cursing had ended when he hauled the drunk by the elbow out of the front door and pointed him down the street. The man thanked Sands in Spanish and wobbled away toward home on uneasy legs.

"The mayor of our fair city," Sands muttered as he headed back inside. "Poor bastard."

Jack decided to check out the town a little bit more, not bothering to dash between awnings to avoid the rain. He didn't give a shit if he got wet. He was already battling a blinding depression from Liliana's death, but Sands's warnings to stay off the mountain had infuriated him.

The rest of the street was a series of small shops, crowded tenements, and improvised housing. An endless stream of bedraggled miners and their women shuffled through the muddy street. Drunks and addicts clustered in knots in the alleyways, either standing in the rain or lying beneath plastic sheeting hung from ropes strung between buildings. The stench of human waste and burnt wood and old cooking grease dogged his steps. Whatever beauty or charm this place ever had was swallowed up by the hopeless desperation of grinding poverty. His already bad mood worsened. He decided to turn around.

As he approached the front of Sands's bar again, an unmarked bus rumbled to a stop at the gas station. The door clunked open and a bearded Hispanic male descended. He glanced up and down the street. He and Jack locked eyes for a moment, then the man turned away, heading for a fuel pump.

Suddenly, a teenage Quechua boy leaped out of the bus door and sprinted toward Jack, his young face a mask of terror.

The man at the pump shouted **"¡Alto!"** at the boy as he pulled a pistol from beneath his raincoat.

Jack started to bolt toward the terrified kid, but a strong hand grabbed him by the shoulder and spun him around—

"Stay the hell out of this," Sands growled.

"But that kid—"

A gunshot cracked behind them.

Jack whipped around just in time to see the teenager skid to a halt in the mud, his trembling hands held high. The man who fired the pistol in the air grabbed him by the scruff of the neck and hauled him back toward the bus.

"This is bullshit—" Jack said, shaking Sands off.

But Sands grabbed him again with both hands and pulled him close.

"Getting yourself shot ain't gonna help that kid

or nobody else on that bus or your friend there hanging around your neck! You fuckin' feel me?"

Jack wanted to throw a punch at Sands to put him on his ass and go after the kid, but Clark's voice in the back of his head told him to stand down.

Another man with a short-barreled carbine stood in front of the bus now as the other man with the pistol dragged the kid up the stairs.

Sands released his grip. Jack's eyes raged at the former Ranger.

"You want to tell me what that's all about?"

"Go get something to eat and bed down for the night, then head back home tomorrow. There's nothing here for you except misery and maybe a bullet in the back of your skull."

73

Jack begrudgingly took Sands's advice to grab some grub and headed for the restaurant he'd recommended. It was in the best part of town, which wasn't saying much. But the place was clean and the steak and eggs were good—better than he'd hoped for, actually—but he couldn't take his mind off his troubles or the hellscape outside. Whatever was going on in that bus with that kid wasn't good, but there wasn't anything he could do about it at the moment.

He thought about calling the American embassy on his cell phone, but besides the fact that he couldn't get a cell signal up here, what could he say? "I saw a guy grab a kid and threaten him with a pistol?"

He had nothing to offer by way of clues or evidence or even a license plate number. And what could the State Department do anyway? This place was clearly beyond the reach of the local authorities. Maybe when he got back to Lima he could figure something out.

He felt like shit even thinking that, but he really

was out of options. That poor kid was scared out of his mind, but for all Jack knew, he was a criminal being transported on a police bus.

Maybe Sands was right after all.

"You loser," he muttered to himself as he dropped the fork onto his plate. He'd failed Liliana, and he'd failed that kid.

Nothing he could do about any of it. Yeah. He got that.

But they were just as screwed.

Jack headed back to the bar. The rain had slowed to a fine, watery mist. With any luck, it would stop soon.

Self-flagellation worked up a thirst in any man, especially one who thought he had the blood of innocents on his hands. He shook off the rain and stepped inside.

The same fat mestizo woman smiled at him again, her eyes hopeful and despairing all at once, but Jack ignored her. Her male companion was gone.

Jack changed his mind.

He approached her table. Her face brightened with surprise. Jack pulled out his wallet and tossed her a one-hundred-**soles** bill. She stood eagerly to service the big American in a room upstairs, but Jack waved her back down. "Take the night off, honey. On me."

She didn't understand a word. Confused, she

glanced over at Sands behind the bar, his nose in a paperback. He shook his head in disbelief and muttered something in Quechua. She snatched up the money with a frown and stormed past Jack and out into the cool, damp night, angry or grateful, he couldn't be sure.

Maybe both.

Shit. He couldn't do anything right.

He ambled over to the bar and perched on a stool. He and Sands were the only two people in the joint.

"Beer or whiskey?" Sands asked, setting the book down. Steinbeck's **Travels with Charley**. A poodle and a pickup truck.

"Both."

Sands smiled. "Good choice."

Sands pulled bottles and glasses, and the two of them drank and talked about the finer points of football, landing on the Super Bowl prospects for Jack's Redskins and Sands's Chicago Bears. From football they turned to baseball, and as the booze kicked in, they took a sudden swerve into Steinbeck—the book was still on the bar—and then Hemingway, and somehow they landed on the Lake Poets, especially Wordsworth.

Then the conversation died, and the two men sat in a silent, shared grief for sins neither man confessed, mirrored images of each other—the past on one side, the future on the other.

A couple rounds later, two men pushed their way into the bar. They had the rolling gait and

easy confidence of men who knew their way
around trouble. One of them was the bearded
man with the pistol from the bus. The other was
taller, but Jack didn't recognize him.

As they took their stools on the other end of
the bar, both men greeted Sands with a silent nod.
Jack saw pistols in their OWB holsters.

"**¿Qué quieren beber?**" Sands asked.

"**Cerveza,**" the shorter man said.

"Coming right up."

Sands opened two bottles of beer and set them
in front of his armed customers. He didn't move.
The three men locked eyes. Finally, the taller man
glanced over at Jack and gave him the once-over,
then turned back to Sands. Sands leaned on the
bar close to the two men and whispered something in Spanish Jack couldn't hear.

Sands stood erect again, then came back over
to Jack.

"Another round?"

Jack lowered his voice. "That was the guy at the
bus this afternoon."

Sands leaned on his elbows, his reddened nose
inches from Jack's face, stale alcohol on his breath.

"You didn't see shit, and you don't know shit,
and you're not gonna try any shit. Understood?"

Jack started to turn toward the other two men.
Sands laid a firm hand on Jack's forearm.

"What would Midas tell you to do, right here,
right now?"

Jack stiffened, but Sands's grip tightened. "Jack, listen. You got no weapon; they do. These are two rough hombres not to be fucked with. Trust me on this."

Jack was drunk, but not so badly that he couldn't read the writing on the wall. He nodded curtly, hot shame burning his neck.

The two men stood. The shorter man tossed coins onto the bar and waved a hand over his head as if to say **Adiós**, and the two of them disappeared into the night.

"What the hell was that all about?"

"A friendly warning to get out of town. I suggest you take it."

Yeah, a friendly warning. But from them or you? Jack wondered.

The three men obviously knew one another. For all Jack knew, Sands had called them in while he was at the restaurant.

"I'm leaving tomorrow." Jack stood and reached for his wallet. His head spun. He wanted to puke, but not from the booze.

"Forget it, kid. I'll put it on your tab and we'll settle up before you get on the bus. Better yet, let me run you down the hill in my Jeep. I'm heading that way for a resupply anyway."

"I'll take the bus. Where's my room?" Jack picked up his pack, woozy and exhausted.

"Follow me."

74

Fung had accepted Dahm's offer, of course. The chance to build his own empire proved irresistible.

He stood framed in the large picture window of his condo overlooking the bay. Men younger and less talented than himself were billionaires already. Why couldn't he achieve the same heights? Indeed, why **shouldn't** he?

Perhaps then his father would finally approve of him.

His private cell phone broke the reverie. An unknown number. A call, not a text. His tingling spine told him who it was.

"Yes?"

An electronically altered voice answered, male and alien. "This is CHIBI. Lawrence, we have a problem."

Fung's heart sank. "Oh, God."

It could be only one thing.

"I have reason to believe you have been discovered. We need to take action immediately."

Fung trembled. He'd feared this day for months.

He tried to calm himself and clear his mind. He'd made plans for just such an occasion, hadn't he?

Time to put it into action. Fake passport, the Cayman accounts, a bug-out bag with important papers, gold coins—

"Are you listening to me, Lawrence?"

"How close are they to closing the net?"

"Twenty-four hours at most. For all I know, they are on the way over to your place right now."

Fung's doorbell rang. He nearly jumped out of his skin.

"They're here!"

"No. I took the liberty of sending over my very best agent. Let her in and follow her instructions to the letter."

"You're bringing me to the Chinese embassy, right? I'd be safe there."

"Federal agents are already there waiting for you."

"Oh, no, no, no."

"Do not worry. I anticipated all of this. I have a plan. But you must trust me."

Fung's lightning-fast brain made a calculation—

another scenario he'd played out if things went sideways. He could testify against CHIBI if he confessed his crimes, even show the government how to defend against men like him. They'd be lenient. Hell, they'd pay him good money to save them billions from cybercrime.

The doorbell rang again.

"Lawrence, now is not the time to improvise. Either let me help you now or face the consequences."

"How can I be sure you're not just trying to protect yourself?"

"Lawrence, how can you say that? You are my most important asset and I would never want to lose you. But you are also my friend. You can trust me."

"I just don't know what to do."

"Think about your parents. Think about Torré. How can you help them if you are hanged for treason?"

"Oh, jeez . . ."

Fung took a slow, deep breath. CHIBI was right. Getting arrested would shame his parents, and poor Torré would be utterly lost without him. CHIBI was his best option. His only option.

He headed for the door.

"I'm opening it now."

"Excellent. Soon your worries will be all over."

Fung yanked the door open.

A young Chinese woman in dark glasses and

a smart suit stood in the doorway, carrying a leather laptop bag and an aluminum attaché case in leather-gloved hands.

"Do exactly as she says," CHIBI said.

"I will."

He did.

CIELO SANTO, PERU

Jack slept like the dead in the broken-down hotel bed, anesthetized by copious quantities of Sands's cheap whiskey and beer.

He dreamed he was falling, until his face smashed against the floor. The sharp pain woke him just in time to feel a boot crash into his ribs. He grunted with the kick and doubled up instinctively. A second kick to the gut drove him to reach out to snag the other foot planted near his face. A sharp blow to his cheek by a heavy fist stopped him short, followed by two other hands pressing his shoulders against the floor and a cloth shoved onto his face until the sharp, sweet acetone smell in his sinuses brought on the dark.

75

Jack forced his eyes open.

His face was smashed against the filthy hotel carpet, head throbbing, ribs stabbing him with every breath. His mind was fogged with whatever had knocked him out.

He climbed to his unsteady feet and sat on the creaky bed. Harsh sunlight kept him blinking, but he could see that his room had been trashed.

What time is it?

He reached for his watch on the near nightstand. It wasn't there. Neither was his phone—he checked his pockets. **Shit.**

He stood and scanned the room for his backpack. He didn't see it.

He flung the closet doors open. Only old wire hangers and someone's abandoned shirt.

He dropped down on his knees and checked under the bed. Nothing.

He ran to the bathroom. Not there, either.

Gone.

Damn! Everything was in it.

He glanced down at his stocking feet.

The bastards even stole my hiking boots.

He felt for his wallet.

Gone.

Panicked, he clutched at his throat for Cory's ashes.

Gone!

Rage and nausea flooded him. He grunted through clenched teeth.

Motherfuckers!

The rage turned inward.

Sucker-punched him in the gut.

He had screwed it all up.

Again.

Jack dashed over to the cigarette-burned night-stand on the far side of the bed. An ancient clock with flip numbers read 11:35 a.m. The bus back to Anta would be arriving at any minute.

But what caught his eye was his passport and return bus ticket lying next to the clock.

Message received.

Yankee, go home.

A crumpled ball lay next to the passport. Jack knew what it was before he even opened it. He tried to smooth out the picture of Cory's dad standing on the top of La Hermana Alta, but it was ruined.

He shoved the wrinkled Polaroid into his pants pocket and stumbled toward the tiny bathroom with its filthy tiles and rusted sink to splash water on his aching face. A clouded, cracked mirror revealed a black eye above a swollen cheek and a fat, split lip, which explained the coppery taste of blood in his mouth.

Jack buried his face in his cupped hands and let the cold water cleanse his skin and clear his mind. Then cupped his hands again and drank until he slaked his searing thirst. He dried his face with a paper-thin towel and smoothed out his matted hair. His bladder ached. He pissed and washed his hands, then rinsed out his mouth with tap water, since his toothbrush had been stolen along with everything else.

His stocking feet were wet from the sink water splashed on the floor. How in the hell was he supposed to get around without any shoes, let alone any money?

He snatched his passport and bus ticket from the nightstand and pulled open the front door. He glanced up and down the hallway—a half-dozen rooms on either side, and a door at the far end. Probably a maid's closet.

Jack darted as quietly as he could on the stained hallway carpet and flung the door open. It was a closet, for sure. Stacked with towels, tiny wrapped soaps, and 200-grit toilet paper. But there was also a broom, a bucket, a mop, rags, and an old-fashioned push sweeper. He kept rifling around, hoping beyond hope.

There.

A pair of old, battered brown wingtips. He blew the dust off them and raced back to his room, where he fell on the bed and pulled the shoes on over his wet socks. They pinched his feet, but beggars can't be choosers, he reminded himself. He loosened the laces as far as he could and tied them. That would have to do.

That's when he realized they had even stolen his jacket.

The numbers on the old digital clock flopped over with a mechanical click.

Time to go.

Jack came down the one flight of stairs and into the empty bar. Sands wasn't there.

Of course not.

Damn snitch. Worthless drunk.

Sore as hell from the beating and queasy from the booze, Jack stepped out into the light. The sky was cloudy and the air was cool.

At least it wasn't raining.

The bus from Anta came rolling up into town just then, its groaning engine and crunching leaf springs inching toward the gas station. Another busload of miners. He headed that way.

By the time he got there, the passengers had unloaded and the driver was refueling the bus. Jack queued up behind a half-dozen locals, beaten down, haggard, and filthy, their dreams of golden riches shattered by the harsh reality of this hellish place.

After refueling, the driver paid the gas station owner, climbed aboard, and fired up the engine. Jack's peripheral vision caught sight of the two men he saw in the bar last night, watching him and the bus from a distance. No surprise there.

The bus did a one-eighty and headed back down the hill past Sands standing on the last corner of the last street, arms folded and eyes watchful. Jack had half a mind to jump off the bus and beat his drunken ass. But the look on Sands's face held him back. The ex-Ranger was feeling sorry either for Jack or for himself.

Either way, it didn't matter now. Sands and his buddies saw that they had won when Jack climbed onto the bus.

Jack hadn't made it to the top of the mountain and he didn't have Cory's ashes to scatter even if he went there now. What should have been a simple, final act of friendship and respect had turned into a bitter failure amplifying Jack's already out-sized sense of guilt over Liliana's horrific death and the tragic turn of fate now crushing her sweet, orphaned son.

Hurt, tired, and utterly defeated, Jack knew it was time to get the hell out of Dodge.

76

Jack figured ten minutes had passed since the bus left town.

Plenty of time.

He made his way forward and asked the driver in his broken Spanish to pull over. At first, the driver refused. Jack pulled off his last remaining possession, his Georgetown class ring, and handed it to him. The driver flashed a gap-toothed smile that wrinkled the leathery skin around his black eyes. He pocketed the ring, pulled over, and cranked the doors open.

Jack jumped out, his toes smashing into the end of the too-small shoes when he landed. The doors slammed shut behind him and the bus roared away as Jack turned and headed back up the hill toward Cielo Santo.

It was going to be a long damn walk from here to there and then to the top of La Hermana, Jack told himself.

But he was going to do it, come hell or high water. If he couldn't spread Cory's ashes on top of the mountain like he had promised, at least he'd still make the trip and bury the photo. He'd stop by Cory's grave when he got home and explain it all to him and ask his forgiveness for failing. But he sure as hell wasn't going to apologize for not even trying.

Jack didn't have much of a plan. Sands and the two assholes that jumped him saw him leave, so they wouldn't be expecting him to make the trip back up to the town, let alone the mountain. He found the location of the trailhead on an old topo map stapled to a wall in the restaurant where he ate dinner last night, so he didn't need Sands's help on that account. If he hurried, he could make the mountain summit by dark, then get the hell off the mountain, climbing down the worst part of it in the twilight. The crescent moon would provide enough light for the rest of the trip, so long as the clouds went away, which they were supposed to. After that, he'd figure out how to get back to Lima, one way or another.

By the time Jack got back to town his feet were already beginning to blister in the cramped shoes. At least Sands had disappeared, and the two thugs were nowhere to be seen. Since he had no idea who else in town was connected to those jokers, Jack did everything he could to stay out of the street and out of eyesight, trying not to draw any attention to himself.

Twenty minutes later Jack was on the edge of town and near the trailhead. He spotted a couple guys with guns on their hips and smoking cigarettes, clearly guarding the entrance and exit to the narrow mountain trail. They were sitting in green plastic chairs and playing cards, laughing and cursing.

A stand of gnarled paperbark trees on one side of the road provided cover. Jack snuck down below the road and around the sentries, and climbed his way back up a steep, crumbling slope, slipping and sliding until he reached the trail a half-mile farther up and out of their eyesight.

Already tired from the short, steep journey and parched by the dry air, Jack pressed on. At least he was out of the running sewer known as Cielo Santo and on the trail toward the giant, flat-headed granite mountain looming high above. The higher peaks around him were capped in blinding white snow. It was as beautiful a sight as he had ever seen, much like the Julian Alps he had witnessed in Slovenia last year.

The top of La Hermana Alta had to be nearly fifteen thousand feet, he reckoned. The thin, cool air had gotten even thinner and cooler since he jumped off the bus. He was already feeling a little light-headed.

At this height he was in danger of altitude sickness, or at least the mild form of it. The good news was that he was already suffering the symptoms of altitude sickness—aching muscles, headache, and nausea—from his hangover and beating.

How much worse could it get?

Jack picked up the pace. He'd be damned lucky to reach the summit in five hours at this point, but even if he didn't, he wasn't turning back, even if he had to climb in the dark.

The farther he climbed, the steeper and narrower the trail became, even as the rocks and boulders shouldering it grew in size. Patches of plants with long, green leaves like palm fronds became smaller and less frequent. The twisted, rust-colored paperbark trees had disappeared altogether.

Thirty minutes past the trailhead he felt like he was marching through molasses, his oxygen-starved brain thundering with a vicious headache. This only drove Jack harder, each step a penance for his past failures, each footfall the chance to stomp away the guilt that wracked his soul.

Without water or food and with his bruised ribs aching with every breath, Jack suddenly realized that there was a very real chance he wouldn't make it to the summit after all.

The sky roared overhead with a crushing boom like an artillery shell, so close he felt the sonic pressure. A spear of jagged lightning tore across the sky.

And then the rain came in cold, chilling sheets.

What little rain gear he had was stolen with the backpack. He was soaked instantly, chilled to the bone.

Jack trudged on.

77

WASHINGTON, D.C.

The NSA's counterintelligence directorate, the Q Group, was still badly shaken by the Snowden fiasco. They'd chased the traitor all the way to Hong Kong but never did find him, even though he was in a hotel just blocks from the U.S. embassy, spilling his guts to a reporter before escaping to Russia.

The director of Q Group was determined not to let Fung be a repeat.

The call straight from Director Foley to the director of the Q Group rang alarm bells throughout the unit. They tapped their best bloodhound, Lynette Fortson, a month shy of early retirement, to lead the investigation, which could take weeks, months, or even years to resolve. There was no one better in the business, and she wouldn't quit until Fung was captured and questioned, retirement plans be damned.

She began by filing the necessary documents with a FISA court judge favorably inclined toward national security matters. The documents were based on the data provided by Jesse Benson's office and Amanda Watson's sworn statements regarding her strong misgivings about Lawrence Fung.

If Fung were smart enough to compromise the IC Cloud without getting caught, he probably had early-warning safeguards in place to alert him if the NSA—an IC agency—was hot on his heels. Fortson went old-school: phone calls and couriers only.

If she were Fung, her first thought would be to flee to a country without an extradition treaty with the United States. Currently, there were more than seventy such governments, including Russia, which was one reason Snowden went there. The Vatican was an unlikely option, as was China, because it seemed the most obvious. Burkina Faso, Yemen, and a few dozen other hellholes were also on the list. If it were her, she'd head to Andorra, a slice of heaven in the Pyrenees, wedged between Spain and France. There was no way to know which one he'd choose. Alerts were put out with private and public air carriers, as well as with TSA passport control stations deploying facial recognition. She hoped Fung wasn't monitoring TSA priority alerts, but it was a risk Fortson was willing to take.

She need not have worried.

Fortson got the call from the team in California. Lawrence Fung had been found dead in a Lake Arrowhead cabin, a suicide, according to the note on his laptop, which also contained both a confession and an explanation of how he'd committed his crimes.

A preliminary investigation by the forensic data analyst on scene confirmed that Fung's laptop contained the necessary links to the comms satellite portal he had gained access to and, subsequently, the details he'd laid out in his confession.

Fortson's first call would be to Foley to deliver the good news. Closing Fung's case was a glorious capstone to Fortson's already remarkable career.

Fortson's second call would be to her husband to start packing the RV. Their retirement plans were back on track and there was a brand-new grandson in Idaho they were both dying to meet.

ON THE SLOPES OF LA HERMANA ALTA IN THE PERUVIAN ANDES

Jack's oxygen-deprived brain throbbed with every heartbeat, his lungs gasping for air like a landed carp. Slightly delirious from hyperventilation, his monkey mind went into overdrive, and regrets stabbed his heart like blunt screwdrivers.

The deaths of his cousin Brian Caruso and Sam Driscoll, two of his best friends from The Campus, flooded him with sorrow. He missed those guys every day. Paul Brown's self-sacrificing death in Singapore brought on another pang of self-loathing. It should've been him and not the heavyset forensic accountant who died that night.

But it was the constant flashbacks of Liliana's drowning that dogged his every step, hearing in his mind her final, desperate cry of her son's name. He was grateful for the pain wracking his body; each agonizing step dulled his mental anguish. The pain also helped with the growing cold. The clouds blocked what little warmth the sun offered. At least the rain had stopped, though the dark, heavy clouds promised more to come, and soon.

With the sun blocked and without a watch, he could only guess the time. It felt like he'd been marching for two weeks, but it was more likely only two hours, the elevation increasing with each faltering step. The trail now proceeded along a narrow ridge with steep, grassy slopes strewn with boulders that rolled all the way back down to the valley below. He was, by his reckoning, about half-way to his objective. It would be just after sunset when he reached the summit, but that would be okay, especially if the clouds passed and the moon could light his way, if only dimly.

And if not? Well, he'd manage somehow. If David Goggins could do 4,025 pull-ups in seventeen hours and run hundred-mile-plus ultra-marathons, he sure as shit could walk just a few more hours.

For the first time, Jack wondered if he'd pushed beyond his physical limit. Shivering and exhausted, he had at least two more hours ahead of him, and then the long, five-hour hike back down in the dark without food or water. He began to despair. Not because he might die—an even bet, especially if the temperature dropped much further—but because he might not reach the summit and finish the job.

Something told him this was all a very stupid idea that Cory would hate.

But this really isn't about Cory anymore, is it?

Something yelped up ahead, knocking Jack out of his delirium. He glanced up in time to see a young girl, dirty and dark-haired, her eyes wide with panic, staring straight at him.

Before Jack could call to her, she bolted off the trail and down the slope, crying and yipping as she stumbled and slid down toward the valley floor.

Suddenly, a teardrop-shaped OH-6 Cayuse appeared out of nowhere, its rotors beating the air.

It swooped hard and fast out of the sky, tracking the girl.

Automatic rifle fire erupted from the chopper. Bullet strikes burst around her, cutting her down in a dead run. She tumbled like a rag doll facedown, her twisted form coming to rest in the grass and rocks. The chopper hovered over her above the boulders, unable to land. Satisfied, it rocketed away, back toward the La Hermana Alta summit.

Jack sprinted off the trail and down toward the girl, his weakened, exhausted legs nearly collapsing underneath him on the steep slope. He stumbled over a rock halfway down and tumbled forward, smashing his arm against yet another stone lying in the grass. He grunted with the pain but regained his footing and raced ahead for the girl, praying she was still alive.

He fell down next to her shattered, bleeding body. Her face was intact, her unblinking eyes opened to the sky above. Jack felt for a pulse but knew before he touched her that she was gone.

Jack wept.

Beyond the bullet wounds he saw a body brutalized. Her nails were torn away from bloody and callused fingers, and her bruised flesh scabbed and purpled.

The girl was fleeing the mountaintop, terrorized and terrified. She might have escaped if she had stayed on the trail, hiding among the boulders. But she saw him and thought he was chasing her, too.

In a way, he'd caused her death.

Jack glanced up at the summit.

Whoever had killed that girl was on top of that mountain.

Something broke in him.

He stood, trembling with rage.

Suddenly his mind narrowed, his focus singular and pure.

All of his life had led him to this moment.

And if it was his last, so be it.

Somebody had to pay.

For all of the evil, and all of the pain, and all of the hell on earth, or at least his corner of it.

Right here. Right now.

He knew he didn't stand a chance. He had no weapons, no food, no strength.

There was only one thing he could do.

Fight like hell anyway.

78

CYBERSPACE

CHIBI's computer received the last of the four acknowledgments. With four—well, technically five—proof-of-concept demonstrations, each of the four bidders—Iran, China, Russia, and the Iron Syndicate—now understood the value of what was being put up for auction.

The time—two days from now—was set, as were the place and conditions. Everything had gone according to plan.

How high the bidding would go was anybody's guess. But that was the point of a blind auction, wasn't it? What would America's fiercest enemies be willing to pay for unlimited and undetectable access to the totality of Western intelligence—past **and** present—twenty-four hours a day, seven days a week?

A billion?

Ten billion?

More?

However high the bidding went—and truly, the

sky was the limit—all of it would land in CHIBI's digital pocket.

More than enough money to disappear, to re-invent, to resurrect in a new face, a new body, a new reality.

Good-bye, CloudServe.

Jack scrambled back up the slope and onto the trail.

The Cayuse had disappeared and was out of earshot; whether it landed back on the moun-taintop or flew away, he didn't know. It could re-appear at any moment, and the trail was probably monitored. He began using whatever cover he could, crouching low and scrambling fast among the jagged boulders through which the trail now threaded.

Up ahead, heavy boots scuffed in the dirt and rocks, heading his way. No doubt somebody sent down to verify the kill and dispose of the corpse. Jack ducked behind a boulder just off the trail and held his breath.

A voice crackled on a radio as heavy footfalls crunched past. Jack timed his swing perfectly. A sharp, softball-sized stone in his hands thudded hard into the soft flesh of the bearded man's tem-ple, spraying hot blood onto Jack's numb face.

The bearded man hit the ground face-first, dead

before his forehead broke open against a jagged stone embedded in the trail.

Jack scrambled to pull the corpse off the trail and back behind the boulder where he'd been hiding just in case another man was following behind or someone was watching up above.

The bearded man was Jack's size—a little taller, actually. That was lucky. He stripped the man of his camouflage coat and pulled it on, along with his black woolen watch cap. The cool breeze had picked up and blew colder, dragging black clouds across the late-afternoon sky.

Jack secured the man's Glock ten-millimeter pistol and tossed it into the coat pocket along with the two extra mags he was carrying. Jack quickly unlaced the man's boots and pulled them off. He stripped off his own wet socks and pulled on the man's dry but stinking woolen socks, then pulled on one of the man's unlaced boots. It was a near perfect fit for Jack's swollen, blistered foot.

He slipped on the other boot, snagged the handheld radio, and headed up. Voices chattered on the speaker, mostly in accented English.

He heard a name—Rodrigo—called out three or four times. Must've been the name of the guy he'd killed. Jack lifted the radio and clicked the transmit button on and off like it was broken, and muttered gibberish until he finally heard the response, "Damn radios. Never mind. Just get your ass back up here. Rain is on the way. Out."

Rodrigo won't mind the rain now, Jack thought.

And soon enough, the asshole on the other end of the radio won't be worried about it, either.

Nothing had changed. In fact, things had gotten worse.

The temperature had continued to fall, the trail had gotten steeper, and the last three hundred feet was just as Cory had promised—a steep, hand-over-hand climb over tall, jagged granite stones.

But his singular mission had focused all of Jack's depleted energy, driving his blister-bitten steps one after the other up the steepening incline like a shot of pure adrenaline. All that mattered now was stopping whatever the hell was going on up top and seeking vengeance for the young girl murdered down below. He knew the killing couldn't change the past, but it might change the future for somebody up there—if he succeeded.

If not, his death was a penance.

Either way was fine by him.

The light rain that began thirty minutes ago turned to ice crystals that whispered against his jacket. He counted at least a dozen different voices on the radio, probably all contract killers like the one already dead on the trail below. He killed the radio. No point in making any more noise than he had to.

It was dark now, the crescent moon well hidden behind a bank of heavy clouds, but enough to see a few feet ahead of him. He was a hundred feet below the tabletop summit. Diesel motors rumbled above, no doubt the source of incandescent light glowing above the rocks. Convenient for Jack. The first sentry he spotted was silhouetted by the generator light that didn't reach down to him.

The sentry smoked a cigarette listlessly. Jack climbed higher, carefully navigating the slippery granite beneath his frozen hands, trying not to kick anything loose beneath him and give himself away. He worked his way up and around a hundred feet to the left, out of the man's line of sight. Jack peeked up cautiously between the rocks.

His heart sank.

The tabletop summit was a temporary mining operation. Or, more accurately, a revitalized one. New equipment was scattered among old facilities—rusted tin roofs, weathered lumber. The whole area was about two football fields long and three wide.

On one end of the summit was a wooden structure over a shaft of some sort, Jack presumed. Dozens of miners milled about, carrying heavy sacks lifted up from the shaft or pushing rock-laden wheelbarrows over to sorting and washing tables. Two guards with rifles stood in the mouth of a nearby cave, sheltered from the freezing rain beginning to fall, cursing and cajoling.

On the other side of the camp stood a half-dozen temporary prefab buildings. Housing facilities for the guards, Jack guessed. One building was brightly lit. A belching stovepipe on the roof told him it was probably the mess hall. A huge steel propane tank behind the building confirmed it. A giant lean-to, little more than a corrugated tin roof on poles, might have been for equipment storage, or shelter for people treated worse than cattle.

Careful to avoid detection, Jack caught sight of oxygen and acetylene tanks for welding, assorted tools, and plastic storage tanks for water and fuel. Even a mini–Bobcat excavator. Everything he saw could have been hauled up here by the big Russian chopper he saw yesterday.

A woman screamed. Jack's head swiveled. A laughing guard was dragging a young girl by the hair into one of the shacks. Another guard whistled and egged him on, shouting in Ukrainian.

Jack's body tensed. He wanted to charge forward now. But even his rage couldn't override his training. He needed to finish counting targets, then formulate his plan.

And then it would be time.

79

The light, frozen rain had warmed to a liquid downpour. A biting wind swept the plateau.

Forty-two miners huddled in threadbare rags, shivering together around a cookpot simmering over a jerry-rigged gas burner beneath the giant lean-to. A lone guard hovered near them. An Indian woman ladled the pot's contents into tin bowls as miners shuffled past her, sitting down exhausted on the cold, hard ground to eat.

Jack crouched beneath the rim in the drenching rain, hidden behind the rocks. He had a plan. All he needed was the opportunity.

Suddenly, he heard it.

A dinner bell clanged on the steps of the mess hall trailer. Eight armed men ambled in that direction.

So far, Jack had counted twenty men guarding the compound. He didn't stand a chance.

But he didn't have a choice.

Time to roll.

———

Fried steaks sizzled on the grill, filling the trailer with the sweet smell of burnt fat and cigarettes.

The eight guards inside talked and smoked as they sat at the tables in the cramped but warm little mess hall, wolfing down steaks and pinto beans, and washing it all down with cans of soda. The rain hammered on the trailer's metal roof.

The cook—a Canadian Army deserter—circulated in the cramped space with a platter of more steaks, forking them over as requested, the butt of good-humored jokes about his food.

A single ten-millimeter pistol shot rang out a second before the propane tank erupted just outside the trailer's thin walls. The guards not killed by the concussive blast were gravely wounded by the steel shrapnel or burned alive.

Three more gunshots took out the generator powering the overhead lights. The camp went dark, save for the burning mess hall.

A guard in his skivvies raced out of an adjacent trailer at the sound of the propane blast. He was cut down in mid-stride by a single shot from Jack's ten-millimeter Glock.

The unit commander stood back in the shadows of the cave's mouth, trying to assess the situation. Who was attacking? How many? From where?

He called for sitreps on his handheld radio, but no one replied.

"Merde," he cursed.

The blazing mess hall flames spread to the nearest trailers. The burning buildings lit up the entire camp in a flickering, orange fire that hissed as raindrops spattered on the hot sheet metal.

Two more pistol shots rang out in the noise of the rain. Oxygen tanks exploded like artillery shells just as three men were running past, shredding them into smoking chum.

Suddenly, one of the commander's men shouted in German and fired off two three-shot bursts from his Steyr AUG 5.56 Bullpup machine gun—at what, the unit commander wasn't sure.

But two sparks from a pistol thirty yards behind the guard was the answer, tossing the big German backward into the dirt.

The commander couldn't help but laugh.

He knew exactly who it was out there.

Thirty seconds later, another guard in a poncho and boonie hat and carrying a pistol-gripped Benelli M1014 shotgun barked in pain as a blade severed his spinal column where it attached to the base of his skull.

His body dropped behind one of the big sorting trays.

Jack stripped off the poncho and hat, pulled them on, then grabbed the semiauto shotgun and charged back toward the Bobcat for protective cover. Three guards had ducked behind one of the unburnt trailers, hoping to circle back around the perimeter.

Trusting that the poncho, hat, and Benelli gave him cover as one of the guards, Jack sped across the compound and ducked behind the shack, calling out to the others, "Hey, assholes!"

The three men turned around in unison. Jack recognized two of them from the bar. Before they could raise their weapons, Jack cut them down with eight rounds of double-aught buckshot in less than two seconds, flinging their shredded torsos to the dirt, with the smoke still curling from the barrel of the Benelli.

"JACK RYAN! CAN YOU HEAR ME?"

Out of ammo, Jack tossed the shotgun aside and pulled out the Glock. By his count, only three guards remained. He edged up to the corner of the trailer.

"JACK RYAN! LAST CHANCE FOR THIS GIRL! COME OUT NOW OR I KILL HER!"

The voice sounded vaguely familiar. A European.

Jack peeked around the corner. Slashing rain made it hard to see clearly.

In the flickering firelight, Jack saw a man holding a pistol to the head of a woman kneeling in the puddle in front of him. Beside the man with the pistol, a dozen other miners knelt in the mud at the mercy of a second gunman armed with a rifle. And behind them, the remaining miners were huddled in the lean-to, covered by the third guard.

"JACK! I see you! You have three seconds to come out from behind that trailer! Or the girl dies! One . . . two . . ."

Damn it.

If he came out, they'd cut him down. No question.

But if he didn't, that girl would die, and so would the others on their knees.

Fury overwhelmed him again. He was trapped. But he had no choice.

"Wait! I'm coming out."

Jack held his hands high, still holding the Glock. He stepped toward the man with the pistol.

An LED tac light popped on, nearly blinding Jack as it swept over him.

"Drop the pistol, Jack. And keep coming forward."

Jack tossed it aside. He closed the distance. The rain splattering against his boonie nearly deafened him.

Jack couldn't believe his eyes.

"Jack Ryan. You act as if we've met before." The man scratched his beardless face with the barrel of his pistol.

Jack was sure they had.

Except . . . the tattoo. It was in the wrong place. The sword-bearing winged arm was on the back of his gun hand instead of his forearm.

But it was the face of the shitbird who killed Liliana.

Wasn't it?

Not quite. Nearly the same face. A fraternal twin or maybe a cousin.

"No, we haven't met. How do you know me?"

The man—also named Cluzet, like his younger brother—said, "Your friend Sands ratted you out."

Cluzet saw Jack's reaction. "Don't be angry with the old drunk. He saved your life, actually. My men were sent to kill you, but Sands said you were an American tourist with curious and important friends. Too bad you didn't go away."

"I'll be sure to thank him when I see him."

Cluzet grinned. "I doubt it."

"That tattoo. Where have I seen it?"

Cluzet twisted and turned the loaded pistol in his hand to flash the tattoo. "French Foreign Legion, Second Parachute Regiment."

"Is it a rub-on from a cereal box? Or did your boyfriend buy it for you?"

Cluzet roared with laughter. "So funny, and such a killer, too! You wasted some very hard men tonight, Jack. No easy feat. I'm impressed."

He stepped closer to Jack. Rain poured off his

nose and chin. "You're a real badass, aren't you, Jack?"

He stepped even closer. Almost nose-to-nose.

"You think you can kill **me**?"

Jack threw a punch, but he was totally spent. The adrenaline rush of the last fifteen minutes had completely exhausted itself, robbing him of any strength.

Cluzet easily sidestepped the weak jab and returned the favor with a hard fist into Jack's gut, doubling him over.

Jack's knees splashed in the mud.

The crown of Cluzet's pistol pressed against the top of Jack's head.

"I'm sorry," Jack whispered.

Sorry for the girl down the hill, and Liliana, and all the others he had failed over the years.

Especially his father.

Cluzet laughed and pulled the trigger.

The pistol report near Jack's face stabbed his eardrum like a hot nail. His throbbing headache only worsened, and a high-pitched whine screamed inside his brain like a bad radio wave.

The nine-millimeter bullet splashed harmlessly next to Jack. To his credit, he didn't even flinch, but mostly because he was too damned tired.

"Tie him up," Cluzet said to the two men who

approached. Jack glanced up and saw that he had miscounted. There were five men left, not three.

"What about them?" Jack asked, nodding at the miners still kneeling in the mud.

"They have work to do tonight."

Cluzet leaned close to Jack's other ear. "But in the morning, they shall all be killed. We're starting a new mine tomorrow because this one is all played out, just like they are."

He grinned in Jack's face, daring him to do something. But Jack's eyes focused on Cory's hollow wooden amulet hanging around the man's neck.

80

Jack lay soaking wet with his back against the cave wall, hands tied behind him, ankles bound with rope and legs stretched out in front. A Coleman lantern lit the space. Rain still fell in sheets outside. One of Cluzet's four remaining guards stood at the entrance, facing out.

Cluzet had told Jack that in the morning the Russian heavy hauler would arrive to take him out to the ship in international waters that was carrying the precious cargo mined in these mountains.

"And after that?"

"You will either travel a very far distance or, because of the trouble you caused tonight, a very short one," Cluzet said, grinning, as he headed back out into the rain, leaving the American to ponder his fate.

Hog-tied and humiliated, Jack was out of cards, his hand played out.

He called to the guard, a narrow-shouldered, five-foot-eight Che Guevara wannabe with a scraggly beard and a short-man's complex.

"Hey, I gotta piss."

"Then piss," the guard called back over his shoulder.

"C'mon, man. You got the gun. I ain't going anywhere."

The man turned around. Hatred dripped from the guard's exhausted eyes. Jack had killed several of his friends tonight.

"Piss yourself, **singao**."

"Look, help me up. I can't run away tied up like this."

"Even if you are standing up, how are you gonna piss with your hands tied?"

Jack shrugged. "Well, if you're nice, you can hold it for me. But you're gonna need both hands, if you know what I mean."

The man charged over and swung a heavy boot at Jack's face to kick it like a soccer ball. Jack barely managed to duck out of the way. The guard's boot crashed into the rock wall, knocking him off balance. Jack saw his chance. He rolled like a log, his two-hundred-pound bulk smashing against the man's leg still planted on the ground. It was just enough to knock the little man off balance, but not down. He stumbled backward.

Jack's plan to head-butt the guy and maybe find a way to cut his ropes was dead in the water.

So was he.

The guard roared, ready to launch another kick at Jack's exposed face. But a strong hand wrapped around his forehead, pulling it back. The man's shocked look gave way to agony as a knife blade punched through his throat, the drop-point tip a steel tongue beneath his larynx. He gurgled and gasped, clutching at the wound as he dropped to the ground, drowning in his own blood.

Sands knelt down, pinned the guard's head to the ground, and jammed the bloody blade back into his neck, severing the spinal column to finish the job.

Sands said, "Sorry, slick. It's been a while."

The former Ranger was dripping wet, dressed in a well-worn hiking coat and a faded Browning ball cap.

Jack's eyes narrowed. "What the hell—"

Sands wiped his bloody Ka-Bar on the dead man's coat, then stepped over and cut Jack's ropes from his ankles and hands, and then killed the Coleman lantern.

"What are you doing here, Sands?"

"I like the night air. Went for a walk."

"I don't get it."

"No time for touchy-feely shit right now, kid. We gotta get you the fuck out of here." Sands pulled his pistol, a heavy, all-steel Beretta 92FS.

"Not yet."

Jack knelt down and picked up the dead man's weapon, an AK-103 with a folding stock. "They're going to kill the miners in the morning."

"Let's get you back down the hill first."

Jack stood, checked the weapon, racked a round. "I won't keep you."

"I ain't leaving without you."

"Then follow me."

Jack and Sands reconnoitered the mining camp. Someone had restored the diesel generator. The lights were back on. That wasn't good.

The miners had been put to work gathering and disassembling equipment, putting out the remaining fires, and anything else they were directed to do by the barrels of the rifles pointed at them.

Jack and Sands took their time, working their way around the periphery, as far away from the light as possible. The sound of the ceaseless rain and the rumbling diesel covered their tracks, but the cold air turned their breath into steaming vapor.

They caught the first guard by himself taking a leak. Sands seized him by the skull and twisted. The man's neck broke with a muffled crack.

His partner was next, taken down by the butt of Jack's rifle to the back of his head and then Sands's knife across his throat.

The two of them dashed across the compound, where Cluzet and the last guard hovered over a group of miners filling sacks with processed material.

Sands fired his Beretta, putting two nine-millimeter rounds in the guard's forehead.

"Don't even think about it," Jack said as the Frenchman reached for his pistol.

Cluzet's tattooed hand froze in place. He smiled as Jack and Sands stepped into the light, Jack's rifle and Sands's pistol both pointed at him.

"You wanna fill in the details?" Jack asked, grabbing Cluzet's pistol from its holster.

"I'm a working man, hired to do a job, that's all."

"And killing innocent people is part of the job description?"

"Who is innocent in this godforsaken world? Nobody gets out of here alive, anyway."

"Great. A fucking philosopher," Sands said.

Cluzet turned to Sands. "I didn't think you had any game left in you. Tonight truly is full of surprises." He grinned widely.

Sands's pistol cracked. The Frenchman's head snapped backward, the smile still plastered to his face. He toppled over, splashing into the mud on the flat of his back, his arms flung wide.

"We could have questioned him."

"Yeah. We could have," Sands agreed, holstering his weapon. "Now can we go?"

"What about them?" Jack nodded around the camp. The miners had dropped to the ground or crouched behind equipment, terrified, when they heard the gunshots.

Sands sighed. "Let's get these people organized. See if you can find a sat phone or a radio in one of those trailers while I go talk to them." Sands stomped off toward a knot of miners, speaking Spanish in a friendly, comforting manner.

Jack had other business first.

He stepped over to Cluzet and snatched Cory's amulet off the lifeless neck.

He still had a promise to keep.

81

Jack drank enough water from the storage tank to fill an aquarium, or so it seemed, before heading over to the undamaged office trailer, where he found a fully charged sat phone. A call to Gerry set everything in motion, including notifying the President.

Jack and Sands spent the next hour caring for the miners, first by getting them out of the rain and cramming them into the remaining bunkhouse trailers where the guards had been. Sands managed to fire up the heaters while Jack distributed warm blankets and spare dry clothing.

Sands learned in Spanish that all of these people were taken from clinics in Lima, La Paz, and a few other cities. These drug addicts, alcoholics, and prostitutes were all given promises of a brighter future and worthwhile employment until they arrived at La Hermana. Starved, beaten, and, in the case of the women, raped repeatedly, they had no recourse but to work or die digging. As society's castoffs, no officials bothered searching for them.

The rain stopped just before dawn as the first

of two MH-60R Seahawk ("Romeo") helicopters roared into view, flown in from the flight deck of the **Ticonderoga**-class guided-missile cruiser, **Belleau Wood** (CG-74), docked at Lima's naval port as part of a Latin American show-the-flag mission for the Fourth Fleet.

The helicopters were normally fitted out with antisubmarine gear and weapons. Because the choppers had to fly beyond their rated altitudes, only volunteers were allowed on the op. The captain ordered the ordnance stripped and the two ASW aircrewmen debarked. A half-dozen Spanish-speaking Marines and Navy corpsmen crammed into each aircraft with medical supplies, blankets, and MREs.

"I've got orders from the CMC directly to load you onto my chopper, sir," the Marine lieutenant shouted over the idling turbines on the windswept plateau.

Jack shrugged. "Sorry, Lieutenant. My dad was in the Corps, not me. You can tell the commandant I'm not moving off this mountain until those people get their ride first."

"He said you'd say something like that." The lieutenant smiled. His lance corporal tapped the Stinger missile on his shoulder. "We'll sit tight until the Peruvian Air Force arrives, but if the Halo or Cayuse you reported show up, Corporal Hernandez will send them a high-explosive greeting card."

"I'll hold you to that," Jack said. "Until then, I'm gonna find me a cup of coffee."

An hour later, the first silver rays of the sun pierced the low-lying clouds.

Best sunrise I've ever seen, Jack thought. Mostly because he didn't think he'd live to see it.

Jack stood at the place Cory's father had been so many years before. He opened the small wooden amulet and said a silent prayer as the light breeze scattered the half-ounce of Cory's ashes over the granite rocks below, then knelt down and buried the crumpled photo in the wet dirt.

Behind him, twin GE turboshafts roared as the Peruvian Air Force SH-3 Sea King helicopter lifted off, carrying the last of the miners off the mountain.

Sands and the Marine lieutenant approached.

"Does that satisfy you, Mr. Ryan?" the lieutenant asked hopefully. "My ass is already in a sling."

"I'm ready to roll if you are. Hey, question. You bring a cell phone with you?"

"Yes, sir. Why?" He handed it to Jack.

"I've got some pics I need to snap. I'll bring it right back. Five minutes, tops."

The lieutenant nodded as he stepped away, calling up one of the Seahawks circling overhead to prepare to pick up HAMMER, Jack's code name.

"You did good," Sands said.

"Not good enough, but it'll have to do."

They stood on the edge of the plateau. Cielo Santo was a dirty smudge far down below.

"We'll head back down there and grab your stuff, then we'll catch my plane in Lima back to the States."

"No, but thanks." Sands pointed back down the mountain toward Cielo Santo. "I'm gonna make my stand down there. Maybe help turn things around for those poor folks."

Jack understood. Sands had filled him in on a few details in the last hour.

The former Ranger's personal descent into hell began years ago when an Iraqi translator and his family he had recruited were brutally tortured and killed before Sands could get them out of the country. He had blamed himself for breaking faith with the family he'd promised to protect. Their murders broke him. No longer caring about anything, especially himself, he drifted around until he washed up at Cielo Santo.

Sands told Jack he knew bad actors were up on La Hermana Alta, but he swore he didn't know about the specifics. "Mostly because I didn't give a shit," he'd admitted, shame cracking his voice.

Seeing Jack reminded him of his younger self, and Jack's determination to keep faith on a promise to a dead friend rekindled something deep inside he'd thought he'd lost.

"I owe you one," Sands said.

"Other way around, I think." Jack nodded toward Cielo Santo. "Won't be easy."

"Nothing good ever is. But you can do me one favor."

"Name it."

"Tell Midas that Brick still has a few rounds left in the chamber, will ya?"

82

ON BOARD THE HENDLEY ASSOCIATES G550

Beyond logistics and scheduling, Lisanne Robertson was responsible for Campus crew and aircraft security, a skill set she acquired on tours of duty with both the Marine Corps and the City of Alexandria Police Department.

But as good as she was to have in a fight, she also knew her way around a galley. While Jack showered in the Gulfstream's small but adequate bathroom and changed into fresh clothes, Lisanne began preparing the waffles, bacon, and eggs he'd requested.

Remembering Clark's visit to his apartment a few days ago—which his aching body told him was more like a few years ago—the first call Jack made was to his dad on his private number, assuring the old man that he was tired but fine and would be back in the States that very evening.

The second call he made was to Gavin Biery, The Campus's IT genius. "You get those photos I sent you?" Jack asked. He'd used the Marine lieutenant's phone to grab pics of the dead French merc, along with the Foreign Legion paratrooper tattoo on his hand, and forwarded them to Biery.

"Sure did. Helped me narrow down my search results from three hundred and twenty-seven to just two, both ending in the name Cluzet. And your hunch was right, they're brothers, separated by eleven months."

"I know one of them is in a metal drawer in a Lima morgue right now. Where's the other **enculé**?"

"Still working on it. I've got a few databases I'm about to raid. I should have an answer by the time you get back to the office."

Jack thanked Gavin for working his digital magic once again and rang off.

Lisanne arrived at his seat with plates of steaming-hot food and cold, fresh-squeezed orange juice, but Jack had already passed out and was snoring like a bandsaw. She set the tray down, covered him with a blanket, and sat in the seat across from him, keeping a careful watch over her exhausted passenger.

SAN FRANCISCO, CALIFORNIA

The CloudServe Bombardier Global 8000 lifted off at five p.m. PST. Capable of carrying up to seventeen passengers, today's flight included just

Elias Dahm and Amanda Watson, along with the flight crew. From San Francisco they could reach Sydney or Moscow without refueling, but a flight plan was filed for London Heathrow, arriving by noon local tomorrow, just in time for the Tech-World conference kickoff.

Watson was grateful for the Bombardier's separate en suite arrangements. Elias had already retreated to his cabin, presumably to write his speech. He had arrived at the charter terminal in a strange and irritable mood, barely greeting her or the crew, as was his habit. She assumed he was still brooding over the French Guiana disaster, but his moods were as hard to read as Kierkegaard.

It could have been far worse for him. Watson barely convinced Foley to keep the Fung matter between themselves, arguing that the fewer people who knew about it, the better. She promised Foley she'd inform him immediately after the conference, a delay of just a few days.

"And frankly, Mary Pat, I need Elias focused on London. It's our most important annual event. This news will send him over the edge."

Foley understood her concerns and reluctantly agreed, but only because Watson had been responsible for first finding Fung. "I want you both in my office the day you get back from London."

"We'll be there. You have my word."

Watson was relieved Dahm had sequestered himself away for the long plane ride. After dinner, she would finish up her final notes for Foley and turn in. Given the events of the past few days, she could use a good night's sleep, and she needed to be fully rested for the world's most important industry conference.

She had a feeling London was going to be eventful for them both.

ALEXANDRIA, VIRGINIA

Jack sure as hell didn't feel like one, but Clark and the rest of the Campus operators—Ding, Dom, Midas, Adara, and Gavin—greeted him at the Hendley Associates charter hangar like a returning hometown hero with smiles and hugs and claps on the back all around.

The Campus had been briefed about the events of the previous twenty-four hours, including the successful evacuation and hospitalization of all forty-two miners from La Hermana Alta.

Clark noticed a marked difference in young Ryan since their last conversation. Quiet, but in good spirits. Apparently, Jack had taken a good look in that mirror they had talked about back at his apartment, and he must have fixed whatever he had seen down in Peru.

"Any line on Cluzet?" Jack asked Gavin, who was munching on a jumbo-sized Snickers bar.

"Yes, as a matter of fact. That Iron Syndicate outfit that was hunting you last year? The one

Clark told me to keep an eye on? Well, I found an Interpol internal memorandum linking the Cluzet brothers to it, thanks to those funky tattoos."

"So I take it you contacted Interpol for a line on him?"

Clark answered, "We talked about it. But the Iron Syndicate is global. They've got agents and informants planted in every major security agency. It's better if we go after Cluzet ourselves, and maybe build a case that helps unravel the organization while we're at it."

Jack had read the 2018 DNI Worldwide Threat Assessment. It listed organized crime, a $2 trillion global enterprise, as a serious American national security threat. He wanted Cluzet dead, but he was all for taking down the Iron Syndicate in the process if at all possible.

"If we're not going to Interpol, our only shot at finding Cluzet is the Czech."

"That's exactly why we're here," Clark said.

"Where is he now?"

"At home, in Czechia."

"He's making it kinda easy, isn't he?" Jack asked.

"'A dog always returns to his vomit,' the Bible says," Gavin offered, wiping the chocolate from his lips.

"And you don't trust the Czech government to round him up for us, either, I take it."

"I think it'll be better if we talk to him ourselves. I'd hate for the old fart to accidentally get a bullet in the face and his secrets die with him because we tipped off the wrong person."

"Then let's go talk to him."

"We're already planning on it. You want in?"

"Do you have to ask?"

"It involves another long plane ride."

"I can use the miles."

"Are you one hundred percent? This thing might get a little hairy."

Jack's eyes narrowed. "Don't even think about cutting me out of this."

Clark recognized the determination in his eyes. He also understood it. He had the same fire in his belly when he reaped bloody vengeance for Pamela Madden's murder four decades ago.

Clark threw a thumb over his shoulder. A stack of mission gear stood in the corner of the hangar. Something serious was about to go down.

"Brought your kit along, just in case. We're saddling up right now. Wheels up as soon as the plane is gassed and the preflight completed. I'll brief you on the ride over."

"Thanks. I appreciate it."

"You earned it, kid. You did a heck of a job down there."

Heads nodded all around.

"No," Jack said. "The job just got started. Now it's time to finish it."

83

WASHINGTON, D.C.

Case closed.

Fortson at Q Group had signed off, as had the IT division heads from each of the IC departments. So had Watson.

Foley sighed with relief. The intelligence community had dodged a bullet. No, an artillery shell. For a terrifying moment, she envisioned shutting down the entire IC Cloud, currently processing more than a thousand terabytes of video and audio surveillance data each day, and trillions of pieces of metadata from phone and computer records from around the world. Intelligence collection and processing as it was currently practiced would have ground to a halt. The damage to American intelligence credibility would have been devastating, perhaps insurmountable. No ally would ever trust the United States again.

Fortunately, the leak was cauterized.

Fung had been the lone perpetrator, and his breach had been severely limited in scope and time. The forensics on his laptop had been completed and confirmed Fortson's initial conclusion. Watson immediately and secretly patched Fung's breach with the CIA comms satellite.

She then helped design a secret emergency security audit, searching desperately for any other signs of a breach in the IC Cloud. If some other party had broken in and saw what they were up to, they'd go to ground. The bigger challenge was to keep the IC Cloud humming along while the investigation was going on. Too many other critical, real-time projects were at stake, and even the hint of a possibility of a breach would have put their allies—particularly the Five Eyes members—in a panic.

Foley was grateful for Watson's Herculean efforts. Judging by the time stamps on her calls, texts, and e-mails, Watson had worked around the clock for the last forty-eight hours. Now she was off to a conference in London but promised to be available 24/7 should any need arise.

Watson and the experts all agreed that Fung's breach had been something of a fluke and not indicative of a larger security problem. Foley worried about Watson. She had taken the news about Fung's espionage particularly hard and counted it as both a personal and professional failure. In a sense, she was right on both counts. But Foley was equally culpable. It had all happened on her watch.

The most obvious question that plagued her

was how had Fung managed to evade the regular security audits of critical IC contracting personnel. Were they not being conducted as often and as thoroughly as she assumed? Or relying too heavily on polygraph testing—easily defeated by proper coaching? She would need to address the issue as soon as the dust settled.

Now all that was left was for Foley to put together an executive summary of the Fung incident and call the President. As a former national security advisor and deputy director of Central Intelligence, he would appreciate both the severity of the crisis and its rapid resolution.

As POTUS, she imagined he would be furious. But Foley didn't believe in hiding the dirty laundry, come what may.

Sunshine was the best disinfectant, especially in her line of work.

KLATOVY DISTRICT, PLZEŇ REGION, CZECHIA (FORMERLY KNOWN AS THE CZECH REPUBLIC)

The barrel of Clark's Colt .45 pressed against The Czech's knee as he sat in his favorite high-backed office chair. Like the rest of his massive hunting lodge, the log walls featured trophies of game he had killed in the surrounding forest.

"Really, Mr. Clark? Such dramatics?"

"Last chance, buddy. If you ever want to dance the cha-cha again, you better tell me where we can find Cluzet."

Jack was in the room as well, Glock 19 in hand, along with Gavin, who was already rooting around the gangster's laptop.

"We've both seen this movie before. If I tell you, you'll kill me anyway."

Jack said, "We just want Cluzet. Not you."

"Is that what you told my guards outside before you killed them, too?"

"They didn't cooperate. That made them collateral damage. Now it's your turn to choose," Jack said.

The owlish eyes behind the glasses studied Jack's face.

"Cluzet has wronged you personally, hasn't he?"

Jack charged forward, gun up. He jammed the barrel against The Czech's skull, knocking his glasses off his nose. "Cluzet! Where is he?"

"Jack—"

"Last chance, asshole!"

The Czech saw the murderous rage in Jack's eyes. "I'm not a micromanager. I honestly have no idea."

"Then there's no reason for you to waste any more space on the planet." Jack's finger slid over to the trigger.

"No! Wait. Perhaps I have something more valuable than Cluzet to offer."

Clark pushed Jack's pistol away from the old man's forehead. "Like what?"

"Your country has a problem. A very large problem. A problem only I can resolve. But I will need to speak to Director Foley."

"You're out of your fucking mind," Jack said.

"Why Director Foley?" Clark asked.

"Trust me, she will want to hear what I have to say."

WASHINGTON, D.C.

Mary Pat Foley frowned with confusion when The Czech told her about the BKA agent murder in Berlin. That it was all based on intel provided to him by CHIBI.

"I'm sorry to tell you this, but CHIBI is dead. Killed himself. The leak has been sealed."

"It's not possible. My representative is meeting with him tomorrow. The confirmation came just an hour ago," The Czech said over the phone.

The blood drained from Foley's face.

The Czech finished her thought for her. "You were meant to believe the leak was sealed. Whatever corpse was conveniently provided to you was a ruse, and, judging by the sound of your voice, a brilliant one."

Fifteen minutes later, The Czech handed Clark's phone back to him with a triumphant smirk.

"Mr. Clark, Mary Pat here. I'm afraid we're going to have to agree to his terms. Complete amnesty, in exchange for that algorithmic key."

"You trust him, ma'am?"

"Unfortunately, yes." His knowledge of the BKA murder was all the proof she needed.

"Now what?"

"I need you to sit tight. I'm going to put you on a conference call. I have an idea. I'll call you back in twenty minutes. Secure our friend in another room out of earshot. And don't hurt him."

"If you insist, ma'am."

The Czech sat back in his chair, satisfied he'd cheated death once again.

Clark wanted to wipe the smile off the old man's face with the back of his hand, but he had his orders. He had to admit, though, the gangster had pulled a fast one. The Czech told Foley about a man named CHIBI and a secret, silent auction being held in London tomorrow night. One bid only, in person, by an authorized representative. The winning bidder would receive a special algorithmic key that would unlock the entire IC Cloud—and the IC would never know about it.

The Czech proposed that in exchange for his life, he would provide the encrypted passcode that allowed his representative to bid. "They don't know who's coming. The only ID needed is the passcode."

Clark was no security expert, but Gavin's drop-jawed response told him it was all pretty serious.

"You know, if you screw us on this, you'll wish I'd let Jack blow your brains out," Clark said.

"I have no loyalties to anyone or anything other than to myself, Mr. Clark. My intense desire for self-preservation is your best guarantee."

Dom and Adara kept watch over The Czech in another room while Gavin, Clark, Jack, Mary Pat, and a couple NSA cyberwizards conferenced on Clark's phone.

The plan they came up with was rough around the edges, and more likely to fail than not.

But it was their only shot.

And it all depended on Gavin Biery.

84

LONDON, UK

The TechWorld conference was held in a soaring glass tower hotel and convention center in the Canary Wharf section of London adjacent to the River Thames.

Gavin was dressed in a hastily acquired Savile Row suit. He sat in the back of a rental van with Clark and Adara. Midas was at the wheel. Dom and Ding were still in Czechia, keeping the old gangster under wraps until the mission was completed, after which he was free to leave—a decision Clark couldn't abide but didn't argue, because it wasn't his call to make.

Jack and Foley were already in the hotel. Foley had flown a red-eye government jet with her hastily assembled team, arriving early that morning.

"You're sweating buckets," Adara said, wiping Gavin's portly face with his handkerchief. "You might short out the microphone."

"Really?"

"Joking," Adara said. "You'll be fine."

"Look, Gav. This is a cakewalk for a guy like

you," Clark said, trying to calm the man down. "A tower full of computer geniuses jabbering about bits and bytes? And all the free cocktail weenies and soda pop you could ever want?"

"But . . . I'm not really a field operative."

"But you've always wanted to be one. And you've been out with us a bunch of times now. You'll do great," Adara reassured him.

"But this is really, really important. I'm not IT support for the mission this time. I **am** the mission."

"And you'll kill it," Clark said.

Gavin blanched.

"Figuratively speaking. This is all IT stuff and IT people. No guns, no goons. Okay?"

"Okay."

"We'll have eyes on you the whole time," Adara said. She adjusted the tie clip with the embedded miniature video camera and microphone. "And no one more than one floor away."

Clark checked his watch. "It's time."

Gavin paced inside the hotel room The Czech's people had reserved for the conference, as per their instructions from CHIBI. At precisely eight p.m., CHIBI's representative would arrive. Gavin would provide The Czech's encrypted passcode to authenticate his false identity, and then hand over an envelope with The Czech's bid.

Gavin didn't care about the technical side of this meeting. That was as difficult as pulling twenty dollars of cash out of an ATM. Playing it cool was the challenge. Like he was actually the bad guy, and not some sweaty, fat techie playacting like a spy.

Gavin practiced his breathing exercises and tried to think about his favorite beach. When there was a knock at the door, he nearly fainted.

"C'mon, Gav, you can do this," he whispered to himself.

He opened the door.

He nearly wet himself.

"Uh, please. Come in."

CHIBI smiled and entered. Gavin shut the door.

"Something wrong?"

"Wrong? No, not at all."

"You have something for me?"

"Yes."

He pulled out The Czech's thumb drive from his pants pocket and inserted it in the reader in CHIBI's hand.

"Excellent. And the bid?"

"The bid? Sure." Gavin reached into his pocket and handed over the sealed envelope.

"I'll be in touch. Good luck."

CHIBI turned to leave and pulled the door open.

Mary Pat Foley stood in the doorway, furious.

She slapped Amanda Watson hard across the face.

"You treasonous bitch!"

85

oley, Clark, Jack, and Gavin stood over Watson, seated in a chair, her face still beet red from Foley's slap.

"When and where's the next meet?" Foley demanded.

Watson checked her watch. "Ten minutes from now, two floors up."

"How many more are left?"

"You got lucky. You were the first. Three to go."

"Here's the deal, short and sweet. You're going to do exactly as I say, and in exchange, I won't toss your ass off the tenth-story balcony myself. Does that work for you?"

"You can't do that."

Foley leaned on the chair, got right in her face. "Just fucking try me."

Watson blanched.

"What do you want me to do?"

Foley stood. "Do exactly what you planned to do. Meet the other three, collect their bids. But then tell them this: The winner will receive a text

tonight to come to a London location at a specified time, and that's when you'll hand over the
algorithmic key. Are we clear?"

"Clear."

Foley called over her shoulder. "Jack?"

Jack stepped over and wired Watson up with
a Bluetooth ear device that doubled as a video/
audio unit.

Jack touched his earpiece. "Say something."

"Something."

Jack nodded. "Loud and clear."

Foley said, "If the mic and camera go dead, you're
dead. Give us up, and you're dead. Do anything
stupid and give yourself away, you're screaming-
in-agony dead."

"I won't screw it up. You'll see."

"Yes, I will," Foley said. "Now move your
sorry ass."

An hour and a half later, Watson was back in
Gavin's room, seated in the same chair. The
others were gathered around Gavin's laptop, scrub-
bing through Watson's first-person video. They'd
seen it all live but wanted to review just to be sure
Watson hadn't pulled a fast one.

"Well?" Watson asked.

"You think you sold them?" Foley asked.

"I sold you, didn't I?"

Foley's jaw clenched. "Yeah, I guess you did. You sold a lot of us."

"I'm thirsty. Can I have a water or something?" Watson asked.

Jack grabbed a bottle of water out of the minifridge and handed it to Watson. She cracked it open.

"Why'd you do it?" Foley demanded.

"Does it matter?" Watson took a swig.

"Humor me."

"Multiple reasons."

"Starting with?"

"First of all, because I could. The idea of outsmarting the entire western IC seemed like an immensely satisfying exercise."

"Was it? I mean, until we caught you red-handed?"

"Yes, entirely."

Foley turned to Clark. "If I ask for your weapon, turn me down. Understood?"

"Yes, ma'am."

"Why else?" Foley demanded.

"Elias Dahm."

"What about him?"

"While he was out banging teenage interns on his boat, I was building his goddamn company. Everybody knew Elias Dahm. He was the rock star. I never got invited to an owner's box at the Super Bowl or asked to toss out the first pitch at a Giants game, or hang out with Oprah in Maui. Instead, I got hit with questions all the time. 'Where's Elias? What's he like?' 'Can you tell him "hi" for me?' 'Can you tell him I'm a big fan?' Made me want to puke."

"You used to be in a relationship with him."

"Yeah, for a while. Talked me into walking away from my dream NSA job by offering me his bed. But then, after I got fenced in, he moved on to greener pastures."

"You mean younger ones," Jack said.

"You'd risk the security of the United States because your feelings got hurt?" Clark asked. Jack watched his face redden.

"Why'd you stay around?" Foley asked.

"The stock options, mostly. I mean, CloudServe really was my company. I did most of the important work. Elias was just a salesman. Like I told you with Fung, Elias kept us all on a tight leash by keeping our stock options in escrow for five years after we left in order to guarantee the NDAs and noncompetes we signed. So if we left under bad terms, we couldn't earn a living and we'd lose everything we'd worked for."

"Your stock options must have been worth tens of millions."

"Try hundreds."

"But doing this would kill the company, and your stocks would crash."

"That's why I needed the auction. I could destroy the company and get rich, all at the same time."

Foley asked, "Any other reasons?"

"My brother."

"The Ranger? Killed in the line of duty?" Jack asked.

"He was my hero, my life. And Ryan killed him."

"How did the President kill your brother?" Foley asked.

Watson's icy composure melted away.

"What the hell was my brother doing fighting in Ukraine? Or Afghanistan, Iraq, Niger, the Philippines?"

Her rage escalated. "Why does Jack Ryan think America needs to fight everybody else's stupid wars? Wars that we cause to begin with? I'm sick of all the patriotic, flag-waving bullshit. It just gets good people killed. And for fucking what? Tell me why, goddamn it!"

"Your brother was a soldier," Clark said. "He swore an oath. He obeyed his orders. Maybe he didn't even agree with them. Hell, most of us in uniform don't agree with them, at least not all the time. But that's the job. And your brother did his job. He sacrificed his life for his country—a country you've betrayed."

"Which means you betrayed his sacrifice," Jack added.

"I still can't figure out why you decided to do the London meet yourself," Foley said. "That was risky."

Watson slowed her breathing, fighting to regain her composure. "Trusting people is even riskier, isn't it? It was safer to do everything myself."

"You didn't kill Fung."

"No, I didn't."

"But I'm guessing you had the job hired out. Probably the Dark Web, paid in Bitcoin so nothing could be traced back to you."

Watson smiled defiantly. "Good luck proving that."

"I won't bother trying. You did us a favor by hauling out the trash."

Gavin glanced up from the desk where he sat, the bid letters all opened. "Looks like the Iranians put in the highest bid."

Foley frowned. "Not the Chinese?"

"China was a close second, and Russia third."

"The sanctions must have really put a hurt on old Yermilov," Clark said.

"The Iranians obviously found other investors to sweeten the pot," Jack said. "Or sold a shit-ton of weapons-grade uranium."

Foley turned to Watson. "You would have turned over our national security apparatus to the Iranian mullahs?"

Watson fought back a grin. "I was planning on

giving all four of the bidders the algorithmic key. They would have been as busy screwing each other over as you guys."

"And made a lot more money for you," Jack said, "collecting all four bids."

Watson smiled defiantly. "You're damn straight."

"Eventually, they would have figured it out and come hunting for you," Foley said.

"With the kind of money I would have made? Good luck finding me." She took another sip of water.

Foley checked her watch and said to Clark, "An hour before the Iranians arrive. We need to get moving." She said to Watson, "We're going to wire you back up, so don't get cute."

As per Foley's instructions, each of the three bidders were texted that they had won the bid, and each was scheduled to arrive at a different time and a different location around London that Foley had prearranged.

To protect Watson from kidnapping by a bidder too cheap to pay up, Clark would drive Watson to each location, using SDRs to avoid any chance of a tail, while the rest of the team would screen in two other cars for further protection.

Foley also couldn't allow the three bidders to tail one another. She mobilized local CIA assets to ensure this didn't happen. Her plan would only work if each of them thought they had won the bid exclusively.

Foley handed Watson three thumb drives.

"Each of these contain an algorithmic key that will give them limited access to a controlled area of the IC Cloud. When they log on, they'll see they've purchased the real deal."

"Let me guess. You've put something else on those drives."

"When they connect to our cloud, our cloud will connect to them. We're the ones who will gain unlimited access to **their** computer systems."

"Cyberjudo," Gavin said, chuckling. "Pretty cool."

"They'll figure out what you've done, eventually," Watson said.

"Not before we've raided their cookie jars."

"So after I've held up my end of the bargain and pulled off this intelligence coup for you, what do I get out of all of this?"

"A traitor's noose, I hope," Clark said.

"I doubt that will happen. Hanging women isn't very politically correct these days," Watson said, smirking.

"There's an alternative solution that'll never make the papers," Clark said. "Trust me on this."

"Or you can take my offer," Foley said.

"Which is?"

"You're not going to like it. But it beats an early grave."

Foley was right. Watson hated it.

But she took it anyway.

86

THREE HUNDRED MILES DUE WEST OF THE AZORES

Foley flew back to D.C. on the same Boeing C-40B jet she'd borrowed from the 89th Airlift Wing at Joint Base Andrews the day before.

The C-40B was the military version of the 737-700 business jet and, like the President's much larger Air Force One, deployed secure data and comms for the fifteen cyberwarfare experts she brought on the flight over to London. Between them and the hastily assembled working group at the NSA, they had managed to build, test, and deploy the three algorithmic keys with the worm needed to carry off Foley's espionage coup: the penetration of the Chinese, Russian, and Iranian computer intelligence systems.

The cyberwarfare experts—men and women, mostly in their twenties and thirties—specialized in offensive cyberoperations. Several were elite members of various armed forces Cyber Mission Teams, in joint service to U.S. Cyber Command.

The only addition to the flight manifest was the new passenger, Amanda Watson, cuffed and secured by two of Foley's security detail.

Watson tried to convince Foley that in five years, the knowledge she possessed would be utterly useless to foreign governments.

Foley countered that high treason was a death-penalty offense.

Watson responded by describing in detail the secret portal she had carved into the IC Cloud that her auctioned algorithmic key would open. She even patched it right there on the airplane under the supervision of Foley's top cyberwarriors, who confirmed the fix.

Foley's best and final offer was thirty years in a federal minimum-security facility with community-service privileges. She suggested it was still a better deal than a visit by John Clark in the middle of the night.

Watson agreed.

"Director Foley? You're not going to believe this," Sergeant Molly Houk said, the blue glow of the computer screen reflected in her glasses. Her baby bump hardly showed in her maternity battle uniform.

"What is it?"

The petite twenty-three-year-old airman

beamed. "We're already inside the Iranian mainframe."

"They didn't waste any time, did they?" Foley said. She called over to the steward near the galley.

"You guys got any champagne aboard this bird?"

TWO HUNDRED FIFTY MILES DUE WEST OF THE AZORES

The Hendley Associates G550 was on nearly the same flight path and just under six minutes behind Foley's aircraft.

The Campus team debriefed the events of the last few days, compared notes, and discussed options for future action, but it was difficult to lay out any specifics without hard data.

Hard data that suddenly became available when Gavin shouted, "CRIKEY!" from the back of the aircraft near the galley.

Hunkered over The Czech's laptop for the last three hours and connected to his own personally designed computer network via the onboard encrypted satellite comms, Gavin had unearthed a gold mine of data.

"Hey, Jack! Come over here and look at this. I think I've finally found an answer to that question you had."

Jack scrambled back and dropped into the seat next to Gavin. He scrolled through pages of account numbers, deposits, and receipts. Jack clapped the IT director on his soft, round shoulder.

"Gavin Biery, Resident Genius."

Gavin beamed with pride.

The two of them spent the remaining flight time assembling a document that would rock Capitol Hill like a high-magnitude quake.

87

WASHINGTON, D.C.
OVAL OFFICE,
THE WHITE HOUSE

Mr. President," Senator Dixon said, flashing her best Chamber of Commerce luncheon smile.

Dixon was a very attractive woman, President Ryan had noted on previous occasions, but her arrogance diminished it considerably for him.

"Madame Senator, I appreciate you coming on such short notice." President Ryan gestured toward one of the chairs. She took one of the long Chesterfield couches instead. He didn't bother offering her anything to drink.

"It must be urgent, Jack, so I came right over. I'm here to serve."

More like here to measure for curtains, Ryan thought. **Don't get too eager just yet.**

He took one of the chairs, a file folder in hand. The seat gave him a slightly elevated position. Not that he needed it.

"Where's your lapdog, Arnie? It won't be the

same without him here, slavering on the leather and nipping at my heels."

"We have a problem I'd like to discuss with you, and I wanted to do it in private."

Dixon pointed a finger at the ceiling. "We're not being recorded, then, I take it?"

"Never without asking permission, and I'm not asking for it. This stays strictly between us."

Dixon brightened. "I'm all ears."

Ryan opened the file folder and handed her the inch-thick report. "You'll find an executive summary on the first page."

Dixon took the document in hand cautiously, her eyes locked on Ryan's.

"Why don't you ballpark it for me? I know you're good at summarizing."

Ryan fought back a smile. His son Jack had already ballparked it for him less than an hour ago as his plane was landing. He and Gavin had put together one heck of a document, with every **i** dotted and every **t** crossed. He was damn proud of both of them.

"Bottom line? Your son, Christopher Gage—"

"Stepson."

"—has been connected with an international criminal organization known as the Iron Syndicate. He's also partnered with a Chinese national by the name of Hu Peng, the son of one of the directors of a state-owned bank and a high-ranking CCP official. The two of them have been running point for a drug-smuggling operation distributing chemical precursors along with processed heroin and methamphetamine all over Europe. They've hidden their activities behind a series of shell companies that take advantage of BRI trade treaties that Peng's father helped negotiate."

Dixon flipped a few pages, scanning numbers.

"That's a fascinating story—sounds like a Clive Cussler novel. Even if it's true, what does it have to do with me? I have no business or financial relationships with my stepson. If he's guilty of anything like you're describing, that's his problem, not mine."

"By the way, where is Christopher? We've reached out to him but can't seem to locate him."

"I have no idea. Like I said, his business affairs are his own and no concern of mine."

Ryan sat back, tenting his fingers in front of a satisfied smile.

"You put on a brave face, Deborah. I think we both know what kind of political damage this will do to your presidential run, even if you are legally innocent, which, in fact, you might be. This report screams 'Swamp' on every page, and you and your family are neck-deep in it."

"My husband's affairs are his own. I file a separate tax return from his and make it public every year, and have done so for the last twenty years. I have nothing to hide. My affairs are in order."

"Then you might want to turn to page thirty-seven of that report, where it begins to lay out the financial accounts of the Dixon-Gage Charitable Trust, something I know you're very proud of."

"Why shouldn't I be? We've done important work for poor and disadvantaged people all around the world, not to mention our brave veterans here at home, too."

"And Christopher has been intimately involved with your charity, hasn't he?"

Dixon stiffened. "Yes, he has. For years. He's told me on more than one occasion that the work he's done there has changed his life."

"I'm sure it has."

"Meaning?"

"Unfortunately, Christopher was using your trust to launder his dirty money, making millions of dollars of annual contributions through thousands of fictitious donors."

"I can't be responsible for the origin of anonymous monies donated."

"No. But the story doesn't stop there. Christopher then funneled that dirty money into 'clean' projects, especially ones in Africa, where there is very little government oversight, and where, coincidentally, the Peng family has significant resources invested. Christopher was buying charity goods and services at exorbitant prices from shell companies that he and Peng secretly owned. All of those water wells and tractors and schools you thought the trust was building all went instead into the pockets of your son and your husband and, it turns out, at least one high-ranking official in the Chinese Communist Party.

"Even if you can prove at trial you didn't know about any of this, you're still going to be found guilty by association in the court of public opinion, and worse, it makes you look like an idiot or a dupe."

Dixon's heart rate fell. The arrogance around her Botoxed eyes faded away.

"Not exactly a winning platform for a presidential campaign," Ryan said, just to twist the knife.

"You'll have a hard time bringing any of this to court. I doubt it was legally obtained."

Nice bluff, Senator. Glad I never played poker with you.

"I'm willing to take the chance. Even if we lose in court—and my AG insists we won't—it will still ruin your reputation and take years to litigate. And we haven't even begun really digging yet. That report just scratches the surface."

"Well, speaking of reputations. I have evidence of my own suggesting that your son Jack, Gerry Hendley, and, by implication, you, are associated with an organization engaged in questionable activities. I'll use my information to help launch impeachment proceedings against you."

"The Chadwick stuff again? How'd that work out for her?"

"Chadwick is an idiot. I'm not, and you know it."

Ryan shrugged. "Do your worst. I'm not going to be President forever, anyway."

"A congressional investigation might determine that you and your associates are guilty of crimes for which you can be prosecuted."

"In theory, yes, but I doubt it. But even if that were to happen, **in theory**, there could be a stack of presigned presidential pardons sitting in a safe somewhere, written up for just such a contingency."

Dixon's shoulders slumped, defeated. She stood, her voice softening.

"Well, then, there's nothing more to be said. I agree to resign from my office if you drop all of this nonsense."

"On what grounds would you resign?"

Dixon smiled cynically. "'To spend more time with my family,' of course. Isn't that what they always say?"

"Sit down, Deborah. We're not through yet."

His commanding voice dropped her back onto the couch.

"It's high time we remind ourselves in this country that nobody is above the law, especially the people who write it. That's why I'm instructing the attorney general to prosecute your family to the fullest extent of the law possible."

"Jack—"

"Unless you agree to this."

Ryan stood, retrieved a bound document from his desk, and handed it to Dixon. He didn't bother to sit down.

"What's this?" Dixon said, opening it.

"I'm sick and tired of the corruption that plagues this town. It's corroding the confidence of the American people in their government. Trust is the glue that holds a democracy together, and you people on the Hill are destroying that trust. Far too much legislation is passed that only benefits the few at the expense of the many.

"What I just handed you is my proposed legislation to clean it all up. The sweetheart deals, the revolving doors, the family loopholes—all of it. Get this bill passed and on my desk in its present form for me to sign in the next sixty days or I'll see you in court."

"And if I get it done? Then what?"

"Then I memory-hole that report I handed you. And **then** you can resign to spend more time with your family. Whatever you decide to do after that is up to you."

Dixon smiled a little. "You know, an anticorruption bill like this **would** make a great presidential platform to run on."

Arnie was right, Ryan thought. Dixon was pure ambition, even in the face of disaster.

"You may not be on Beijing's payroll but you

killed the Poland treaty because you're dancing to their tune. Was it all that Chinese money your husband made that flipped you, or something else?"

"Money? Don't be ridiculous. What matters is something Sun Tzu called **shi**. Do you know the term?"

"Momentum, advantage . . . power."

Dixon shook her head, incredulous. "Always the professor. Then you also know that the world's changing, and China is the future."

"My future is whatever we have the courage to make of it. My job as President is to create change, not follow it."

Dixon lifted the heavy file folder. "How do I know you still won't release that report after I get this legislation passed?"

"If everything in that report all came out, it might do more damage to the country than to you, and, frankly, you're not worth it. More to the point, once you get that legislation passed, you have my word I won't use anything we discussed today to sabotage you or your family, as much as that idea sickens me."

At that moment, Dixon hated Ryan's guts more than any person she had ever known.

But she agreed to his terms.

Because as much as she hated him, Dixon still knew that Jack Ryan was an old-fashioned patriot and, indeed, a man of his word.

EPILOGUE

WASHINGTON, D.C.

With President Ryan's blessing and an executive order in hand, Foley put every available resource at her disposal into dismantling the Iron Syndicate, now deemed a high-priority national security threat.

Within weeks, significant Iron Syndicate assets were uncovered and identified. Foley personally contacted the heads of the Chinese, Russian, and Iranian security agencies to provide them the names of the criminal elements within their respective governments, "in order to stem the tide of illegal drugs and human trafficking around the world," she assured them.

It was also a ploy to throw them off the scent of her recent espionage coup—perhaps the greatest in modern history.

But the cancerous tendrils of the Iron Syndicate ran deep. Removing them proved difficult and painful. Investigators raced against Iron Syndicate bosses desperate to cauterize leaks, cut away evidence, and tie off loose ends.

Both President Ryan and Foley expected unintended consequences would follow.

They did. Sooner than they'd anticipated.

SAN FRANCISCO, CALIFORNIA

The bankruptcy judge banged her gavel.

CloudServe, the most powerful cloud company on the planet, was dead. The circling vultures would soon divide the remains among themselves.

The disappearance of Elias Dahm had raised alarm bells all over Silicon Valley and Washington, D.C., though for entirely different reasons.

Locals assumed Dahm's disappearance was connected to the suicide of Lawrence Fung, whose troubled life and financial difficulties were detailed in a poignant exposé that relied heavily on unnamed government sources.

The locals were only half right.

Despite Watson's fervent denials, the Feds feared Dahm was somehow connected to her plot and fled the country to avoid questioning and, worse, found asylum with one of America's strategic competitors.

Foley suspected Dahm was merely a coward, abandoning responsibility for his failed dreams.

Weeks passed before a New Zealand widow sailing solo across the Pacific Ocean sighted the wreckage of Dahm's yacht, **Prometheus**. Investigators concluded it had been swamped and broken apart by a recent tropical storm.

His body was never recovered.

GDAŃSK, POLAND

The theme-cruise pirate ship sailed slowly under engine power, with tourists on deck sipping hot mulled wine and shivering in the cool air. "What Do You Do with a Drunken Sailor?" blared in Polish over the loudspeakers.

Two retired schoolteachers from Knoxville, Tennessee, stood on the forward deck, searching TripAdvisor on their smartphones for a seafood restaurant along the well-lit Motława riverfront.

Both of them felt the same **thunk** in the soles of their shoes as the pirate ship bumped into a heavy object in the water.

The puffy-sleeved pirate crewman standing nearby shot them both a nervous glance, then leaned over the side to see what the ship had hit.

An hour later, the police coroner's van hauled away the decomposed corpses of Christopher Gage and Hu Peng, bound together by ropes and drowned in the same canvas bag.

CARPATHIAN MOUNTAINS, ROMANIA

The Czech stood on the edge of the forest, the pine-scented air crisp and cool in his nose. His favorite rifle in hand, his best dog at his side, and a guide's recent sighting of fat boar in the area promised a perfect day.

He hadn't been this happy in years. Retirement, though forced, had suited him, he decided. No more burdens of running a vast criminal enterprise.

His Bohemian pointer began barking wildly, his bearded snout aimed at the stand of trees ahead of them in the far distance.

"Rexi! Good boy! What do you see?"

The Czech heard the familiar crack but didn't bother to move. In truth, he'd been expecting it for some time now.

Two hundred grains of steel-jacketed lead split the mountain air some six hundred meters distant. The bullet struck The Czech's forehead cleanly, but the back of his skull erupted in a gory cloud of blood, bone, and brain matter.

His corpse tumbled into the tall grass, Rexi barking and whining at his feet.

On the other side of the clearing, the Polish ABW sniper and his spotter slipped away, headed for their exfil point. Vodka would flow like tap water back at their barracks tonight.

Foley had agreed to spare The Czech's life, but she never promised not to track him or convey his indirect responsibility for Liliana Pilecki's death to the Polish government.

Liliana's actual killer remained unknown to the Poles.

But not to Jack.

BENGHAZI, LIBYA

News of his brother's death had only just reached him.

Cluzet had been on the run for several weeks now. He was holed up in a fourth-floor apartment of a bombed-out six-story tenement building built with oil money by the Ghaddafi regime decades ago. Ghaddafi's death and the ensuing chaos transformed the richest country in Africa into an impoverished hellscape within a few short months, tortured and divided by rival Islamic factions, drug runners, and human-trafficking syndicates. It was in the midst of this chaos and death that Cluzet finally found sanctuary—and kindred spirits.

With only intermittent water and electricity, his apartment was less of a home than a concrete cave, but useful for his current, desperate circumstance, hunted by hostile governments and vengeful enemies alike. Its singular virtue was an unobstructed view of the Mediterranean on the far side of the coastal road.

He got word out to a former Iron Syndicate colleague in the city, a gun runner named Tóth, that he was in town and available for the wet work Cluzet was famous for. Today, his friend would arrive within minutes, bearing good news, he promised.

Broken glass crunched beneath Cluzet's boots as he stood in front of the shattered window overlooking the parking lot and the street beyond, careful to remain in the shadows. No telling who was lurking out there with a sniper rifle and a bullet with his name on it.

A cool breeze chilled the skin of his tattooed arm. A short burst of automatic gunfire echoed in the distance, a common sound in the shattered, seaside city.

He studied the trash-strewn parking lot, flooded by the morning rain. A rusted, bullet-riddled car squatted on blown tires near the next building, home to an elderly woman even more desperate than he.

A white Toyota Hilux sped in off the street. The 7.62-millimeter machine gun mounted in back was crewed by a man in sunglasses and wearing a black-and-white keffiyeh wrapped around his face, just like the driver.

The Hilux charged toward Cluzet's building,

its knobby tires splashing away the cigarette butts and soda cans floating in the puddles. It skidded to a stop just below his balcony.

His friend Tóth, a fat, knife-scarred Hungarian, leaped out of the passenger seat, his boots splashing in the filthy water. His round, bearded face was uncovered for the Frenchman's benefit.

"Cluzet!"

The blond legionnaire stepped out of the shadows and onto the balcony. "Tóth, you old wolf! You came!"

"Of course! Why wouldn't I?"

"You risk a lot, knowing me."

Cluzet's eyes drifted toward the man on the machine gun, staring at him behind his dark glasses. He hadn't moved.

"We are all being hunted, my friend," Tóth said. "That is why we must stick together."

"I need work. What do you have for me?"

Tóth planted his hands on his broad hips and shook his head, smiling. "Yes, you need work. But someone else, I'm afraid, must speak with you first."

"Who?"

"Me, asshole."

Cluzet spun on his heels, pulling his SIG as he turned.

Jack's Glock fired first, putting two slugs into the bridge of Cluzet's nose, killing him instantly.

Cluzet's SIG fired as his hand spasmed.

The nine-millimeter round plowed into the peeling paint of the moldy wall just inches from Jack's head.

Jack stepped over to the corpse and put two rounds in the blond skull, then two more into the lifeless heart, shredding it.

He stared at the ruined man, satisfied.

Jack holstered his weapon and stepped over to the balcony, his eyes drawn to the wide horizon of the boundless sea. A wheeling gull cried in the distance.

The man in the back pulled off his headgear.

"All good, kid?" Clark asked, leaning on the machine gun.

Jack nodded.

"Yeah. All good."

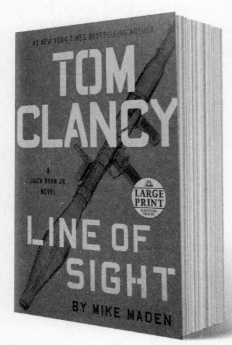 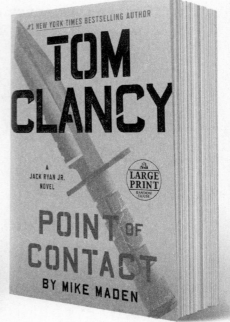